Imagine…

You lost the Death Man Game but then decided you still wanted to live.

To find out who God really is, you become a God Hunter.

How do you know if your god is speaking to you?

Suppose…

You could travel into other galaxies through a wormhole, but you might not come back alone….

You love your wife—only she has been dead since she was an infant.

What if your religion protected your kind but condemned everyone else?

Dream…

What if there existed a group whose total purpose was to ensure a perfect world, by controlling events going back through time?

How many times must you go back and relive the past to undo a terrible mistake?

Could black magic be the answer when all else fails?

Wonder...

The lonely orphan child finds she has magical powers and a destiny to match....

Where do religion and science really meet?

There are three kinds of people in the world. Which one are you?

What has been said about the
L. RON HUBBARD

PRESENTS
WRITERS OF THE FUTURE
ANTHOLOGIES

"The most enduring forum to showcase new talent in the genre."

"The series continues to be a powerful statement of faith as well as direction in American science fiction."

—*Publishers Weekly*

"These stories push the boundaries—entertaining, creative and greatly varied. A feast for short-story lovers."

—Gregory Benford, Author

"L. Ron Hubbard's *Writers of the Future* anthologies are a roadmap—they show the future of science fiction by showcasing tomorrow's writers today. These are the best of the next generation, and their stories are a heck of a read. But they also point the way to the writers who are pushing to come next. My own achievements in Writers of the Future opened a path of success that I'm still exploring—if you want to follow that path, read the book, enter the Contest, grow with the winners."

—Jay Lake, Author

"Prior to L. Ron Hubbard's Writers of the Future Contest starting, there was no field which enabled the new writer to compete with his peers—other new writers."

—Kevin J. Anderson, Author

"Winning the Contest was my first validation that I would have a career. I entered five times before winning and it gave me something I could reach and attain. It kept me writing and going for something. Reading the anthology is important. Writers of the Future is a market and you have to KNOW your market if you are going to submit and win. I had the first four volumes of *Writers of the Future* and just read them over and over before I won and was published in volume five."

—K.D. Wentworth, Author

"The L. Ron Hubbard Writers of the Future Contest has carried out the noble mission of nurturing new science fiction and fantasy writers for a decade now with resounding success."

—Dr. Yoji Kondo, Author

"An exceedingly solid collection, including SF, fantasy and horror…"

—*Chicago Sun-Times*

"A first-rate collection of stories and illustrations."

—*Booklist*

"Some of the best SF of the future comes from *Writers of the Future* and you can find it in this book."

—David Hartwell, Editor

"L. Ron Hubbard's Writers of the Future Contest and the *Writers of the Future* anthology represent not only the premier showcase for beginning writers in the field of speculative fiction, but also a wonderful teaching tool for aspiring authors."

—John L. Flynn, PhD
Professor of English and Modern Languages
Towson University, Maryland

"Not only is the writing excellent…it is also extremely varied. There's a lot of hot new talent in it."

—*Locus Magazine*

"This Contest has changed the face of science fiction."

—Dean Wesley Smith, Author and Editor

For Doug & Helen,
All Best Wishes!

KDWentworth
Coordinating Judge

SPECIAL OFFER FOR SCHOOLS AND WRITING GROUPS

The twelve prize-winning stories in this volume, all of them selected by a panel of top professionals in the field of speculative fiction, exemplify the standards that a new writer must meet if he expects to see his work published and achieve professional success.

These stories, augmented by how-to-write articles by some of the top writers of science fiction and fantasy, make this anthology virtually a textbook for use in the classroom and an invaluable resource for students, teachers and workshop instructors in the field of writing.

The materials contained in this and previous volumes have been used with outstanding results in writing courses and workshops on college and university campuses throughout the United States—from Harvard, Duke and Rutgers to George Washington, Brigham Young and Pepperdine.

To assist and encourage creative writing programs, the *L. Ron Hubbard Presents Writers of the Future* anthologies are available at special quantity discounts when purchased in bulk by schools, universities, workshops and other related groups.

For more information, write:

Specialty Sales Department
Galaxy Press, L.L.C.
7051 Hollywood Blvd., Suite 200
Hollywood, California 90028
or call toll-free: 1-877-8GALAXY
Internet address: www.galaxypress.com
E-mail address: sales@galaxypress.com

L. RON HUBBARD

PRESENTS

WRITERS

OF THE

FUTURE

VOLUME
XXII

To Doug & Helen,

Do your Dream!

L. RON HUBBARD

PRESENTS

WRITERS

OF THE

FUTURE

VOLUME
XXII

The Year's 12 Best Tales from
the Writers of the Future®
International Writing Program

Illustrated by the Winners in
the Illustrators of the Future®
International Illustration Program

With Essays on Writing and
Art by L. Ron Hubbard • Bob
Eggleton • Robert J. Sawyer
• Orson Scott Card

Edited by Algis Budrys

Galaxy Press, L.L.C.

Advice to the Word-Weary: © 2006 L. Ron Hubbard Library
The Sword From the Sea: © 2006 Blake Hutchins
Broken Stones: © 2006 Judith Tabron
Games on the Children's Ward: © 2006 Michail Velichansky
Evolution's End: © 2006 Lee Beavington
The Red Envelope: © 2006 David Sakmyster
Schroedinger's Hummingbird: © 2006 Diana Rowland
On the Mount: © 2006 David John Baker
Life on the Voodoo Driving Range: © 2006 Brandon Sigrist
At the Gate of God: © 2006 Joseph Jordan
Balancer: © 2006 Richard Kerslake
The Bone Fisher's Apprentice: © 2006 Sarah Totton
Tongues: © 2006 Brian Rappatta

Illustration on page   22 © 2006 Nathan Taylor
Illustration on page   91 © 2006 Alex Y. Torres
Illustration on page 119 © 2006 Miguel Rojas
Illustration on page 156 © 2006 Melanie Tregonning
Illustration on page 209 © 2006 Laura Jennings
Illustration on page 239 © 2006 Daniel Harris
Illustration on page 302 © 2006 Tamara Streeter
Illustration on page 335 © 2006 Katherine Hallberg
Illustration on page 349 © 2006 Eldar Zakirov
Illustration on page 406 © 2006 James T. Schmidt
Illustration on page 440 © 2006 Kim Feigenbaum
Illustration on page 486 © 2006 Osbaldo Rodriguez

Cover Artwork: The Once and Future King © 2006 Stephen Hickman

This anthology contains works of fiction. Names, characters, places and incidents are either the product of the authors' imaginations or are used fictitiously. Any resemblance to actual events or locales or persons, living or dead, is entirely coincidental. Opinions expressed by nonfiction essayists are their own.

ISBN: 1-59212-345-7
Library of Congress Control Number: 2006929955
First Edition Paperback 10 9 8 7 6 5 4 3 2 1
Printed in the United States of America

CONTENTS

INTRODUCTION

by
Algis Budrys

ike other author-adventurers with names like Melville, Twain, London and Hemingway, L. Ron Hubbard's experiences and travels—as an explorer and prospector, master mariner and daredevil pilot, philosopher and artist—found their way through his writing into the fabric of popular fiction and into the currents of American culture for fifty years. Distinguished editor, literary critic and grand master of science fiction Frederik Pohl said of L. Ron Hubbard: "There are bits and pieces from Ron's work that became part of the language in ways that very few other writers managed....He had a gift for inventing colorful pictures that still stay with me....Pictures that stayed in your head." At the same time, his unique voice and style helped reshape and establish new literary trends for many of the popular genres he wrote in— from science fiction to fantasy, and from horror to adventure—resulting in a compelling literary legacy. And what a legacy it was: Nineteen *New York Times* bestsellers, stretching over fifty years from his earliest commercially published story, "The Green God," in 1934, to the completion of a mammoth ten-volume novel, *Mission Earth*, in 1987. His most signal talent, however, was perhaps the ability to create rich characters and place them in unusual circumstances.

In his 1940 horror classic, *Fear*, Hubbard frames an unrelenting nightmare of the macabre around bookish and mousey James Lowry, Professor of Ethnology at Atwater College, who after publicly debunking the existence of demons and devils finds himself confronted with unexplainable and ghastly real-life evidence to the contrary. Horror/suspense giant Stephen King acknowledges *Fear* as "one of the few books in the chiller genre which actually merits employment of the overworked adjective 'classic,' as in 'This is a classic tale of creeping, surreal menace and horror'...This is one of the really, really good ones." Works like *Fear* etched Hubbard's place among the greats of contemporary suspense fiction including legends like Ray Bradbury and Stephen King. But his storytelling expertise was not limited to suspense.

Hubbard also excelled in other fiction genres, including fantasy, "future-history" science fiction, space-travel adventure and frontier fiction, while still showcasing his unforgettable characters in desperate—or hilarious—but always original circumstances. In *Typewriter in the Sky* (a satiric, story-within-a-story, literary fantasy), he engages the reader in a what-if tale of a piano player suddenly finding himself part of an adventure novel written by his writer friend, Horace Hackett. As if that weren't enough, he is trapped in the novel as the villain of the piece and discovers that he has to suffer through Horace's hackneyed writing and threadbare plot—knowing that his character is going to be killed off at the end. In *Final Blackout*, the apocalyptic science fiction adventure set in the aftermath of total war, the story focuses on an enigmatic, post-modern guerilla fighter, who is the least likely to lead a nation back from oblivion, and yet finds himself stuck with the problem. *To the Stars* is yet another beautifully crafted novel of future space travel and adventure that explores the sensibilities of a man shanghaied into becoming a crewman on the "long passage" of extended travel across the universe, while time goes forward normally on Earth.

All are examples of Hubbard's unique approach to fiction and his unmatched storytelling ability, crossing multiple genres with ease. From horror and suspense, to action-adventure and, of course, science fiction, he blazed a wide path of fiction output rarely matched by either his contemporaries or literary followers with over 250 novels, novelettes and short stories to his credit. Not surprisingly, L. Ron Hubbard's life was an adventure story in itself.

His real-life experiences began in rural Montana where he grew up on a ranch in the early 1920s and formed an early and lasting friendship with the Blackfeet Indians. By the late 1920s, he left the country to serve aboard a coastal trading vessel operating between Japan and Java in the Pacific. On his return in 1927, Hubbard studied engineering and took one of the earliest courses in molecular phenomena. Later, he went on to achieve renown as a pioneer aviator, famous in the air meets of the day, and became a master mariner—licensed to sail any ocean, and was three times a flag-bearing expedition leader of the Explorers Club (as recounted in George Plimpton's *As Told at the Explorers Club*). All the information gleaned from his experiences growing up and his personal interactions with the characters he met during his travels found their place in his various works: stories of civilians' narrow escapes from marauding warlords and vindictive Japanese generals during the Sino-Japanese war; men being trapped in the Sahara under the guns of the enemy without enough ammunition or water—or relief—in sight; or tales of danger and the risks taken by those who had to test airplanes for the military before such could be put into active service. During this period, his editors noted that his name on the cover of a pulp magazine would greatly boost its sales, so compelling were his stories, and he became a frequently featured writer.

As a consequence, novice writers who hoped to learn his storytelling and story-selling skills often consulted Hubbard for advice. He was happy to offer suggestions and so he began sharing his hard-earned experience with creative writing students in speaking engagements at institutions such as Harvard and George Washington University. In 1935, he was named president of the New York Chapter of the American Fiction Guild, where he made it easier for new writers to join the guild and readily shared his knowledge of writing and publishing with others who sought his help.

Hubbard also generated a series of "how to" articles that appeared in a number of writing magazines in the 1930s and 1940s, offering guidance to help new writers navigate the rough waters they were likely to encounter. Included in this volume is his wry article, "Advice to the Word-Weary," a compilation by Ron of advice letters not previously published. In 1940, as a feature of a radio program he hosted in Ketchikan, Alaska, while on an Explorers Club–sanctioned expedition, he offered advice for beginning writers and went one step further, initiating the "Golden Pen Award" to encourage listeners of station KGBU to write fiction, and he awarded prizes for the best stories submitted.

Years later, in 1983, in recognition of the increasingly difficult path encountered between first manuscript and published work, particularly in an era when publishers devoted the lion's share of their promotional budgets to a few household names, L. Ron Hubbard "initiated a means for new and budding writers to have a chance for their creative efforts to be seen and acknowledged." And so were born the Writers and Illustrators of the Future Contests. These Contests have continued to expand and now receive entries from all over the world. Recently, the Writers of the Future Contest was acknowledged by *Publishers Weekly* as "the most enduring forum to showcase new talent in the genre." At the Awards Ceremony for *Writers of the Future Volume XXI, Library Journal* presented the following award:

THE *LIBRARY JOURNAL*
AWARD OF EXCELLENCE

Presented to L. Ron Hubbard's
Writers and Illustrators of the Future Contests

In recognition of XXI years of discovering, fostering
and nurturing writers and illustrators of
speculative fiction and successfully infusing new
talent into the fields of literary and visual arts.

Library Journal
August 19, 2005

These Contests have become today the standard by which any aspiring writer and illustrator in science fiction and fantasy should measure their work. And, as the past twenty-one years have proven, the writers and illustrators you will meet in this twenty-second volume will be the names you will see in the years to come.

So read and enjoy *Writers of the Future Volume XXII* and see for yourself why Orson Scott Card says, "Keep the Writers of the Future going. It's what keeps sci-fi alive."

THE SWORD FROM THE SEA

Written by
Blake Hutchins

Illustrated by
Nathan Taylor

About the Author

The son of a diplomat, author Blake Hutchins grew up in Finland and Sweden, where he developed a love of folklore, foreign cultures and rugged landscapes. When he encountered Andre Norton's Star Rangers in fourth grade, Blake became hooked on speculative fiction and began exploring the worlds of Le Guin, Tolkien, Heinlein, Zelazny and many others.

Notwithstanding his early start, he managed to sidetrack himself from serious writing for thirty-odd years during which he earned a law degree, traveled abroad, and ran a couple of marathons. He also dabbled in a variety of occupations including teacher, firefighter, computer-game designer, entrepreneur and public defender. He has recently stepped away from software and law to pursue his boyhood passion and begin his newest occupation: writer. When he is not writing full time, he volunteers at his daughter's kindergarten or chops wood. Blake lives in Eugene, Oregon, with his wife and two daughters. He is a member of the Wordos, Eugene's local writer's group, whose members are regular participants in the Contest.

About the Illustrator

Like most children, Nathan Taylor started drawing at three. Unlike most children, Nathan stuck with it. His first art instruction came from animated Disney cartoons on TV and comic strips published in the local Anchorage Daily News *in Alaska. As a young illustrator, Nathan wanted to be an animator, studying movement, action and figure drawing. Somewhere along the way, he started being pulled toward science fiction and fantasy scenes (probably because his own parents loved science fiction). At twelve, Nathan won first place at the local Fur Rendezvous arts festival. In college at Washington State, Nathan earned a BA in fine arts while penning a comic strip called* Simon. *Nathan has since relocated to Redmond, Washington, where he works as a freelance illustrator and assistant manager of a printing-press shop. When he's not drawing, Nathan enjoys writing, backpacking, poker, photography, strategy games, fencing and guitar (not all at once). He's currently working on at least a half-dozen fiction stories and plans to eventually enter them in the Contest.*

Keeping herself small and quiet, Gull crouched behind a tall clump of russet-bladed warden grass and spied upon the men as they gathered around the body. It sprawled near the twin gray spurs of the Offering Rock, which thrust man-high from the beach.

The sea boomed its endless song as the waves rushed in to spread salty fingers across the sand, and the Mad God's breath blew a buffeting chill from the gray expanse of water. Gull shivered; she should have worn more than the thin shift that covered her body, but the heavy wool cloaks favored by the villagers dragged at her and made it hard for her to climb on the rocks. Normally, she stayed off the beach and away from the worst of the wind. That morning, however, the sighting of a sail—a sail!—had roused the village in fear and excitement. Now there was a body sea-cast upon the beach, and she was curious. Let Old Kàpala curse and beat her for disobedience. Gull didn't care. There was something here. She felt it with her eyes, tasted it with her ears. A change was coming.

The men were talking. She stilled her breathing and listened.

"Alive," she heard the priest Varyaden say in his resonant voice. "The God has been merciful."

The other men shuffled in discomfort. "Mark the

blood on his head," the fisher-sentry Gefhan said.
"He may not yet live through the night."

"We should leave him for the *merren*," said
sallow-faced Tùulsin, the village oil-maker. He made
the sign to ward against evil. Gull narrowed her eyes.
She didn't like him. There was darkness there. He
smelled rank, and when she ran errands in the village
that took her near his shop, his eyes scuttled over her
like beetles.

Sandmouse stepped forward, the smith. A man of
good heart, he was dying of a secret sickness. Hale
now, he would go to the God before the end of the
year, though no one but Gull knew. She saw it like
ashes in his blood, darkening his skin beneath the
long gold hair. She felt sorry for his children; they
were less unkind to her than others. Foam laced the
smith's shoes as he crouched by the body and took the
stranger's hand in his own enormous paws. When he
spoke, his voice was low, and Gull could barely hear
his words over the pounding of the sea. She made
out "scars" and "foreign marks." Then Sandmouse
showed the other men something that made them
start, something about the stranger's hand.

Tùulsin stepped back in alarm and looked around,
his face twisted in fear. "Cursed!" he said. "The man
is cursed!"

Gull flattened herself and lost sight of them for
a moment as she wriggled carefully forward and
extended her hands to part the warden grass at the
base, just enough to let her see. All the men except
Tùulsin were now bent over the body. She heard
them mutter to each other, but could not make out
the words. Tùulsin kept back and wrapped himself
in his cloak.

"It is growing dark," he said. "I say we leave him."

Sandmouse stood and squared his massive shoulders. "The sea spared him. I say we take him to the temple."

"He is cursed!" Tùulsin insisted. "The God rejected him."

A seagull shrieked overhead, and all the men raised their heads to watch its flight. Gull watched it herself, knowing it for an omen. The gull arced low over the water, then wheeled and flew inland, shrieking again and disappearing in the direction of the village.

Varyaden sighed and held his open hands toward the crashing waters. "The God has spoken. Take the stranger to the temple and we'll send for the woundwitch."

Tùulsin tried to protest, but Varyaden cut him off. "Na, na, I have said it. He is under the God's protection for now."

They worked willingly, for none of them wished to remain this close to the sea and risk the God's wrath, in the form of the *merren* or a robber wave, or, be merciful and holy, a Godwave, though none of the last had been seen in years.

Under the priest's direction, the men took Sandmouse's cloak and spread it out on dry sand. Then Sandmouse and Gefhan lifted the stranger and carried him gently over to the cloak. Once they had him properly arranged, each of the four men took a corner and lifted, even Varyaden with his weak leg. They bore the stranger away, the wind buffeting them as they struggled up the long dunes past the thick walls of warden grass. Gull watched them go, waited until they vanished from sight, then counted seven crashes of the surf. When they did not reappear, she ventured out of her hiding place.

The beach was an expanse of brown sand flattened

by the constant attention of the sea. Driftwood in the form of logs and great chunks of logs littered the beach like bones from some great beast, stripped of bark and smoothed in the tumble of sand and saltwater. A deep slate sky hung over cold gray green waters. To the right, the beach curved north into a steep granite cliffside, atop of which Gull could see the stubby shape of the Seal Tower. To her left, the sands stretched away south for a long span before the river broke through from the land. On the river's far bank, the beach was little more than jumbled stones and boulders, and it faded into a broken shoreline. In the summer, the River People would come down the river and anchor their brightly painted boats at the mouth, and they'd celebrate the Festival of Deliverance with the villagers. During the three nights of the festival, there would be driftwood bonfires and mummers' plays and wild music and dancing. Many a child was a Deliverance Child; Gull was one herself. She wondered who her father had been, but her dreams remained silent, and the villagers had nothing to say. Except for Old Kàpala, who pinched Gull and told her her father had been a shiftless Riverman who offended the God. Gull often wished the *merren* would take Old Kàpala, but they never did.

Gull ran to the spot where the stranger had lain once the sea released him. Saltwater ran cold around her shoes. There was nothing but the barest hint of a depression where his body had pressed into the sand. She sniffed the air. Something…that something was still nearby. The different thing. It tasted like the brazen tone of the bells Varyaden rang at evening tide, but wetter and older, a sharp melody with thrumming notes of red.

A fresh wave foamed across her feet, soaking her

shoes and her woolen stockings. The white foam separated as the water slid back, and for a moment, the bubbles formed lines and shapes like the runes Varyaden carved on the temple pillars. Gull frowned and tried to understand, but the runes bled away into the sand; she stamped her foot in frustration. She couldn't read runes like Varyaden did, anyway, so what was the use?

Stupid gods. She opened her mouth to berate them, but only produced a shrill squawk like the cry of a gull. As ever, words remained beyond her.

She kicked at a piece of shell and watched it bounce across the sand. Her nose was running. She dragged a sleeve across her face and tried to push the bell tones and sense of whatever-it-was away. It was getting dark; even she had to return to the safety of the village sometime. The *merren* came at night, along with ghosts of people drowned in the Godwave. Gull was a practical girl; despite her curiosity, she'd not come down at night-tide to try to spy on *merren* or ghosts. Yet.

She flipped a damp lock of black hair away from her face and glared at the ocean, then at the Offering Rock. She snorted. They thought she didn't know.

A gull wheeled out of the dusk and glided by her, coming to alight on the sand a short distance away. She hesitated. Time to go back to the village now if she wanted to avoid a beating. The gull hopped a few feet, then turned and looked at her, cocking its head.

"Here," she heard it say. "Here."

Gull licked her lips and darted over. The place where the seabird stood was littered with pieces of driftwood, many of them smooth and painted, some of them sticky with caulk. Her hand played over the surface of one. It was made for the sea, she

knew. Was it part of a ship? The idea excited her.
Ships were blasphemy. Ever since the coming of the
Godwaves, ships were a violation of the Mad God's
rule, a defilement of the ocean. Men were to cling
to the land like barnacles. They could feed from the
sea, bathe in the surf, travel the rivers, but they were
denied travel upon the body of the God.

This wood was unholy, Varyaden would say.
Cursed. Gull held it to her budding breasts and stared
down the weave of the southern coastline while
her heart beat in hope of something she could not
name. Somehow, somewhere, there were still ships.
Somehow, somewhere, men still dared defy the gods.

The gull had gone; evening was closing in, and
there was no moon to light her way if she tarried
much longer. Gull tucked the piece of wood into her
belt and started back to the village. The ragged hem
of her shift caught on something. She turned to pluck
it free and her fingers brushed across something cold
and hard in the gloom. A deep bell-tone tolled red in
her eyes, dazzling her for a moment. The thing was
slender and jutted out like a stick jammed deep in the
sand at a sharp angle. She explored it with her hands,
smelling the shape of it in her nose and across the
back of her mouth. Long and curved and sharp and
dull all at once, brimming with whispers of blood.
With a burst of strength, she pulled it free, falling on
her backside as the beach finally released its grip. The
thing clinked and clicked as Gull got to her feet. Its
voice was ancient and strong and crusted with blood,
and it filled her vision until Gull had to drop it and
clasp her hands over her eyes to shut the noise out.

"Huh-huh-nuh!" she shouted, and the volume
of the thing's presence fell away. She blinked and
lowered her hands.

Hear me, thing, she thought. *If you want me to take you away from the sea, you'll not push me so.*

Silence. She breathed salt air, heard the crash of the waves. It was dark now, but she had no trouble finding the thing. She knew just where to reach. It shuddered under her touch, and the red whispers were muted.

It was heavy despite its slenderness, this thing. Like a long knife or one of Sandmouse's scythe-blades. A sword. She had heard them described in the tales Varyaden told in the temple meeting hall on cold winter nights. Heroes carried them. Her exploring fingers told her it was covered with fine markings and lines that tasted a little like Varyaden's runes, but smokier and deeper. This thing was *old.* She wondered how many lives it had taken, and her breath quickened.

She clutched her new treasure to her chest and turned away from the sea, following her instincts to make her way through the dark through the warden grass, away from the endless angry speech of the sea, onto the sea-path that ran through the hillocks and rolls of the land up to the fields and turf-walled cottages of the village. When she saw at last the lights of home flickering behind the ring wall, it occurred to her that this sword might not be welcomed. After all, no priest had blessed its recovery. No sign was given to the men that they would permit this thing to come among them. They might throw it out. They might throw it into the sea, or even bury it in one of the barrows on the northern shore, where the spirits of the dead would guard it until the Mad God rose for the final time and drowned all the land forever.

Gull stopped. No. The sword was hers. She had found it. The God—or maybe the Goddess, if there was such in the world—had shown it to her. Turning

her feet from the path, she crossed the northern field to
Tualoth, her favorite of the four guardians ensorcelled
to hold back the sea's rage. She walked on the turf path
to keep from leaving tracks, and once she reached
the shadow of the great stone, taller than a tall man it
was, she pulled up turf until there was room to tuck
the sword into the soil and cover it with the blanket
of grass. Tualoth would keep it safe, she knew. She
patted the rune-carved side of the stone in thanks, felt
the slow pulse of magic there, and took comfort in the
lights and shapes that passed through her mind's eye.

Then she roused herself. Voices in the village were
whirling through the air, scraps of sound with her
name attached. Chief among them was the thin sound
of Old Kàpala's cursing and promises of a beating
for the stupid orphan girl. Gull sighed and hugged
herself, swaying in the night chill. Time to go home
and be punished. But she'd never reveal this, her
secret. Na, never, never, never, *ever*.

•••

Sandmouse and his daughter Shona were waiting
for her at the sea door of the ring wall that protected
the village. Shona was of an age with Gull, but heartier
of build, with golden hair and ruddy skin as opposed
to Gull's raven hair and sea-foam pallor. Shona held
her little brother Sohan in her arms, the boy wrapped
in a blanket against the night. Sandmouse held a torch
aloft in one hand. In the other he held a cloak. Gull
accepted it gratefully and wrapped it about herself.

"You're late, girl," he said. "Don't be staying
without so long, eh?"

The sea door had its own lantern hanging in the
wooden arch that bridged the gap in the stone wall.

A small shrine occupied a niche by the heavy wooden door. This held offerings of dried fish and flowers and a cup of sweet water to the Mad God and the Sib-Shankar, the Guardian of Safe Travel. Gull stood before it and touched her heart and lips dutifully with her fingertips before following Sandmouse and Shona toward the temple.

They walked in companionable silence, neither the smith nor his daughter being given to idle speech. Gull leaned close to Shona, who smiled and showed her Sohan's sleeping face. She cooed and grinned. Then Sandmouse shot a look at them and scowled. Shona's smile vanished, and she shifted Sohan to her opposite shoulder. Gull watched her feet until the temple steps appeared in her vision and the heavy iron knocker boomed against the door. The latch thunked, the hinges creaked, and Old Kàpala's voice grated across the threshold.

"So you found her, our idiot."

"Na," said Sandmouse. "She found herself. Come to the sea door like a wet cat with mud on her hands and without a cloak, but she's well enough for all that." He shifted. "We'll be away back to the house now. Gods spare ye."

"Our thanks for finding her."

"Aye." Gull heard the crunch of retreating footsteps. Then Old Kàpala grabbed her by the hair and yanked. It hurt, but Gull stayed quiet and kept her eyes on her shoes even as she was pulled into the temple.

"Come along with ye now, fool. Should have stayed out there and let the *merren* take ye. Varyaden has enough to do without you traipsing about at mischief and wickedry." A bony hand gripped Gull's arm and slammed her down onto a crude bench. "Shoes off, girl. You're in the house of the God."

A lantern's fickle light cast fitful shadows about the boot room. Gull felt her secret stir in her heart, and hugged herself to keep it from flying out. Her feelings swirled up in a storm of confusion and outrage and glee. She started humming a little lullaby to herself to put them to sleep. Old Kàpala was shouting something from somewhere, but Gull concentrated on the more important task of her feelings.

Her cheek brushed rough wood. She blinked and felt Old Kàpala pull off her second shoe. The old woman was muttering something dark green and spiky about idiots. Gull's strong feelings had gone to sleep; she was thirsty and ready to eat. She could just see the stew pot with its thick mixture of mutton and onions and herbs. It was still hot. She sat up and pointed at her mouth.

"After all this, ye think I'm feeding you this eve? Ungrateful wretch!" Old Kàpala threw the shoe down and clambered stiffly to her feet. She was a gaunt old woman, gray hair hidden under a faded blue scarf, her body covered by a nondescript woolen smock over a heavy woolen shift. Her hands were gnarled and callused. To Gull, they were like angry ravens ready to swoop down and pinch or slap or pull hair at a moment's notice. One of the ravens made a claw and stabbed out to grab Gull's hair, when the voice of Varyaden called for more hot water from the inner room of the temple.

Old Kàpala lowered her hand and wiped it on her smock. "Aye, then, I have work to do." Her lip curled. "There's stew. Feed yourself."

She turned and vanished into the back rooms, leaving Gull alone with the flickering shadows of the boot room. She watched them and felt for the piece of driftwood under her shift, thinking of men on the sea. Then the shadows curled and twisted, turning into men boarding shapes that raised sails and tilted across black waters to a great city with seven towers. Then the forms of *merren* rose from the waters and pulled them all down. A *merren* poked its head above the waters and turned. Its eyes gleamed amid the shadow shapes, searching the room as though trying to find who watched it.

Gull shrieked and threw her arm across her face and fled across the threshold into the God's room, where people worshiped on the holy days. She barked her shin on a bench and tumbled onto the cold stone floor, gasping in pain. Behind her, she could still see the *merren*'s questing gaze; she kicked the door shut, but as it swung closed, the *merren* locked its eyes onto hers. She tasted the tang of surprise, then the bitter bite of a deep, red-tinged malice. Foreign syllables hissed and uncoiled in her mind, forming words.

Where is the sword?

The creature's thought pushed at her, parting her efforts of resistance as though they were naught but curtains of gossamer. Its claws scratched in her head for secrets. The pain was terrible. She tried to run, but her body refused to obey. She opened her mouth to cry out, but could not utter a sound beyond a sharp gasp.

Then the good wood of the door came between them, and the shadow-*merren* was gone.

For a long moment, she lay there breathing, feeling the bleeding of her inner worlds, the cuts opened in her thoughts, the jumble of images and sounds spilled by the ravages of the intruder. There was Old Kàpala, with less gray in her hair, burying her granddaughter and weeping, then turning red, angry eyes on Gull. There was happy warmth before a fire,

and giant arms that held her close. There was the
boom of distant waves during a storm, and the rage
of the Mad God's song behind it, his face dim and
huge in the sky beyond, his beard of fog and surf
reaching to the shore. There was the feeling of sand in
her toes, the joy of digging up tide-berries from the
hidden pockets only she could find. There were the
faces of the villagers, more closed and resigned every
year, and finally, the secret many of the adults held
in their hearts, the secret they thought Gull could not
taste or know until it was too late: the Offering Rock
and its rusted manacles. Even Shona and the older
children of the village held this one close. But the
secret darkened their eyes and hid in each notch of
care etched on their faces—Gull knew it as well as she
knew her own hands. It would wait until she became
a woman, then it would be released, and Old Kàpala
would have her revenge.

That secret kept. In the meantime, there were all
the others, the ones that fluttered and lurked and
danced between earth and sky. Gull collected them all
like a magpie, effortlessly, thoughtlessly, as though
they were her due. It didn't matter that she found the
lost amber piece Terowen's wife had misplaced one
summer after Deliverance. It didn't matter that she
knew the exact day when the fish would swarm up
the river in the spring or where the woundwitch's
starfoil bloomed in the deep wood every harvest. It
didn't matter that she always knew how to find the
lost children. What mattered was that she always
found the drowned ones or the ones broken after a
fall upon the rocks, that she knew who of the village
was next to die or fall to misfortune, that she spent
hours staring into empty air and crooning, that she
looked upon the villagers with knowing eyes, that she

could speak no tongue of man, and ever and foremost that she was not afraid of the sea.

She wanted to tell them they had nothing to fear from her, wanted to act as the other children and not be caught up by the sudden sweet taste of birdsong or the swelling music of a cloud in the summer sky. She wanted to share what she knew, to save those who were doomed, to comfort those who sorrowed. She did not want the dreams of others to disturb her sleep. She did not want to listen to the voices of the dead whispering old cares to her in the shadows of the day. And she did not want the *merren* to know her. And yet one did. Knew her and hunted her.

"What's gotten into you, girl? Another fit?" Old Kàpala's toe jolted her. "Up with you. The woundwitch calls for hot cloths steeped in coltsfoot. Have you wit to fetch them? Coltsfoot is in the second jar from the right, third shelf."

Gull took a deep breath and managed a nod. She scrambled to her feet and trotted for the kitchen. She knew her herbs and had shown she could be trusted with them, fey as she was in other respects.

Water was hot already, and the thick woolen cloths were soaking. Gull used a stick to fish them out and lay them on a flat stone. Using a board, she pressed them to squeeze the steaming water out. She measured out the coltsfoot into linen pouches and tucked them into the hot cloths, then placed them in a basket before carrying it out to the sanctuary behind the God's room. There on a blood-soaked palette before a shrine of the God, Varyadan and Old Kàpala and the woundwitch, a stout woman named Madhu, worked on the stranger.

The woundwitch shot a quick smile at Gull. She wasn't like the other villagers, even though she held the same secrets and some of the same fears as they did.

There was kindness there too, and warmth. Once, Gull had dreamed of becoming an apprentice woundwitch, but the secret and the distrust of the village had closed that door forever. Instead, Madhu had taken Torilan's daughter Nisha, upon whom calm waited as sweet scent upon a flower. But Nisha wasn't here this night.

Gull crept to a corner and made herself quiet and still. If she tried very hard, people no longer noticed she was there. The memory of the shadow-*merren* haunted her, and she didn't feel safe going far from people.

The stranger had been stripped down to naked skin above the waist. Gull had seldom seen a man's bare chest before; the families took their sweats together, and the men and women took their sweats separately on holy days, so she was well acquainted with the bodies of women and girls, but men and boys were another matter.

Even so, she knew this man was different. His skin was darker, almost the color of honey, his body nearly absent of hair. More remarkable, however, were the marks and lines that swarmed along each arm and crossed his chest, writ on his skin as though they were runes painted on one of the wooden pages in the temple's holy book, except that these were finer and more flowing, with curves and arcs wholly unlike the straight lines yielded by Varyadan's painstaking efforts with chisel and hammer. They reminded Gull of patterns she'd sometimes glimpsed in spider webs on dewy mornings. Some of the marks, however, were like the runes and stood independent of the flowing spider lines. The more she looked at them, the more the marks seemed to stir, to demand understanding, but she closed her eyes and tucked her head into her knees until the urge faded. Then she peeked to finish her examination of the stranger.

A darkening of stubble covered his scalp, and his face was beardless. He was not young, but neither was he old. Gull could not guess his age. Certainly his body looked strong. His chest was deep and slabbed with muscle. His arms were thick, his shoulders wider than any man she'd seen save for Sandmouse the smith. His stomach was flat and wound about with linen that held the bandage on his right side.

The lines on his skin began to demand her attention again, so she looked away. The woundwitch pressed the coltsfoot cloths onto the stranger's chest.

"The wound is clean now," she said. "The bleeding has stopped. 'Tis a miracle he survived it, truly."

"His head?" Varyadan asked in a flat voice.

"Not broken, at least. I don't know if whatever blow he took scrambled his brains." The woundwitch indicated the shrine. "That's in the God's hands now."

The Mad God, thought Gull. The God who hates people.

Varyadan ran a hand through his gray-shot beard and nodded. "Aye. The God's hands. Tell me, woundwitch, have you ever seen a man such as he?"

"With the markings?" She shrugged and traced one on the stranger's shoulder with a thoughtful finger. "Somewhat of the River People wear them. Not like these, I'd guess. The skin be darker, aye, as though touched by hotter summers than ours."

"What of the hands?"

"Hmm." She sat back on her haunches and rubbed her face. "Na, I've not seen scars like these. Thick and between all the fingers on each hand. 'Tis a mystery."

Varyaden sounded bitter. "Aye. A mystery." He

looked about to continue, but then clamped his mouth shut. Gull watched the thought beat at his lips in an effort to escape, then slide back defeated into his heart.

The woundwitch chuckled. "The other scars on his body, they tell me better tales. This man is a warrior. Too many of these are healed from cuts that would come from such things as spears or swords. The wound in his side, though, that was made by a beast with claws."

"Truly?" said Varyadan, the motion of his hand in his beard stopping short. "The *merren?*"

"So I would guess, though I'd not swear to it."

The stranger stirred and groaned, but did not wake. *"Tiruvalluvar,"* he whispered. The word fell from his lips like a jewel and spread shining, golden wings across the room. Gull gasped. The stones thrummed, her blood sang, and a tide of unaccountable elation rose in her heart, as though something she had longed after all her life had touched her at last, like a long-forgotten promise. Gull sighed as the word faded. Tears made salty trails down her cheeks.

"Eshàlon," the stranger continued, twisting with agitation. *"Kandoth agru tal…!"*

The woundwitch leaned forward and produced a sachet from the purse at her side. She held it under the stranger's nose and chanted a quick charm. Gull saw the magic puff from the woundwitch's lips like rose-colored smoke. The stranger breathed in deeply and relaxed.

"There," said the woundwitch. "He needs rest, whosoever he be."

The priest leaned against the wall and fingered the whirlpool sigil that hung at his breast. "He said *Eshàlon.* Did you hear it?"

The woundwitch nodded.

"I thought Eshàlon lost in the wrath of the Godwaves. That is the end the tales tell. Could it still exist? The city of the seafarers?"

"Maybe." The woundwitch's voice was calm, but Gull detected a thread of wonder in it, purple like the thrushblooms that were first to open in the spring. "What was the first word he spoke? The one like a bit of song?"

"The name of a hero from the elder days, I think," said the priest. "Of the blood of Eshàlon, they say—"

Old Kàpala snorted from where she sat on her haunches by the doorway. "Fools' tales! Next ye'll be squawkin' like that idiot girl! Be warned, Varyadan. The God won't be liking that kind of talk."

He regarded her coldly. "Don't speak to me of what God likes or does not like, Kàpala Fisherwife."

"Why not? You don't beat the girl. You let her run all over the heath and shore with her hair unbound. You let her make her impious noises and throw her unholy fits here in the God's sanctuary. Now you take an enemy of the God Himself here in His place set aside in His honor. You burble about blasphemous stories. Why should I be silent, you?"

He drew himself straighter. In Gull's eyes, his beard bristled and his thinning hair seemed thicker. His gaze snapped like the crack of a stone splitting under a hammer.

"Because I am the voice of the God here. The girl's days are numbered. Her life belongs to the God. Why should I not let her run unhindered?" His gaze softened. "She had nothing to do with your grandbabe falling in the well, Kàpala. Surely you kn——"

"I know naught of that! Naught but that she was the

one who knew where my beautiful Asha lay bloated
and blue when none of the rest of us did. How should
she know that unless she had done it, eh? Eh?"

"We've talked on this before. She was little more
than a babe herself."

Old Kàpala stood, trembling. "She's a darkwife in
the making. A *darkwife*. She feeds on evil. And you
know it, priest—and *you*," here she pointed at the
woundwitch, "the God will take her life soon, and I'll
rejoice, that's what I'll do. Rejoice! I'll burn a candle
in thanks when she's gone."

Before he could respond, she wheeled and stalked
out of the sanctuary toward the hearth room, leaving
uncomfortable silence behind her. Though Gull had
known Old Kàpala's heart for years, she had to resist
the urge to keen and rock at the taste of the woman's
hurt, so deep it was, and bitter.

"There's naught more for me to do here," said
the woundwitch at last. "I should go." She pulled a
blanket up over the stranger and stood. "Send for me if
something changes. Keep him warm and keep water
nearby. That's most of what he needs now, along with
the favor of the gods."

"Aye. Thank you, Madhu."

The woundwitch put her hand on the priest's arm.
"You're a good man, Varyadan. But Kàpala is right:
the time is coming near. Gull is close to becoming a
woman."

He closed his eyes. "I know."

"Will you do what must be done?"

"I serve the God," he whispered.

She patted him and retreated, bowing to the shrine
on her way out. Gull caught an odd look on the
woundwitch's face, the glitter of tears in her eyes.

Then she was gone, and Gull returned her attention to the priest.

He knelt by the stranger's head and faced the shrine, his voice full of emotion. "Guide me, O Yashaskar, O God of the Great Waters and Giver of Life. Let me be the vessel of Your Will." He remained there for a long time, head bowed, and then he too rose and touched his heart and lips. After checking the stranger's breathing, he limped out of the sanctuary.

Gull pressed her hands against the floor, felt Varyaden's footsteps recede through tiny shivers in the stone that spoke of his weariness. Poor Varyaden, she thought.

The lantern threw faint light on the shrine, across the stranger and Gull's toes, which poked out of the blanket of shadow that had pooled in the corner of the room where she sat, tasting and retasting her memories of the words spoken here, and watching over the stranger for want of anything better to do.

Eventually she slept.

•••

She woke to the sound of the stranger groaning again. It was still dark, and the lantern had burned down. She made her way to him in the darkness, watching for the burst of his speech to play across her vision. She didn't recognize the words, but she understood he wanted water. She fumbled for the beaker in the dark and put a hand on his shoulder to steady him. He was hot and damp to her touch. She held the beaker to his lips, and he settled to drink greedily from it. She refused to allow him to have all of it, remembering that people who suffered from

Illustrated by Nathan Taylor

great thirst often needed to let the water settle in their stomachs before taking more.

"Kra-Shaloth," he croaked before lapsing back into sleep. She guessed he meant to thank her.

The water bucket was nearly empty. She refilled the lantern, lit it, and then padded out to the well behind the temple to refill it. It was dark outside, but the clouds had cleared so that the sky was a dark blue and spattered with countless stars. A sickle of moon provided a thin dram of light and set the frost aglitter on the grass and the edges of the well. She returned with the bucket sloshing gently at her side, eager to return to the warmth of the temple.

The stranger was awake. She knew it as soon as she approached the door into the sanctuary, though he still seemed to be asleep. His breathing was deep and slow, but he was awake just the same.

She put the bucket down quietly, thinking she would fetch the priest. But then the thought struck her: how would an enemy of the God act? But an enemy of the God might also be an enemy of the *merren*, and thus a friend to her. If the priest and woundwitch spoke truly, she would be a woman soon, and then she'd go to the Offering Rock. This stranger might be her best hope. She'd thought once to run away, only to find she could not. There was a geas upon her that kept her from going too far. But if someone *took* her—

The priest would not bestir himself much to hinder her, but Old Kàpala would, that was sure enough. Gulping a deep breath, Gull leaned on the doorjamb and closed her eyes, concentrating, peering inward to see the way forward. Sometimes she could see, most times not. This time, she saw three paths clear before her. One led to the manacles of the Offering Stones. A darker one led to Old Kàpala strangling her—no, *drowning* her—in the sea. The darkest led to the *merren*, and she could not look well upon that one. As she watched, the paths swam together and braided into one, and she opened her eyes in fear, unwilling to look further, the vision replaced by the cool stone of the sanctuary.

Death. Yet she could not run. She could not run. The geas upon her was too strong.

She slid to her knees, a lump in her throat. Her hair brushed across the backs of her hands where they pressed onto the cold stone. Never had she felt so alone. The feelings rushed through her like wind, a long, sobbing noise came from her throat. Her fingertips dug at the floor. The stranger was her only hope, if hope remained to her.

Well then, she told herself.

She rubbed her sleeve across her face. When she was sure she had pulled her heart back into its harness, she stole into the room and made her way toward the stranger. She went to kneel at his side when his hand shot out and gripped her arm. His eyes gleamed like pieces of green glass and seemed to shine with their own light. She tried to pull away, but he was too strong. The markings covering his forearm jumped and twisted over the bunch of his muscles, and for a moment, they gleamed and chimed in her sight like the tiny silver bells of the Icebegone Festival.

He whispered something to her in a gold-flecked tongue she did not understand. But she grasped his meaning: *Where am I?* She couldn't answer. Instead, she shook her head and made the various nonsense noises she was capable of, and her heart sank as she watched the frown settle across his features. With a fit of strength born of despair, she wrenched her arm free and shrank back against the wall.

"Na!" he called. Wincing, he pushed himself to a sitting position. He held his hands out and spoke a gentle word: *hànatu*. She saw it open in a twining burst of silver and green. *Friend*, she guessed, or *safe*.

The fear bled out of her. She inched closer and reached out to take one of his hands in her own. He dropped his other hand into his lap and waited.

Thick calluses greeted her touch. At the base of each finger, his skin was as hard as a shoe sole. That wasn't unusual, but the thick line of scars between each finger caught her attention. The scars ran in a line from thumbtip along the web of his hand and then up to end at the fingertip of his index finger. Then they began again from fingertip to fingertip. She traced them and drew comfort.

"*Selkhen*," he said, pointing to his hands and then himself. Then he patted his heart and said, "Borakai." The words tasted crisp and briny, like the open sea, perhaps. She smiled.

His voice was deep but gentle, reassuring despite its strangeness. The light continued to pour from his eyes. Gull swallowed, hearing the peal of distant music in that light.

He pointed to her.

Gull flushed and shook her head.

He lay back down and felt along his side and said something in a thoughtful tone. Then he pantomimed bringing a cup to his lips.

Gull scrambled to the bucket and hauled it over, then filled the cup and offered it to him. He accepted it and struggled to a sitting position again to drink. He drained it three times before he was done.

He thanked her—she didn't need to speak his language to understand that—and returned the cup to her. Then he eased himself down and closed his eyes. But he did not sleep, at least not in a way Gull understood. Instead, he began to whisper to himself in the language she could not grasp. She settled down to listen and perhaps learn more, but her own weariness caught up with her, and she fell fast asleep.

The dream struck her hard, knocked her sprawling on the sand under a huge, sharp-edged moon. The blood ran from the Offering Stones across her hands, completely covering the left one. Over her stood a shadowy figure holding a long curved blade. Behind her something came from the water. The *merren*. She rolled over, heart thumping, and watched the shadowy figures emerge from the water with burning, coal red eyes.

The girl is ours, man of Eshàlon, said the *merren*. Their laughter gurgled out of their throats. *The sword is ours. You cannot prevail. Do not stand in our way.*

They raised great clawed talons then, and fell upon her. She shrieked and tried to fight back, but they were too fast, too fast—

The cry of "Tiruvalluvar!" burst across her vision like the sun at noontide, and then someone was shaking her, and her eyes opened. Before her loomed the figure of the stranger. His green eyes were hard. The air smelled of salt tang, as though the sea had come to the temple's very door, but there was something oily in it, something foul that clung to the roof of her mouth and made her want to spit.

"Tiruvalluvar?" he asked, then added a stream of liquid words Gull watched without understanding. His nose wrinkled. "*Merren.*" The accent was different, but it was the same word. He looked up at the shrine.

She sat up and pushed his hands away. He glanced at her.

"Tiruvalluvar?" he asked, more gently. The word

dispelled the noxious stink from the air, but her heart
still sped from the darkness of her dream.

Gull stared at him, then pointed at him.

He shook his head and tapped his chest. "Borakai.
BOH-ruh-kye."

He reached out and touched her lips, then tapped
her between her breasts. "Tiruvalluvar." He mimed
someone shouting and pointed at her.

She said nothing, simply sat in disbelief. Her?
Speak? She shook her head violently and scrabbled
away from the stranger, this Borakai. He frowned
and reached for her, but she hissed at him, leaped to
her feet, and ran. Out of the sanctuary, through the
worship room into the boot room, where she flung
open the door and raced outside into the chill and the
morning mist, heedless of her bare feet slipping on
the grass.

• • •

The Seal Tower offered a familiar haven, high on
a bluff overlooking the sea. She clambered up to the
topmost chamber where the great seal-oil lamp used
to burn in the old days before the God's Wrath, when
ships still sailed between the lands of the world.

It was round and open to the wind, though the large
windows were covered by a slatted frame of wood
that in years past had held sheets of oiled sailcloth to
protect the flames from the wind. A polished bronze
mirror bolted into the mortar behind the flame pit once
cast the light out to sea, she had heard. The sailcloth
and the mirror had been taken down years ago, and
the slats had fallen into disrepair. Now the tower was
used only in spring ceremonies or as a trysting point
for the young lovers of the village. Children were

discouraged from playing there after a boy fell to his death one year. Gull found it a reliable place to be alone, where she could think without the full flood of visions and sudden insights that made it so hard for her with the villagers.

In the lee of the raised firepit, she huddled in her cloak, feeling heavy and tired. The sea wind snaked through the slats and around the firepit to slip cold fingers through her hair and hiss names of far-off places into her ears.

Eshàlon. Grundamir. Zanetavaleska. Corume of the Red Towers. The Weeping City of Threnody. Erigal the Golden, with its fabled Gate of Lions…A cascade of images came to her, of great walls and columned houses and fleets of ships, of tall people, clear-eyed, sailing upon the back of the Mad God. She shook her head and covered her ears. All gone in the God's Wrath, all gone, all lost.

Weren't they?

But the wind was insistent; it kept whispering, conjuring names and visions in her mind's eye, tugging at her cloak as if it had hands, trying to get her to stand and embrace it, to dance about the tower. She shut her eyes tight and shrieked to drown out the whispers.

The wind dropped suddenly, and the whispers stopped. Gull peeked out of her hands. Nothing. The air was silent save for the distant *shush* of the surf. Even the gulls paused in their eternal squabble.

She rolled to her hands and knees and spat. The heavy feeling hadn't gone away. It was as if she'd taken a stone into her gut. After a time, she got up and went to the sea side of the tower and looked out. The sky hung over the sea like a leaden curtain and darkened at the horizon. Far out at sea, the surface roiled under the whips of an oncoming storm. She knew the signs well, but today there was something else, something more menacing than mere weather. She read it in the shadows staining the water in the distance, how they looked like claws stretching for the village. She read it in the way the sky itself seemed to spread like water above her, in the way the gulls and fisherhawks stayed over the shore, not daring to venture out over the waves. But mostly, she knew it from the sudden, brittle stillness of the wind, as if the world held its breath in dread or in prayer.

The *merren* were coming. Gull wasn't surprised, truly. They were coming. For her. For the sword. Perhaps for the stranger's life. Her heart beat faster, and she clutched at the edge of the wall. Maybe they'd take Old Kàpala at last. But then they might harm Sandmouse and his family, who had done her no harm. Or Varyaden, who was as close a thing to a father as she had. Or Madhu the woundwitch, who had been truly kind to her. Or the other children and babes of the village, who knew no better.

She cursed her soft heart, then, for a moment wishing she was in fact the darkwife Old Kàpala thought she was, for then she could break the geas of her childhood and turn the harm and scorn back on everyone, and fly away on a cloud or in the shape of a gull for true, not just in name, and leave all to the mercies of the *merren*. Especially Old Kàpala. Gull entertained a brief daydream of the old woman groveling at the feet of taloned monsters, begging for her life, but then she released it. There was other work to do.

But what could she do? She was weak of body, a child still, and her inability to shape words meant none of her secrets could be shared, even if she possessed any scraps of knowledge that might be of use. She growled in frustration and beat at the stone beneath her hand until her palms stung. The silence in the air bore upon her like barrow stones.

The sword. The thought flitted in from amidst the despair. The woundwitch had described the stranger Borakai as a warrior, and he had seemingly spoken the name of a great hero. If he had his sword, could he not fight the *merren?* She screeched in excitement. Even so!

Hope rekindled, she descended from the Tower and ran toward Tualoth, where she had hidden the sword. Down from the bluff along the Tower path she fled, beneath a roof of windswept branches formed by the trees that clung to the shore. Dirt spattered under her feet as they beat away the distance between the treeline across the meadow toward the ring wall and the guardian stones. She met Old Kàpala and another woman of the village on the meadow path, carrying laundry to the stream. Scowling, Old Kàpala balanced her basket on her hip and caught Gull by the arm as she tried to fly by.

"And where be you off to, eh?"

Panting, Gull tried to pantomime needing to go to the privy. The other woman rolled her eyes and said, "Ay, let her go, then. Since when has this one thought on being clean?"

Old Kàpala's eyes slitted. "Na, the brat is up to somewhat, I'll say to ye." She shook Gull. "What is it now? What are you plotting, you evil thing?" Her birdlike eyes darted over Gull, demanding. Gull looked away and stilled herself, hoping Old Kàpala would be satisfied by the submission. To her surprise, the old woman uttered a gleeful cackle.

"See here, Ulryka! See here! The time has come at last. The Gods are good."

Startled, Gull followed Old Kàpala's leering gaze down, down to the parting of her cloak, where a narrow strip of her shift showed from neck to knee. There, between her legs, were two bright spots of blood. She raised her eyes to stare dumbly at Old Kàpala's triumphant expression.

Her old enemy laughed, a black sound like bones rattling in a pot. "You're a woman now, you evil thing. Prepare to die at last, as it has been sworn."

Gull wrenched away with all her strength, surprising Old Kàpala, who staggered as she lost her grip. Freed too suddenly, Gull stumbled back and tripped over a rock that fetched her tumbling into the wet grass at the side the path. She rolled to come to her feet, but Old Kàpala fell upon her with the laundry basket. Hissing and biting, Gull kicked and struggled to escape, sending dirty clothes helter-skelter into the grass and the path. But Old Kàpala was heavier than she looked, and she fought just as desperately. The last thing Gull saw as she sat in the path, half-tangled in a blanket and trying to free herself, was the old woman rearing up with a stone clutched in her scrawny fist. Then it was a red flower of pain and a dive into waterless depths where even Gull was beyond the reach of vision or dream.

•••

Awareness returned slowly, by degrees of blackness rising into pain cut by the murmur of voices. Her head throbbed.

A man's voice was saying, "...rag has been taken to the sea. The *merren* will come and we will fulfill our oath, but I say it is an evil thing we do."

A woman's voice, full of sorrow, replied, "Ay, and we gain nothing by this shedding of blood. Why, the girl is only half-alive now, no thanks to you."

A snort and soft, hate-filled laughter. The malice in it beat at Gull's head with heavy wings.

"The stranger is asking for her, I think," said the man. "We cannot speak each other's tongues, but he says his name is Borakai. It seems he knows our Gull."

"He sleeps now," said the woundwitch. "He heals quickly."

"Doubtless they spoke of evil deeds in the night," came a bitter voice, one that stirred Gull's blood with anger. "Doubtless they were about some dark magics to curse us with."

"Kàpala…" said the man. "Stop now. Ye'll get your heart's desire soon enough, black though it may be."

"So you do say, though ye be weak-gutted about it. What of the sea-cast, I say! Why has he been sent if not as a sign that the girl's time has come? Why should he too not be placed as an offering to the God?"

Other voices murmured agreement, some sighed.

"I mislike this," said a deep voice. Sandmouse. "But we swore the tithe to the God."

"Ay, one child from each of our towns," said Old Kàpala. "One from each of our steads upon the shore, freely given. Is that not the desire of the God?"

"We shall honor our oath," Varyaden said. "As to the stranger, the God bid us take him in, and so we have. I'll not break hospitality to feed your bloodlust, woman. If the God gives us another sign, we'll heed it. Until then, still your tongue!"

"As you wish, O priest." Old Kàpala's words dripped honey, but Gull could taste the poison beneath it. "And yet a storm comes. A great dark storm, the God coming for His offering, yes?"

More noises of agreement. A man's voice, thick and hot. "Are we to send her unspoiled?" Tùulsin. Gull recoiled as the words prickled across her skin. A woman. She was a woman now, subject to men's desires.

Old Kàpala cackled. "'Twould make her a better offering, perhaps, if she were filled with seed."

"No," said Varyadan flatly.

Never, Gull thought. Never. The throbbing in her head rose and broke in red waves through her body. A groan bobbed out of her as nausea uncoiled from her stomach. Retching, she rolled onto her side. Her eyes felt sticky and opened only after great effort, but the light, even of the temple's shadowy worship room, was too bright.

"Easy, my girl," said the woundwitch.

"'Ware her evil," said Old Kàpala. "She attacked me on the instant I saw her woman's blood. I say she is coming into her power. I say we should gag her so she cannot shriek her spells at us. I say—"

"Be *silent*, Kàpala." Varyadan's voice was iron, accompanied by the sound of a fist striking wood and something clattering to the floor. "I'll hear no more of this in the God's house! No more, or I'll call the God's curse upon you. As it is, had you killed the girl, we'd all have been foresworn, and you'd hang for murder. Think on *that*."

Then the woundwitch's arms held Gull. "Here, there's a spewpot for you." Gull retched and the effort caused the pain to explode in her head again. Gasping, she leaned into the woundwitch's bosom, feeling the tears leak from her eyes. So helpless, but there was something she had to do—

The sword! Her eyes snapped open. She had to get the sword. For Borakai. Before the *merren* came.

Breaking free and rolling away, she tried to get to her feet and run, but the nausea and white pain in her head slowed her. The woundwitch caught her easily and held her back. Thunder rolled in the distance, heralding the storm.

"Na, na, come here, you. It's all right. It's all right." The lies fluttered around Gull's face like white-furred moths, and she spat at them to drive them away. A knife drove behind her eyelids, but she continued to struggle. Others came to assist the woundwitch, and powerful hands held her down. Sandmouse's stern face hovered over her, his mouth shaping the words, "Be still, girl. It'll be done soon."

Then the woundwitch was there again, lifting Gull's head and holding a cup to her lips. Something bitter wafted from the cup. A potion for sleep. Gull knew it as soon as it touched her tongue, and spat it out. Sleep was death. Sleep was the Offering Rock.

"Nuh-nuh-nuh!" she managed, struggling to shape words with her traitorous tongue. "Nnnnnhhh…!"

"See how she treats kindness," observed Old Kàpala, but she stopped at a glance from Varyadan.

Then the woundwitch's fingers pinched her nose and Gull was choking on the potion, until her body betrayed her and the muscles of her throat made a great swallow. The woundwitch let go, and everyone relaxed, including Gull. Then she thrashed and threw her head back and forth until the red pain sailed out again and she threw up in great spouts that wracked her body and spattered the contents of her stomach on the woundwitch and Sandmouse and even somewhat on Varyaden, who held her ankles.

Old Kàpala made a quiet, scornful sound. The woundwitch's mouth tightened as she wiped off her cheek. She reached again for the cup.

"Hold her head this time. We'll keep her still until the potion takes effect."

"*Errak-tol ganadu loh?*" someone said, and people fell silent. Borakai stood in the doorway to the sanctuary, a blanket draped over his powerful shoulders and covering him to the knees. Sandmouse took a step forward to put himself between the newcomer and the table, arms half-raised.

"Nai, nai," Borakai showed white teeth in a wide smile and held up a hand in a plain gesture of friendship. He pointed at Gull and added something else no one understood, except that it ended in "Tiruvalluvar."

She looked at him with pleading eyes, the throbbing in her head fierce enough to keep her from wanting to shake it again.

Save me! she thought at him. *Take me from this place!*

"This girl is sick," said Varyaden, advancing around the table to greet Borakai and stand next to Sandmouse. "We wish to ease her into sleep, that is all." While he was speaking, the wind howled outside and he had to raise his voice to be heard.

Borakai frowned, his eyes moving from Gull's back to Varyaden's. At last, his face closed, and he gave a little bow and said something everyone took as an apology. Gull moaned, then spat at him.

Then the hands pressed her down again, and this time she did not resist. The woundwitch pinched her nose and again the bitter drink burned over her palate and down her throat to settle in her stomach with a deadly warmth that sent its tendrils through her body, relaxing her and stilling her, heartbeat by heartbeat, until the world hazed into a blur of color, and she slipped away into a darkness as deep and cold as the sea.

● ● ●

Gull swam in luminous green depths, past the bodies of the drowned. There were many, countless many, and they clutched at her and mouthed entreaties as she passed, gliding through their outstretched fingers as though through soft tendrils of seaweed. She felt calm and clear, and as she reached through the water, she saw that webs of flesh joined her fingers like the paws of a sea otter or a seal's flipper. Around her moved swift shapes, great darting shadows in the water. One swung close, and she saw it was a sea lion that regarded her with a gleaming black eye before shooting ahead through the water.

The seals led her in a path through the drowned spirits until they came to a small girl who drifted with her stubby arms and legs curled in tight. Her hair was brown and curly, it opened in the water about her like a flower. Her eyes were wide and staring, her mouth half-open. As Gull approached, the girl extended her limbs and righted herself.

"You're not my grandmama," she said, her voice distant and hollow.

No, said Gull, only slightly surprised that she could speak in this place. *Do I know you?*

"Once you did," the girl replied. "Not your fault."

Gull knew she should know this girl, but she could not pin the memory. At the same time, she knew how dreams were and decided not to strain for it.

"Grandma hates you," said the girl. "But she will redeem you. Be kind to her. She misses me, and blames herself."

Who are you?

"Can you not guess?" The girl pointed up, and there

above them the shadows formed circular walls that ended in a spot of watery sunlight crossed by a bar.

A well. Gull nodded. *You're Old Kàpala's granddaughter.*

"Be kind to her. Please." And then the girl closed her eyes and turned and somehow Gull lost her.

Wait! Please…! But the waters darkened and tossed her in unknown directions. The seals were still there, guiding her, but she did not know where to go. Then she saw them, three forms moving through the water, shaped like men, but swimming more as fish, with an undulating side-to-side motion that was wholly not born of men's bodies. One of them turned to look at her, and she felt his malice cut through the water like a spear. But then the seals were there, pushing and pressing her, and she sped away upward, a bubble in a rising wave. And then she burst out of the water and flailed through the air, fumbling, with her toes slapping the waves. But her arms lengthened and her fingers spread into feathers, catching the sea wind as her body tucked up beneath, and she wheeled high on the teeth of the wind with a cry of triumph, surrounded by gulls. Lightning flashed behind her, followed by a rumble of thunder. Ahead waited the green swell of the coast, Seal Tower high on her left and the river low on her right. She gained height quickly and saw the village before her, shadowed in twilight. Swiftly, she covered the distance and passed over the guardians Tualoth and Siraloth and Maja and Kol, the stones covered with burning runes and spirals and spell-wards in her sight. She circled over the ring wall and the sharp-peaked roof of the temple at the village center.

Though she wanted to fly more, to exult in the freedom of the high places and the lofting hands

of the wind, she felt herself pulled down, spiraling,
crying in frustration. The shingles of the roof creaked
as she passed through them, and beneath her she saw
Borakai sitting with his legs crossed. A strange heat
played around the marks on his arms and body, and
he glanced up at her passage as she flew through the
wall into the worship room. There a pale girl lay on
a pallet, fast asleep, clad in a beaded sky-blue dress,
her hands folded on her breast, her long black hair
braided and bound with red ribbons. At her feet was
folded a dirty white shift. Gull thought her pretty but
somewhat thin, and she had an ugly bruise on her
forehead.

An older woman leaned over the girl then, and
Gull smacked her lips at a sudden sour/smoky taste
that splashed onto her tongue. She lost all ability to
fly in the next instant, and plunged with a cry into
the girl and a turgid, billowy blackness that resolved
into a peculiar clarity. She tried to move, to open her
eyes, but nothing happened.

"Do ye hear me?" whispered the familiar hated
voice. Old Kàpala. "Aye, I know you do. That
woundwitch be not the only one who knows herb
lore." A rough thumb peeled her eyelid back, and Gull
saw the seamed face of her enemy glowering over
her. Then Old Kàpala let go and darkness returned.

"You'll not be asleep for *this*, you evil thing, na,
na. You won't be stirring hand or foot, but you'll feel
it sharp and hot as the God takes your foul life, as the
saltwater fills your lungs and the *merren* tear your
guts out for the fishes. You'll feel it very well." A
cackle, and bony fingers pinched her cheeks together
painfully. "I've waited so long for this, ye ken. I'll not
be cheated."

The hand left her face, and Gull felt their touch linger, the pain of it slow to ebb.

"I'll be watching, my girl." And then Old Kàpala was gone.

• • •

They made ready to carry Gull down to the beach at nightfall, when the tide was returning. They lifted her onto a blanket-covered plank and conveyed her gently out of the village by torch and lantern, which she knew as a flicker on the inside of her eyelids. Her senses felt sharp, uncommonly, exquisitely sharp. She felt the rough woolen blanket beneath her, the skirl of chill air on exposed skin, the musky, brown-tinged smell of the men carrying her mixed with the brittle salt grumble of the sea, the shuffle and scrape of feet on the earth and the sniff and occasional cough of the villagers who watched as they passed beyond the ring wall.

That was not all. She knew too the thrum and moan of the guardian stones, the scent of lightning pregnant in the air, the swirl of the wind as it stroked the feathers of an owl in the great wood. She felt the strength of the land pulsing with its own heartbeat, stretching skyward through root and branch. She felt the seals sheltering in their rocky caves to the north, bobbing their heads up to bark and sniff the sea air, and most of all she felt the *merren* approaching like a sore ready to burst, a hunger knifing toward her with implacable intent.

And she could neither scream nor struggle. For long moments, she sank into formless panic. Then she grew angry. The village was taking her to her death,

and she had never done anyone harm. Good people
like Varyaden and the woundwitch and Sandmouse
were caught up in an evil vow to an evil god. And
there was Borakai. What had he been trying to tell
her? Tiruvalluvar? If only she could have taken the
sword to him. Or him to the sword...!

The anger built, built, built, filling her until she
felt ready to explode. Yet her traitor body would not
move. She cast about then by instinct, looking for
some way to release that anger. Her thoughts went
to the sword, where it lay buried under a thin layer of
turf at the foot of Tualoth, perhaps to lie there forever.
Unless the *merren* found it.

No. That must not be.

No.

No. No. NO.

Far above her, her anger found kinship in the
tumult of the storm. Around them, the wind rose to a
shriek, causing the men to stagger, and the rain hit in
the next instant, hissing down in a torrent, the drops
rattling against the rocks. Gull felt it tinkle across her
exposed skin even as she felt it stream into the sea
below them and splash across the broken slats of the
Seal Tower.

"Gods be merciful!" shouted one man.

"Hellshades!" swore another.

"Hurry!"

"Watch that step!"

"To your left, you!"

Gull's anger peaked, seeking release. In her mind
it was hot and huge and burned in her blood like
firewine, flaring with enormous wings that beat at her
eyelids and mouth.

The sword, she told it. *Go*.

A brilliant light erupted across the sky, blinding even Gull behind closed eyes. A huge thunderclap followed, violent enough to shatter eardrums. The men shouted and stumbled, and Gull slid off her board to flop loose-limbed on the path. Her leg cracked painfully against a stone, and she lay in the cold mud while the rain tore at her. Then small hard things pelted her back and legs, some of them sharp. The men cried out in fear.

"Tualoth! Look! Tualoth is broken!"

It was true. Gull felt the death of the guardian stone like a sudden candle flame gone out, and it grieved her, but her anger was spent.

Varyaden's voice boomed over the wind and fear. "Go on, now! Pick her up! To the beach!"

Desperate hands clutched at her and hauled her up. Someone lost his grip on one arm, and she half-fell into the mud again. Hard beads of rain entered her open mouth.

"Don't bother with the board or blanket!" shouted Varyaden. "Sandmouse, carry her!"

A strong grip took her and cradled her to a hard chest. Her head lolled forward and she felt as though a giant carried her, moving in long, steady strides. For a time, she took comfort in the rise and fall of the great chest she leaned into, but then she remembered the *merren*, and it was all she could do to push the fear away.

They were very close.

A change in Sandmouse's gait told her the men had reached the beach; his steps slowed and required greater effort that she felt in the muscles of his stomach. The rain continued to tear at them. And then someone else held her while Sandmouse extended her arm over her head. Something cold and hard clinked around her wrist, and Sandmouse repeated the action with her other arm.

Only one man held her now. A wet beard itched at her jaw. Varyaden said, "May the God be with you, dear Gull-girl. I am sorry. Know that you were always good in my eyes." He lowered her until her toes touched the sand and his arms fell away. Her body dangled in the manacles, limp in the wind, her chin pressed into her chest. She felt the men withdraw, felt their fear retreat toward the safety of the ring wall, and she wanted to laugh. There was no safety from the *merren*, but they didn't know that.

She dragged her eyes open, saw the pale blur of her bare feet and shins through a wet sheet of hair. Mud and sand splattered them; the pretty dress was filthy and slicked to her legs. Her wrists and shoulders ached under her weight, the cold bit at her, and the rain embraced her like a live thing. Hanging there, she wondered whether Borakai would find the sword, whether Old Kàpala would feel better on the morrow, whether her—Gull's—death would make things better for the village. To her surprise, she hoped this would be true. She would look into the eyes of her death, she decided. She wondered how long it would take and how much it would hurt. Would it hurt more, or less, if she could not scream?

The tide had reached her knees when the *merren* came at last. She was able to lift her head a little by that time. Her wet hair stirred only a little under the sea-wind's whips. Her body shivered from the cold, but not from fear. For the first time in her life, she felt truly at peace.

She saw them clearly despite the darkness. Three forms loomed from the surf, each taller than a tall man, even without the crests that sprouted from the crowns of their heads. Their mouths were broad and lipless, showing sharp teeth. Their eyes glowed with reddish light. A ridge of sharp-spined fins ran along their scaled forearms, and their fingers were long and taloned. They approached in long, clumsy yet powerful strides that betrayed their unfamiliarity with the land, the water roiling around their hips where they rose from the water.

Their leader smiled, his mouth stretching into a sharp-toothed grin wider than any face of man could.

At first Gull looked away, then she remembered her vow to herself, to look into the eyes of her death, so she stared back in defiance. The thing waded closer, its gaze burning into hers, a hiss uncoiling like a long serpent from its mouth and snaking across the distance to rear up before her, forked tongue darting at her eyes. The *merren* came closer, malice stinging the air around them. Gull held her breath. The surf had reached her thighs.

Sssso close, the leader of the *merren* spoke into her mind, its words fat with satisfaction, like worms crawling through her head. *And so far.*

The *merren* stopped, their attention sliding away from Gull. She sagged in the chains, shivering in the chill water.

Another figure splashed into her field of view, a man whose upper torso and arms burned and rippled with markings of sunlight and wind. Gull could almost taste their meaning, bright and bitter all at once. One of the stranger's hands held a long, curved line of similar marks, though these tasted older, mustier, redder, and touched her ears like bones struck against metal drums, whispering to her in a language she knew yet did not understand. Pale, mistlike streamers steamed off the curve, moaning and weaving ghostly faces in the air, minding Gull of lives lost and fates severed.

Borakai. And the sword.

And the *merren* knew him. She saw it in the sudden tension of their monstrous forms as they straightened and spread out, raising their taloned hands above the roiling water and flexing them. Words boiled from the leader, dark and spiny and writhing with menace, but Gull could not understand them. Borakai responded with bright flickers of speech like those she had seen before. One word slipped its meaning to her memory, swimming through the wind and rain to her ears: *selkhen*.

The knowledge came to her then, that the blood of white-walled Eshálon was known to all things of the sea, and Borakai's ran strong. But though he was a man reckoned powerful among men, she knew as well how the *merren* possessed the strength of the deeps, enough to rend a man apart like a boiled pig if they but seized him.

Beside, Borakai was hurt, was he not? And the water stood at his thighs. Despair wrapped icy coils about her heart even as the *merren* attacked. The runes burned like brands on Borakai's skin and the sword's ghosts fluttered in the gloom as the man slashed arcs and flat, sudden lines through the air. The *merren* fell back, one reeling as its blood smoked hot into the sea.

Then Borakai stood before her, rising like a ghost himself from the dark and the surf, his face as tight as an oilskin tarp. The sword flashed up, its marks dazzling and murmuring, and sharp red pain shattered down Gull's left arm. Her body lurched to the side, her weight hanging full on her right wrist even as Borakai turned again to face the coal-eyed shapes that loomed behind him.

Hand! her body screamed.

Gone, her mind whispered back. *Gone. Gone.*

Warmth pumped across the front of her dress where she cradled her left arm. She swung in the grip of the chain and watched dumbly as Borakai fought the *merren*. The tide rose higher and she let her stump fall into the water, gifting the sea with her heart's blood.

Then someone else was there. She felt hands at the remaining manacle, felt the iron click open, staggered against the unyielding face of the Offering Rock. She tried to step back, thankful to her rescuer, but a hand knotted in her hair and lips touched her earlobe.

"I'll not let ye be saved," snarled Old Kàpala. Remorseless hands drove Gull's head underwater, backed by the hatred of years and the weight of a grandmother's grief.

Gull tried to struggle, but her body was still lulled by the potions and cold and blood loss. She might as well have been held by one of the *merren*. Chill water filled her lungs, and she choked out the last of her air, her screams stillborn in the roiling saltwater. Her body lost its buoyancy and sank under Old Kàpala's pressure. Everything was cold and black and cold and black and *nonononononono—*

"I mislike what we do," rumbled Sandmouse from somewhere.

"Naught but a darkwife," Old Kàpala said. "I'll light a candle when she's gone."

"She was always a good girl to me," said Varyaden.

"Not her fault, Grandma," pleaded dead Asha.

Mother! thought Gull. Father! If only…

She felt herself come unknotted then, as if it were someone else dying. Her spirit wafted up, up, up from the boiling waves, up past the woman drowning a girl, up over the man who staggered amid tearing

claws, up over the Offering Rock, higher than the Seal
Tower. She watched as the sparrow's wingbeat of her
heart slowed and stuttered, and finally uttered a final
defiant beat. Then all motion ceased, all light sluiced
away from the world, and she felt herself falling,
falling through starless, soundless waters. Somewhere
far away her cheek settled against the tide-packed
sands beneath the Offering Rock. Water tugged her
hand as it drifted down to her side. Strands of hair
swirled about her neck, mixed with her blood. Her
world ended in dark and cold.

● ● ●

Darkness whirled a turn with silence. And in the still
mortality of her heart a seed quickened and sprouted
a flickering tail of light.

She opened like a springtime flower. Broadened
under the touch of saltwater. The tresses of her hair
rushed over the sand across the beach and across all
the beaches of the world, across temple steps in broken
cities, across the hulks of ancient ships mouldering
in drowned harbors. She opened her eyes and saw
emerald waters and sunlight and the forms of seals
swarming around her, buoying her up and uttering
joyous barks that broke the silence. She tasted the
wind as it sang across the seas and teased foam from
the waves.

She felt the waters stroke the shins of a young
brown-skinned boy standing in a distant lagoon, a boy
who whispered a prayer for bounty and protection,
a prayer of a single word.

Tiruvalluvar.

The word unfolded and unlocked worlds within

her, opened palaces and chambers within glittering chambers of memory.

Tiruvalluvar.

She stood with that boy and with all people in whom the brine of their blood passed through their hearts with reverence for the sea.

Tiruvalluvar.

She flew with every sea bird, swam with every seal and porpoise and whale, felt the nets tug under her hands, felt schools of fish dart through sapphire waters and colder gray ones, felt the sun spread warm fingers on the waves and the whips of lightning and the slowly yielding resistance of stones where the sea made music upon the land.

Tiruvalluvar.

She felt the heart's loss of an old woman, the tears of anger spent and the heart not yet freed from blame.

Tiruvalluvar.

She felt the blood of a kinsman mingle with the black blood of the ancient enemy, servants of her mad brother.

Tiruvalluvar. She knew Herself again at last, reborn after so many years. Returned from murder to hold the world in Her embrace once more.

Tiruvalluvar! She laughed, filled with joy and sorrow to the very marrow of Her being, and reached through all the waters of the world to the frail form of Her rebirth that rested amid the sand and surf, and there She moved its heart again and raised it up with gentle hands.

•••

Gull opened her eyes and found herself standing,

the sea wind lashing her hair, a glow like moonbroth lighting the night about her. Her left hand ached, but she felt whole. She coughed out a bitter gout of seawater, and another, and then a third, before she regarded the old woman who gaped in awe by the Offering Rock.

A sound behind her caught at her ears with hooks. Gull turned. The *merren* leader cast Borakai's torn body into the water between them, the surf lacing with red for a long moment.

"You are…too late," Gull said. Her first words scratched her throat as they escaped her lips. She smiled, sensing the new presence within and around her as it silenced the waters about them, the waves in the harbor flattening to a glassy smooth surface like a midnight pool. The wind fell away in reverence. In an instant, silence reigned.

The *merren's* red eyes narrowed. *You cannot deny me with the reach of power, Goddess. You know the one I serve.*

"I need not act…thusly." Gull bent and reached beneath the water with the stump of her left wrist. Ghost fingers curled around the hilt of Borakai's sword, and she drew it from the placid surface.

Kra-Shaloth, it whispered to her. *The Key of Oaths.* She raised it and pointed it at the sky. Though it had been heavy before, now it felt light as a feather in her hand.

Sword or no, you are but a girl, the *merren* said as it prepared to leap.

"I am not alone," Gull replied.

Around them a host of shadowy forms broke the surface and a hundred eyes shone green in the moonlight. A bull seal roared a challenge that was taken up by other throats so that the noise filled the air like sharp stones.

Toothy maw agape, the *merren* leaped. The seals hurled themselves forward and battered the *merren* aside with their bodies. It reared up in rage, its talons red with seal flesh, and Gull stepped forward and swept Kra-Shaloth through the *merren*'s neck as though it were naught but mist. Blackness erupted skyward, and the *merren*'s body splashed back into the still water in a ripple of bloody foam.

•••

Dawn. Gull sat on the beach watching the tide recede. With the first rays of the sun, her ghost hand lost its grip on Kra-Shaloth. She still felt the hand, could flex it, but it could no longer touch things of the world. The sword lay upon the sand next to her, silent and waiting. On the other side of it stretched Borakai, who had crawled onto land with terrible scars marring the sigils and scripts tattooed on his skin. The Goddess had healed him, too. A short distance away cowered Old Kàpala, rocking with her arms wrapped around her knees, staring at Gull with wide, white eyes that trilled with fear.

"Tiruvalluvar was the Goddess from years agone," Borakai began after his strength returned. His words had not changed to Gull's ears, but they were no longer strange to her ken. "A foe of the *merren*, a friend of men," he continued. "It is written in the Books of Maana-Pelaku." He examined the scar ridges between his fingers and closed his dark hand into a fist. "*Selkhen* blood, from those beloved of the Goddess. The pure blood of Eshàlon."

"Why did you come?" asked Gull, listening both to his words and to the rippling flash of her inner eye. The Goddess was a part of her, but a distant part now, and the knowledge and the fearsome understanding that went with it had receded as well.

"I was following the signs in the stars, as were my brothers, that foretold of the return of the Goddess. Three times before my line has failed, to its shame, but now the Goddess is come again, and the world is changed at last."

"How did you come to this?"

"My name is Borakai, son of Alakai, son of Amanakai. I am a mariner of white-walled Eshàlon, and I do not fear the sea. It is the nature of our people to go forth into the world, to dare the wind and sea and even the Gods with courage and hope. When they do not do so, they are dead, and might as well cover themselves with earth. It was our task to herald the Goddess, to help her if we could."

"Why was I chosen?"

He laughed then, a rich sound redolent of spice and tarry smoke. "Goddess knows. I think the blood of Eshàlon must flow in you as well, in small but potent measure."

"Why didn't you find me sooner?"

Borakai levered himself up onto one elbow. His sea green eyes kindled with regret. "The signs are not easy to follow, and come clear only close to the time. Had I come sooner, you would not have died, and She would not have come forth."

She nodded and poked a stick at her toes. "What comes now?"

"What do you wish?"

Gull considered that. Now that the world was

open to her—she felt certain the geas held no further power over her—she could not decide. The village was all she knew.

"Eshàlon is open to you," Borakai said. "You would be a great lady there. We would take you to all the fabled cities. They will wax again now that the seas are freed. All the world waits at hand for you."

It was true. Gull sensed it in the boom of the waters. The inimical darkness of the sea was still there. The Mad God still dwelt in the depths, but now His Sister, too, was in the world, a merciful presence to counter His spite and rage.

"What will you?" Borakai asked again.

A shout from the path above came to them. Varyaden and the men of the village were making their way down to the beach. Gull looked at them, then to Borakai, and finally to where Old Kàpala shivered by the tall blades of warden grass.

Borakai's question hung in the air, like fruit ripe to be picked. Gull thought upon it. What had she always wanted? She looked out to sea and saw a solitary gull gliding in the distance. She got to her feet, turned toward Old Kàpala, and held out her stump to one who waited there unseen. Her ghost hand closed gently around small, cool fingers.

"First," she said. "I will mend what I can mend." And she started across the sand, her hair whipping about her in the clean wind.

For Doug & Helen,
Thanks for encouraging
children to read!
Judith L. L.

BROKEN STONES

Written by
Judith Tabron

Illustrated by
Alex Y. Torres

About the Author

Since earning her doctorate, New York resident Judith Tabron has published a comparison of Nigerian, Australian and American literature, formally analyzed Buffy the Vampire Slayer, and is about to weigh in on the economics of TV and the selling of Stargate SG-1. Her past teaching assignments covered formal composition and literature, but her current position is in academic computing. Judith's literary aspirations began as a teenager. While many teens ignore the sage advice of a parent, Judith took to heart her mother's critique ("people don't talk like that") of one of her earliest works. As a result, Judith was a semifinalist in the 2004 Academy of Motion Picture Arts and Sciences Nicholl Fellowship competition for her screenplay Jailer. She recently finished her first novel and is busy turning it into another screenplay.

About the Illustrator

When young Alex Y. Torres's kindergarten teacher called his parents to class, Alex had no idea why. "Look what your child has done!" exclaimed the teacher. She pointed to a clay figure Alex had just made of a little boy sleeping in bed, sucking his thumb, with a tiny layer of clay sheets and a pillow. Alex's father was proud but not impressed—he'd seen Alex do better! It was at that moment that Alex knew he wanted to be an artist. Son of a silkscreen-artist father and a sculptor mother, Alex never lacked for artistic expression. Today, our winning illustrator is in his last year at the School of Fine Arts of Puerto Rico earning a BA in digital arts. On the side, Alex is a freelance designer and illustrator. He has just begun his fantasy illustration portfolio and has had one cover illustration published in Puerto Rico. He believes that the purpose of his art is to "solve the enigma of creation."

1740 A.H.

"We won't need you next year."

She heard Aki but she didn't answer. She stared into her palm, where she was holding a rock she had picked up hiking the previous year. It was razor-edged, as were most of the broken boulders of the sahel that surrounded the border town. Her blood was on the stone, sinking in, absorbed like the precious moisture it was.

"We're not renewing your contract."

"I heard you, Aki." She gave him a look he remembered for the rest of his life; much, much later, the memory of it frightened him.

She said, "Sorry. I have to go. My students are waiting."

• • •

It was only after the students had filed out that Sharwah remembered again that it had been her last class. Wait, she wanted to call after them, even Hamed Keboushi who hated her so painfully. He had made every class a struggle and she suspected he had something to do with her contract's cancellation. She watched him go, short curly black hair disappearing in the sea of other heads, and wanted to hug him. She wanted to hug all of them. I've got so much to tell you. I should have been more honest. I still want to know what you think, too.

The last of the only children she would ever have trailed out the door and, slowly, motivated by a gentle cross-draft, the door closed. Snap.

Sharwah thought several curses, in Arabic, so much more mellifluous a language for unhappiness.

• • •

In her office she put a box on the floor and dropped things into it, hoping they would break. A stylus. A cup. A photograph of her and parents: father alive, mother sober.

She picked up the perpetual calendar: a hadith a day. She hated these things. She should have wiped it long ago, reused the frame. She looked at the quote for the day, the perpetual An-Nawawi:

> That which is lawful is plain, and that which is unlawful is plain.

Surely her least favorite hadith, simplistic and unhelpful. She was undoubtedly being dismissed because she had been too vocal at one too many meetings. She had known this could happen when she had opened her mouth, and yet, to be quiet was far too painful to be allowed. Her dismissal, which chipped at her ribcage, was lawful.

She dropped a memory link, full of the semester's assignments, into the box onto the calendar. Neither cracked.

The knock at the door interrupted this activity.

Ghibet waved an arm through the door. The Ch'fia were not so constructed that sticking a head in a partially opened door was feasible, and this was their substitute.

"Ghibet. What can I do for you? I was just heading out," Sharwah added shortly, thinking ungraciously that she might've found something that would produce a satisfying crunch if she'd been left alone another five minutes.

The Ch'fia entered, with Mig'sa right behind him. "We have your present now, Teacher."

Ashamed and afraid she might burst into tears, an action that would obliterate her hard-won tough classroom facade, she sat. Ghibet and Mig'sa entered like a pair of badly calibrated rotary mixer beaters, legs intertwining and untangling as they crowded each other. The office wasn't small, but a couple of Ch'fia pretty much filled it to capacity.

"You don't need to give me anything," Sharwah told them, and was happy she had one last opportunity to tell them something she could feel with sincerity. "You've both been delightful students and I've enjoyed having you in the class." Smiling at Ghibet, she said, "And your English has improved tremendously. I really hope you're proud. You've worked a lot." Winking at Mig'sa, she added, "And one suspects your English has improved too, but one cannot tell, since you never speak in class."

Ch'fia couldn't blush, and Sharwah wondered if the nervous shuffling of feet Mig'sa now demonstrated was an equivalent. "Sorry," Mig'sa offered.

"It is all right."

Surprisingly, it was Mig'sa who continued. "We give your present now, please."

The Ch'fia tended not to be good with conditional

phrasing, but Sharwah could tell from the tone Mig'sa meant to be pleading, not ordering. Ghibet's next words confirmed it.

"Elders approve gift then."

The elders had approved the gift? Why would they need to?

"You are terribly polite then-now-will."

Sharwah interpreted this confabulation of tenses as meaning that Sharwah had always been terribly polite—a tremendous compliment among the Ch'fia. She thought for a second that she *was* going to cry. Well, she told herself, if you must, do it in front of these kids. They probably won't even know what it means.

"It is rare then-now-will. It is not given to Outsiders then-now-will."

"Ghibet, that was beautifully done. A passive verb!"

Mig'sa was fairly vibrating up and down with excitement now. "Teacher, listen!"

"Excuse me. Bad habit. You don't need to give me anything. But if you want to," she repeated the conditional again slowly, "*if* you *want* to, if it is a desire that you have now, please give it. To me."

"Your gift. A gift to you. Your gift," Mig'sa repeated, as if memorizing the possessive again—which, quite frankly, he had failed to do when it was homework.

"We would like to give this gift to you now," said Ghibet, and along with this elegantly composed and obviously memorized speech, he rotated to reveal an arm that had been behind him all this while, and held out a small box.

"Thank you," and Sharwah took it, opened it.

Inside was a dull stone, the length of her finger and even thicker. Surprised, Sharwah took it out to examine it closely.

"Who told you I collect stones?"

"You make jewelry then-now," Ghibet observed, showing signs of excitement himself now. "We ask Mrs. Diya then, what Miss Sharwah likes will. She tells stone-story then."

"Ah, she's very flattering. I make jewelry sometimes. I will make something very nice out of this. But why did the elders need to approve the gift?"

"Not to Outsiders," Mig'sa repeated vehemently.

"What, not ever?" Sharwah's tone was teasing.

"Never."

Something about the way he said the word melted Sharwah's temporary smile. His tone was final, and almost…vindictive? Sarcastic? Her brow furrowed.

Ghibet added, "Outsiders are rude then-now-will."

Her conciliation was automatic. "Don't make sweeping statements, boys. I'm an outsider, after all." She stood, and hugged each Ch'fia awkwardly.

"Our boys how know you now?" Mig'sa teased.

"I've been calling you boys all semester. You mean I'm wrong? Fine time to tell me."

"Boxes carry you now?" Ghibet pointed at the box on the floor.

"Yes, I'm taking things out to my bike. Do you want to help me?"

•••

The setting sun turned the gray green omnipresent lichen lightly gold. Here and there, where a garden had recently lived, the blood red loam of the vast alluvial field that was the human colony formed a dark spot without reflection. In the distance, the tumbled boulders of the sahel, all razor-edged and heavy, slouched into the dirt and hid the living spaces of the Ch'fia, who traveled over and through them with ease. And while the town itself consisted primarily of low-lying buildings, adobe walls built of loam and glue and spotted with opportunistic lichen here and there, the mosque's towers soared beautifully upward, built of stone cut from the sahel that sparkled in the sun's last rays, studded with decorative blue tiles hand-carried from the one large city of Madinah.

The house was right where she'd left it. So many other things had changed in her life during the day, she half-expected it to be gone. But there it was, adobe outside, painted pressboard inside, smelling just slightly of alcoholic death. The gravel lawn looked just the way she left it. Someone had left her some fresh eggs, in the basket by the door.

She left the box of her office things on the back of the bike. It would have been pointless for anyone to try to steal in this small colonial town, and there was no rain due for months. The dew that fell each night and fed the native lichen that coated the ground as far as the eye could see wouldn't harm the belongings in the box, made as they were from sturdy recyclable polymers. This was a practical town, a practical home, a practical life.

When the evening call for prayer came, the muezzin's voice electronically amplified to carry to the edges of town, Sharwah dropped where she was, bent her head to the ground, and wondered if she dared ask God for guidance.

Mecca's location had been deduced upon planetfall, and even light-years away the inhabitants of this world turned their faces toward that place five times a day.

After prayer, Sharwah sat in a low chair inside the living room of the house and stared at the walls, feeling her life leak out of her through her toes, wondering what she would replace it with.

•••

She dreamed that night of the Qa'aba, left behind on Earth, toward which they prayed, and dreamed of the pilgrims on the hajj that no one on her world had ever made or would ever make. The slow turning wheel of human bodies surrounding the square black rock looked like some ancient organism just learning to move. Sharwah woke crying.

•••

Long afterward, Sharwah could not remember anything of the time that followed, except the developing cold. Logic dictated that she must have graded exams and papers, spoken to the officials at the madrassa, wrapped up the details of her contractual obligations. She must have eaten and washed; she must have moved. What she remembered was sitting in her house, wondering whether or not she should paint the pressed fiberboard that formed its inner surfaces, listening to the rising winds that sounded as though the rocks were breathing onto the crouching little town. As the temperatures dropped below zero each night, the water level in the cistern dropped, but not dangerously. The condensers still worked during the day.

She sat and thought of the time that her mother had drained the cistern and let it dry completely, then had announced that the cistern was now clean. Water apparently had represented dirt to her mother, some form of invisible uncleanness that Sharwah did not

understand but would have liked to discover. She
wanted whatever her mother had feared.

• • •

When she started to wonder what she was going
to do to support herself, her brain started to spin like a
buttered ball bearing and she had no way of stopping
it. She had to try not to let it start, or else she would
be awake all night, and then, unable to sleep during
the day, she would feel even more depressed.

She had been used to running outside every day;
now she did not always run. Why bother? But because
not running made her feel even more sluggish and
stupid, eventually she resumed the habit. She changed
her clothes less frequently, learned, for the billionth
time in human history, the practicality of underclothes.
She became familiar with her own smell, or rather,
finally admitted that she had always liked it and now,
with no one else to see her or talk to her for weeks at
a time, she had no reason to pretend to avoid it.

Why hadn't she learned more about classical music?
She should have been a musician the way her mother
always wanted. Perhaps she should not have spent
her younger years on the building crew. It had given
her practical experience that seemed to be no use now.
She'd thought she could always go back to building if
she decided she didn't like teaching. What an arrogant
child she'd been, to think she'd have a choice about
what to do with her life. That was her father's fault.
He'd always said she could do anything she wanted.
If he knew the secret to making that true, he'd taken
it with him to his grave.

She should read more about Earth history. Would

things have been better if her family had never emigrated? Why was she stuck here on this mudball of a world? Why were they all stuck here?

No, there was nothing wrong with the world. It was her.

She deleted newspapers unread.

When she realized one afternoon that her last three meals had consisted of yogurt and honey, she decided that she would soon have to leave the house.

• • •

She found herself at Esi's house without planning it.

"Hold the baby," Esi said unceremoniously as Sharwah walked over the yard's immaculately kept gravel. Sharwah's gravel was raw and pointed; Esi's, of course, was lovely tumbled quartz, because Esi was a much better and more interested housekeeper. Sharwah suddenly remembered for the first time the stone the Ch'fia students had given her. She smiled into the tiny soft brown face of the baby.

A little girl with thick twisted curls flying to all directions from her head came whipping around the house at top speed.

"May I have a hug?" Sharwah asked politely, bending down, but the little girl shook her head and, with an impish grin, tore off again.

"She's learned that hugs are currency. We're all on tight rations. I hope she gets over it soon," Esi informed her. "You can give me the baby back." Esi's skin, sheened with sweat from the coal fire, glowed deep black, and Sharwah imagined how water would shine in a similar way on the face of the Qa'aba, if it were wet. How often did a desert stone get wet?

"She's fine. Warm enough to sit out here for now?"

"Oh yes. It hasn't even dropped below zero yet."

Sharwah sprawled on a low bench, also a sturdy polymer but one into which a medallion had been carved, one of the words of the Prophet. The baby sprawled across her chest. The baby smiled at her, then spit at her. Sharwah laughed.

Esi decided to rescue her friend from the spit. "I'm sorry. She thinks it's hilarious."

"She's right." Sharwah accepted a rag from her friend and wiped the moist baby. "I can't think of anyone I would rather have spit on me." Sharwah rubbed her eyes. "You know the madrassa released me from my contract."

"I know."

"So everyone knows."

"Anyone who cares to gossip."

Sharwah looked up at her friend's face, so honest, so open. "Will anyone tell me why?"

"Not officially. You regret what you've been saying about the Ch'fia?"

"Not one bit. They've been admitted at the madrassa since settlement. Who are we to rescind that right?"

"You think of it as a right; others think of it as an incorrect precedent."

"Everyone is a sheik in their own imagination."

Esi didn't want to let it go. "I think you should talk to the imam about Hamed Keboushi."

"Why? What law has he violated? There's no law against hating Ch'fia." Sharwah allowed herself to sound bitter.

"Yes, there is." Esi was firm. "He introduces strife into the ummah. He rejects part of the ummah, which he may not do."

"The Ch'fia aren't part of the ummah." Sharwah started to heave the baby a foot or two up in the air, then lower her again to her chest. She checked out the corner of her eye to see if Esi, a ferociously careful mother, would allow this play. Esi ignored it. Sharwah went on, "But the Sudanese, the Kenyans, the Nigerians, they *are* part of the ummah."

"Oh, haven't you heard the latest? The 'black ship' caught more radiation on the crossing than the others. That's why Africans are defective. Or darker. They're not sure which."

Sharwah stared, open-mouthed. "Please tell me you're joking."

"Isn't that a charmer? The kids at school told that one to Alia. She came home crying."

"What did you say?"

"I asked her if she thought it was nice for them to say that. She said no, it made her cry. I told her that it seems clear to me that making people cry is a bad thing to do, and that people who do some bad things like that might do other bad things, like saying things that weren't true."

Sharwah shook her head and suddenly cuddled the baby close, but the baby, warm and happy in her fleeces, had no interest in being cuddled. She wanted to be flung around in the air a while longer, and squirmed and squeaked to say so. "Esi, your family is Nigerian. You have to teach your little girl to fight back when people say such things to her."

"I don't want her to fight back." Esi's braids fell across her face as she bent over the barbecue, obscuring her expression. "I want her to be happy."

Sharwah sighed. "Me too."

"The Ch'fia don't fight back, and they seem happy."

"Even Ch'fia must have their limits. Hamed just insulted the ones in my class. What if he had attacked them?"

"That's unthinkable! What's the first hadith every child learns to recite? That our laws determine our fate, and the fate of Islam is to settle this world—"

"—honorably and peacefully," they finished together, which made the baby laugh.

•••

She walked home by the women's path, which cut wide around most of the buildings and curved around the outcroppings of the sahel. The women's path provided great opportunity for gossip and for spending just that extra ten minutes outside the home, but Sharwah met no one. Instead she saw a sign painted roughly on the side of the fruitshop, the last shop in the street whose flat side faced all the traffic heading into the thicker part of town. "Ch'fia keep out," it said in both English and Arabic.

•••

The warmth and light of Esi's home was long gone by the time she reached her house. The chill the sign had given her stayed on her skin, throwing into harsh relief the empty cold corners of the rooms. Why was this furniture here? Sharwah had never liked it. It wasn't hers. It was her mother's, as the house had been. Her father used to joke that he'd married her mother for her money; and just because he used to joke about it, Sharwah knew it wasn't true. But it was certainly the case that he'd made a good match for himself, better than a poor man usually made. It was only one of the small things that gave Sharwah the impression that they had married for love.

The poets insisted that love lasted forever, but that didn't seem to be true at Sharwah's house. After her father's death, her mother had spent all her love on liquor. The black-market price of the alcohol had measured the quantity of her sin but not its perverse quality. The liquor hadn't loved her back, gifting her with a slow painful death as its dowry, the price of a love forbidden by God. Sharwah's mother had seen the death coming; she went to it, arms open, as to the most beautiful lover she could imagine.

And Sharwah's husband. What had he loved? It was Sharwah's opinion that no one would ever know. As a younger woman, she had been entranced by his mystery. It was a decade before she decided that "mystery" in a human being meant either shallowness or a stubborn opacity that couldn't be penetrated, not even with the sharpest objects. She still didn't know which description would apply properly to her husband. He went back to engineering in the big city clearly relieved to be rid of the responsibility his wife represented. And Sharwah, who had never considered herself a burden, developed a prickling knot of fury deep in her belly that she had not yet let go.

She lavished her love on her students, but since in her case love took the form of firmly insisting that they learn rather than spending their time doing whatever they would rather be doing, few of them recognized it as such.

It didn't seem as if anyone who had so much contact with other human beings ought to properly be called lonely, so it was a long, long time before Sharwah put a name to the feeling with which she spent most of her time. It had been several years now since she had known its name. She felt she should paint it, in beautiful calligraphy, on one of the blue Iznîk-style tiles and embed it in the wall to permanently mark its home.

•••

One day Sharwah started putting things in bags. In a fit of voracious simplification, she sold or threw out most of the things in the house. It was not until she had cleared out almost all of the furniture and all of the other chests and presses that she ran across a flat wooden box her mother had kept in the bottom of her clothes chest.

There were photographs in it, none of them older than planetfall, obviously, but at least a hundred years' worth of family was stored in that box.

Sharwah took out one photo of a great-grandmother she remembered. The woman was lethally thin, with beautiful dark jewels for eyes. Sharwah cradled the physical connection between her and this ancestor, dead these twenty years. The great-grandmother, who had been from France, wore hijab. Sharwah felt a dire need to brush her hair for her. She wanted to see it and touch it and compare it to her own.

•••

Sharwah dreamed that night again of the great black stone, the house of God, but this time it was floating in a sea of stars, in space, and there were no people surrounding it or touching it. It sailed, alone and sterile, through the vacuum.

• • •

It was the next day that Sharwah sat for an hour on her lawn, feeling the sharp edges of the local stone trying to cut into her even as they were defeated by the artificial fibers of her fleeces. When her feet grew numb, she turned up the temperature in the fleeces. She sat staring at one stone for so long that she forgot where she was, and when her unconscious started to unfold her limbs, desperate to get more circulation in them, she cut an ankle badly. Her blood soaked into the stone, and this time she noticed that it looked more wet than red.

That was when she went inside and unpacked her old stonecutting tools.

It had been a childhood hobby, cutting and polishing pretty rocks, making rough jewelry pieces from them. Her eye for design was not good; all her pieces lacked some sort of harmony. But she liked them anyway, and they gave her something to do while she was thinking. Her father, proud of her in this as he had been in all things, had bought her ridiculously good equipment, capable of professional-grade cutting and polishing, and the software to plan it.

She cut a small face off the stone the Ch'fia had given her. The interior of the crystal was a shockingly pure blue, a color Sharwah had never before seen in nature. Chipping a tiny piece off the opposite side, and placing a backlight behind the stone, Sharwah examined it more closely.

She couldn't see any inclusions or impurities. Such a clear stone might refract very prettily if it were faceted. Faceting was careful, tiny work; Sharwah was pleased to have the challenge in front of her.

She wasn't quite sure of the best way to cut the

stone, but decided she could get it into three large pieces without sacrificing much of the stone. A professional stonecutter could have saved more carat weight, but Sharwah was determined to do this herself. She got a large piece that was almost twenty carats uncut, and two smaller pieces that were about twelve carats apiece in their raw form. She spent days with software modeling the cuts she would make before she made even one more slice.

• • •

She had finished cutting a full dozen faces on the pure blue stone when Ksh'tu came to call. Sharwah was happy to put down her tools and uncross her eyes for a few moments, but Ksh'tu, who had simply walked into the house, came right over to the workbench and bent an eye close to the stone.

She looked up at Sharwah and blinked, the single eye disappearing for a second behind the dilating lid. "You make of it a thing it would never occur to us to make."

"Really? You must cut the stone, otherwise you would never appreciate its properties."

"Such an emphasis you put on the way things look. We know what the stone is. We appreciate it for that reason."

"Are you cold? Are you hungry?" Sharwah decided to get the traditional greetings out of the way.

Ksh'tu waved a hand impatiently, bending several other legs to get her eye even closer to the newly faceted stone. "It is a beautiful color."

"Do you think we see colors the same way?"

"Does it look beautiful to you?"

"It does."

"Then I venture to guess, we perceive it similarly."

Sharwah touched the blue face, expecting it to be cold, but it was still warm from her hands. "I've never seen a color anywhere like this in the world. We synthesize something like it for our ceramic work, but that is a lighter, yellower blue."

"Some humans have eyes this color."

"Very few. It is a recessive trait. It rarely surfaces."

"And so with this stone. It rarely surfaces."

Sharwah smiled. "A poetic turn of phrase. Your English is so very beautiful. You remind me of the poorness of my Ch'fia."

The clicking sound Ksh'tu made was in lieu of a chuckle. "Students are not always poets. Mig'sa will never be an English poet."

That idea made Sharwah snort. "But Ghibet could be. His English is good, and getting better."

"Bah. By the time I was their age I had already given up the tense marker that they cling to. They're lazy."

"Perhaps you are extraordinarily good at languages," Sharwah hinted graciously.

Ksh'tu clicked again. "Perhaps."

"Perhaps the boys will do better with Arabic."

"They will not have time to learn Arabic."

Sharwah ran her hands through her hair, rubbed her scalp—a habit she had when she was both tired and tense. "Why not? Don't tell me they won't be allowed to go back to the school. I thought it was just me they wanted to get rid of."

"By the next school year, the fence will be up."

"What fence?"

"Cutting off the sahel from the town."

At that, Sharwah couldn't help but laugh, even though it sounded unpleasant even to her ears. "What are you talking about? The sahel *surrounds* the town. That's what it means. The edge. Where the alluvial valley ends and the containing rocks begin."

"But the sahel does not go on forever. And the engineers from Madinah want to build a railroad through it, to get to the other side, where they can build more towns."

"Why? The valley is thousands of kilometers in every direction. It could support three times the current population."

"Your people thirst." Ksh'tu retreated from the workbench; the Ch'fia could do this, moving in any direction, and she kept her forward eye on Sharwah.

Sharwah shook her head. "This is ridiculous."

"Nonetheless true."

"And the fence?"

"I think they are afraid of us. That we will come into the town and cause trouble if we can."

"Will you?"

"Of course. The railroad plan violates our treaty."

Ksh'tu settled down on all five feet; she had no other need to sit. Sharwah sank into one of the low chairs.

The Ch'fia continued. "To block off our homes is against the spirit of the treaties. But not the letter. We cannot stop your people from doing what they want; we never could."

"Why not?"

"War has never been much of a hobby with us. Whereas with your people, it has been an overwhelming vocation. It's no secret we come to your schools and read your books to find out more about you. And these things we are sure of."

Sharwah glanced over at the workbench, where a

splinter of light was piercing the cut face of the stone, which scattered it through its other facets in several directions. The stone was quite refractive, Sharwah noticed. Light that passed through it was separated into its constituent colors, giving it flash and fire.

"Why did the elders approve giving me this stone?" she asked Ksh'tu.

"It would not remain hidden for very much longer. And they had other reasons. You should ask them."

• • •

The cut she had made on her own palm, gripping the sharp stone in Ahmed's office the day he had let her go, made a scar. Sharwah found this puzzling. She had other cuts; why didn't they all scar? Why this particular one? Had she not kept it clean enough? Had she moved her hand too much while it was healing?

When she dreamed now of the Qa'aba, she woke not with tears, but with longing. She felt an ache in her body that her own hands could not touch, and often woke to the sound of small noises she herself was making in the back of her throat while she slept.

• • •

"As-salaam alaykum."

"Wa alaykum as-salaam."

The imam seemed quite comfortable, seated on the rug after the midday prayers; Sharwah felt extremely tall and awkward as she lowered herself down opposite him.

"I have a question."

"Well, get on with it, child. My dinner will get cold."

Sharwah grinned at him. She had known him since birth—or more correctly, he had known her. "It is needful to correct someone doing wrong, is it not?"

"I don't have to tell that to a teacher."

"My kids have said…well, a few have said some funny things. I am disturbed."

"Then I too am disturbed. Explain."

Sharwah related the stories of Hamed Keboushi, and the children in Alia's class. "Where could they get the idea that they aren't African? It troubles me."

"Shouldn't children be proud of their Arab heritage? You are Arab yourself, my child."

His answer prickled on her skin; she said nothing, but he saw the expression on her face.

And he said, "Just because God tells us not to discriminate, that doesn't mean we don't do it. Still, the children will learn. These are examples of children who need to be taught, not some radical disaster. I will speak to their parents."

Immediately Sharwah felt a lightness under her chest. All could be made right in the world after all. Things *would* fall into their proper places.

"And about the Ch'fia?"

"What about the Ch'fia?"

"Haven't you noticed? The sign that was on the fruitshop three days ago. I heard the railroad company was planning to build a fence against the sahel to keep the Ch'fia out of town."

"The Ch'fia are not part of the ummah."

And just like that, Sharwah's happy little bubble was gone. She had said the same thing to Esi, but she had not meant it. "And yet, as a wise imam once told me, we should not discriminate, even if we do."

"All humans are caliphs of God. We must honor them all as God's representatives on this plane of existence. The Ch'fia are not caliphs of God, nor are they believers."

Sharwah's brow furrowed fiercely. "When the Jews and Christians lived in our lands, they had dispensations. So do the Ch'fia. If they live in our towns, they pay taxes. We owe them charity. The land we live on is theirs."

"Demonstrably, the land we live on is ours. We have lived on it for generations. Our blood and flesh are now within it. We came to this world to establish ourselves according to the laws of God as related to us by His prophets. We are doing this. The Ch'fia have no place in these plans." He tried to smile soothingly at her. "And there are no Christians or Jews on this planet."

The stone of the floor felt like ice even through the thick wool rug. Sharwah could feel it pushing up, up against her, driving her to her feet even though she was shaking and stumbled as she rose. "That is not why we came to this planet. We came because our land, our language, our governments, everything had been taken away from us. All the Westerners gave us in return was money. We took the money and left their world to them because we were sick of drenching ourselves in blood. We were the richest people on Earth. We decided we would rather have a home. We froze ourselves—we, a desert people—in order to reach this place. For more than a century and a half we have lived peacefully on this planet. Will we now empty all the honey jars and start filling them with blood again?"

"Young lady, I did not say that. You asked me a

question about the Ch'fia. I simply pointed out that they are not part of the ummah. They are not ruled by our laws."

"They abide by our treaties. And so should we."

"Our treaties do not require us to mix with the Ch'fia. Nor do they say we must allow the Ch'fia to wander through our streets, take seats in our schools, or in any other way partake of our community."

Sharwah looked closely at the imam. His name was Qasim; his nose was beautiful, grand and hooked, and gave his face an aura of authority. When she was ten, she had decided that she was in love with Imam Qasim Abdallah Singh and that she would grow up to marry him. She had learned almost all she knew of Islamic law and faith from this man.

And yet, at some point, he too had slipped away from her, like all the other necessary pieces of her life.

"'*That which is lawful is clear; that which is unlawful is also clear,'*" she said softly.

"Don't you remember the rest of the verse?"

"No, I don't. Do you remember this one? '*Coexistence with the Ch'fia is as necessary to our survival as our care of the land and soil. We must husband our faith with them as we hoard the water that falls from the sky. God gave them this world first, as he gave us this world last. We are brothers.'*"

The imam bowed his head. He had taught her the hadith that she had just recited.

She went on, "I know what that means, no matter what you say today. I think you do too."

Raising his eyes again to hers, Qasim nodded, very slightly. "God also requires that we avoid that which he has forbidden, and do that which he has ordered. And we will."

"He doesn't order us to break faith. We do that by

ourselves." She was shaking so hard that she had to push herself into motion by shoving against a wall. As she walked out of the mosque, she said over her shoulder, "Watch us become the people who drove us out of the world in the first place."

As she left the mosque, she had a feeling in her gut that she would never be back.

•••

She was almost finished with the largest of the three stones. She had given it a fat cushion shape, wasting a good deal of the gem material, but the curved shape of the stone appealed to her. She had about six carats in the final cut stone.

As it turned out, the stone did have an astonishingly high refractive index. Light that passed through it caused it to burn, and the fire it had contrasted with the cool blue color of the stone in a way that was hypnotic.

Sharwah couldn't make much of a guess as to the makeup of the crystal. It wasn't pure carbon, and it wasn't corundum either, though its hardness and toughness were more similar to the latter than the former. If it had been diamond, she wouldn't have been able to cut it.

It was a forgiving enough stone to drill. She couldn't decide whether or not she wanted to risk it.

•••

Eight months after the madrassa had terminated her contract, the railroad crews came. They had rented several warehouses by the terminus; one they converted into a dormitory, the others held vast shipping containers of poured steel, tools and supplies for the workers.

Her husband did not come to visit. Instead, she saw him, as she was running by the terminus. Her five-kilometer runs had become ten, then twenty. The long winter was drawing to a close; it was easier to get out, more pleasant to let the sun beat down on her head, warming her brain. As it began to grow warmer, she found she did not want to give up the longer runs. Her body craved the exercise, and she had now gone from simply thin to sinew and bone. She no longer menstruated, which gave her a secret thrill, perhaps of smugness, when she saw him, and helped give her the strength to speak to him.

"Mehrhaba!" she said, her voice loud and strong, and she slowed her pace to walk the last few steps toward him.

Startled, he turned. "Mehrhaba," but he said it absently. Did he even remember who she was?

"Where will all this new track go?" she asked.

"In sh'Allah, through the sahel," he said. "You look thin, Sharwah."

Ah, he did remember her.

"I always did. I hear your new wife is delightfully plump. Any children yet?"

He had the grace to blush. "Two."

"Healthy?"

"Yes."

Good, she thought. Let him look uncomfortable. He had never wanted her children; and now she was running out of time to have any. To hell with him.

"How nice. I hope you aren't going to be involved in building the fence."

At that he looked grim. "What fence?"

"You and I both know what fence. I should think you'd be ashamed to give those pretty little children such a fence for their inheritance."

He was shaking his head and staring at her. "When did you get like this?"

"I'm just like I always was. A little sharper."

Just then someone shouted for him from across the railyard. Sharwah saluted him. "I'm on a run," she said by way of goodbye as she picked up her pace again.

• • •

That night, Sharwah felt so good she even remembered to cook lentils and rice to go with her yogurt and honey. She felt so good, in fact, that she began the cuts on the third stone.

She had never brought herself to drill any of the three. The cushion-cut lay naked on her worktable. The second stone she had cut into a relatively sophisticated teardrop shape, and had traded her mother's cooking pots to a jeweler in Hadrassah to set it in an onishi setting, one that cupped the stone without tying it heavily down to earth. The third one she wanted to cut in a classic Tiffany shape, and it really required the skills of a far more practiced cutter. But she had nothing but time.

• • •

In her dreams, she faceted the Qa'aba, and light glowed from it, falling on her face and the faces of her children.

•••

Esi brought her goat cheese, and Sharwah, who had nearly forgotten it existed, almost drooled. It was packed in tight cloth; if she stored it under the house, it would keep for quite a while.

They didn't talk much. Sharwah asked if Alia were still having trouble with the other children; Esi shrugged.

"You're Arab," Esi said. "Your people remember when they had an empire that spanned the world. My people damaged each other as much as we were damaged. Before the hejira, your people still lived in their own lands, even when they spoke only English. My people were killed and maimed by their Christian neighbors, and we killed and maimed them back. Nothing is worth that."

Sharwah rubbed a bit of cheese against the roof of her mouth with her tongue. It was luxurious. "What will she ever fight for?"

"I told you, I don't want her to fight. You can't imagine what it's like to see your little girl cry. I just don't want her to cry."

When Esi left, Sharwah gave her a bunch of carrots, turning the cheese from a gift into a poor trade. Esi didn't visit again.

•••

"I can't," she gasped as Ksh'tu's last furry foot disappeared over the boulder above her. Her hands and feet were sore, and she was out of breath.

"Don't be absurd," Ksh'tu's susurrus voice

whispered back over the stone to her. "You are not even tired. You are simply lazy."

"Humans can't go through the sahel."

"No, it's not that they can't. It's that they don't. But you are doing it."

As the stones grew more vertical, Sharwah found she could lever herself forward through the clefts between them primarily by simply pushing out with her arms and swinging her body.

"Why are we doing this?" she called after Ksh'tu again.

"Because it's the only way to get where we want to go," Ksh'tu said reasonably.

It seemed to take forever to travel to a bowl that had been formed by the collection of smaller stones between the clefts of larger ones. Much later, Sharwah would know that it was less than two kilometers from the edge of the sahel to this place, and that she had been unforgivably feeble that day, taking nearly two hours to make the trip. In later years, she would be able to make the trip in twenty minutes. In later years, she would be able to find this place in the dark, by the smell of the blood that had dried here, when it was moistened so very lightly by the night's fallen dew. In later years, she would pray here, and cry. Much later, she would order a retreat that fell back to this spot.

But on this first visit, she merely sat down and emptied some pebbles from her boots.

There were several Ch'fia whom she did not know waiting in the bowl. One was delicately picking meat from a rockbug and placing it bite by bite into its mouth. Ch'fia mandibles bothered a lot of humans, but not Sharwah.

Ksh'tu waved a limb. "Ask them about the stone."

Sharwah's brain was so full of stones that she had to think. The blue stone. The one Mig'sa and Ghibet had given her. For politeness.

"Are you cold? Have you eaten?" one of the Ch'fia said formally, in a rote way that made Sharwah think it was probably the only English he or she knew.

"I am quite comfortable, thank you," Sharwah nodded. "Shall we speak English?"

"Ch'fia to you improves will; speak Ch'fia now," said another.

Ksh'tu said something in Ch'fia, her tone conveying the meaning, which said "Don't be ridiculous" in a formal mode that Sharwah could hardly follow. To Sharwah she said, "Just talk. I will translate when necessary."

"I am curious about the blue stone Mig'sa and Ghibet gave me then," Sharwah said, automatically adding the Ch'fia tense marker even though she suspected that it made her the equivalent of the tourist who speaks louder and slower to make herself understood.

The formal Ch'fia pronounced a word, something that sounded like water running, and Sharwah realized that must be the name of the stone.

"Why have the humans never seen this before?"

"Humans are tragically rude," another Ch'fia with excellent English said apologetically.

"I apologize for missing the connection now?"

The formal Ch'fia let loose a torrent that Ksh'tu translated. "It is the mark of a frozen moment of correctness, of rightness. It is a badge of clarity, of politeness, of those qualities which do not translate well into English words but which you know we share. A sense of the fitness of things." Ksh'tu was clearly struggling, trying out a few combinations. "Ecological justice."

Sharwah's eyebrows raised. "Then I am doubly honored. Then and now."

"A quadruple formulation. Are you trying to kill me?" Ksh'tu muttered.

"There must have been other humans equally deserving at some point in the past."

"Undoubtedly," said the good English speaker.

"And yet you chose to give it to me."

"We needed someone of whom we could ask a question," Ksh'tu translated for the formal one.

"Ask of me any question you like," Sharwah spread her hands expansively.

"Will they kill us for it?"

Sharwah sat, turning up her fleeces. She regarded each Ch'fia silently. Several blinked their forward eyes at her. Humans, Sharwah mused, would either sound afraid or angry if they felt the need to ask that question. The Ch'fia sounded neither.

"This requires thought," she answered.

She knew that such an answer formally ended the conversation, but though the Ch'fia stirred, they did not leave. They wanted an answer now.

Sharwah said, "The humans do not need such things, but they may want them. Still, I do not think they would kill you for pretty blue stones."

"We disagree." The good English speaker rustled his or her limbs. "We think they would kill us for much less. They push on us, and we don't know why. Could it be for these?"

Sharwah's denial stuck in her dry throat.

There was silence for several minutes. This was not unusual in Ch'fia conversation, and there were formal ceremonies for celebrating extended silence, but in this place, at this moment, even among the Ch'fia, there seemed to be a sense of unease as the silence dragged on and on.

Sharwah had never felt more alien in her life.

"It is not impossible," she finally said, "that humans would want or value the stones. We do value such things."

"As in the case of your gold. A conductive metal used for currency because of its appearance."

"Yes. Although that predated systems that allow value to be communicated rather than indicated by objects."

"But began because humans liked the look of the metal."

"Yes. They did."

"And will they like the look of our stone-of-frozen-rightness?"

Sharwah felt her shoulders slump. She didn't know as much history as she should, but this answer was obvious. "Yes. They will."

"They have already decided they must go through the sahel. Someone may have discovered this stone. It may be an incentive of its own. Otherwise, how can we explain them?"

"Yes," said Sharwah, reaching for words. "There are historical precedents. They must have something in mind...."

The Ch'fia rustled. "We appreciate when you say 'they,' as we do."

And just like that, Sharwah realized that she had left the ummah. The ummah was defined by faith. Sharwah still had her faith, in tatters, at the back of her soul. But the ummah itself had receded from her like a wave, leaving her on a rocky beach, stranded.

She shed the first of her tears that would soak into the gravel of the bowl. As it turned out, Sharwah cried easily, something she had not known when she was younger.

• • •

She came out of the stones and paused at the tip of the boulder that hung over the end of the human's path. She looked out over the town. The solar lamps glowed by doorways and studded gardens like globular flowers. She knew from experience that their warm light gave no heat.

She surveyed the scene as though her eyes and her brain were a new set of tools, with new edges, new handles, a new heft in her hands, and she asked herself: what was she willing to break?

• • •

Two days later she went to the railroad construction site. She found her husband manipulating a digging machine. She crooked a finger at him, and he came, turning off the machine, climbing down. She was astonished that he simply did what she wanted him to do. She wondered if he realized it.

"I want to know why this railroad has to go through the sahel, and I want to know now," she told him.

He looked at her, his sad eyes, a browner green than the valley lichen, sliding over her and back as if they couldn't rest yet couldn't pass. "That's not for discussion."

"I don't want to discuss it. I want to know it."

"Decisions have already been made."

"But not told." Trying a different tack, she cocked

a hip, waved an arm. "Come on. What does it matter if they've already decided everything? I live here, you don't. Why not tell?"

"There's a plan—"

"You won't even tell *me?*"

It was a dirty card and she could tell as she played it that it had no value. Now he pitied her. "If you spent any time in town, you'd already know."

"Huh. It's not on the nets, but everyone knows. What a surprise. Might as well help me back into the world. Poor me."

"Sharwah." He sighed, but she could tell he was going to tell her. "We have to make the hajj."

She was shaken, thoroughly shaken. Could he see her dreams?

No, she could tell by looking at him. He wasn't talking about her.

"No one on this world will ever make the hajj."

"God requires it. Once in one's lifetime, if one can, one must make the pilgrimage."

"Shari'yah has been reinterpreted many times. God says we must if we can. We cannot."

"We can."

"How? How?" She didn't care how shrill her voice had become. "It took us a hundred years to get here. Many died in the tanks. Families had time to grow to love, then hate one another, the ones who stayed awake to guide and protect. Their service to the ummah was infinite, and God's mercy will be just."

"We can go back. We have improved some technologies."

"We left that home."

"No, Sharwah." His eyes were soft and sad. "No one chooses where home is."

She rubbed her scalp, squeezed her head; she thought this level of insanity might cause her brain to burst. "What does this have to do with the sahel? I can guarantee you the Qa'aba isn't over the ridge. Why bother the Ch'fia?"

Now he looked not just sad, but uneasy. He could not keep his gaze anywhere near her face.

She stared at him, and thought out loud. "The old ships are still in orbit. They can be refitted. New tanks, new equipment would be built in Madinah. The facilities there need to be expanded. You can synthesize any tools, any building materials you need—"

"But not power." He was a big man, as tall as she was but much broader, much heavier. His head tilted toward the ground as if gravity were tugging on it; his eyes stayed on the loam. "The solar collectors cannot gather the power we need for the building, Sharwah. Orbital surveys indicate there are deposits on the other side—"

"FUEL?" She screamed it at him, and he looked around quickly. Some other engineers and builders stared at the two of them. He held out a hand as if to shush her, but the sound exploded out of her. "You're going through the sahel for *fuel*? For *fuel*?" Another bomb exploded in her head. "Are you mad? Is there nothing to eat in Madinah but insanity?"

"Enough of us want this, Sharwah. Don't you want it? Can't you feel the pull?"

"We've never lived on Earth, any of us! We've been on this planet for generations! If the center of our faith is not the ummah here, we will not find it on some other world that tried to grind us down and spit us out!"

"But it's not here. We all know it."

He was hustling her out of the building zone, his big warm hands under her elbows, half-pushing, half-nudging her along. "You know it too, Sharwah."

He turned and left her outside the digging zone, her feet on the gray green lichen.

• • •

At home she stared into the empty spaces and they felt too cold and too warm by turns. She was desiccated, her skin cracking open; she was drowning in a thick choking fog.

It can't be, she thought to herself. It can't be. It can't be. It can't be.

The cushion-cut blue stone sat in her hand and she rubbed it with her thumb, its smooth purposeful edges reminding her that matter existed, at least in crystalline form.

You can do anything you want, her father's voice said again in her head. You can cut stone. Just think of that. With tools and planning. If you want to.

• • •

It was another three weeks before she left the house again.

• • •

Four months later, she still felt her brain was split in half. There was the part that had heard insanity, and did not believe it; and there was the part that was considering going mad, every second, every minute, and constantly finding reasons to reject that path. She could find no solution to the discontinuity, just as she could find no solution to the clean pattern of the link fence that was erected, all along the sahel, around the edge of town.

The engineers in Madinah, apparently, had not considered how good the Ch'fia would be at climbing. Clearly they did not encounter Ch'fia as often as the citizens of the outlying towns.

Four meters of regular link did not give the Ch'fia much pause. They appeared now in town always in groups, usually three or four; they went to stores. They stopped attending school, but Sharwah heard from a neighbor, when she traded some extra water for some goat cheese, that the Ch'fia had walked all around the perimeter of the madrassa, visible from every window to the students and teachers inside.

Her next-door neighbor told her all about it when she came to trade some eggs for water.

"Good," Sharwah said, and the woman looked taken aback. Sharwah wondered why.

Sharwah cradled the eggs in her hands. She had not bothered to put a robe over her fleeces to receive company; she'd brought the can of water outside. "We should see whom we are cheating. We cannot hide from our breach of good faith. If we are going to do evil, we should not pretend we cannot see the actions of our own hands.

"'That which is lawful is clear; that which is unlawful is also clear,'" she told the older woman, who shook her head and retired to her own house.

•••

The next time Sharwah went out running, she went

nowhere in the town. Instead she followed the train tracks out, out across the flatness so far that no one from the town could see her, kilometers out.

And Sharwah knelt, and dug under the rails with her hands, looked at the ties, and wondered what kinds of tools could be used to separate them.

•••

It was not long after that—she could not remember, later, how much after—that Sharwah was out running again, in the dawn light, and found the body.

Two of Mig'sa's legs had been crushed, each pseudovertebrae snapped so that they could be pushed through the chainlink and tied in a knot, suspending his body about a meter and a half off the ground so that he was easily visible.

The forward eyelid was dilated, and the eye it usually protected had also been crushed, its internal fluids leaking down over the fur of the head/body like tears. It had not been cold enough to freeze them nor dry enough to evaporate them.

Sharwah knelt on the ground. She did not want to touch him, neither did she want to leave him. She knelt, and she prayed.

Mig'sa's body, and its kneeling attendant, were quite visible from the main street through town. People stopped to speak to her, but she did not answer.

When the muezzin called for the evening prayer, she had already spent the entire day on her knees, in humility to God.

•••

To Doog: Thanks for your support

Illustrated by Alex Y. Torres

Someone left a bowl of water; someone left lentils. She did not notice, though occasionally, as if subconsciously, she would be driven to consume a mouthful of one or the other. She was neither a hermit nor a saint, she wanted to scream at them, but she was too busy concentrating to indulge that part of her. There was a light, a hard, faceted light, deep inside her, and she had to see it.

•••

After several days she felt the light infusing her. It did not come from outside of her. It was of her very essence, and she knew she should mistrust it, but if she mistrusted it, she would have to mistrust every atom of hard reality, every word she had ever heard, and everything she still felt.

She did not.

•••

On the fourth day she stood up. She fell over. Some watchers who were waiting to see if her vigil would end helped her up. She did not see them.

It was hard to see. She was blinded by the light from within her. Maybe it was shining out of her eyes; maybe that was why it was so hard to see through them.

She saw bent backs and kneeling bodies. A few meters away Esi knelt with her husband. Within the circle of their arms Alia and her baby sister cuddled, asleep.

And Sharwah, who had never felt such an emotion before, envied them with a bitterness that threatened to flood the hard light inside her with green swampy emotion. No, she thought, rocking herself on the balls of her feet and letting the bitter green bile leak out of her into the ground, too late for that now.

• • •

"Here is my will and testament," she said, and all the surrounding people turned to look at her.

"My house I leave to the ummah, except for what I will remove from it. It is my last tithe; it will have to last my lifetime.

"Look at the blood on our hands." She spread her hands before them. "Keep showing it to everyone. They have it too.

"The law is clear; the right thing to do is clear. Are you avoiding the doubtful area in between? Have you forgotten?

That which is lawful is clear; that which is unlawful is also clear. Between the two are doubtful matters of which few people know. Whoever avoids these doubtful matters absolves himself of blame with respect to his religion and his honor. Whoever falls into doubtful things will fall into what is unlawful, just like the shepherd who grazes his flock too close to a private pasture is liable to have some of his flock stray into it. Truly every king has a private pasture, and truly God's private pasture is what he has forbidden. Truly, in the body is a small piece of flesh that, if it is healthy, the whole body is healthy and if it is sick, the whole body is sick. This small piece of flesh is the heart.

"You are killing my heart. I will take it into the sahel and try to do that which is lawful. Please. Please."

And Sharwah walked away from the people because she could no longer speak.

• • •

She went to her house. The hands of many townspeople touched her as she went, wiped tears from her face, but she did not stop for them. Inside, no one saw her take the three stones—the two smaller ones beautifully set, the large one still bare—and stuff them in the bottom of a travel pack, underneath two sets of fleeces, extra underwear and sandals. Then she took the sandals back out again and left them on the floor; they were suitable for the smooth alluvial plain but would do nothing for her in the sahel.

She only paused once more, at the house of her friend Esi. She went in and came out again almost immediately, walked off into the stony verge, and never came home.

1873 A.H.

"Don't you kids ever turn those nets off?"

The little boy never took his eyes off the screen. His sister, older by ten months, turned her face back over her shoulder to answer her dad.

"We have to watch this, Papa. It's an assignment. A program about Sharwah bint Razieh. Did you know she was from right here in New Jeddah?"

"I didn't." Their father settled back in his chair.

"I did." Their mother had come in just in time to hear them. "I think we're descended from her, through my maternal grandmother."

"For pity's sake, don't tell them that," her husband squawked. "The last thing they need is to think they're descended from a guerilla fighter."

"I bet the kids at school would think we were cool if we told them that!" the boy said, his eyes shining as he finally turned around.

"Would they?" The little girl didn't sound sure. "Anyway, Mom, if we were, we'd have the magic stones! Do you have the magic stones?"

"What magic stones? We have your grandmother's shitatsuhiaya necklace, that's in a vault, and you can wear it when you're twenty and not a day sooner."

"Sharwah had three of the shi——"

"Shitatsuhiaya," her mother supplied.

"Yes, those," the girl went on, "she cut them herself, and the Ch'fia blessed them, so they had magic powers. And one's in the museum at Madinah, and one's lost, and one's in a cleft in the stone somewhere in the sahel, marking Sharwah's grave." The little girl's brow furrowed. "So I guess we don't have one. Unless we have the lost one."

"I doubt it."

"I don't know what they're teaching at the madrassa these days," the father grumped. "Sharwah bint Razieh was a traitor, a murderer, a terrorist. She'd slit your throats in your beds if you crossed her. And Ch'fia can't bless things. They can't speak human languages, for one thing. And they aren't Muslim."

"I'd like to talk to one anyway!" the little girl enthused.

"Don't sound so negative," her mother chided the father, "you've never even seen a Ch'fia, how do you know what they're like?"

"I've never seen a rat but I know I don't want one in my home. It took a hundred years to get them out of the territory; why would we invite one back now, just to chat with a little girl who's really up past her bedtime?"

The mother nodded at the little girl, who officiously hustled her brother up and out of the room for the unpopular evening ritual of toothcleaning.

"For pity's sake," the father said again once the children had gone, "don't encourage their fantasies. They've got a short enough grip on reality."

"They're children. They have imaginations."

"*You* have imagination. Descended from Sharwah on your mother's side. Your mother would faint if a tea leaf were out of place on the table. She's not descended from a Ch'fia guerilla fighter." He sipped at the cup. "I doubt Sharwah bint Razieh was even human, if she existed at all. But if she did, I doubt she cared about place settings."

"Maybe my mother's braver than you think. After all, her mother went out in the *Mi'raj*."

"And died on it, leaving your grandfather to raise four children alone. You think that's brave? Don't you try it."

"It's what they call a pioneer spirit, you flathead."

"No. The pioneer spirit is to new lands, not to go back to the rock you came from."

"Someday people from this world will make the hajj, you'll see."

"I can't imagine what for." He squirmed comfortably in his chair, settling his buttocks into the grooves that he had worn into the cushion, balancing his cup of tea on his knee.

"Once upon a time, every faithful person did it. God asked it of us." Her brow was furrowed; she felt she wasn't getting anywhere, but she wasn't willing to give in yet.

"Once upon a time, every faithful person lived in a tent in the desert, too, but darned if I don't like a nice cozy apartment better."

"You have no poetry in your soul; what's worse, you have no interest in what's sacred." Still feeling that this made for a rather weak exit, she nonetheless sailed out of the room, head held high, past the Arabic calligraphy that hung, beautifully framed, on the wall above his head. Neither of them could read Arabic, but they knew what it said, because there was a translation on the back into English; the father had bought it on a trip through the Ridge to Bida. The framed piece said

It is clear what is lawful; it is also clear what is unlawful. Avoid the doubtful areas.

ADVICE TO THE WORD-WEARY

by
L. Ron Hubbard

Once upon a time Ye Ed wrote me a letter in which he stated that he did not want a dissertation upon the way Keats used a comma. He wanted, he claimed, an article in which there was a great deal of sound advice about writing and a number of examples.

While cleaning my files I ran across the following letters and carbon copies. If I wanted to be grasping, I could write two dozen articles using this material.

Instead, by cutting out the funny sayings and things, here is raw, solid meat as handed out to certain gentlemen and ladies who, somehow or other, obtained the address and thought, for some reason, that I could write.

• • •

L. Ron Hubbard
New York City

Dear Mr. Hubbard;

For a long time I have been writing fiction. Most of it came back and lies neglected in my files along with letters from editors and plain rejects.

I have not managed to sell a single line. Of course

I had some published in the school paper and a few places like that, but I think that if I could get at it right, I could earn a good living by writing.

The man down at the service station has read a lot of my stories and has given me quite a lot of good advice on them. He took a writing course, I think, or maybe it was journalism, at the local university.

Is it asking too much for you to answer this question? How did you start to write and sell?

Respectfully,

Jim Higgins
Cornshuck, Iowa

• • •

Jim Higgins
Cornshuck, Iowa

Dear Higgins;

It isn't a question of *how* I started to write, it's a question of *why*.

There's a world of difference there. I take it that you have a job, otherwise you wouldn't eat and if you don't eat, you don't last long.

We assume, therefore, that you are eating. That is bad, very bad. No man who wants to start writing should be able to eat regularly. Steaks and potatoes get him out of trim.

When a man starts to write, his mental attitude should be one of anguish. He *has* to sell something because he *has* to pay the grocery bill.

My advice to you is simple. If you have the idea that you can write salable stuff, go off someplace and get short of money. You'll write it all right, and what's more, you'll sell it.

Witness the case of a lady I know in New York. She was plugging at writing for some fifteen years without selling a line. She left the Big Town with her husband. In the Pacific Northwest her husband died and left her stranded.

She went to work in a lumber mill and wrote a book about it and sold it first crack out. She worked as a waitress and wrote a book about that and sold it.

Having succeeded with two books, she went back to the Big Town and got herself a job in the library until the returns came in. She wrote all the time after that but she was eating. In sawmill and hash house she wasn't living comfortably. She needed the extra.

She hasn't sold a line since.

The poet in the garret is not a bad example, after all. Personally, I write to pay my bills.

Jack London, I am told, plastered his bills over his writing desk and every time he wanted to get up or go arty he glanced at them and went right on grinding it out.

I think if I inherited a million tomorrow, my stuff would go esoteric and otherwise blah.

I started to write because I had come back from the West Indies where I had been hunting gold and discovered that we had a depression going on up here. Dead broke and with a newly acquired wife I had to start eating right away.

I started writing one story a day for six weeks. I wrote that story in the afternoon and evening. I read the mag I was to make the next day before I went to bed. I plotted the yarn in my sleep, rose and wrote it, read another mag all the way through, went to bed....

Out of that month and a half of work I have sold

fiction to the sum of nine hundred dollars. At the end of the six weeks I received checks amounting to three hundred and two dollars and fifty cents.

Unable to stand prosperity, I left for California. I got broke there, wrote for a month without stopping to breathe, sold eleven hundred dollars' worth.

Nothing like necessity to take all this nonsense about how you ought to reform editors right out of your head.

As far as that guy down at the service station is concerned, he may be okay, but remember this: You are the writer. You have to learn your own game. And if he's never hit the bread and butter side of the business, he knows less about it than you do, all courses to the contrary.

Write me again when you've gone and done some tall starving.

Best regards,

L. Ron Hubbard
New York City

•••

L. Ron Hubbard
Podunk, Maryland

Dear Mr. Hubbard;

I have always felt that I could write if I tried, but somehow I've been so busy during the last few years that I haven't had much chance.

I was married when I was very young and every time I started my writing, Joe would either move (Joe is my husband) or we'd have to both work because of the bills.

Most of my children have grown up now to a point where they can take care of themselves and although I have some time now I don't seem to be able to get down to work. I have a lot of stories in the back of my head but I just can't find time or ways and means of getting them down on paper. I feel that this is mostly mental.

Would you tell me how you write?

Wishfully,

Mary Stein
Swampwater, Florida

• • •

Mrs. Mary Stein
Swampwater, Florida

Dear Mary Stein;

Remember when you read this that I didn't ask to be appointed your psychoanalyst. I am nothing but a hard-working writer, after all, using fictitious characters and working them over. When real people get planted in front of me I stand back and gape and wonder if it can be true.

Let me tell you about Margaret Sutton. She writes some of the best children's books being written today. She has five kids, I think. A lot of them need plenty of attention. She has to support them and do her own work and everything.

One day somebody asked her why she didn't get

a maid now she had so much royalty money. She blinked and said, "A maid? Why, what would I do with my extra time?"

Well, there you have it. Maybe it *is* mental.

From Crabtown to Timbuktu, when I have been introduced as a writer, somebody always has said, "Well, now, I could write too if I just had some time."

That is a queer mental quirk with people. If a man is a writer, he is doing something everybody thinks they can do. A chap who is the head of a big insurance company, highly successful, once said to me, "I would like to write, but I never seem to be able to find the time."

It's their way of apology, I guess. Nearly everyone makes that remark and, to be brutally frank, it is a source of much merriment in the professional ranks.

I am not one to talk about working and writing in the same breath. I have a law around the house here which says that writing comes first and to hell with everything else. The lawn grows into an alfalfa field, the pipes drip merrily, the floors need paint, but I turn a deaf ear to pleas and go right on writing.

I have found this to be the case. My time at the typewriter is worth, per hour, what the average artisan gets per week. I do not work the same hours he does. I work far less, but I work much harder.

Therefore I paint my floors and fix my pipes with the typewriter keys, if you get me. One short story will pay for all the work to be done around this house in a month including the maid's wages.

People let petty things keep them away from a typewriter. I think that is true because they *want* to be kept away from the machine. When you start to write there seems to be an invisible wall separating you from the keyboard. Practice is the only thing which will dissipate it.

If you make yourself write during trying times, you are doing a lot toward whipping your jinx.

Recently I was very ill in a New York apartment. My agent, Ed Bodin, and his wife came in. My wife had been there with me for several days and was worn out. Ed and Juliet wanted to take her to a show.

They left at 8:45 p.m. They returned at 11:30. In the interim I had grown restless. I felt that I was stale, would be unable to write anything for months. Then I got mad at such a traitorous thought, climbed out of bed, sat down at the mill and wrote a story which I gave to Ed upon his return.

I knew, of course, that the story would be rotten. Half the time I couldn't see the paper, I was so dizzy.

But I guess I was wrong. Ed sold it almost immediately to *Detective Fiction Weekly*. It was "The Mad Dog Murders."

My contention is that, if you have the stuff on the ball, you can write anytime, anyplace and anything.

Best regards,

L. Ron Hubbard
Podunk, Maryland

• • •

L. Ron Hubbard
Unusualado, California

Dear Mr. Hubbard;

I been pounding out a lot of western yarns and shipping same to certain editors located in New York where the only horse in town is located on a whisky bottle.

These gents claim, per letter and returned stories, that I haven't got any real feel of the west.

The same irritates me considerable. I spotted a yarn of yours and you seemed to know hosses hands down and guns likewise and that don't measure like most of these western yarns.

I think maybe I'd better go back to wranglin' hosses because maybe I don't know how to put it in stories. I sure do know something about putting them in corrals.

I thought it was about time somebody wrote some western stories that knew what they was writing about. I still think so.

The question is, what the hell can I do about it?

Yours truly,

Steed Monahan
General Delivery
Stud Horse, Arizona

• • •

Steed Monahan
General Delivery
Stud Horse, Arizona

Dear Steed Monahan;

You have laid the finger on something. I'm not sure what. I wouldn't go as far as to say that you have the dope but lack the knack of writing fiction. You know there might be something in that. Anyway, I'm no judge because I never read any of your stuff.

This question once leaped up at a New York Chapter meeting of the American Fiction Guild. Clee Woods,

Al Echols, Sayer, and maybe Tom Roan got pretty deep into the argument about whether or not you had to know the west to write westerns.

I wasn't so very interested because my forte is adventure and such, but I listened because I had been raised in Montana but had never been able to sell a good western story.

These lads who knew the west had it all settled to their satisfaction that you had to have the dope and data before you could put down the words and syllables.

Then Frank Gruber stood up and said he'd sold a few westerns that year. Fifteen or so. And that was odd because, he said, he had never been closer to a ranch than editing a chicken paper in the middle west.

So there you are. The dope and data does not outweigh good story writing. I can write stories about pursuit pilots, stories about coal miners, stories about detectives, stories about public enemies, G-men, arctic explorers, Chinese generals, etc.

Which doesn't mean that I had to shoot down another plane to get the dope. I have never: 1. Been in a coal mine. 2. Been a detective. 3. A public enemy. 4. Been a G-man. 5. Explored the Arctic. 6. Been a Chinese general.

And yet I am proud of a record which was only marred by one inaccuracy in a story, and that was very trivial. By getting experience somewhere near the field, I can exploit the field.

For instance, of late, I have been looking into dangerous professions. I've climbed skyscrapers with steeplejacks, dived with deep-sea divers, stunted with test pilots, and made faces at lions. But at no time was I actually a member of that particular profession of which I was to write. I didn't have to be because the research enabled me to view it from a longer, more accurate range.

The only thing you can do is try hard to write a swell, fast-action western yarn. Peddle it to every western book in the field. Ask for some honest comments on it.

But before you do this, be sure you are writing what these magazines are buying.

A good story comes first. Information comes second. An editor of one of our best books recently told me, "Accuracy be damned. Very few gentlemen will know you're wrong. Give us the story. We can buy the accuracy from a twenty-five-a-week clerk with a library card. You don't have to *know*. You can *write*."

Ride 'em, cowboy, and don't pull any leather until they spot your trouble for you. But if you can't write, you can't write, no matter how much you know.

And I guess that's all I know about that subject.

Best regards,

L. Ron Hubbard
Unusualado, California

• • •

Mr. L. Ron Hubbard
New Orleans, Louisiana

Dear Mr. Hubbard;

During the last few months I have managed to sell some of my stories to magazines located in New York. I have every assurance that I can keep right on selling these stories of mine and I think it's about time I made a break for the Big Town.

I've been reading the writers' magazines and I think you have to know all about New York and the markets before you can really get places in this game.

I've been making over a hundred dollars a month in the writing game and I've sold stories to_____, and_____. I asked one of the editors about this and he told me by all means look him up when I got to New York. As that sounds encouraging, I'm planning on leaving.

Jeb Uglook wants me to go with him to Baffin Land on his whaler this summer, but I think I better give my writing a break and go to New York instead.

But I thought, before I made a decision, I'd better write to some professional writer like you who's been in New York a lot and ask him what conditions were there.

My stories are mostly about this part of the world as I am always cruising around or trekking off someplace with guys like Jeb Uglook, or Biff Carlson (he's the Mountie here), but I think I ought to have a wider field for my work. Detective stories, for instance, and things like that.

Would you tell me about New York?

Sincerely,

Arch Bankey
GeeHaw Factory
Hudson Bay

●●●

Mr. Arch Bankey
GeeHaw Factory
Hudson Bay

Dear Arch Bankey;

A few years ago I knew a beachcomber in Hong Kong. All he ever talked about was the day he would go to New York. That was the place. New York!

But he was smarter than the rest of us. He never went. He just talked about it.

There's nothing like knowing your editors, of course. Editors are swell people as a rule. Nothing like getting their slant face to face. Increase your sales no end.

But if you think you can go to New York and live there on a hundred a month, you're as crazy as a locoed wolf. Think about it from this angle:

In New York you'll have noise, bad living conditions, and higher expenses. You will have to keep right on writing to keep eating.

You are used to writing where the biggest noise is a pine tree shouting at its neighbor. That is the condition you know. You can write there.

Chances are a hundred to one that you won't be able to turn out a line when the subway begins to saw into your nerves, when the L smashes out your eardrums overhead, when ten thousand taxi drivers clamp down on their horns.

If you can't write, you can't eat because you won't have enough reserve.

Besides, the markets you mention are not very reliable. Those eds are the brand that want something for nothing. Wait until you sell the big books in the pulp field. Wait until you crack into at least four of the big five publishing houses. Wait until you are pretty sure you know what you're doing in the game before you make a change.

I've wrecked myself time after time with changes just because I have itchy feet. I have just come from New York. I got along all right, for a very little while, then the town got me. I had a big month and managed to get out.

But once New York gets you, you're got.

Some of the swellest guys I know are in New York. Also some of the worst heels.

Here's my advice, take it for what it's worth to you.

Jeb Uglook and the whaler will provide you with lots of story material. Go with him and write it. Trek out with that Mountie and study the way he goes about it. Take your trips with your eyes open for data.

Neither Jeb nor Carlson will let you starve. If you can't put out the wordage, you'll find editors far from interested in you.

Write everything you can, study the mags you're sending stuff to, collect every scrap of story material from GeeHaw Factory. Collect yourself checks to the amount of one thousand dollars, no more no less. With that all in one piece, shove off for New York.

On arrival, get yourself the best clothes you can buy. Register at the Waldorf-Astoria. Take editors out to lunch in a Cadillac taxi.

Stay in New York until all you've got left is your return trip ticket to GeeHaw. Pack up and leave right away quick for home.

Don't try to work in New York. Don't try to make it your home. Go there with a roll and do the place right, then grab the rattler for Hudson Bay before the glamor wears off.

Sitting in a shabby room, pounding a mill with the

landlady pounding on the door is fine experience, but I think gunning for whales up off Baffin Land is much more to your liking.

Best regards,

L. Ron Hubbard
New Orleans, Louisiana

• • •

And this, my children, endeth the lesson. Any questions?

GAMES ON THE CHILDREN'S WARD

Written by
Michail Velichansky

Illustrated by
Miguel Rojas

About the Author

When Michail Velichansky was just five years old, he left the former Soviet Union with his family bound for Austria and Italy. Receiving political asylum in the United States, the family eventually ended up in Maryland. Admittedly, this was much less intriguing to young Michail than graspable objects like LEGOs, gum and ripe bananas (which were all quite new and delicious except, possibly, the LEGOs). It's also where Michail's love of reading and the fantastic began after he came across his school library's worn copy of J.R.R. Tolkien's The Hobbit. Michail began writing in high school and quickly discovered it was absolutely the most difficult thing he had ever tried. Based on this realization, he decided to devote much of his life to it. Michail recently graduated from the University of Maryland, College Park, with a BA in English, concentrating on mythology and folklore. In 2003, he attended the Odyssey writers' workshop and recently made his first professional sale to the horror anthology Corpse Blossoms.

About the Illustrator

When illustrator Miguel Rojas began drawing, he relied on how-to-draw-super-heroes books. Yet he never liked the idea of drawing figures like Spider-Man or Batman. Instead, Miguel created his own characters. Later, as video game graphics became more sophisticated, he learned that such games began with concepts from illustrator/concept artists. So he decided to go for a degree in multimedia and animation, which he recently completed in San Diego. He's currently working as a graphic designer at a print graphics company in Southern California, and continues to improve his craft by drawing every day. Much of Miguel's artwork is influenced by comic book illustrators like Keon (Incredible Hulk), Capullo (Spawn), Maduriera (X-Men) and Pacheco (X-Men), who deliberately overexaggerate for effect but maintain a strong sense of realism. He would love to do book illustrations and appreciates the opportunity the Contest has offered him.

There were games the children played on the ward. First lying in bed recovering from surgery, then slinking around the common room, Shawn had plenty of time to see them all. They played with cards limp from years of shuffling and set up board games that the nurses brought them.

Sometimes they played "Sally Ate My Dessert!" in which you ate your pudding as fast as possible and tried to convince the nurse that Sally had come out of her coma and stolen it. A game for one, though there were always spectators. Others, like "Code Blue! Code Blue!" could involve any number of people. "Don't Let Them Know" involved everyone: if the doctor comes in barking orders while a nurse takes you away on a field trip, if when you get back there's one less on the ward and the nurses struggle to smile in their colorful smocks—then you can't let them know you know. Everybody wins if nobody cries. "IV Racing" required at least two people, unless it was timed. And then there was "The Death Man Game," a complicated game of cards and dominoes that Michael had made up. On the rare occasions that Michael ran the game, every long-term patient played.

But not Shawn. Why make friends when he was leaving soon? Any day now he'd be better, and his parents would come to take him home. He'd been on the ward before. He knew that only the sick let the ward become home. He remembered the catheter in his chest, the dialysis sessions, the shunt in his stomach, so they could pour the fluid in.

No more of that. He had a new kidney.

Yet he was still here, tired, hurting, staring out the window of his and Michael's room. He imagined the feel of pine needles against his skin, of rough bark and sticky sap. He remembered how a spider's web stuck to his fingers when he broke it and the smell of mold after the rain. Outside, the world seemed full of life. Inside, the walls were covered with smiling, dancing cartoon animals. He smelled medicine, and it made him sick.

"You really getting out of here soon?" Michael asked.

Shawn nodded. "Real soon."

"The doctor tell you that?"

Another nod.

Michael made a fish-face, then said, "Did he have that look when he said it?"

Shawn didn't answer. He knew what look Michael meant: the same look the doctor gave when he talked about ninety-five percent success rates.

Michael said, "We're playing the Death Man Game tomorrow. I could teach you."

"No thanks," Shawn said.

He tried hard not to learn any of the games they played, but already he knew too many by heart. He was glad Michael's Death Man Game was too complicated to take in accidentally—with its dominoes and marbles, with cards moving from hand to table to hand. He was glad he could be ignorant of that rite.

•••

Shawn slept less and less each night. Now he wondered if he would fall asleep at all.

The ward changed with the rising of the moon. Trees cast shadows on the walls, and the cartoon animals turned into shades—where there had been a smile, in moonlight shone pale teeth. Machines hummed, giving off red and green lights like false stars. Shawn could make out the voices of nurses and doctors through the walls. He kicked his blankets to the edge of the bed and wiggled out of his gown. He shivered and squeezed the clump of hair he held in his left hand even tighter.

A few feet away, Michael's lips were moving: he was doing math problems in his sleep again. Shawn left their room and waited for the Blue-sky Woman in the game room. He saw her sometimes, walking through the ward at night, but she no longer stopped at his bed. He missed her touch like he missed the wind on his face, a touch that went through his skin to something deep inside him. Something deep inside…something dead, most likely. Something broken or cut out by the doctors, something the drugs didn't like. Whatever it was, it was probably killing him.

Shawn followed the Blue-sky Woman past the empty tables into Sally's room. She ran a transparent hand over the comatose girl's brow and whispered in her ear. Then the Blue-sky Woman faded away, as though Shawn had only imagined her in the moonlight shadows of tables and IV stands. Shawn knew what she said: It'll be all right. You'll be fine.

His left hand shook and his nails dug into his palm. Shawn was glad she didn't visit him anymore. The Blue-sky Woman was a liar, taunting him with recovery, with going outside. He told himself again and again how much he hated her.

Of those staying on the ward long term, Sally was the only one the Blue-sky Woman visited anymore. The doctors still thought she might wake up, and he wondered if in her coma dreams she thought the same.

Shawn returned to his bed. Because he could not sleep, he waited.

If you stayed up late enough on the ward, you would see the Death Man with his dingy rags and mismatched shoes, his eyes that wouldn't look away. Even with the lights on, Shawn could feel the Death Man hiding behind the pictures on the walls, breathing down his neck, thick air that left him shivering and covered in cold sweat. If he didn't leave soon, the Death Man would visit his bed, and they'd wheel him out at night while the ward played Don't Let Them Know.

Shawn stuck his fist into the pillowcase and hid his face.

• • •

The next day a nurse wheeled in a bald, skeletal girl who couldn't have been older than seven and looked small and fragile enough to be four. Beneath her gown one of her legs was little more than a stub and the other a shriveled twig. Kids were always coming on and off the ward, but she looked like she was there to stay.

"This is Wendy," the nurse said.

The kids mumbled a bored hello, hardly looking up from the Death Man Game.

"Would you like to join their game? You can for a few minutes, if you like. Then I'll take you to your bed."

Wendy shrugged. The nurse smiled and patted the

Illustrated by Miguel Rojas

girl's shoulder—"Make some friends, dear"—and walked out.

"So what've you got?" they asked. The usual greeting for a newcomer on the ward.

"Cancer," the girl said.

Rubbing his own bald head, Tim asked, "How long?"

"Year and a half."

"You have surgery?"

"Two."

"I've only had one. How many pills they giving you?"

They spoke as the game went on, comparing cancers while the girl watched the game, perched like a gargoyle on her wheeled cathedral. Her eyes were too large on her sunken face, her jaw bony and hard-set.

"What game is this?" she asked.

"The Death Man Game," Michael said, pressing his lips together as he smiled. "I made it up."

Losing interest, Shawn walked back to his bed. He stopped outside Sally's room. The curtain was drawn, but he could see her parents bending over her. He strained to hear their words.

"Love you…"

"Miss you…"

"We've kept your room just the way it's always been, only we've got some machines there now, we—"

"Maybe you'll wake up at home," Sally's mother said. "The doctor said it hasn't been too long, that you could still wake up. He said your…your brain is…fine. There's no reason…We'd like you to wake up again. You remember how she would sit up in bed blinking and rubbing her cheeks, always smiling…like…like she was rubbing the smile in…I…"

Behind the curtain their silhouettes reached out, touched, and came together.

"We brought you something from home," Sally's father said, his voice almost level, while the girl's mother set an object on the bed. Then they walked away, too absorbed to notice Shawn. In the bright light that fell from the window, Shawn thought he could see the Blue-sky Woman whispering into their ears.

Shawn looked around and sneaked into the room, peeked behind the curtain—Sally lay sleeping like Snow White, only her pale face was not beautiful. Shawn had seen too many pale faces to find Sally's beautiful. An IV ran from the back of her hand, a catheter tube from under her sheets. Her parents had set a fuzzy brown bear next to her head. With its stubby paws spread wide, it waited for its hug.

Shawn felt nauseated from the pills he had to take. Using the wall to keep himself upright, he walked back to his room and told himself he didn't care. He knew his parents wouldn't come. They were playing their own game: "Sorry We Couldn't Make It."

• • •

They were still playing the Death Man Game when the nausea passed, but the silence that had settled over them told Shawn that they neared its end. When it did, only Andy still held any cards. From his spot next to the window, Shawn watched Andy walk back to his room—shoulders sagging and staring at the floor, toying with a smooth, sandy-colored stone.

The rest of them sat together until the nurse came to take Wendy. As she was wheeled away, she told the nurse to stop and called to Tim. Shawn watched her face soften, and for a second she looked almost like a little girl.

"Tim," she whispered, "do you…do you get scared?"

The boy shook his head. "I'm gonna be fine." He rubbed his head.

"I just feel—"

Michael appeared behind them, and instantly Wendy's face became a skull again. Michael didn't notice. "Hey cancers, how's it going?" He chuckled and rubbed Wendy's head. "Tim's always rubbing his head like that, have you noticed? He's been without hair so long, it'll probably be weird if he ever got it back. You should play with us, we'll teach you how."

"Michael, don't talk like that," said the nurse, a voice of pleading command. The nurses never could bring themselves to discipline any of the long-terms on the ward.

Ignoring her, Michael looked at Shawn and giggled. Touching Wendy's shoulder, he said, "Or you could just sit and watch, like him." Michael's eyebrows furrowed. "Hey Shawn, you look like you're losing some hair yourself. I thought you were kidneys—they don't put you on chemo for that, do they?"

"My hair's fine," Shawn said. Walking away, he made sure not to run to his bed, not to peek at the bear still waiting for its hug, not to slam the door. Alone, unseen, Shawn held his head in his hands. He could feel the blood pounding above his right hip where they'd put his father's kidney. Frustration bent his back and turned his breathing shallow. He couldn't resist. He clutched his hair and pulled.

It had gone from the color of flame to the color of mud. Had become broken and thin. Another part of him was dying. Just a minor side effect of the drugs, the doctors told him; and the nurses said, "You have to take more of them, or else your body will try to reject your dad's kidney again—you remember how that felt? Do you want that to happen again?"

Breathing heavily, shaking and dizzy, Shawn hid his fistful of hair inside the pillowcase with all the rest.

●●●

But the next day, Shawn returned from the tests to find his sheets had been changed, his pillowcase cleaned. The nurses had taken his hair. Again and again he reached inside the pillowcase to see if any hair remained, but there was nothing. They had taken his health, cut him open, taken parts of him away, and now they took his hair—he fought to keep from pulling out more, instead running his hands through his hair again and again.

It was starting to show. He looked sick again.

I'm healthy, he told himself, *I have a new kidney, I'm going to leave soon.*

Michael was absorbed in an old college math book one of the doctors had brought him, busy scribbling numbers and figures in the margins. Shawn was glad. He didn't want to talk. He was leaving soon. He was healthy.

He hadn't peed in over a day. His forehead was hot. Sweat rolled down his body, yet he shivered. His side ached with a dull, continuous pain—the same pain that haunted him before it sent him to the hospital, before machines cleaned his blood. His old kidneys withered in his back. Time flowed by in sickly waves.

"You're going to be all right, we'll take care of you— Nurse!"

They gave him shots and spoke to each other in terse commands. "…hundred-two degrees…Shawn, does this hurt? Shawn?…blood pressure…three hundred milligrams Cytoxan…" He hardly knew what was happening.

Then he woke in a soft chair with a dialysis machine humming next to him, choking him with the smell of soap and urine. He knew this. He'd been here before. From the wall, the Death Man stared back.

And while Shawn was sitting there a day later, Andy's heart gave way, and when they wheeled him out the children said that he'd gone home. Everybody won.

• • •

"You need anything?" Michael asked, leaning against the wall next to Shawn's bed.

"Leave me alone," Shawn whispered.

Michael sighed. He ran a finger over the bed's metal railings. "You're in this with the rest of us. You think you're leaving? I got here almost a year ago, and I heard the doc talking—she said I wouldn't make it two weeks. But here I am. Here, on the ward. We're not going anywhere, and neither are you." He flicked his finger against the railing—*ping*. Then he sighed, and smiled without opening his mouth. "Come on, you need anything?"

Michael's face was wrinkled from pain, yet relaxed. Eyes splotched red with broken blood vessels moved without hurry, as though he didn't care that he was on the ward.

"Do you ever see the woman?" Shawn asked. "The woman who walks around, blue like the sky, like a ghost, only…"

"Only she says nice things to you? Tells you it'll be all right?"

Shawn nodded. "She's a liar." He reached under his back and took out another clump of hair. He held it out to Michael. "Could…could you put this where they won't throw it away?"

Smile unchanging, Michael took the hair.

Shawn watched him leave, then drifted off to troubled sleep. He didn't wake until he heard them playing the Death Man Game again.

• • •

In a few weeks Shawn felt better, though his legs still shook as he walked toward the other kids. They were dealing cards and setting up dominoes. With Andy long gone, and another girl dead a few days before, there were only five left to play. No, six—Wendy was playing now, craning forward in her wheelchair. She stared at her cards as though there was nothing else.

"Can I play?" Shawn asked.

They looked up at him, then at Michael.

"You don't want to just step in without knowing the rules," Michael said. "Maybe later."

But Shawn knew this game: if you didn't know the rules, you couldn't play; if you didn't play, you weren't a friend. Only a friend was taught the game. It had always been that way at school.

"It's no big deal, it's just cards," Shawn said. "I've seen you play. Just…just tell me as you go."

"Are you sure?" Michael asked. "This is kind of like a tournament—like a math competition at school."

"I want to play."

"Let him, Michael," Tim said softly, looking at his

cards. "The rest of us pretty much just started playing too. He'll do fine—beginner's luck."

"You sure?" Michael said, raising his eyebrows. With a bit of hesitation, they nodded, except for Wendy, who just shrugged her shoulders.

Smiling his tight-lipped smile, Michael shrugged too. Their circle spread to let Shawn in. He was glad to sit down—he felt so tired, and walking upset his stomach. He made sure to keep on smiling as they dealt the cards and flipped over the dominoes.

So he learned to play the Death Man Game. Cards moved around the circle, parts of people's hands rotated, cards were set aside and put back in the deck. Each card had a point value, and at a certain score—based on your revealed hand—you had to reveal the rest of it; then, if you had another certain score, you left the game. If not, you lost cards. There were ways to force moves, to steal cards or unload cards on another player. Dominoes could be bought by revealing cards. Yet, it was a card game. It was chance. You drew from the deck, you shuffled an opponent's hand before stealing.

It was not an easy game, but Shawn learned quickly. It didn't matter that he played badly, for Wendy struggled with the cards almost as much, though she seemed furious about it—a frail thing stooped in her wheelchair, glaring at him over her cards.

And for the first time, Shawn noticed there was something different in the way they played. Though they joked and teased and laughed, there was something serious in the play. Sarah's hands clenched too tightly, bending the cards. Tim constantly clicking dominoes together. Tapping feet, cracking knuckles, the shuffling of cards. And Michael, smiling, his eyes darting about like sparks.

For a while Shawn did well enough that Wendy fell behind. But there was no beginner's luck. Tim dropped out, then Michael, then Sarah—until only Wendy and Shawn remained. Then, missing clues, misunderstanding, he forced her score to twenty. She stared at him and threw down her hand. Thirteen. He'd lost.

Wendy didn't seem happy, though. Tim patted her shoulder, and at his touch she yanked her wheels, turning away from him. Without looking at the players she drove her wheelchair from the room.

"Here," Michael said, holding a smooth stone out to Shawn.

"What is it?"

"Loser's rock. You keep it till the next game." Michael shrugged. "It's just a thing we do."

Shawn took the rock. It was cold, colder than the doctor's stethoscopes—he thought Michael must have kept it next to one of the air-conditioning ducts. It sucked the warmth from his fingertips, from his lips and tongue. Shawn tried to ignore the sensation. "That…was a good game, yeah?"

"It was fine," Michael said. "Keep the stone near you, all right?"

"Sure thing…" The cold faded, and Shawn thought he must have imagined the sensation. He must have. And if he told the nurses, they'd do more tests, they'd—Just a cold stone, that's all.

"Next time someone else is getting it," Shawn said, passing the stone from one hand to another.

Michael smiled and said, "Of course."

• • •

The others insisted on giving Shawn some of their

pudding to make him feel better about losing. He told them he didn't mind, it was all right.

"No, no," they said, "you were a beginner, don't worry about it."

He took one cup of pudding from Tim, but refused any more. "I lost fairly," he said, laughing. "I knew how to play, and I lost."

That made them feel better—they loosened up, started joking with him again. They went back to playing their games, and this time Shawn played with them. Go Fish, Monopoly, Code Blue! Code Blue!…He had friends on the ward now, and that day he was happy.

•••

That night Shawn still couldn't sleep. Instead he closed his eyes and counted—it could only be so long before day came. One…two…three…He thought about the time he got to take a train, when his grandfather died. He'd stared out the window counting farmhouses. Twenty-one…twenty-two…

He heard a soft rolling.

A hundred and nine…a hundred and ten…

He opened his eyes and looked up: Wendy thrust her wheelchair forward with more strength than her hands seemed capable of. She scrunched up her face like Shawn's little brother did when he was angry, only her face was thin, and dark. It reminded Shawn of the Death Man.

"What?" he asked.

She breathed out through her nose. She whispered, "You…you moron. You stupid…stupid…You had to play, didn't you? You had to ruin it. I bet you don't even know what you lost."

"I—"

"Give me the stone. The one Michael gave you when you lost."

Shawn reached behind him to touch his pillow, the stone a hard lump beneath. "Why?"

"Because it's mine! If you weren't so dumb, I'd have it!"

"I'm not dumb," Shawn said. She couldn't talk to him like that. Even *he* could hurt her.

"Yes, you are. You're dumb and stupid. You don't deserve it. You don't even know what it is."

"It's just—"

Her thin blue lips peeled back, her mouth a shadow. "Dummy, dummy—it marks who the Death Man will take next."

"The…what?"

"You know, in the corridors, behind the paint on the walls. The adults don't see him, not like we do. He looks…looks like that one doctor. The one that writes things in his pad right away, more tests, more surgery, and can't look up 'cause he doesn't have a face."

"You're making it up. And he doesn't look like that. I—"

Wendy grabbed the metal rails, his sheets, his arm, and dragged herself onto the bed. Her nails raked across his face as she looked for something to grab. One hand found an ear, the other his cheek and jaw. Shawn made a choking noise. Her nose was against his.

Into his face she spat, "It's mine, it's mine!"

He thought his ear might tear. He couldn't stop trembling. He wanted to kick her off like one of his siblings, to laugh at her until she was nothing. She was shaking all over and twisting his ear. He felt hot breath, felt her weight pulling on his flesh.

"You don't know…you don't know how much it hurts. And it's not going to end. You're just like Michael, like Tim. I want it to end. I should have lost. I would have lost, I was trying to lose, but you had to show up. Give me the stone…." Then Wendy let go and fell to the floor. She was so light the thud was barely noticeable.

Shawn looked over the edge of the bed. She was crumpled up, shaking, sucking in air.

"Wendy?"

She looked up at him, and her face became still and grim, every muscle tense. He stepped off the side of the bed and lifted her up, sat her in the wheelchair. She didn't look at him, didn't move. He reached beneath the pillow and handed her the stone.

Her breath caught. She rubbed it, kissed it, clasped it against her stomach like a stuffed animal. She smiled widely, her eyes straining toward the stone. Shawn had to turn away. He felt flushed, his tongue and lips and fingertips all tingled. He shook his head against the fear that his fever had returned.

Wendy's wheelchair squeaked as she pushed herself away from his bed and out into the hall.

Shawn thought he could see her mouth moving. She was whispering. "Take me away…I'm dying now…take me away, make it stop…."

"Wendy?"

She blinked before looking at him. "Leave me alone."

But he didn't want to leave her alone. There was something wrong with the way she smiled; it made him sick. Like he was looking into a mirror. He wanted her to smile like a little girl again.

"Please stop," he said.

"That's what I'm doing. Making it stop." She waved

back and forth. "I feel dizzy.…I think it's the cancer…it feels just like a carousel."

Her eyes rolled. Shawn became aware of his heart beating too fast, of nausea. He wanted to sit down but instead stepped forward. "Are you…?"

Wendy turned to him and smiled, the area around her mouth wrinkling a little, her eyes closing just a bit—the faintest hints of freckles beneath her pale skin as her trembling mouth bent into a smile."I'm *supposed* to die…it's all right if I'm *supposed* to die.…" She closed her eyes and stared up at the ceiling, and in a whisper to herself she sang, "God takes all the little children up to heaven and makes them angels. They play in the clouds. Such fluffy clouds…to make it stop…"

Slowly, she leaned over in her chair, and the stone fell to the floor with a loud *clack!* Light seeped from the room until it was dark and gray. From off the wall a cartoon rabbit peeled away—a shadow bubbling and billowing out. The Death Man stepped out on the floor. The smell of alcohol made Shawn's nose itch, and the smell of vomit made him gag.

The Death Man knelt. His coat was so long he seemed to have no hands, and the stone disappeared into his sleeve.

Shawn backed away, a scream stuck in his throat.

The Death Man stared into Shawn with bloodshot eyes, and it seemed they would never look away. Shawn remembered the homeless man he had seen the first time he had to walk to school alone, his parents too busy working and taking care of his brothers. The Death Man's cracked lips never moved, but Shawn heard the whisper of wind on rock, of the sea on sand: "So everything must end. All games crumble."

All the light came rushing back. Wendy lay unmoving in her chair, her eyes still open, perfectly still.

Shawn screamed for the nurses and the doctors. They came quickly, pushing him out of the way and calling orders. While they put Wendy's body on a gurney, a nurse told Shawn that he should go back to his room. But instead he followed them at a distance—out of the children's ward, to where the walls were plain. He watched them stick needles and tubes into her, watched them try to keep her heart going. Watched them try to save her life. Watched them fail.

God takes all the little children up to heaven.

He saw the Death Man walking through the corridors and staring out from behind the off-white paint. He was more than mere shadow: he was solid darkness, the darkness of caves, the darkness after every light goes out. The Blue-sky Woman withered in the Death Man's gaze.

It could have been me. It would *have been me.*

The pieces came together, Andy walking back to his room stone in hand. Clues missed, misunderstandings—Shawn told himself he wouldn't let it happen again, no matter what. But still he clutched his blanket and shivered. A few feet away Michael slept soundly with the curtains back, and on his chest, just over his heart, the Death Man had left the loser's stone.

● ● ●

When Shawn woke to find Michael sitting on his bed with the stone in hand, staring at Shawn. There was no smile on his face. When the nurse came for him, he hid the stone in his gown and left without looking back. Another nurse took Shawn. Blood pressure, blood sample, pee into the cup, take your medicine. Shawn was wary—there were games everywhere, trying to trap him.

They met him in his room; Tim closed the door.

"Why aren't you dead?" Michael asked. He clutched the stone in his left hand. "You lost the game. You had the stone." His hand shook. His knuckles turned white. "Why is Wendy dead instead of you?"

Shawn tried to leave, but the circle had closed around him.

"Leave me alone," he said.

"If you lose the game, you're supposed to die," Tim mumbled behind him. "You lost fair and square. You said so yourself."

"Why aren't you dead?" Michael asked again.

The circle shrunk. Shawn said, "She took it from me. She wanted to die."

"That's not how it works," Michael said. "You lost the game. It's your turn to die."

"I didn't—"

Behind Michael, Tim said, "You said it was fair. You said so."

"No!" Shawn cried.

Michael said, "You shouldn't have given her the stone."

"I didn't know," Shawn whispered.

But he doubted the words even as he spoke them. Once Wendy had told him, he'd known, and yet he'd given her the stone. It was easy to disbelieve, because in disbelief, he didn't have to die. He didn't know if he could keep standing. He felt the sick bodies all around him, and he clutched at one to stay upright. There were hands on him, holding him up. "I didn't want to die," he pleaded.

They helped him to his bed, then stepped away. Shawn could only see Michael's rigid face.

"Where did the game come from?" Shawn asked.

"I made it up. But the stone—the stone comes from the Death Man. I made a deal with him. We would play the game, and the loser would be next to die. The rest of us would be safe. We could go on without seeing him every time we closed our eyes."

The Death Man stared at Shawn from the walls. "I saw him. I saw him take Wendy. He told me that all games crumble, that everything must end."

Michael scowled. "No. Wendy had the stone, and Wendy died. The game still works."

"But Shawn lost," Tim said from across the room.

Shawn made himself sit up. Michael paced the room like a wild animal.

"Then he has to die, doesn't he?" Michael stopped pacing. "We'll give him the stone, just like before." He held the stone out to Shawn. "If Wendy wanted to die, it's not your fault. Take it. It's fair."

Shawn stared at the dull, sandy stone, covered with indistinct brown whirls.

"No," he said. "I don't want to die."

With a snarl, Michael grabbed Shawn's hand, put the stone in Shawn's palms and curled Shawn's fingers over it. The warmth left Shawn's body even as he tried to hold it. He squeezed the stone as tight as he could, as though he could force the warmth back into his body. But his life flowed into the stone like water down a drain, and he couldn't stop it.

Michael stepped away. "There. The game's still on. The loser dies next." Smiling, out of breath, Michael left the room. For a second the others stared at Shawn, and then they, too, left, and he had only the stone for company.

• • •

Shawn didn't want to die. If Wendy asked him for the stone again, he'd give it to her. The Death Man hid behind the paint on the walls or between the mattress and the bed. Eyes that wouldn't look away, wouldn't let you go. Shawn knew that even now, even in the day, the Death Man walked the halls.

Shawn got out of bed, his knees wobbling. The air was still, a bit too cold. He touched the walls, ran his hand over the outline of a pond, over the wing of a bird in flight.

In his left hand Shawn held the stone that would be his death.

"Come out," Shawn whispered. "I know you're there. Come out."

The lights went dark and gray. The air grew thick. The Death Man came.

In his windlike voice the Death Man said, "Are you as eager to die as she was?"

Shawn swallowed. "I don't want to die."

The Death Man stared at him.

"I won't die," Shawn said. "I won't."

"Your life is in the stone, and the stone is mine." The Death Man reached out, and Shawn felt cold sweat on his skin, the beginning of another fever.

"I lost before and I didn't die. If it's a game, I…I don't want to play anymore."

The Death Man stared at him. Shawn wanted to turn away, but he didn't.

"Then the game will break. They will live in fear, and feel my breath on their necks." The Death Man bent over Shawn so their faces almost touched. "They will live like you."

Softly, Shawn said, "I don't want to die."

The Death Man's mouth was on Shawn's, his lips dry and dusty. Cold hands on his forehead, sweat like fog on his skin, a dull ache where his kidney struggled. The Death Man's voice swept through all the hollow places in him. He felt the ache in his chest for every time his parents played their games, blaming him, resenting him—even as they worked to pay the bills. Felt the fear of those around him, don't touch the sick or the Death Man will smell you too. And the Death Man's voice asked, "Why?"

Shawn didn't know. "I don't want to die...." He tried to move away, but he could only curl up on the floor and sob, clutching his stone. He heard Wendy's dead voice say that adults didn't see him like they did, and he wished he couldn't see him either. "I won't. I won't play."

He thought he would die now; he trembled and wondered what it would be like. But then the pain receded and faded away.

"The one who lost did not die. Return the stone to Michael. His game is broken, and he has lost his life."

And Shawn was left alone on the white tiles of the hospital floor.

For a while he lay still. Then he grabbed the bed and pulled himself upright. Carefully, methodically, he pulled out all his hair. It wasn't hard. It didn't hurt. Making sure to hold on to whatever was available lest his weakness cause him to fail, Shawn threw the hair into the trash and made his way out to the game room.

Michael was playing Memory with a pack of cards, flipping them over as fast as he could. By the time Shawn reached him, most of the cards were gone.

Shawn dropped the stone in front of Michael.

"He says your game is broken," Shawn whispered. "I'm not going to die."

Michael stared, then reached forward and touched the stone. His hand jerked back. "No," Michael whispered. "No!" He gathered his cards and shot past Shawn without a glance.

Exhausted, Shawn sat by the window and watched as Michael gathered all of the kids who never left the ward. "We have to play again," Michael told them. "We have to play *now*."

•••

Michael shuffled the deck. Tim dealt. Throughout, they were silent. They didn't look at Shawn, though he watched them. The cards were dealt, the dominoes laid. Finally, Michael set the stone at the center of the table and the game began.

They played in silence. They looked only at their hands, only at the cards on the table. Their lives rode on every card they drew. Cards moved around. The points on the table changed with every move. Tim was losing. Sarah looked as though she was trying to steal a card in order to go out. And Michael was somewhere in the middle, his eyes darting to every card, his lips moving.

Somewhere in the middle...

In his head, a pattern dangled just out of reach—dangling in front of his eyes, blurry in the details. Something about the way the game looked after Michael left. All the times he'd half-watched Michael play...He watched the game. Watched Michael's eyes. It reminded him of the way his eyes moved when he was dreaming, when he was juggling great numbers.

And then Shawn saw it. He understood, and laughed. The players shot him dirty looks.

"You know he's never won a game," Shawn said. "He's always second, or third. And he's never lost, of course. And he won't. Because he's playing all of you. He's counting cards."

Michael's gaze jerked up from the game, while all the other players looked at him. His face was twisted up, he was almost out of his seat—then he sat back down and shook his head.

"The dead don't speak," Michael said. He turned back to the game.

But the others had put their hands down. They stared at Michael.

"It's impossible," Michael said, his mouth turning up.

"It's not," Tim said. "I saw a movie where a guy did that. Didn't you say you won some math contest once?"

Michael's smile vanished. "You can't stop playing," he said. But the players didn't pick up their cards. "If you stop, you die. You know what it's like without the game. The Death Man everywhere, you don't know who's next, you—you have to play."

They stood up.

"It's bad enough you're cheating," Tim said, "but letting Shawn play without knowing, giving him the stone even after—"

Michael threw his cards in Tim's face. "Don't blame me for what you did. What you all did. You let him play—you knew what you were doing! You're no better than me. You think I don't see how you shuffle the deck? And Sarah, trying to hold extra cards in her hands, and…"

"Take your stone," Tim said. "We can die without your help."

Michael stared at each of them. He was shaking, but Shawn couldn't tell whether it was rage or fear. Michael took the stone, and winced. His lips turned blue. He spat on the table and walked away.

•••

The children on the ward watched and waited for Michael to die. He was shrunken, pale. He had spasms. He'd tried to get another game going with others, but everyone avoided him. It was as though he reeked of death. As though there were a mark on his forehead. He carried the stone with him wherever he went.

He could barely walk, and still they watched him.

Unable to look anyone in the face, curled up in his bed, Michael hid the stone from them.

"I don't want to die," he mumbled again and again.

Shawn sat in a chair next to Michael's bed, holding Michael's hand. At first Michael cursed him, tried to spit at him. Now Michael had no spit. He couldn't even cry.

"Is there anything you want me to do?" Shawn asked.

Michael shook his head.

"Are your parents—"

Michael tried to laugh, a dry rasp cutting through his throat.

"They left me here. You want to know how long I've been here? Three years. One thousand ninety-five days. Twenty-six thousand and...and..." Michael shook his head. "Three years I've survived. You'd do it too, all of you. They put you in a fridge when you die. They burn you. I've never seen a kid turn into an angel…only the pretty woman who walks the halls, just like the one that gave me candy and never yelled or hit…when was the last time she came to you? Never…not to us…if you play the game, you know you're not going to get better. There's no hope in the cards. There's just…certainty."

Michael fell asleep, and Shawn walked out of the room. His hand shook when he took it from his eyes. Saltwater. His body was crying.

He looked at the children's ward, and saw that Sally's door was open. The bear still sat on her chest, paws wide. Always hoping. Even if she never woke, there was always hope. With a lurch Shawn walked through the door. He picked up the bear and squeezed it tight.

There was something wrong with its back. Shawn turned it over. He pulled at a bit of stuffing poking out from a hole larger than a quarter. Shawn felt inside, and there was something there. He tore the bear open. Stuffing fell like feathers to the floor.

And there, inside the bear: a stone, and hair.

Shawn dropped the eviscerated bear and walked away. His body was experiencing a spasm, but he no longer knew if it was tears or laughter. It didn't matter; both were just games.

•••

"You're a murderer," Shawn told Michael.

"I don't want to die," the boy pleaded. "She's not going to wake up. Why should I die? I bet she wants to die! Just like Wendy, you let Wendy die!"

"It's not up to you to choose life or death for someone. It's not up to any of us. You're still playing games."

Michael whimpered, "But I don't want to die...."

"Don't you ever want to leave? Don't you want it to end? Your players never get better. They never leave. Michael...how many have you killed? How many has your game killed?"

"I won't let him take me. I'll find a way out, just like you did! There's always a way!"

"No," Shawn said. "No, there isn't." He held the stone in his hands, and he could feel Michael's life inside it. He spoke to the walls, "Come out and take what's yours!"

And the lights, the air, the very earth bowed down to the Death Man as he came.

"Greetings, Game-breaker. You have played your part well." The Death Man turned to Michael. "Your game is finished, and so is ours. I have won. Your life is mine."

The Death Man reached out for the stone, but Shawn held it back. "No," he said. "You can't have it. Not like that."

A shadow of a smile, the soulless smile of a photograph or corpse. "It's mine," the Death Man said.

But Shawn just smiled back, and shook his head. "You have no power. You're not real. You're just another game! I feel death, and you aren't it. I've seen death, and it doesn't have a face." Shawn held up a deck of cards and laughed. "This is death. There—" He flicked a card. "And there, and there—" Cards littered the floor. "There is no choice. It's all just games."

He dropped the cards and swung his hand through the Death Man's chest as though slapping him. Like a plume of smoke the apparition broke, still smiling, whispering—only now the voice was just machines. The lights flickered on again.

Shawn squeezed the stone. When he opened his hands, they were empty.

He looked at Michael. Then turned to the foot of the bed where the Blue-sky Woman, a faint outline in the bright white hospital lights, smiled and held out her hands.

"Don't listen to her lies," Shawn said. "The games are over."

He blew on her, and she scattered like a dandelion in the wind.

● ● ●

The doctors told Shawn that he was getting better. The drugs were working; his body was accepting the kidney at last.

The nurses smiled when they saw how he was walking better, smiled when they talked about his tests.

His parents came to see him. He was going home soon.

Shawn sat on his bed, staring out the window. The trees swayed in the wind. Shapeless clouds moved slowly through the sky. The world turned, and the sun made its way through the blue sky. He sat on his bed and knew that none of it mattered. He was alive.

A few feet away, Michael still lived. His disease should have killed him, but instead it receded and waited for another day. If the nurses and doctors thought it miraculous, they had grown used to it over the three years. And if they thought it tragic when one night Sally ceased to breathe, nobody called it unexpected. Shawn sat and flicked cards out onto the bed. All over the world, without regard for hopes or dreams or human games, people lived and people died.

EVOLUTION'S END

Doug +
HEVEN,

Written by
Lee Beavington

EXPLORE!

Illustrated by
Melanie Tregonning

[signature]

About the Author

It's not much of a secret that biologist and winning author Lee Beavington is really more of an arts aficionado than a pure scientist. Even while he was completing his biology degree, Lee Beavington's favorite class was short-story writing. So while he's a lab instructor at Kwantlen University College in Surrey, British Columbia, away from the office he indulges his many passions for writing, music, books, film, running, dancing, badminton, philosophizing, laughing and deeper explorations of myth, the stars and animals (far too many interests for one lifetime, he says). First published at thirteen in a student writing contest, Lee received his first professional recognition years later as a Writers of the Future semifinalist in 2002. His winning entry this year moves him that much closer to his dream of publishing his first novel. Lee's other professed desires are for greater love, owning less stuff, making babies and never owning a cell phone.

About the Illustrator

Like many of our contributing illustrators, Melanie Tregonning has been interested in art and drawing since she was a youngster in Western Australia. She started a comic strip at about ten (Licorice the Cat) and dreamed of being as successful and widely published as cartoonists Murray Ball (Footrot Flats), Jim Davis (Garfield), or the legendary Charles Schultz (Peanuts). While family definitely encouraged her, kids at school (even the ones who didn't like her) admitted that her art was good.

Influenced by Japanese SF graphic novels like Battle Angel Alita, Mel points to the Alien film series as having a profound impact because they were so original and thought-provoking. She's a recent grad from Australia's Curtin School of Design and is currently seeking work as a freelance illustrator. Mel intends to become more proficient in many illustration fields, capable of mastering any illustration technique or style. Eventually, she wants to create graphic novels—writing and illustrating her own original stories full time.

Every cell is formed by the division of another cell. Except the first.

—*Revised Cell Theory*

Fifteen billion years. Barry found it hard to fathom. Trailblazers were usually exact in their work. They couldn't afford to be otherwise. If that timestamp proved accurate, the planet before them dated further back than any age estimate of the universe itself. Its ancient sun would burn out in another 20,000 years.

The *Astral Surveyor*, having just passed through the wormhole horizon a few hours prior, would soon take them in visual range. The Central Bureau for Astronomical Telegrams had designated the planet 2184 ZB178. He hoped to coin the common name at some point during the mission. It would be one helluva way to cap a long career in the Space Science Academy.

"Initiating atmospheric entry sequence," Ellen said, sounding as dispassionate as the computer cross-checking their trajectory.

Subtle wrinkles and glimpses of gray in her curly hair revealed her age, and Barry's as well, for he was her senior. Sarah, nearly half his age, stood glued to the viewport, an unmistakable gleam in her eyes. Fresh out of the Space Science Academy, excited at her first taste of real exploration. In a way, he envied her youthful optimism, not yet faded as a result of experience.

Barry suited up and braced himself. The transition from the upper to lower atmosphere went by in a yellowish blur. Sarah sat transfixed, no less enthusiastic at this development. To Barry, however, this was old hat. Ellen maintained her poise as they went down, eyes peeled to the console. A minute later, their jolting descent came to an abrupt halt.

Barry gave her a round of applause. "Good show!"

Ellen acknowledged his comment with a slight nod.

They set down a kilometer from the shoreline—SSA regulations were sometimes reactionary, but mostly, like this procedure, they were preventative.

Barry unhitched himself and got to his feet, feeling a little disconcerted at his flexibility. These new quintuple-layered suits felt lighter than his summer attire. Comfortable enough to sleep in. But he found something reassuring about the traditionally bulky spacesuits. Going out onto the surface of a foreign planet in this thing felt like jumping into freezing water wearing only a pair of underwear.

Barry checked the fabric for imperfections. Ellen was ready; Sarah wasn't long behind. She looked more at ease than he felt. So much for comfort coming with age.

The two women motioned Barry to the fore. Sarah had explained to him since this was his last mission, she would gladly grant him such honors. Ellen, on the other hand, merely followed another SSA regulation: the most experienced starnaut always took the first step.

"One small step for Barry…" he started to say over the suit's com. Then he hit the 2.4 Earth standard gravity.

"One giant fall for mankind," Sarah finished. "Are you okay?"

"I've only bruised my ego—that is, if I had one to bruise."

He pushed himself off his knees, taking more effort than he wanted to admit. Ellen followed his lead with a far more graceful entrance, then turned to help Sarah off the ship. Retirement suddenly felt obligatory. But it didn't take long to remind himself why he was here.

None of them spoke. There were no words for such an experience. Like the first humans looking back on Earth from outer space...what could they possibly say?

Everything seemed at peace, as though a refined equilibrium had settled over the planet. A light breeze ruffled his suit, failing to upset the barren layout of the land. He was reminded of the mudflats along the California coast. Except here, there was no pickleweed, no crabs, no anything. The terrain looked undisturbed, smoothed over. The few rocks present, none larger than his fist, lacked even the dullest of edges. Wisps of pale yellow cloud drifted overhead in the nearly colorless sky, far too scattered and listless to hold the prospect of rain. He couldn't spot ZB178's satellites; two other planets in the heavens substituted as moons, both gas giants with diameters stretching further than Jupiter's. To the east, the dying sun hung low in the sky, blazing orange.

He didn't let disappointment strike. His SSA training, as it should, erased the wonder of standing on another world. He boiled the visual details down to a fine point: a firm, bare surface, surprisingly flat, with—he couldn't help but sigh—no indication of plant or animal life.

He led Ellen and Sarah prudently around the *Astral Surveyor*, taking small penguin steps. Barry felt his spine arching, forcing him to hunch over as he tottered forward. His interest now lay solely with the vast oceanic regions rolling out of sight. On the opposite side, he could see mountains rising up, looking more like low-lying hills. Taking into account the gravitational pressure they were under, these could probably match the grandeur of the Himalayas.

"We'll need a point of reference," he said, breaking the silence. "Let's call those hills south."

At his words, Ellen broke out of her own reverie and brought out the new-world probe. She dropped down to her knees—by choice—and with some difficulty managed to stick it into the uncooperative ground.

Sarah was still in a trance. "Amazing," she breathed.

Barry chuckled, following her gaze. But it wasn't the planet surface she described. A series of what looked to be standing stones jutted out of the ground. Sinuous, smooth and gray, the dozen or so thin structures resembled single-trunked eucalyptus trees.

"The probe's done," Ellen announced. She retrieved the device and stepped back onto the ship. Sarah didn't move at first, still beaming. Eventually, she reluctantly followed Barry inside.

"What do you make of those?"

"No idea. But we'll certainly investigate them further. How are you enjoying your first mission?"

Sarah opened her mouth and closed it again. "Just amazing," she said.

"We need to get you a thesaurus."

When they were all seated, Ellen started the separation process. He would've offered to help, but she would probably end up spending more time telling him the proper procedure than it would take for her to do it herself. For safety's sake, they would take two-thirds of the *Astral Surveyor* with them, leaving behind the smallest third—which, by happy coincidence, housed Barry's quarters.

The *Astral Surveyor* had all the comforts of a luxury cruiser. Even though this was a biological research vessel, fully equipped with a biolab, viewscopes and quarantine cubes, it reminded him more of a tourist cruiser. Each of them had their own quarters, and all the primary systems were made in triplicate, meaning the *Astral Surveyor* had the capability to separate into three fully functional subcrafts.

It didn't take Ellen long to secure the latches and complete the separation. Then she focused with single-minded tenacity on flying them closer to the shoreline. In the interim, Sarah's swollen eyes led her back to the viewport, while Barry reviewed the probe's assay analysis aloud.

"The surface temperature is over fifty Celsius. The forecast holds sunshine for our four-week stay, with zero percent chance of precipitation. The atmospheric readings reveal few surprises: major constituents of nitrogen, helium and hydrogen, and faint traces of sulphur and...oxygen."

Hmm. With less than one percent of that oh-so-precious gas, it was bound to make evolution of life difficult. Of course, that reading didn't discount the possibility of higher O_2 levels having existed at some point in the past.

Ellen set them down a few hundred meters from the coast. For all they knew, this was low tide, and the heightened ocean could rise up right over their ship. Hence the buffer.

"Oh my goodness!" Sarah suddenly exclaimed from her vigilant post at the viewport.

Ellen was changing suits. Barry looked back.

"What is it?" he asked.

"The ocean. It suddenly turned…green."

He got up.

"But it's not that way any longer," she hastily added.

Indeed, Barry couldn't see any green. He looked sideways at Sarah.

"Don't stare at me like that, Barry. You think I'm seeing things?"

He *did* believe her, but there was no longer any evidence of what she had seen.

"What do your wizened years tell you to do?"

"To get down there as fast as these antiquated bones of mine will carry me."

•••

Standing on the stony shore, the three starnauts remained several meters from the ocean's edge. Until these organisms' secrets were revealed (Ellen was quick to remind him) they were to assume this species posed a threat to human health—and them to it. Thus Barry peered at the yellow green surface from afar.

The reflective glare from the sun followed his gaze. This must be some kind of organic matter. Viscous, almost gelatinous. A nondescript gray.

Sarah began jotting notes into her digital logbook. Ellen pulled a tele-imager from her belt and attached the twin cylinders to her mask.

"Little bacteriums," she commented.

"Don't you mean bacteria?"

"I shouldn't say little," she went on, ignoring Barry's query. "Even though there are millions of them. Oval-shaped. But they aren't small. Definitely not microscopic. Yet they almost look single-celled. Bundled so close together, it's difficult to tell."

Barry thought back to the radiating green Sarah had seen, thinking of the bioluminescence of blue-green algae back on Earth, and how those little dinoflagellates dazzled like living lanterns in the night sea. That bright glow was very conspicuous. It would surely, under normal circumstances, attract predators. Maybe there were no predators present for that to matter. Or maybe these organisms *wanted* to be detected. That's exactly how the three of them had responded, going down to the shore in a hurry. But what purpose did that serve?

"Dinoflagellates," Sarah suggested.

Ellen nodded. "Very similar, yes."

Barry refrained from commenting. Great minds *do* think alike. Instead, he carried their shared idea further.

"Do you think that glow you saw earlier might be some kind of bloom? You know, like a red tide? There are marine coastal species of phytoplankton on Earth that gather this way in order to reproduce. I forget the name—"

"Karenia brevis."

"Thanks, Sarah. Those dinoflagellates are tiny plantlike cells. They create red tides through massive multiplication, disrupting other species, and also pose a significant risk to human health."

"That's right," Sarah confirmed. "From neurotoxins accumulating in bivalves such as clams, mussels and oysters."

"This is our first day here," Ellen reminded them. "We don't want to make any bold comparisons. The red tide on Earth is regulated by a completely different set of biological and environmental conditions." Ellen handed the imager to Sarah, who readily placed it above the nose of her mask.

"It's been a long journey," Ellen explained, "and

past time for me to return to the ship. Be sure you two come back together."

Even this discovery couldn't affect her routine. There was something to be admired in that, even if Barry couldn't see it.

Sarah occupied herself with her precious logbook. Barry, on the other hand, reverted to a skill from his student days to help him overcome obstacles. None, he confessed, were quite this daunting. Whenever his physics instructor gave a particularly thorny question, one to which nobody could work a solution, Barry attacked it from every angle but the obvious. He went home and looked outside the problem, examining the periphery, and other factors indirectly influencing the fundamental variables.

There was no beach. No sand, no driftwood, no pleasant breeze. The hard, rocky ground of the shoreline merely tilted down at an angle just below horizontal until it reached and subsequently slid under those organisms. That didn't offer him much insight. But there was one peculiarity.

A channel, maybe a third of a meter in width, ran up and over the incline. Only a few centimeters deep.

"This little canal is interesting."

Sarah cocked her head. "Sorry?"

"This channel in the ground, running south from the ocean—if you can call it that."

"How far does it go?"

"Good question." He followed it for a way, until it rose smoothly back to surface level. "Maybe thirty meters."

The grooved furrow did not follow the lower contours of the terrain as a river should, its straight path often taking it right over the highest elevation.

Back on the shoreline with Sarah, he looked to the

tiny organisms for answers. A sudden impulse to wade into those depths took him. To submerge his body, and examine them up close.

He quickly dispelled the thought. He must be getting tired. Moving through a liquid of any substantial density, even if his suit *were* featherweight, would be next to impossible on this planet.

"Time to go," he declared.

Sarah fiddled with her logbook.

"Sarah—"

"Just a minute. Let me get this thought down."

He let her finish. She lowered the logbook to her side and, after a moment, took a step toward the living ocean.

"The ship's this way," he stated in a flat tone. She knew better than to take such a risk.

Sarah stopped, staring outward. Then she turned and followed him away from the shore.

"Everything all right?" he asked.

"Everything is amaz——"

"Got it."

But had she felt something similar to him? A longing to swim amidst the green tide? He almost inquired, but decided against it. She'd probably think him a crazy old kook. More so than she already did.

She ended up helping *him* get back to the ship. It took him a minute to find his sleeping bunk—or rather, to remember that his was on the other third of the *Astral Surveyor*—and thus collapsed onto Sarah's unoccupied bunk instead. His mind spiraled with thoughts of the impossible. Discovery of the new and unfamiliar had that effect on the human-centered psyche.

•••

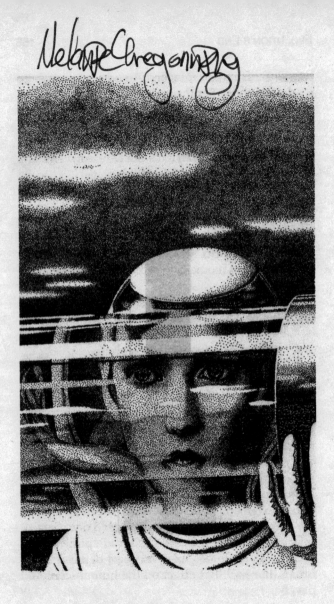

Illustrated by Melanie Tregonning

He woke four and a half hours later. A deep black filled the viewport. Faint stars were visible overhead. Barry peered into the dark, hoping to see that majestic glow Sarah had described. However, the ocean remained unseen. So instead, he sat down in Ellen's coveted pilot's chair next to Sarah.

"Sorry. These old bones of mine needed a good rest. You should've woken me."

"It's okay," she said. "I don't think I can sleep anyway."

"You tend to avoid sleep, don't you?"

"It gets in the way of things that need to be done."

"And what are you doing now?"

She sighed. "Nothing much at all." He looked over her shoulder at the console.

Provisional name: 2184 ZB178

Class/type: terrestrial planet, weak magnetic field

Equatorial diameter: ~ 20,000 kilometers

Sidereal period: ~ 550 days

Perihelion/Aphelion: 1.31 AU

Rotation Period: 0 days, 19 hours, 45 minutes

Satellites: four known

Topography: over 90% of surface oceanic

Barry had read this before. Many times. He integrated the information as follows: ZB178 was about 2.5 times the size of Earth, with an orbit similar to Mars; a rocky planet, with very little land surface area, and a twenty-hour day. He skipped to the final data entry.

Life forms present: Algae-like organism. Olive-colored. Present in all water basins. Depth and range of distribution unknown. Further study highly recommended.*

That was it. They were here to fill in the rest of that

"further study." He didn't recall seeing that asterisk before and clicked it with his finger. A new window popped open.

In accordance with the SSA Statutes, no sample of the "algee" was taken.

Algee? This trailblazer had a sense of humor.

The discovery of the wormhole array had single-handedly created the trailblazing profession. However, it took decades to determine its safety and stability. The first probes put through the horizon—just outside the orbit of Pluto, in a region known as the Kuiper Belt—were never heard from again. Maybe they were destroyed. But if they weren't, where were the probes transmitting *from?* The signals might very well take thousands of years to receive. So they sent a dozen more probes through the array. Each had slightly variant navigational instructions. But all were programmed to return, if they could.

All twelve came back, appearing as though out of nowhere, fully operational, with images of a dozen different solar systems.

Intergalactic exploration exploded. Sending a trailblazer first became a cost-saving measure. For one-tenth the expense of a fully equipped ship and crew, these scouts recorded every piece of data they could gather. Their report ultimately determined if further exploration would take place. Of them all, ZB178 looked the most promising.

The presence of life guaranteed approval, regardless of the other requisites, including safety. Hence Barry found himself here, studying the trailblazer's report. Before all this kerfuffle, the experts agreed that a stable wormhole was only a theorized solution to Einstein's relativistic equation for gravity. Now, they only agreed on one point: whatever, or *whom*ever, had created this impossible anomaly—for it certainly wasn't a natural phenomenon—needed to be found.

"How about Noachia?"

Sarah yawned, and looked at him quizzically. "Huh?"

"The planet name. I think that should be it."

"What is that? One of the Greek gods?"

"No...all of the mythological deities have been taken. It's an allusion to Noah. You can name a planet after bloodthirsty, ravaging gods, but anything religious is taboo."

"I suppose it's appropriate, what with the lack of land. But..."

"What?"

"It doesn't have that *zing* to it."

"Zing? Don't get scientific on me."

"I have something better."

"Really? Spill the beans."

"I didn't say I have it *now*."

Barry laughed. "You'll be the end of me yet, Sarah. I bet Ellen prefers the technical designation."

Most of the time, Ellen was barely human. They were a bit like old friends; they knew how each other would react, without the need for small talk, although he didn't know her at all outside the Space Science Academy. Apparently Ellen had a spouse back on Earth, which was more than he could claim. Sarah and he got along like brother and sister. Admittedly, a much older brother.

"We know why I'm here. What about you, Barry? What first brought you out to the stars?"

"I don't know if I can honestly answer that." He was happy to leave it there. But Sarah just sat there staring at him. "Oh, all right. I do remember one incident early on. One that stuck with me."

"Do share."

"My eldest brother, Jeff, took me down to the beach. We were just kids. Jeff and I spent the day skipping stones, playing in the sand, turning over rocks to find crabs. I guess that's where my interest in science started, there on the seashore. We stayed right into the summer evening. I remember his hand being on my shoulder as we watched the sun set over the waves.

"Of course, he only took me there because our mom ordered him to. We never went again, as far as I can remember. But I never forgot that day." He paused, debating whether or not to go any further. He had never really talked about this to anyone before. What the hell.

"Jeff died when I was thirty. I was on my way to Titan at the time."

He felt Sarah's hand on his arm.

"The life of an explorer isn't an easy one, Barry. How did your family take it?"

"By the time I returned, the funeral was a buried memory and my relatives were reluctant to talk to me about it. I became sort of an outsider then. The thing is, I didn't return early. I stayed with the mission until it was done. That's what you're supposed to do, isn't it?"

"It's in our training."

Barry leaned back in the chair. "It's the life I chose."

"No—it's the life we chose. Now, I better get some rest." Sarah got up, but turned back at the threshold.

"Archeya," she proclaimed.

"Archeya? It's definitely old-sounding."

"I thought you'd like it," she said with a grin, and went to her quarters.

• • •

Sarah's logbook sat on the console. He picked it up.

She was definitely recording too much. A common error among green explorers, noting every trivial detail, although the exobiologists at home would doubtless be ecstatic over Sarah's explicit descriptions. In truth, it didn't add up to anything concrete. To Barry, all one needed was the pertinent information. That usually didn't reveal itself until the end of the mission.

One item caught his interest: *The bacteria appear to be single-celled. They are clearly separate entities. However, it is possible that each bacterium may be synergetic with those surrounding it, like a colony of choanocytes becoming a multicellular unit.*

Hmm. On Earth, multicellular life didn't appear until over 700 million years ago. That meant for more than three billion years, Earth was inhabited solely by single-celled microbes. But with fifteen billion years, didn't Archeya have time enough for evolution well beyond multicellularism?

The next few hours droned by, Barry trying to glean some useful information from the ship's biological database. At one point, he searched for *bioluminescence: Light produced by an organism via a chemical or physical reaction, usually as an expression of circadian rhythmicity. Light emission spectrum falling between 474 and 476 nanometers in wavelength, with an action potential extruding hydrogen ions into outer pockets of the vascular membrane. Leading theories suggest a complex method of maximizing exposure to light, thus providing an adaptive advantage for photosynthesis.*

Barry wondered. Photosynthesis was a biosphere's

metabolic foundation. In a sense, it provided the basis for all life, synthesizing carbohydrates from carbon dioxide and water using light as an energy source, while releasing oxygen as a byproduct. Those carbohydrates were eaten by other organisms, and that oxygen breathed by animals. Without photosynthesis, one could argue, complex life on Earth never would have evolved.

Did the algee carry out something similar to the photosynthesis process? Was it related to the reason the algee were the only organisms on Archeya?

He let out a hearty laugh. If you can answer that, Barry, you'd be done here.

He went to the viewport. With the day cycle here shorter than Earth's, the sun was already cresting the gray horizon. Its rays spread color over the land, ascending into the atmosphere. Black shifted to a surreal green, slowly fading to brilliant teal until the orange ball of flame once again dominated the sky. For the first time in weeks, he felt a stabbing symptom of the chronic disease carried by all starnauts: homesickness.

"Better not let Sarah see you staring out the viewport like that."

Eyes hypnotized by the display, Barry blinked.

"You missed an *amazing* sunrise, Ellen. I'm starting to sound like her too, aren't I?"

"I'll take my watch. You get some sleep."

He almost relented, but at the last moment saw the gleam in her eye.

"I can't sleep. I have a feeling neither of us feel like sleeping any longer."

Ellen licked her lips. He knew the scientist in her couldn't resist.

"Well, what are we waiting for?" she announced, as though she had planned this all along. "Let's suit up."

•••

Before they went to the shore, Ellen went to check on Sarah.

"Where are you going?" he had asked.

"Just making sure she's all right." She evidently had a maternal instinct.

The four moons had shifted position in the sky, having no effect on the mysterious sea. The algee remained abundant, flat, and still. On the sandless beach, Barry showed Ellen the channel running inland.

"What do you make of it?"

"At a right angle from the source, digging along the surface as the crow flies. It almost looks artificial."

"I don't know," he said. "Indigenous animals have done far stranger things on Earth, things that might seem supernatural until they're understood by science."

"You think this was made by an animal of some kind?"

"Maybe something went into that ocean of algee. Or something came out of it."

Ellen ruminated. "If that's the case, it didn't get very far. You head east, Barry. And keep the com open."

"Got it."

They split up. Barry, weighed down further by an imager and atmo-probe, questioned Ellen's diversion from precaution. He quickly understood that wasn't the case.

"0841 Earth standard time. Do you read?"

"Loud and clear."

It was the same transmission from Ellen every

sixty seconds. Except when a discovery interrupted
them. But the only thing either of them found was
more channels. All immaculately straight lines, all
roughly perpendicular to the algee, sprouting from the
shore an average of every twenty meters. He didn't
bother trying to get a dialogue going, because when
Ellen was in research mode, it would be a one-way
conversation.

The coastline intermittently swerved in and then
outward again. He had trouble believing the algee, so
placid and docile, was there at all. Yet that organism
covered the entire surface, from the shore to the far
reaches of the imager's vision, which would've gone
even further if not for the planet's natural curvature.

The repressive gravity started getting on his nerves
more than Ellen. The unchanging scenery certainly
didn't help clear his encroaching boredom. He returned
with weighted steps to the starting point, where he
found Sarah sitting with her logbook. Ellen arrived
soon after.

"I'm going to see if I can find any evidence of these
fossilized rivulets further inland, and then do some
digging around those unusual structures."

Sarah watched her leave, and then turned to Barry.

"This ocean is thriving with life. You would think
dozens of species would be a given. If not on the land,
then somewhere out there."

"A reasonable hypothesis, though I'm beginning
to think this isn't an ocean at all, but a gathering of
algee. Of course, thousands upon thousands of species
evolved on Earth before one of them figured out land
was a door of opportunity. Here, we have only one."

After an hour, he called Ellen on the com.

"Found anything?" he asked.

"Negative," was the entirety of her reply.

The whole afternoon turned out to be a negative. By sunset only Sarah had something to show for the day's work—more in-depth, ineffectual notes. Some part of Barry longed to get inside the ship's stabilized pressure, and shed a few hundred pounds.

"They're turning green!"

Startled, Barry spun to look at Sarah. Her facemask glowed.

The algee had started to shimmer.

"Turn on the recorder," he ordered.

"Done," Sarah replied.

At first he could see very little color change. Just a fuzzy luminescence. Over the next dozen seconds it became clear that something more was going on.

"They're *moving*."

Sarah was right. For half a minute the algee quivered, their vibrations becoming more and more intense. And then, in complete symmetry, they lit into a vibrant green.

The entire ocean glowed. One big writhing mass of green, incomprehensibly bright.

"What could possibly be so…"

"Amazing?" Sarah finished for him with a grin. "Looks like those worn eyes of yours haven't seen everything."

Barry smiled back. But his mind was elsewhere, churning over this dramatic display of life. Trying to accept the startling image.

He had the atmo-probe ready, holding it near the surface. Doing his best to ignore the algee, he watched the readings. The letter O had turned red. The oxygen levels were falling: 0.5 to 0.4 percent.

"My God. They're removing the O_2 from the atmosphere."

The percentage kept declining. A minute later, it

levelled out at 0.1 percent. He lowered the probe. Sure enough, the algee were slowing, their greenish glow dimming.

"Believe me now?" Sarah whispered.

"Fortunately, yes."

"This green tide was definitely longer than the first," she remarked.

Barry had a sudden thought. "What time did they do this yesterday?"

Sarah responded like clockwork. "Just after 1600 hours."

"And the time now?"

"Coming onto 1430."

That didn't help.

If the green tide were following a time-related pattern, he needed more information to plot a graph in his mind, as well as factor in the shorter day cycles. Oxygen had some significance. How were the algee obtaining the oxygen, and what were they doing with it? Did a 0.5 percent O_2 level stimulate them to go into this state? What was bringing up those levels in the first place?

The algee had lost all their radiance now, throwing Sarah and him into twilight.

"There's still something missing."

"What's that, Barry?"

"Huh? Oh, nothing. I just think there's something we're not seeing that's fundamental to understanding the solution."

"The solution to what?"

"The algee. Archeya. Evolution. I really don't know."

"Well, we've got twenty-six more days to find out."

•••

The following morning, Barry slept in.

"Starting without me?"

Sarah answered him on the com. "We thought about waking you. But you look so peaceful when you're sleeping."

Several minutes and several dozen labored steps later, he found the two women on the shore, staring out at the unchanged algee. Sarah was holding her digital logbook, but it wasn't open. Barry trekked to her side. They exchanged a knowing glance.

"What do you think?" he asked her.

"I think," said Sarah, "that we need a sample." Barry smiled. "Whoever said great minds don't think alike?"

They had spent two twenty-hour days on this world. Decisions such as this, according to SSA regulations, were now left to their own discretion. With Sarah on his side, Ellen got outvoted. He turned toward the solitary woman.

Ellen, however, was prepared for him. She held a specimen cylinder in her hands, and a smirk hidden on her face. It appeared he didn't have her figured out after all.

"Just let me know what you discover about these little guys," she said, handing Barry the canister.

Then Ellen turned on her heel and, armed with a trowel and other excavation equipment, headed out onto the plains. No, he had definitely *not* figured her out.

Barry carefully stepped to the edge of the shoreline. Using the attachment, he scooped two liters of algee. They didn't respond. He put the attachment with the algee back into the cylinder. No reaction. Nothing.

"It seems they're happy to be coming with us."

"Let me see," Sarah said.

He held up the cylinder. They both peered through the metallic plastic.

"Not unlike bacilli," she commented.

"Yes. Although these are more oval- than rod-shaped."

"I don't see any conspicuous protrusions, such as flagella. How big are they?"

"Since we can make out their shape without a viewscope, they're definitely larger than the average cell. Maybe ten millimeters."

He stared at the immobile organisms. What made them tick?

"Come on, Barry," Sarah implored.

"Ah, the impetuousness of youth," he teased. "All right, all right. Here, since you just can't wait to pick them apart, *you* can carry this."

He gave her the cylinder, which she in turn nearly dropped. The small container looked to be no more than a few pounds. But of course here it weighed more than ten kilos. Perhaps Sarah had been a little too anxious. That led to mistakes. He didn't tell her that. He was certain she'd learn for herself.

Back at the ship, they went through the double hermetically sealed doors of the biolab, keeping their suits on. The lab stretched right to the back of the ship—it was the primary reason for this vessel. The unused steel surfaces had a sheen to them, reflecting the bright lights overhead, while the sterilized, state-of-the-art equipment awaited a specimen to study.

Now they had one.

Sarah set up one of the viewscopes. Barry was content to watch her work; it gave him a quiet pleasure watching others perform their duties, especially when they did them well. Sarah quickly adjusted the scope's resolution. With a dropper she put a thin pool of water onto a glass slide, and held it out toward him, waiting expectantly. Sarah was happy doing the familiar. The unfamiliar, however, she left to Barry. A smart one, she was.

Before getting her an algee sample, he secured the specimen cylinder into a quarantine cube. More like something Ellen would do. But there would be no contamination on his watch. The three-layered cube—reinforced steel, aluminum and metalloplastic —set aside that possibility.

He used a pair of vacuum tweezers to lift an algee onto a petri dish. Then he shut the cube and transferred the individual algee—once more, he noted the lack of reaction—to the viewscope slide. Sarah placed a coverslip on top, and was on her way to place it under the viewscope when she let out a horrible screech.

Barry saw her drop the slide. The glass shattered, the lone algee twisting and turning on the floor like a dug-up earthworm, glowing green.

"It changed so fast...." Sarah tried to explain, holding her trembling hands together.

Barry quickly cleaned and sterilized the mess. This wasn't like Sarah. As a microbiologist, she dealt with deadly bacteria all the time. Why lose her nerve over this?

"Is anything the matter, Sarah?" She didn't reply. "Are you all right?"

"I think so."

He tried to see her expression through the facemask.

"I'm sorry. I don't know why I screamed. There's something about the algee that I find... disconcerting."

"What do you mean?"

"Don't worry, I'll be fine. Let's continue here."

Barry prepared another sample. Again, the algee reacted to being placed on the slide. This time, he quickly pushed it under the viewscope and put his eyes over the two lenses. Finally, he would see the heart of this creature.

"Well?" Sarah prompted.

"I have to wait for it to stop quivering. Here, I'll put the image up on the monitor."

And there it was. A ten-millimeter organism blown up on the meter-sized screen. The algee's shape slowly came into focus as it stilled and dimmed, revealing a smooth membrane as its exterior, covered in small porous openings much like those possessed by human cells.

"There's more than one membrane," Barry said, using the viewscope's pointer. "I see at least two."

"Maybe three," Sarah answered. "The outer resembles a plasma membrane, the second a plant cell wall—those are usually arranged the other way around. The innermost membrane doesn't look like anything I've seen before."

"I'm not sure it's a membrane. It does surround the perimeter, but…it's not thin enough. Okay, it finally stopped. Now we can see the cell components. See those small granules just inside the inner membrane? It looks like they're using cyclosis to get around."

Hundreds of tiny organelles circled the cell, like microscopic cars on a racetrack.

"Chloroplasts?" Sarah theorized.

"That's as good a guess as any, I suppose." Chloroplasts were the organelle responsible for photosynthesis, and were usually green. "But these are more compact. And dense, like ribosomes."

"Whatever they are, they're sure keeping busy."

Barry shook his head. "We've overlooked the most important feature. It's just like me to get lost in the details. This algee is about the size of my pinky fingernail. And it's a *single cell*."

Sarah's eyes widened, as if seeing the algee for the first time. Then she shook her head. "It's too big."

"So is an unfertilized ostrich egg."

"That's cheating. It won't grow into anything. A fertilized egg, on the other hand, will become a billion-celled bird."

She suddenly looked lost to Barry. And somehow, very frail. Starnauts sometimes started to act strange, especially the inexperienced ones on long voyages. Space sickness some called it. But it had nothing to do with space, and everything to do with being surrounded by the unfamiliar. He couldn't lose her now, just when things were getting interesting. He needed her to be part of the team.

"I'm going to set up the stereoscope so we can see several interacting together. Can you go over the factors that limit cell size for me?"

"Cell size?"

"Yes, it'll help me think." *And help you keep focused.*

She paused, her mind working, moving back to the familiar.

"A cell's surface-to-volume ratio is vital. With the expansion of the cell, its membrane surface area to volume of cytoplasm decreases. Thus the larger a cell is, the harder it becomes for it to balance water and other resources between itself and the outside environment. So it requires a lot more work to obtain nutrients and get rid of wastes by diffusion. Most cells aren't larger than one hundred micrometers; many are only one or two in diameter."

"But what advantages are there for large cell size?"

"There are none," she said matter-of-factly. "Smallness in the cell world means efficiency."

"But there has to be *some* advantage." He saw the thrill in her eyes, trying to make the unknown known. He needed to keep her going. "What about a larger storage area?"

"No, that just means a cell needs to do more work to maintain the same relative amount of material for storage. Yet…one could hypothesize that a large cell size would allow for fluids and signals to be conducted more easily, without obstruction by the nucleus and other cell components. And maybe to help compartmentalize functions. But that's usually where multicellularism comes in."

Barry thought it over. "Maybe this is one discovery that'll put another scientific prejudice aside. Okay, the stereoscope is ready."

He transferred the image. Six algee now quivered and glowed on the monitor.

"The three membranes," Sarah said, "they look like they're lining up."

Barry watched as the outer two walls of the algee shifted, so that their pores overlapped. Then the third membrane broke apart. The fragmented pieces were the same organelles from before—small, granulated, and compact. Some of them quickly moved through the pores from one algee to the next. Any gaps in that third pseudomembrane were quickly filled from the innermost part of the cell.

"Fascinating. Those channels are like plasmodesmata," Barry noted. "Connecting the algee to one another."

"Yes, and those components moving among the

algee remind me of neurotransmitters. They could be signals, coordinating the algee, allowing many of them to work together toward a single purpose—"

Ellen came onto the com.

"You better come look at this," she said, sounding ominous.

"What is it? Found a terrestrial life form?" For that, Barry could forgive the interruption.

"Not exactly," she replied. Ellen's voice sounded strange. Excited. "But maybe evidence of one."

"Okay, I'll be right there." He turned to Sarah, feeling confident now that he could leave her in the biolab. He had bigger things to ponder than cellular structure. "Can you continue on here while I go see what Ellen's unearthed?"

"Sure thing." She didn't even look his way, occupied with her work. Good.

He went toward the doors.

"Wait a second," Sarah called after him. "Come look at this. The algee—it's dividing."

Barry started walking back.

"Hurry! It's almost done."

Almost done? What was she talking about?

He peered up at the magnified image. Right she was: the cell was just finishing what looked like mitosis. One algee had become two. In under thirty seconds.

Astounding. This was one remarkable little bacterium.

"What's the fastest generation time for a cell on Earth?"

"E. coli," Sarah answered, "can divide in eighteen minutes in a nutrient-rich culture. But I wouldn't call this petri dish a rich culture."

"It does have water."

"Wrong. It *did* have water. They've used it all up."

"Thirty seconds. That's fifteen billion years of evolution for you."

"Perfection?"

"We both know evolution doesn't operate that way. But maybe this algee is the closest anything's ever gotten."

•••

Beyond the single-celled issue, there was a much bigger picture to consider. Were these algee the result of an extraordinarily long evolutionary process? All life started out as a single organism, the joining of two amino acids in a gelatinous sea. From there, over innumerable generations of parent organisms passing on their genes, this mother organism diversified into several new forms. Eventually the oceans and continents are teeming with countless different species, each tailored to its own ecological niche. Some use the sun and water to make food, others feed on these providers, while still others prey on them from higher up in the food chain. The balance between plant and animal, predator and prey, was very fine.

Barry brooded over the question that underlined the algee. If you waited several billion years, or in this planet's case, more than *fifteen billion,* did everything go back to how it began? Instead of countless species, did it all return to a single life form? Were these algee the ultimate end of evolution?

Ultimate or not, they would soon be as extinct as Archeya's dying sun. There was no adaptation to escape that fate....

Outside the ship, on his way to find Ellen, Sarah reached him over the com. "Barry, they start glowing and quivering every time I add water. By the time they finish, the water's gone. Those six algee are now thirty. They've stopped dividing, yet they still use up any water I give them. The algee don't increase in size, either. It's like they're not actually utilizing the water for themselves anymore."

"Thanks for the update," he said, annoyed at losing his train of thought, although it gave him a sudden insight. What was in water? Oxygen. That could easily be a critical resource. And from what Sarah had said, it sounded as though the algee weren't simply using it; they were *removing* it. Whenever the amount of oxygen rose to the minimum level required for life, the algee eliminated the gas before anything else could obtain it.

Ruthless competitors. Is that what these algee were? So efficient at eliminating competition that nothing else could survive here?

Humans had done this as well, until we learned to coexist with our planet's biodiversity. The algee didn't have those worries. One cell, no matter how well adapted, couldn't possess sentience. Therefore these algee had no qualms about causing mass extinction. He wondered if they were an engineered bacteria, a biological weapon so powerful it could destroy all life—except for itself. He shivered at the thought. This algee had had a long time to engineer itself through mutation and natural selection.

A memory tried to surface from the well of his mind. No, the algee wasn't a weapon. Something else. Something he'd read, or someone had mentioned to him in passing. Another expedition like this one. A report. Saying something about—

"What do you make of this?"

He had found Ellen near those odd structures

resembling eucalyptus trees, or the upper half of bishop's heads from a chessboard. His previous musings were immediately forgotten. She held an object in her hands, obviously yielded from her excavation. It looked like silver, although it was nearly transparent.

"My God, Ellen. What have you dug up?"

"This was ten meters below the surface," she explained, handing it to him, answering the one question that didn't matter.

The object was exceptionally lightweight, about as long as his forearm. One side tapered to a smooth and unblemished, rounded point. The other end looked the same, except about halfway down there was a clean break in its shape. He had expected her to discover a fossil, not an alien artifact.

"It isn't rusted at all," he said. "Not even here, where it has been severed. You do realize this could be an object of unimaginable power. After all, any sufficiently advanced technology is indistinguishable from magic."

"Clarke's Third Law?"

"You know your history. This might be the first time that law can be tested."

"Or," Ellen replied nonchalantly, "it could just be a vase."

She was precisely correct. They might never figure out what this was, let alone how it worked. But one thing was certain: it was entirely artificial. Could an intelligent being have created this? The idea was hard to fathom. But he couldn't put it aside.

"Do you think this object's maker—the Archeyans, if you will—were advanced enough to stabilize, or even create, the wormhole array?"

"We can't answer that yet."

"Until we find evidence proving otherwise," Barry said, "I think the answer has to be yes. Why else would the array be so close to Archeya?"

"You mean ZB178. Let's see what else we can find."

•••

Over the next few days, Barry acted as a relay station between Ellen and Sarah. The three of them worked well together, efficiently, sleeping only because they knew it was needed. His earlier idea tugged at his brain. What had he been thinking about? He couldn't remember. Oh well, he would just have to work it out again.

Ellen continued with her archaeological dig. She found two more objects in the same area, guiding a geoprobe remotely to excavate them to the surface. These were larger, about two square meters. They looked identical, like simple rectangular containers with rounded corners.

"Would make a nice bathtub," Barry remarked.

He also helped her with the surface-penetrating radar. The reflected signals gave them a global profile of what lay under the ground. The bishop's heads were actually the top of a massive framework of architecture, the foundations of artificial construction. He excitedly proclaimed them the ruins of an ancient metropolis. The find was extraordinary. Intelligent life had been here.

"During its time, this alien civilization must've been far more advanced than we can ever imagine. Yet, at the same time, these Archeyans may have been beaten by the algee in the evolutionary race."

Ellen didn't want to jump to any conclusions.

Meanwhile, Sarah had a much smaller focus. She

had an algee positioned in the electron transmission microscope, down to the last nanometer.

He asked her how it was going.

"What can I say," she said. "This is the most fascinating work I've ever done."

"Fascinating? Your latest synonym for amazing?"

She beamed. This was why she was here. This was why she had come.

"Let me tell you the three most interesting discoveries I've made," she continued, intent on her objective, determined to get results. "The first involves how the algee quiver about so violently. Remember those small, ribosome-like organelles? When the algee starts to glow, these begin to bounce around inside the cell, like a pinball machine. That's what causes them to vibrate. Don't shake your head. I don't believe it either. But that's what happens."

"I'll take your word for it. What else have you found?"

"The algee are definitely multinucleated. I've seen anywhere from ten to fifty nuclei in any particular cell. That's how they divide so fast—they're prepared for it. The nuclear material is ready to be put into a new cell, with new nuclei being formed all the time. Potentially, a few algee could become thousands in a matter of minutes."

"Fascinating."

"Stop that."

"Sarah, I'm being serious. Or can't you tell?"

"You don't make it easy. Now look at this. The ECM is in a vacuum, and the electron beam isn't very healthy for any biological sample. Not to mention that a specimen has to be completely dehydrated before it can be viewed. That's more than enough to kill any cell on Earth. Yet, hours later when I removed the slide, *the algee was still alive*."

"Resilient little buggers, aren't they?"

"To say the least."

"I assume you're taking the proper precautions?"

"Oh, Barry. When it comes to safety, I'm just your average Ellen. I think I can handle a single cell."

"There's a ruined civilization out there that might disagree."

Sarah didn't say anything.

"What about the green tide? Have you figured out the functionality of that phosphorescence?"

"I have no idea how the glow works. Must be a redox reaction of some sort. Why it sheds such a bright color is still a mystery to me. But that does remind me...."

He looked at Sarah, thought he could see concern etched behind her facemask.

"Yes?" he persisted.

"I've been working on a theory to explain how the algee use oxygen. I think they convert two O_2's into an O_4 molecule. I'm not sure if they're adding an electron to each O_4 ion to make it neutral. But *something* masks the oxygen as being oxygen. Maybe there's no other life here, because the algee hide all the O_2."

"No oxygen...no photosynthesis...no simple sugars...no food."

"No diversity."

"That's a frightening thought." Barry considered it for a moment. "But there's a problem. How do the algee use oxygen if they convert it all to this unusable form? Or do they use it at all?"

"I think they do. They just reverse the reaction. But only they know how."

Sarah looked up at the monitor, almost transfixed. This was her new viewport.

"You're doing good work, Sarah. I'm going to head outside. Keep me posted."

Barry often went to the shore to be alone and think. Well, maybe he wasn't alone out here, but the billion or so little guys keeping him company kept quiet enough. He tried to catch them when they "activated" themselves, forming another green tide. The oxygen levels never rose more than half a percent, and never fell under a tenth. Could the algee actually be creating their own energy source, and controlling it as well? Like a virus or a parasite that didn't need a host to survive. Unless you considered a planet a host. A disconcerting thought.

Carefully cataloguing all his findings, he did his best to integrate them with Sarah and Ellen's, trying to link the data, connect it into one whole. Eventually, his growing fatigue and the failing light forced him to resign. Cursing the planet's short day length didn't help.

•••

On the seventh day of their stay on Archeya, Barry woke to an empty ship.

He had taken the dreaded middle watch, and his second shift of sleep was, unsurprisingly enough, far from restful. He kept waking, then falling back into a deep slumber filled with dreams of Earth's oceans. Each time he dreamed felt like days, time stretching as far as the ocean waves.

Sarah and Ellen were both outside. A week had passed since they had arrived, which meant they would be relocating the *Astral Surveyor* to another part of the planet in a few hours, covering ground in a new area.

He gulped down a nutribar, splashed some water over his face, and went to the biolab. The sterilized steel surfaces gently glowed, the night lights still on. Barry turned on the main lights, wanting to observe the quivering mechanism for himself. He opened up the quarantine cube—

That was strange. This cube was empty. Sarah must've moved them. But to where?

"Barry?"

It was Ellen on the com. Her voice was tight, as though she were struggling to keep it controlled.

"What's going on?"

There was a pause before her reply. "It's Sarah."

He knew something had gone terribly wrong.

"Ellen, what's happened? Where is Sarah?"

"She's here, on the shore."

"Is she all right?"

"No, Barry, she's not. I…need your help."

$$\bullet\bullet\bullet$$

He found Ellen crouching next to Sarah's prone body. One of her hands was half-raised, like a mother reaching for a child that was beyond aid. But Ellen's SSA training kept her fingers from reaching Sarah's shoulder.

Then Barry saw the helmet next to Sarah's body. Sarah was dead.

The emotional weight dropped him to one knee. Archeya's gravity seemed heavier, pushing him down, down, down. Sarah was dead. *Dead*. He fought against it, forcing himself to rise, to bottle his emotion.

"What happened?" he finally asked.

"I found her like this," Ellen somberly explained. "I haven't moved her," she quickly added, as though that were important now.

"And her helmet?"

"I haven't touched that either."

He felt anger rising in his belly. How could she be so calm? "Why didn't you try to put it back on?"

She didn't answer him, because she didn't have to.

The lower half of Sarah's suit was practically eaten away, revealing her slender legs underneath. And her face...her face had shrunk beyond recognition. Skin on bone, with little separating the two. Mercifully, her eyelids were closed. There was probably nothing behind them.

"She said she wanted to see the algee in their natural environment. That was the last thing she told me."

Barry sat next to Ellen. "You think she went in there?" he said, turning to stare out at the sea of algee. Silent, still, almost lifeless. Some part of him thought he was still in a dream.

"I think she waded in, panicked, took off her helmet, and collapsed here on the shore," Ellen said in one breath.

"Why would Sarah do that?"

He looked at Ellen, and realized she had had much longer than him to think this through.

"She's withered away," Ellen went on. "Gaunt, emaciated. Her blood is gone."

"Hemoglobin..."

"Hemoglobin?"

"Yes," Barry said, getting his mind on track. "The oxygen carrier in the blood. The algee could be responsible for denaturing its structure, or putting in an inhibitor onto the heme binding site." Those cutthroat competitors. They had eliminated his protege. His colleague. His friend. Barry couldn't hold it in.

"Duty, protocol. How does any of that matter now? There's a young woman beneath that suit. And she's dead, Ellen. Do you realize that? Of course you do. I'm sorry. It's just, I can't pretend any longer that I'm not feeling anything. She loved her life. She loved being in space. I'm the one who pushed for her to be on this mission. Sarah's father asked me to look out for her, for Christ's sake. I failed him. I failed her. Maybe she was too eager, too green with inexperience. She shouldn't have come...."

"Barry, she knew exactly what she was getting into."

Only when she spoke did he realize Ellen had placed her hand on his shoulder. Barry put his hand on hers, and they remained that way for a long moment. He couldn't deny what Ellen said. Just a few days ago, Sarah herself had told him this was the life she had chosen.

He saw Sarah's logbook sitting on the shore. "Oh, God," he exclaimed.

"What is it?"

He had just remembered that first day, the inexplicable feeling he had to submerge himself in the algee's depths.

"Barry?"

"A week ago, standing in this very same spot, I had this urge. I can't explain it, Ellen, but I wanted to swim in that green tide. I think Sarah might've felt it as well. But I didn't say anything."

Ellen faced him. He couldn't make out her expression through the facemask.

"I felt it too," she stated simply.

"You did?"

"Yes, just once. I remember it. You know why I retired to the ship so early that first day? It was for that very reason. Don't try to blame yourself for this."

Barry decided something right then and there. He may have failed Sarah, but he wouldn't let the mission fail.

"Let's get her back to the ship."

It was nearly impossible to haul Sarah's body back. But Barry refused to do it any other way. He lifted, dragged, pulled, stopped…and then started again. Sarah didn't feel real to him. Light somehow, soulless. When they finally had her aboard, Barry sat with Ellen on the bridge, exhausted.

"We have to go," she told him.

"I'm not leaving."

"Barry—"

"No, Ellen." He took a deep breath. "I'm staying on here. You can go, of course. You have to take Sarah back to Earth. Leave the third of the *Astral Surveyor*, the section with the biolab, here with me. Pack everything else and go."

"There's a proven danger on this world. I can't allow it."

"Nothing has been proven, Ellen. As much as it pains me to say it, Sarah may have taken her own life. This is my last mission. I'll take full responsibility for my actions. That's what I've always done."

"Right now, I don't give a damn about responsibility." He was startled by her vehemence. "I care about *you*."

Barry didn't know how to respond.

"If you stay here, you could end up the same way Sarah did."

He understood then, and was touched by Ellen's concern. But it still wouldn't stop him.

"This mission is all I care about. Sarah's dead, it's sunk in now. But I won't abandon the mission. I can't."

Ellen was quiet for a minute.

"This planet holds a secret," she said softly. "I want to solve it as much as you." Then her voice became firm. "We'll stay another day. No more. Then we go home."

•••

Even though they were leaving tomorrow, Barry helped Ellen make all the preparations. Yet he still found time to retrieve another sample of algee. She didn't object to his assistance. She didn't say much of anything, except when he provoked a response by insisting he continue the mission on his own. But Ellen was adamant in her position, and eventually Barry realized how ridiculous he was acting: He would never leave Ellen alone here, either.

Afterward, they were both worn out. Ellen retired to her quarters, perhaps hoping to sleep away some of the emotional demons that must be lurking inside her head. They had certainly found their way into Barry's mind, appearing the moment he saw Sarah lying on the shore. The demons taunted him, digging at his guilty conscience with their claws.

"Don't you go wandering into that algee. And that's an order," Ellen had told him.

No. He could do exactly what he wanted right here.

The sun had started to set, twilight settling over the world. Yet sleep wasn't possible for him now. He had work to do, and his mind refused to shut down. If his time was limited, there was nothing to do but make the best of it. He was ready, in a manner of speaking, to get his hands dirty.

Within the confines of the biolab, Barry organized a series of petri dishes along the steel counter. He was determined to test the algee's resilience. He wanted to break through it. Perhaps his motives were sinister, some form of unconscious vengeance; at this point, he cared little for scientific objectivity. What they had done to Sarah justified it. He would get to the truth of the algee's origins any way he could.

For the first test he went up and down the pH scale, from sodium hydroxide to hydrochloric acid. The base solutions seemed to shy away from the algee, while the acids were actually consumed.

"That probably did you more good than harm," he quipped.

He spent ten minutes scrubbing the countertop with acetone, and put the petri dishes into the autoclave, before beginning the next test. Filling four test tubes partway with algee, he placed them inside the centrifuge, equidistant from one another so as to properly balance the machine. He set the timer for three hours, and let it work its way up to one hundred thousand revolutions per minute.

Moving on, he placed a petri dish with a new sample onto a cold plate. Positioning it under the stereoscope so he could watch the algee respond on the monitor, he lowered the temperature. When he passed the freezing point of water the algee started doing their vibrating dance, the organelles resembling ribosomes bouncing around the inside of the cells just as Sarah had described. But they weren't glowing. As it got colder, the algee suddenly shrank down to half their size, pulling in both outer membranes. When he raised the temperature, the algee became turgid again, seemingly unaffected.

They appeared to freeze, but did not die. Well, Barry thought, how hot do you like it?

After another acetone and autoclave sterilization, he prepared a converse sample for the incinerator. As he transferred the algee, he couldn't help but wonder if they somehow sensed what he was about to do to them. He let the temperature rise slowly, a few degrees every minute, starting at three hundred Kelvin. It passed three hundred fifty, and then the boiling point of water. Only well beyond four hundred did the cell structure begin to fall apart, denaturing into a disorderly mess of subcomponents.

He came to a rather obvious conclusion: there was no easy way to kill these little buggers.

Barry kept working through the dark hours of Archeya's night. The experiment he took the most pleasure in involved the use of a mortar and pestle. It felt more involving on his part. Primitive equipment, perhaps, but by putting a few dozen algee into the bottom of the mortar dish, he was then able to crush them thoroughly with the pestle. He got some satisfaction manually squashing them. The pulpy product Barry put into the spectrograph's chemilyzer.

While waiting for the results to be printed, he came across his most startling discovery.

The centrifuge had finished spinning. He promptly retrieved the four test tubes, thinking he would now be better able to analyze the algee's particular constituents. As he stared at the suspension of fractionated cells, split into a dozen or so layers of sedimentation, he thought he saw movement.

A minute later he had the contents spread on a petri dish, and observed them on the monitor.

Definite movement. But how? And was it random?

No, they were restructuring themselves. These algee weren't dead.

Maybe he shouldn't be surprised. Maybe anything that had dozens of epochs to adapt would become fierce ecological competitors. Maybe when evolution took place over eons, something like this was to be expected.

He watched in fascination as the algee organized their fractured elements. Within a matter of minutes, they had part of their cell membrane rebuilt.

Maybe it was foolish to try and understand them. Cells were the closest living things to being immortal. When they divided, they made exact duplicates of themselves, carrying the same DNA. But the algee...they had attained true immortality.

Barry had a sudden impulse to see them glow. He needed to see that miraculous display of life. He quickly added some water to the petri dish, helping them re-form. Soon there were three complete cells, shining bright and green on the monitor. Then the vibrations started, leaving him mesmerized. But this wasn't enough.

His own thoughts strayed from him, replaced by a yearning to see the green tide of Archeya's oceans. To see the algee *outside* the ship.

Some part of Barry knew exactly what was happening to him. What had happened to Sarah. Yet he didn't fight it. He wanted to experience what she had experienced, relive her final moments. But he wouldn't let Sarah's fate be his own. He would stop before the end.

He almost left the biolab without going through decontamination. A warning alarm sounded, and the doors wouldn't open. So he stood under the sterilizing shower, letting his suit be purified, thinking of the billions upon billions of identical life forms that were waiting for him. There was no hurry.

The orange sun crept over the flat horizon, the encroaching dawn sending an illusion of colors through the atmosphere. But he didn't notice. Walking slowly and steadily over the barren flats, his only interest lay in the phosphorescence. That supernatural glow. Halfway there, he could see the ocean becoming alive again, the green tide returning. It seemed much brighter than before—

"Barry?"

Ellen's voice took him off guard. He had forgotten she was here, thought he was alone. Except for the algee. He couldn't make himself answer, knew she wouldn't understand.

"Do you read me, Barry? Please respond." He could hear the concern in her voice, turning to fear. Why didn't he answer her? He opened his mouth, then shut it. No, he needed to keep going. She must be able to hear his breathing. Long gasps for air. He walked on.

At the coast, he stopped dead.

A river had formed from the ocean's edge. A living river. The algee, like a mass of tiny, writhing worms, were forging their own channel up the incline. They glowed and vibrated more intensely than he had ever seen them. The newly formed river also appeared to be gaining speed, as though the closer the algee got to their destination, the more attracted—eager?—they became.

His mind began to shift back, the scientist in him taking over. He couldn't keep silent any longer.

"Ellen, you aren't going to believe this."

"Barry? Thank God. Where are you?"

"I'm on the shore—"

"Jesus, Barry. What the hell are you doing out there?"

"Listen, Ellen. The algee is on the move. They've come onto the land."

"What are you talking about?"

"Remember those channels all along the shoreline? The algee created them. They're creating a new one right now."

She didn't reply.

"Ellen?"

"You have to return to the ship, Barry. Immediately."

"In a minute. Oh my God. The algee...they've lifted themselves off the ground...."

"What?!" she said in a very unEllen-like voice.

Barry couldn't believe his unblinking eyes. The algee had raised themselves above the laws of gravity. They were in more or less a straight line. The first twenty meters remained on the land, perhaps leveraging the rest into the air. That explained why the channels always had an abrupt end. But there was nothing his educated brain could put forth to account for the algee's levitation. There would be no more testing of hypotheses, not when the odds were billions against one.

"Is everything okay down there?"

"As a scientist, I can't fathom this, Ellen." A thought occurred to him. "Do you know what this means? Maybe Sarah didn't kill herself. Maybe the algee came to her."

"That may be. But where are they headed?" she asked. It was a rather innocent question, but it didn't sink in.

"Headed?"

"Yes," Ellen said. "If the algee have left the shoreline, where is it they are going?"

He paused, just an instant, before replying.

"The little bastards. Are you coming to eliminate us?"

The growing river of algee, leading unmistakably to the *Astral Surveyor*, didn't respond. Barry wasn't going to stay and chat.

"I'm making my way back," he announced.

"Glad to hear it. Do you need me to help you?"

"No."

"Are you sure?"

"Yes, Ellen."

"All right. I'm going to get the other third of the ship. We're leaving."

This time, Barry didn't argue.

He wanted to sprint back to the *Astral Surveyor*. But he quickly realized, after his initial adrenaline rush faded, how tired he actually was. He hadn't slept for what felt like an eternity. Fatigue seized his muscles. His body wanted to shut down. He needed to pace himself. The algee might have a way to defy Archeya's gravity, but his weighted legs certainly didn't. He kept glancing over his shoulder, more often than he should.

His toe hit a crevice and he fell onto his hands. Barry felt his left knee scrape over the surface. God, had he cut it open? He hastily ran his fingers over the area in question. Fortunately, the thin suit was tougher than he gave it credit for. However, when he got to his feet, he found his knee didn't want to bend.

"Damn it."

"How's it going?" Ellen inquired.

"Slower than I'd like. These old bones of mine need a good rest."

His knee still worked, though he had to drag his right leg a little. It helped when he talked, made him forget the pain in his limbs.

"I'm thinking of modifying Clarke's Law," he said to Ellen.

"To what?"

"Any sufficiently advanced *life form* is indistinguishable from magic. Maybe I'll call it Barry's Third Law."

"I like the sound of that," Ellen said. "What's Barry's First Law?"

"Never abandon a mission."

"Hmm. And the second?"

He had to pause for a moment to catch his breath, panting from exertion.

"Under extenuating circumstances, the First Law can—no, *must*—be broken."

"I think this qualifies. Have you reached the ship yet?"

"I'm there."

"And the algee?"

He turned back before shutting the hatch. "I think they want to hitch a ride. But I've got enough time to get the ship going before their little thumbs reach me."

"Okay. There's no time to reconnect the ships. We'll have to do it on the other side of the wormhole horizon. We'll dock together at Pluto's refilling station."

"Aye aye."

Barry locked the hatch and initiated an emergency takeoff. As the propulsion system started up, he strapped himself in, and—after a moment's thought—ejected the quarantine cubes from the ship. Even though the advancing algee were still a minute or two away, he nevertheless breathed a sigh of relief when the ship thrust off the ground.

I'd like to see you follow me now, he thought to himself amidst the roar of the engines, the as-yet-unnamed planet falling further from view with each passing second.

As soon as he cleared the exosphere, Ellen appeared on the com.

"Just checking in, Barry. All systems go?"

"Definitely a go."

He almost drifted off right then and there. But he needed to attend to something else before sleep. The cryogenic pod was just outside Sarah's quarters. Barry sat beside it.

Leaning against the pod, his arms stretched across its width, he thought of the first time he had seen Sarah. Those eager blue eyes so full of wonder. He recalled her enthusiasm during the SSA training sessions, and how they were at ease with one another right off, exchanging friendly banter from the very beginning.

That fresh young face opened something in him. Something that had been closed off for too long: passion. Passion for his work, for science, for discovery. She had given him that gift, and he returned the favor by getting her killed.

"I'll get you home, Sarah."

Leaving the ship on autonav, he went into Sarah's quarters and crashed on the bunk. It felt as though his eyes barely had time to close when a voice lured him awake.

"Barry, come in."

He sat up, head drooping, and glanced sideways at the clock. "Would you mind putting more than ten minutes between your status check-ins?"

Noncommittal, Ellen said, "I'll try."

She sent a transmission every hour on the hour. He groggily replied to each. After the fifth he got annoyed.

"Look, Ellen, I'm fine. Just be warned that my next reply will be an automated response: *1700 and all's well!*"

"We've reached the array."

That got him up. Deep down this was something Barry wished he could sleep through. The wormhole made him nervous. Just a bit.

"Preparing for horizon entry," he announced from the bridge.

As he approached the wormhole, swirling eddies of time mixing with currents of space, the stars began to disappear one by one. Going into a vacuum solution certainly got the stomach butterflies fluttering. He doubted humankind would ever understand this phenomenon they so eagerly exploited. If they couldn't understand the algee, a single-celled organism, how could they expect to understand the stabilization of a cosmic anomaly?

Something clicked in Barry's brain. The final piece to put the puzzle together. His inspiration came, as he had taught himself so very long ago, from the *outside*.

Outside the algee, outside Archeya, outside the wormhole.

He remembered now with perfect clarity reading a paper in the *Journal of Exoplanetology*, written by a trailblazer who had visited another solar system. It described an unusual planet with a thick atmosphere. Human observations were limited to off-world viewing, though the author had made note of one particular detail: periodically, the surrounding atmosphere glowed green from an unknown source. A probe sent to the surface had taken pictures of continents barren as deserts without sand, and vast oceans swelling with countless unidentifiable organisms.

But he knew what they were. Algee.

With that bit of knowledge, he began to wonder which planet could claim origin of the algee. But he realized that question didn't matter. What mattered was that two planets—and who knew how many others—were dominated by this same versatile organism. Such an example of parallel evolution was unheard of; he could effectively discard the idea. Because the algee had arrived from *outside* Archeya.

They had migrated.

"See you on the other side," Ellen said.

"Roger that."

He didn't offer her his theory. He could hear Ellen's condescending tone, telling him it was preposterous. Yet he couldn't shake the idea. The implications of being right were literally on a planet-size scale.

Somewhere in the universe the algee had evolved. Like plants with seeds, spores or fruit, or animals that swim across channels or fly over continents, they must have their own method of dispersal. But instead of spreading from pond to pond, forest to forest, habitat to habitat, the algee had found a way to go from planet to planet. Just like the human race, they were no longer limited to their home world, traveling to other solar systems. How? The answer was simple. He had almost done it himself.

The mountain of evidence—both circumstantial and otherwise—rose to a point. He could almost see the peak, just needed to clear away a few clouding facts. The alien container Ellen found on Archeya, the presence of another planet with algee, the proximity of both planets to separate ends of the wormhole array. No matter how implausible, it was the only explanation that let all the puzzle pieces lock together to form a whole.

They were sampled. That's how the algee colonized and then terraformed other planets.

That green glow. The algee *wanted* to be seen. Most animals kept out of sight. To hide from predators, and stay alive. Or from prey, and then make a meal out of them. But the algee was letting its presence be known. Not a warning color, like red on a venomous snake, but a friendly, non-threatening green. Of course, the idea that they had adapted to colonize planets was ridiculous. Initially, it must've evolved for a separate function entirely, perhaps to be consumed by predators and then deposited by local dispersion elsewhere. Or maybe the algee glowed to attract their prey. Because everything was prey to them, a competitor, something to be eliminated.

Barry felt sure planetary colonization was happening. The super-adaptive algee had clearly shown an extreme mobility for their size. Once taken to another world, they spread throughout the oceans, stole the atmosphere's oxygen, depleted the water basins, out-competed every native species, and obliterated an entire bionetwork. Survival of the fittest on a galactic scale.

The magnitude of this mission suddenly hit him. The algee had almost used his ship as a dispersal mechanism.

"Ellen, do you read me?"

There was only static.

"Ellen, this is Barry. Please respond."

She still didn't answer. He realized then that she had already entered the wormhole, skipping forward hundreds of light-years in the process. A moment later, he followed.

Jumping transversely through space felt strange more than anything else, like he was plunging downward in an elevator. Then it changed direction. Left…right…up…until he seemed to be moving in every direction at once. A spellbinding display of shifting colors met his vision, going through every shade of the rainbow and beyond, and then there was no color at all. Everything blended to black. He shut his eyes, could feel his body inversing.

But it was all in his mind. Before he knew it, he appeared in the Kuiper Belt, not far from Pluto.

Slightly nauseous, he did his best to go swiftly through all the requisite diagnostics. Ellen would demand he do so before talking to him. His eyes were still readjusting, making it seem as though a pale light surrounded him.

An indicator light began to flash. The ship's O_2 reserves were at sixty percent. The readings plummeted as he watched. Fifty, forty, thirty…Did he have a hull breach on his hands, or just an instrument problem?

Then his vision cleared. That pale light turned out to be bright and green.

Barry turned in his chair. A river of algee snaked across the floor of the bridge toward him. He didn't move, but simply watched the algee spread and multiply. Divide and conquer. His disbelief slowly left him, replaced by a steady resolve of what his new mission objectives must be.

"Ellen, they're inside the oxygen tanks."

"Oh, God, Barry. Can you contain it?"

"Not possible. They're everywhere. My air's depleted."

"Then you'll have to eject. I'll pick you up."

"No, Ellen. It's too late for that. This ship is contaminated. I don't want to contaminate yours."

"What are you saying, Barry?"

"I'm saying goodbye. From the tests I did, there's only one sure way to kill the algee. I'm assuming ten million Kelvin will be hot enough."

He waited for Ellen's response. She knew there could be no other way.

"Your company has been a pleasure."

Despite his situation, he smiled at his co-worker, composed until the very end.

"Can I ask a favor?"

Ellen consented.

"Make sure the planet is officially named Archeya. It was Sarah's idea."

"Archeya it is."

He switched off the com. "I'm sorry, Sarah."

The algee were quivering about his ankles. Barry transferred all the data from his ship to Ellen's. Then he composed a message for Sarah's father, erased what he wrote, made it two words, and sent it off, knowing forgiveness was too much to ask.

Altering the ship's course, he locked on the autonav. Even at this distance, the glare from the sun forced him to shield his eyes. It reminded him of that day on the beach with Jeff. His brother and him together, staring at the sunset.

THE RED ENVELOPE

Written by
David Sakmyster

Illustrated by
Laura Jennings

About the Author

As an impressionable five-year-old, David Sakmyster would sit transfixed as his father read him horrific H.P. Lovecraft and Edgar Allan Poe stories. Seeking to vindicate his oft-scolded father for scaring him, our winning author began penning his own tales of the macabre during the late 1970s and early 1980s. After giving up pen for a Macintosh, David's career nearly ended after a hard-drive crash wiped out an epic novel in progress. A new PC soon replaced his Mac, and David never looked back.

David has since sold twelve short stories to semipro and smaller outlets. He briefly broke from fiction to write a history of a haunted upstate New York castle after David and his wife witnessed its famous ghost (or a very impressive local prank). David is now back on the fiction circuit while currently paying the bills as a financial manager for a New York phone company. He lives with his wife (his editor), their one-year-old daughter (his assistant editor), and family dog (his current agent—until a more reputable one turns up).

About the Illustrator

If her name is any indication, artist Laura Kathryn Dabney Jennings reflects many influences. Born in Maryland yet naturalized as a Texan at three, Laura has always had plenty of interests—from animals and nature to illustration and literature. She particularly remembers believing in magic, myth, and toys that could come to life. Growing up, she absorbed ideas from video games, film and comics, to which she's added the more recent influences of the Internet. Currently she lives on five Texas acres where she's surrounded by pets.

An avid reader, writer and dreamer, Laura remains focused on her goal of becoming both a writer and illustrator of fantasy novels. To that end, she taught herself how to draw with pen and ink. In fall 2006, she'll attend Texas Tech University to start her dual English and studio arts majors.

Thirty years from the day I found the red envelope lying on the narrow dirt street, I returned again to the village of Sanzhi. With one exception, I had been visiting every five years since, making the long trip to northern Taiwan from America, each time leaving from different parts of the country as time chipped away at my foundations, leaning me this way and that.

My nomadic lifestyle was Zhen-Lang's fault. Wherever I went, she flooded the earth beneath my feet so I couldn't put down roots.

On each of my previous four visits, I met with my in-laws in their central hall, gave them gifts, and respectfully lit joffa sticks as offerings for their ancestors. Then, I walked over the hill to the small grove protectively shrouded by drooping red cypress trees. I marched past the family's headstones, through the well-manicured plot and the perfect hydrangeas, lilies and cherry blossoms, and I trod where no one else ever came, past the prickly vines and beetle-chewed bushes to a corner beside a gnarled pear tree. There, I talked with Zhen-Lang. Told her of my life and the world. Reassured her of my constant faithfulness.

I did my duty and kept my pledge. Four times I've visited, at great expense. This time, I did not come alone. Julia was at my side, although quite ill herself, in midstage chemotherapy recovery. I told her not to come, but she insisted.

"I may be weak," she said, her green eyes sparkling under the fake auburn strands in her wig. "But you, Brian, my poor, good man, are not strong enough to do it."

"I am," I assured her, but I knew she was right. It wasn't my age—at fifty-two, I was still in good health. She was talking about something else. I'd had my chances. Four other opportunities to do this in person. But the image of that single red envelope always held me back, flaring up in moments of weakness, sounding the echoes of my promise down through the years.

Like the time I returned to New Orleans after my third year abroad. Taiwan had been the first and only stint of my overseas assignment. Exxon decided a desk job might suit me better.

The first week back, in February of 1975, was Mardi Gras. Coming out of a jazz club was Evelyn, beautiful in every way the partiers out on Bourbon Street were not. Curly brown hair, almond-shaped eyes. She bumped into me. Our eyes met, we smiled, and she dragged me back into the club. Six drinks later, we were in her hotel room. Slanting shadows bisected the walls, and the bed glowed from the revelry outside.

"What's wrong?" she said, after getting over her initial giggles. Her hands were skillfully but ineffectively moving under the sheet and her slick body roamed over mine.

"I'm sorry," I whispered, retreating to my side of the mattress. Her skin felt cold, and my flesh crawled. I smelled something like decayed flowers and muddy grass.

"Come on," Evelyn whispered. "Don't you want this? Or did you drink too much?"

I told her that was it. One too many. I feigned illness, ran to the bathroom and turned on the shower. When I finally came out, she was sleeping with her back to me. I crawled under the sheets and breathed slowly, hoping to sleep.

When I finally drifted off, Zhen-Lang was there waiting, standing perfectly still in the misty shadows, head bowed with sticks in her hair and her hands crossed in front of her. I bowed to her, or at least I think I did, and she made some nominal noise, like the hissing of a cat, and my blood went cold—and I shot up in bed, screaming. Evelyn backed away from me at first, then moved to put her arms around me. Haunted by that lingering image, I knocked her away, roughly. She screamed, then cursed at me. All I remember after that was sitting on the bed as she dressed, shouting at me and pointing to the door. I think she called me a freak, and worse things.

She wouldn't be the last woman to send me packing.

On my way out, she asked me who Zhen-Lang was. I froze in the doorway.

"Who is she?" Evelyn demanded. "You called out her name several times before you woke yourself up."

I shuddered.

"Girlfriend?" she accused. "Or is she your wife?"

I hung my head as I stepped out into the hall.

"Should have told me you were married!" she shouted, and threw my shoes after me. "Or had the decency like any other guy to lie about it and—"

The door slammed—and strangely I don't remember touching it, or hearing Evelyn move. It just closed with a jarring thud.

Ever since, I've had problems with women. With relationships, with my entire life.

Julia says it's guilt. Maybe it's my old Catholic

upbringing taking hold—the sanctity of the sacraments and all that. But I think there's more to it. It's who I am, and what once I promised Zhen-Lang. What I continue to promise her every five years. Against the wishes of her family, even, but I can't help it.

I love her.

• • •

My first trip back to Sanzhi, on our fifth anniversary, was in 1979. It was a crisp fall day, and the Pacific breezes blew a chill over the hills and the storm-dampened rice fields on Zhen-Lang's family plot.

When I arrived, Zhen-Lang's brother, Ho-Jin, was in the fields, working beside his father, Wey-Tan. They were surprised to see me. "Did you bring the tablet?" my father-in-law asked, and I was grateful I could still understand the language. It helped that in the darkness of my room during sleepless nights, I sometimes spoke to my wife. In my head, in her language.

"Of course," I said, and turned my face to the cloud-riddled sky and felt light sprinkles tenderly anointing my skin.

"That is good," Wey-Tan said. "But you do not need to come."

"I think I do," I said as I carefully removed Zhen-Lang's ancestral tablet from my backpack. I knew they wouldn't want it in their house, but I didn't realize how completely they had put the whole business behind them.

"You can honor her in America," he whispered so his son could not hear. The deep lines in his forehead crinkled as he spoke, and raindrops trickled off his hard chin. "She is gone from here. It is what you did for us, and we are grateful, but we do not wish old memories brought back."

"But she is not gone," I insisted, pointing toward the grove to the east. "And...she is your daughter."

He hung his head. Over his shoulder I could see the house, and in the doorway, two women emerged. Mingmei-Chow, my mother-in-law, and Gengi-Sun, her other daughter.

Wey-Tan sighed when he saw his wife. "Very well. Come inside. Share tea and a meal. Tell us of yourself."

Inside, over a cup of bitter green tea, Mingmei-Chow asked if I had married again. Her eyes were bright, her face hopeful. She seemed in much better health than when I had last seen her.

"No, not yet," I said, shifting uncomfortably in my seat. Ho-Jin glared at me. Nearly twenty now, the boy must be nearing his own time for a wife. I looked around. "You all seem well."

Mingmei-Chow lowered her eyes modestly, but she nodded. "Yes, thank you."

I ate some rice and swallowed some more tea. I breathed in the incense from the joffa sticks, and I stared at the tablets on the mantle in the main hall. Their ancestral tablets. Husband and wife, son and daughter.

I recalled the first time I stood before that shrine. On my wedding day. How I teetered on wobbling legs, terrified and morbidly disturbed. I stood before the *Tang-ki,* the oracle of the little god, as he performed the ceremony. Zhen-Lang's family stood in attendance, looking grim and haggard. Each of them sick with various diseases the *Tang-ki* could not cure. The fields outside, too, were sickened, polluted as the well water.

It was the only way, her father told me as I held

that envelope in my hands. It trembled in my fingers the same as it had when I found it on the road six months before.

A common trick, and had I been a native I may have thought twice before picking it up. But that is all ancient history. For whatever reason, by whatever fate, I came across it first. Oh, the *Tang-ki* claims only the intended groom would be drawn to the envelope, only the man Zhen-Lang desired.

On my usual morning bicycle ride, I stopped and picked it up. I opened it and saw the money—fifteen thousand Kuai, which was about four hundred dollars—plus some fine blond hair, like wisps of golden thread. Wey-Tan sprang from the bushes and pronounced me the lucky man who had earned his daughter's hand.

Of course I refused. Simply not possible, I said, without even considering the dishonor I might be causing. I tried to give back the envelope, but he wouldn't have it. Said he'd wait, his family would wait, but I was the intended for his daughter, and she would bring me to her one way or another.

He went on to explain his family's plight—the sickness of his two other children, the flu that struck without mercy. His wife, ill to near-death, and he himself wracked with chest pains. The *Tang-ki* tried everything, every known medicine, every prayer and invocation.

In the end, a dream told young Ho-Jin that his dead sister was not at rest. She was exerting her power from the land of the shades, stirring up the elements here and clamoring for notice.

Her mantle was empty, her tablet kept in a spare closet in the dark. She had died, Wey-Tan told me, when she was still an infant. Nineteen years ago. Now, she would have been ready to marry, to bind herself to a man and produce descendants who would honor her for all time. But today, she had no one. She was the *Guniang*—the "Lonely Maiden." Many families had them; many villages likewise sought this solution.

Wey-Tan begged me, and later, at the hospital, his entire family came, along with the gnarled old *Tang-ki*, to plead with me. "She has chosen you," Mingmei-Chow said with a raspy voice, white blotches on her skin, and her eyes red.

They looked like they belonged here beside me. As it was, I had been struck by a tough strain of malaria a week after I had refused Wey-Tan, threw down the envelope and ran from the village. Three months had passed, with my business counterparts noticeably concerned.

"It is the *Guniang*," the *Tang-ki* said. "It is Zhen-Lang. Powerful spirit, this little one. She will not rest until you concede."

"Please," Wey-Tan implored. "Just agree to the ceremony. That is all. You will be wed in a simple ritual, and then you may leave. You can marry again, a normal human wife. Have children, go on with your life. This is only for Zhen-Lang."

"And for us," said his wife, trembling.

So, finally exhausted, I surrendered and said yes, convinced that something so superficial would hold no meaning for me and I could, as they said, go on about my life. Wey-Tan, grinning, left the hospital after setting that red envelope down on my bedside stand.

In the darkness after the nurses extinguished the lights, I imagined a thin, wraithlike figure in the shadows, watching over me. I felt a strange attraction to that nebulous shape in the corner, then a stirring in my heart, a trembling throughout my body. I looked away, closed my eyes and tried to sleep; to my surprise, I found myself drifting off easily, comfortably. I imagined a soft breathing on my neck, and whispers of affection tingling across my skin.

I was well enough to leave four days later, and the next week, I married Zhen-Lang while seven incense burners puffed their offerings into the stale central hall of Wey-Tan's home. On shaking legs, trying desperately not to look at the grotesque contraption they had put together as a stand-in for my bride, I took the oath and went through with the bargain.

Beside me, a paper-stuffed red and white dress hung on a chair, with a magazine photo face taped onto a balled-up newspaper head. Everyone in attendance wore grim expressions, and no one made eye contact with me or my bride.

Afterward, as instructed, I pulled out Zhen-Lang's tablet from inside the dummy, then Wey-Tan and I took the surrogate out back and burned it, dress, necklace and all, as a final offering to free the poor girl's ghost.

Julia says I should write a book on the whole psychology of these "ghost marriages"—how the interplay of rigid cultural mores work on the subconscious until such beliefs can cause physical symptoms. She thinks that Zhen-Lang's family became ill from their concern over her spirit's restlessness. Living day after day not only with the tragic guilt of losing an infant, but also being forced by society to deny her existence; out of shame, to hide her tablet so as not to admit the reality of an impossibly unmarried daughter. Under all that stress, was it any wonder physical symptoms could arise?

To Doug and Helen,
Thanks for your continuing support.

Laura Jennings

Illustrated by Laura Jennings

Whenever Julia talks like that I keep quiet. I don't ask about the failure of the crops, or their miraculous recovery after the wedding. And I don't bring up my malaria. Of course there are coincidences, but maybe there's more.

I also never speak of my dreams. With Julia, I don't need to. She knows.

Just as Zhen-Lang's mother knew. That first visit, after dinner, Mingmei-Chow took me to the grove, and we stood beside the tiny, unmarked headstone. "She comes to you, doesn't she?"

I could only nod.

She looked at me intently. "And…you talk to her?"

"Yes."

"You…love her." It wasn't a question. She knew.

"Yes," I admitted, my throat dry, glancing away as if accused of some great perversion.

Mingmei-Chow shook her head slowly. "Always feisty, that one," she said.

I smiled, as I already had that impression, without ever a word spoken by that figure in my dreams. I knew enough, by the way her presence weighed on my actions, on everything I did, everyone I talked to. *Especially women*. Finally, I told Mingmei-Chow that her daughter was very jealous.

A shadow crossed her face. "Too young, she doesn't understand. The strongest of our needs is for offspring, to have descendants to keep our name alive, to honor us."

I told her *I* understood all this. It was why I agreed to the marriage, after all.

Mingmei-Chow shook her head and made bony fists out of her hands. "You have to see—it is not only the marriage that matters. You must have children."

That notion, so simple and obvious, sent me backing away from the little white stone. I turned, and caught my arm on a thorny branch below a single red rose.

I left, fleeing apologetically from their home, and I pondered the implications of Mingmei-Chow's words and rubbed away the blood that continued to flow from my arm.

•••

During the next five years I dated four different women. I was living in Los Angeles, working now at a bank. Better hours, no travel. Great climate. I was making good money, and had a decent house in the hills. I never tried purposely to meet anyone, but in a big city, it just happened.

Jennifer and Diane I met through friends at work. Both were similar—dark skinned, blond and pretty, but not stunning like those movie stars out at the clubs. They both wanted to settle down. At first, they liked that I didn't try anything on our dates. The perfect gentleman. I wished our relationships could have stayed at that stage.

At some point with women, hormones and long-range planning take over. Excuses burst from my lips at every chance. When I didn't call them back, things quickly ended. Diane tried to kiss me in my car, and I reacted by leaning on the horn. Jennifer surprised me once by showing up wearing only a bathrobe. I faked appendicitis and went so far as to call an ambulance.

Next came Maria. We met while volunteering at the Red Cross. One Saturday night we went to a show, and she gave me an ultimatum. She had horseshoe diamonds in her ears, and her lips were a strange shade of red. When I stared at them, all I could think of was *that envelope*.

She wanted us to move in together, and she wanted to kiss me, in that order. I told her I'd think about it, then never called, and never returned to the Red Cross. I ignored her calls and turned off my lights once when I saw her parked outside. I sat in the dark and whispered promises of love and adoration to the shadows.

It took several minutes before I realized the words were in Taiwanese.

•••

In 1984 I went back to Sanzhi. It had been ten years since the marriage. In that time, I reflected, I had never been sick. Nothing worse than a cold. I felt great, my job was going well, I had a new car, and money enough to travel first class.

Smiling, I trod up the path where long ago I had ridden a bicycle and found my destiny. At Wey-Tan's home, I was greeted with less enthusiasm than before. Ho-Jin was no longer there; he had married last year and lived at the other edge of the village. Wey-Tan and Mingmei-Chow greeted me at the door while their daughter sat in the shadows near the back, near that empty closet where once Zhen-Lang's tablet had been stored.

"Why do you come?" they asked me.

I opened my mouth, and felt the warm sun at my back, prickling the hairs on my neck. "I want to see her," I said.

Mingmei-Chow put her fingers to her lips and

backed away. "It is wrong," she whispered. "Do you
not have a new wife? Children?"

"No," I said. "I...cannot." How could I explain
this? How could I tell them of Zhen-Lang's hold on
me, how she had so firmly captured me, body, soul
and heart?

"Go," said Wey-Tan. "Do what you must, then
move on, as we have done."

I turned from them and started toward the grove.
Before I reached the great swaying cypress trees and
the gardens, the blossoming hydrangeas and the wall
of greenery, I heard footsteps. Gengi-Sun approached
quickly, caught up, then walked beside me. Without
a word, the young woman pushed aside the prickers
after first plucking a rose from above her head.

I followed, and together we stood at the small
headstone. I knelt, placed three joffa sticks on the
ground, lit each one, then set her ancestral tablet beside
her headstone.

Gengi-Sun and I stood there for a half-hour, not
saying a thing or even looking at each other. When
the sticks were done, I retrieved the tablet, placed it in
my pack, and followed Gengi-Sun out of the garden.
Head bowed, she returned home. At the doorway she
gave me a backwards glance, and the sun danced on
her face and I thought I could see a smile.

●●●

On my next visit, in 1989, I reflected on the
intervening five years. Walking up a paved road that
had once been an old dirt path, I thought of the women
I had met in Detroit since the last visit. Nancy, Alice
and Christy. Each one a disaster of epic proportions,

complete with vile breakup letters and accusations of infidelity.

As if they could understand what faithfulness meant.

Alice even suggested I was gay. Probably because I never touched her, never touched any of them. Not even once. And when we talked, I was distant—or so they said. Fear of intimacy, Nancy told me, and suggested I seek help. Blamed my mother or some nonsense.

I stopped dating around 1987. I stayed home a lot. Rented videos, and read. And I talked with her, even if she didn't answer. No one could accuse me of being distant with *her*. And intimate? There wasn't a secret I didn't share with Zhen-Lang. I told her everything during our nights together. In the darkness, with her tablet on the nightstand beside me, I spoke to the shadows, and revealed everything about myself.

I imagined her responses, tender urgings to continue my stories, subtle hints at her own gentle character; I sensed her adoration, felt her tangible overwhelming desire for me. It burned at my soul, the need I felt from my shadowy bride.

Once, out of weakness, I rolled up old newspapers. I bought a dress and some costume jewelry from a thrift store—but I couldn't do it. I had a chair ready for her, and even thought of pulling back the sheets and placing her next to me in bed.

In the end, I burned the newspapers and the dress, and tossed the jewelry. It's better this way. Sometimes in the dark, I swear I can see her outline in the corner between the wall and the bedroom door. The glint of light on the sticks in her hair, a flicker from her eyes. And I know I've heard her nails tapping together, and her teeth clicking.

I'm never afraid though, not when I've been so good to her.

So I returned to her family home in 1989, and walked in on a scene of mourning. Ho-Jin's funeral had been two years earlier, and this day was his anniversary. He was killed in the Sino-Vietnam Conflict. At the border, blown to bits by a grenade.

He had no heirs.

His ancestral tablet, I noticed, was no longer on the mantle. The *Tang-ki*, a new one, was in the home talking to Wey-Tan and Mingmei-Chow. Gengi-Sun was nowhere about, and I wondered if she had been married in the meantime. When they saw me, the mother cried, and the *Tang-ki* commanded me to him.

I answered his questions as best as I could, and he only nodded after each response, as if anticipating my words. He seemed happy that what I said supported his own conclusions.

"She is not yet at rest," he announced, clapping his hands about the room, as if scaring off sensitive bugs. It made sense—I had been selected to marry the girl, and naturally they assumed I would indirectly provide her with descendants.

"We must try again!" shouted her father to the *Tang-ki*. I pictured Wey-Tan preparing another red envelope.

"No!" I heard myself answering. "She chose *me*, remember?"

"A mistake," said the *Tang-ki*, and Mingmei-Chow sobbed again. My mother-in-law did not look well—and in fact seemed as ill as the first time I met her.

I glared at the men, then lifted my bag. "I have her ancestral tablet," I said. "And it stays with me. Your current problems have other causes. She is happy."

"How can she be?" hissed the *Tang-ki*, his long gray hair flapping as he moved. "No heirs, no bloodline!"

"It was never her blood to begin with, damn it!"

I regretted the words even as I spoke them. To deny these people their cherished traditions was reprehensible. I wanted to beg forgiveness, but it was too late. I was thrown from the house, banished. Before leaving town, however, I stopped at her stone.

No roses were blooming, no flowers of any kind. Only thorns, prickers and brown vines. I lit the joffa sticks, renewed my vows to her, and quietly left as the sky, a bitter mass of gray black clouds, simmered overhead.

•••

In 1994 I returned, cautiously making my way up the hill. The village homes were decrepit, roofs sagging, embers rotting. The hills were barren of all but pockets of rice paddies, with swampy marsh covering the rest. Floods had ravaged the area for months, and before that, drought.

Bad weather and difficult soil, compounded by inefficient land reform, had made life hard. Or so Julia would later tell me, insisting there was no supernatural force at work. Of course, most of the villagers, those that were left, believed otherwise.

Dread had taken root in my heart long before my plane touched down, and my worst fears were soon realized. Gengi-Sun greeted me at the door; she had a baby boy nursing at her breast. Her husband was away in the distant fields.

Mingmei-Chow had died two years ago. A long sickness, at last claiming her life. My father-in-law appeared suddenly. Nearly eighty, the old man hobbled with a cane; he looked at me and shook his fist. Out of a hoarse throat came what sounded like a command to leave. But his energy was spent, and he gave up quickly, returning to sit at the main table beside the family altar. I looked and saw that Ho-Jin's ancestral tablet was back on the mantle.

"How…?" I asked.

Gengi-Sun saw my glance, and sighed. "I let him adopt one of mine," she said, bobbing the boy in her arms. "I had twins. The other is fast asleep. And I have two other sons—four and three years old, and a daughter."

"So, your brother—you gave one child…?"

"To him, yes, so that his spirit could rest. I know it seems strange, but my husband and I will still raise the boy. He will still be our heir. He is only dedicated to Ho-Jin, and will make offerings to him in life."

I told her I didn't think it that strange, considering.

She gave me a soft smile. "It is not so different, is it? Only, you have done something unheard of. You fell in love with your Lonely Maiden, and you are remaining honorable to her."

A cool wind blew through the doorway, nudging me inside to do what I came here to do. I produced an envelope—a red one. I knew it was their custom when giving gifts, and wasn't just for trapping bridegrooms. I knelt before Wey-Tan and placed the envelope at his feet. With a bow to Gengi-Sun, I left.

Inside the envelope I had left the equivalent of two thousand dollars—something I'd been saving away for many years. I felt it was what Zhen-Lang would have wanted.

I told her so at her grave, amidst the dead plants and the overgrown moss. I had to clear away many years' growth of weeds from her stone, but I did it; and afterward, I lit the incense and I said goodbye, even though I knew she was coming with me.

•••

In 1997 I met Julia. I was living in Boston, running my own business. I consulted on business mergers and acquisitions. Nothing to it really, much like the *Tang-ki*'s role—find out the synergies between bride and groom, determine which qualities match up, check the stars and the birthdays and all that—and then make the deal.

Julia was one of the partners at a client's firm. We worked so well together, it felt so natural being with her, I couldn't pass up this chance. So, for the first time in almost a decade, at almost forty-two years old, I asked her out. Divorced but with no kids, she was a bit wary to try again, but she was impressed with my honesty.

"Intimacy issues," I told her over a shared set of lobster claws one night. "And…I'm married." At that one, she nearly slapped me. But then I told her the whole story, and her anger turned to disbelief, then to empathy.

She said all the right things. She never resorted to condescension, never accused me of believing in nonsense. She said she understood, especially about the intimacy. She'd had her own scars, deep wounds that left her unable to connect. In a sense we were perfect—and it was that shared aversion to closeness that actually drew us inevitably closer.

It happened slowly, over many months, nights together, days spent at the Cape, on the beach, on my boat. We talked about everything and anything. We slept in a huge king-sized bed, on opposite edges. We blew kisses across the room.

And yes, as terrible as it sounds, I began to sleep with a night light on in the corner, banishing the shadows. And I soon spoke very little to Zhen-Lang. Just a few tame whispers when Julia was in the shower. I still kept her tablet in the room, but it moved to my desk, opposite from the bed stand.

Two years later, I missed the trip to Sanzhi. I just didn't think about it. I was knee-deep on a new assignment, and spending every free moment with Julia. She brought it up once, and offered to go with me if I wanted to, but I said no. I gathered up my courage, sought out any feelings of anger or jealousy, and finding none, I decided against it.

And that night, in bed, I reached across the mattress and took hold of Julia's hand. In her sleep, she gripped me back, and we slept the entire night in that pose.

Once during the night, I thought I heard nails clicking together; the night light flickered, and the darkness around the door seemed deeper than usual, but I ignored it, gathering strength from Julia's touch.

● ● ●

The next month, Julia started feeling weak. On Monday night, our usual night to go out and catch the football game over a plate of fried wings, she called me from the hospital. They had checked her in after she fainted at work. Irregular nosebleeds, dizziness and spotty vision.

Two weeks later, they confirmed the brain tumor. About the size of a marble. Treatments were set to start the following week. In the discharge room, she came out to me in a wheelchair, and for the first time in my life, I held a woman in my arms.

The first night after returning alone from the hospital where Julia had to stay for a few days, I moved the tablet back to the bedside stand. And I turned out the night light.

Zhen-Lang didn't come. There was nothing but silence. My dreams were cold and empty, like a dry wind over a barren field.

The chemo treatments worked, and Julia went into remission.

For a year.

Then it came back, showing up on a routine test. And worse, another tumor—this one in her stomach.

Treatments, then surgery.

I prayed every night. To my god, to the little god of Sanzhi. To Zhen-Lang.

The doctors were successful, but poor Julia had been through hell. Her eyes held a beaten look, her beautiful auburn hair was gone, her body weak and withered.

And, the doctor told us gently: children were out of the question, if we were considering it. Not possible now.

"Let's get married," Julia said, dreamily, on the way home.

"What?" the word came out in a whisper, and I imagined I heard long fingernails scraping against the back window.

"Let's do it, Brian. I love you. I know you love me, even though you'll never say it." She closed her eyes, and her pale lips trembled. "Because of her. But please, for me, don't miss out on this too."

Outside, at an intersection, the red light swung in

a breeze, hypnotically catching my eye. "Married," I whispered. "Yes, but…"

Julia reached over and took my hand, prying it from the steering wheel. "I know," she said. "You have to go. Back there. Return the tablet. Speak to the father."

"Divorce," I thought with a chill.

The light turned green, but I couldn't move. Horns shouted at me, cars tried to drive around. When I started to move, the light had cycled to red again.

•••

Thirty years from the day I picked up that red envelope, I returned to Sanzhi. This time, Julia was with me. We took a taxi part of the way, then made the slow walk up the crumbling road, past the now barren fields where thin ravens bathed in puddles and drank from the clouds' reflections.

At the home I saw several young children outside, playing with sticks. Julia gave me a worried look and reached for my hand. We hadn't touched since the hospital.

I pulled my hand away and used it to knock on the weathered front door. Gengi-Sun opened immediately. Her hair was thin and gray, lines circled her tired eyes, but she smiled for me, and when she saw Julia, her face brightened.

We were brought inside, and she instructed a pretty young woman to bring us tea. "My family," she said, this time in English for Julia's benefit. "I learned your language from my children, who went to universities. Jin-Chan lives here with her husband. My two boys have moved to the mainland and have families there. I have fourteen grandchildren."

I smiled and glanced at the collection of tablets on the mantle. "And your father?"

She lowered her head. "Passed on, six years ago." When the tea came we all took a sip. My hand trembled, and Julia looked despondent.

"You are not married," said Gengi-Sun. It wasn't a question. She knew. After I nodded, she said, "No children, and you…" She pointed to Julia. "Are sick."

We both nodded.

"Do you wish for me to send for the *Tang-ki?*"

I opened my mouth before I really thought about it, but a sound from Julia stopped me. She set down the cup with a bang, steadied herself in the chair, then looked up. "Send for him. If he can perform a divorce."

Gengi-Sun's eyes widened, and she sat up stiffly. "You think this will help?"

"Can't hurt," said Julia. I saw her eyes roaming the mantle, seeing the altar. She had the look of someone thrust into a fictional world she had only read about.

"Yes, it can," Gengi-Sun said, head bowed. "She chose him, she brought him to the red envelope. It is a thing not easily undone, especially after all these years. She has grown old with him, borne his life as surely as she had lived her own."

I kept my eyes down, sure that I could not meet Julia's. I sensed her despair, and knew the next words from her lips would be ones of defeat, an acceptance that the cancer would return, and this time she would not fight it.

I took a deep breath and looked around the shadows of the central hall. Gengi-Sun's eldest daughter stood in the corner, hands folded together, head down. Chills ran across my flesh.

"There's another solution," said Gengi-Sun, motioning toward her daughter. The woman stepped out of the shadows. There were tears on her cheeks, her lips were shaking, but she seemed beautifully radiant.

"I have four boys," the young woman said, in very strong English. "And three girls."

She let the phrase hang in the incense-soaked air for a minute. "Girls," she repeated, "are not fondly sought after. Especially by my husband, who is still dedicated to the old ways. He wants boys, and would have preferred all seven to be male."

Gengi-Sun leaned forward, and the lamplight caught in her brown eyes, flashing. "What she is asking, what she is hoping, is that you two will help. We had hoped you would have come five years ago. We were ready even then. But you did not. Now we have another chance to set things right. Help us."

"How?" I asked, but my heart was pounding. I glanced at Julia, and her eyes were wide with excitement, and longing.

"Adopt a girl from us," Gengi-Sun said. "Otherwise my granddaughter will have to go to strangers."

Julia gasped. I met her eyes, and our hands reached for each other. "Would it work?" I whispered.

"Boy or girl doesn't matter," Gengi-Sun said. "She will be a descendent. Your descendent. And better yet, Zhen-Lang's blood will be in her veins." She smiled, and her daughter held her hand.

"Yes," said Julia with a choking cry.

•••

We visited the headstone one last time before leaving. Julia and I, Gengi-Sun and her daughter and three granddaughters. One of them, named Lien-Tao, was only two.

I held her tiny hand as Julia lit the joffa sticks, then stood behind me and slipped her arms around my waist. I felt her breath on my neck, her warm tears on my skin.

• • •

We returned to Boston and made the adoption official. An hour after Lien-Tao was asleep, Julia and I made love. I think I cried, and afterward, as Julia slept peacefully, I peered into the shadows near the door.

Nothing was there. The slanting darkness seemed sublime and shifting, but no outline caught my imagination.

The next afternoon I took Zhen-Lang's ancestral tablet and set it on the top shelf in the closet in Lien-Tao's room. While she slept, her second nap of the day, I stroked her hair and thought of how I would one day take her back to Sanzhi to meet her aunt.

• • •

That day came five years later. With Lien-Tao's hand in mine, we climbed the hill along the freshly paved road as small cars drove by. The fields were flourishing, and laborers dotted the countryside. Sloping new roofs were on most of the homes, and several unfamiliar buildings had been erected.

I went first to the grove and had seven-year-old Lien-Tao light the incense sticks. I noted how she prayed, with the wind tenderly tugging at her thin black hair, and the grasses caressing her legs.

As I looked around the garden, breathed in the flowers, listened to the birds, insects and scampering creatures, and as the beautiful cloudless sky stretched peacefully above, I thought of Julia.

And I despaired that in a week I'd be doing this same thing for her. Standing with Lien-Tao at another grave, on a landscaped cemetery hill back in Portsmouth.

It didn't surprise me that Sanzhi had changed so much, that the village had been freed of its sickness and thrived once more.

With Julia it was different. It always had been.

My wife, after all, is a jealous, lonely maiden.

ART IS A JOURNEY

by
Bob Eggleton

Bob Eggleton is the winner of nine Hugo Awards in the field of Science Fiction and Fantasy. He also won twelve Chesley Awards, two Locus Awards and the New England Science Fiction Association's Skylark Award. Bob has worked in the film industry, most recently on the Warner Bros. animated film The Ant Bully. *He has an asteroid named after him—113562bobeggleton—and is an expert in all things relating to Godzilla and giant monsters and was an extra in a Godzilla film. He is married to artist Marianne Plumridge from Australia. He has been a judge for the L. Ron Hubbard Illustrators of the Future Contest since 1987.*

"Art? So you want to do **art** for a living? Do you know what the chances of success are?"

Those words echo in my head, some twenty-seven years later after my last year in high school. They were the words of a provincial and so-called "guidance counselor." Whenever anyone suggests they'd like to have a career in the arts, specifically art and illustration, it is often met with such sarcasm and negativity that one can only feel sorry for the lack of wonder and vision in these people. After all, haven't all manner of people been bombarded with some form of advertising art over the last one hundred years or so?

Perhaps, had I listened to this person, had I followed his suggestions, I would be in some highly "safe" but dismally predictable job. I might never have found out the extent of my reach or potential if I had taken his advice to heart. I don't know, and frankly, I can't picture myself any other way than I am now.

Encouragement in the arts is an uphill battle. Putting it simply, to some, art—writing, music, and also entertainment—is seen as some kind of marginal and dispensable need: something that is not necessary for day-to-day living. Those people do not know how wrong they are, because without it, they are not living. Art enriches lives with understanding and communication on a very basic level. As L. Ron Hubbard once said: "ART is a word which summarizes THE QUALITY OF COMMUNICATION. It therefore follows the laws of communication." And truly, being an illustrator is being a communicator in a visual language all can understand.

There are many ways for someone to recommend "tips" and suggestions on success in this chosen field. Some are general ideas that will work, and still, for others, it is a case of what works for another may not work for you. A lot of it is a combination of drive, talent, and most of all, luck. But then I believe in creating luck—by being determined to succeed.

A suggestion that I found worked for me early on (and I still stand by it), after I found it led to essentially dead ends was: **never work for free**. Even in this book that you hold in your hands, the writers were paid for their stories and illustrators for their illustrations. But that's all beside the point in this case, as in both instances, winners and finalists got a wealth of suggestions and critiques worth far more than money, and, well, the thrill of winning a wonderful accolade. So, that said, they can't now retreat and do something for nothing; this is, unfortunately, a world where there are unscrupulous people who will **surely** take advantage of an illustrator/writer/creator inexperienced in business. I'm not saying don't give of yourself to your favorite good cause or charity—something where the reward is in the helping. I am saying: don't do a fantastic piece of artwork and then simply sign away your rights as having created the work, and someone else goes on and makes money off your labors. Donating your talent and time to a good cause is just being a nicer human being—and that comes back to you, I have found. However, being taken advantage of is another thing. There is nothing more discouraging than that.

Achieving fame is another issue. What's important is not whether you are famous, but rather do you love what you do? And, if you do achieve a kind of fame, I warn you, never ever believe your own press. That is to say, let nothing go to your head too much, positive or negative. Salvadore Dali did his epic painting *Persistence of Memory* (the one with the melting clock) and critics praised this as some life-changing, almost existential, self-defining work of inner truth. In reality his entire inspiration was from…**Camembert cheese**. That was it. It does not detract at all from this fine work, but some people who wanted to read something more into it felt betrayed.

This also means avoiding being "lofty" or "high and mighty." How can you be in the business of communication, as Mr. Hubbard reminds us, if you don't communicate in a way people can **understand**? To some it seems to be the way to more wealth and power, but, in the end, it's a losing game to pursue. And I also warn you, should you reach the heady heights of success and/or popularity…there are those few in the shadows who delight in trying to destroy that. It's called "Tall Poppy Syndrome" and is usually practiced by those who are in opposition to what you do, are trying to make themselves feel superior by belittling your creation, or are jealous, or just petty. There are still others, in all ignorance, who, no matter how much money you make or how happy you are, will never see "art" as a "credible living." They'll forever see it as a hobby and possibly ask when you are going to get a "real job."

The "up" factor is that the majority of people will find something that "speaks" to them in your work.

And it's always exhilarating, no matter how much you achieve in your life, to see an image or written piece you've created in print form. Hold it in your hands and say, "I did that." It's also nice to get paid for it.

I'm often asked about techniques and ways I work with materials. My reply to that is: each to his, or her, own. There is no instruction manual; learning what is right (or wrong) for you is just trial and error —experimentation. However, I will add that art is a journey—an ongoing learning experience—one that will probably consume the rest of your life. My usual answer to "What is your **best** piece?" is "My next one!" because for me, it's a quest to see what I can do next. I try to use different media—pencils, pastels, oils, collage, acrylics, gouache, watercolors and markers—simply because it motivates me to explore. Finding ideas in the paint and the paper itself. At least that's what I tell myself, and it keeps me going. It is always the next piece that will be better than this one. You hope, anyway.

The idea of "the next piece" suits me well in meeting deadlines. I don't have time to fuss around wondering if this will be the defining piece of my life. It's due Thursday and that's what's more important at that time. Deeper works will come with more time and in perhaps creating something just for oneself.

Recently, there is another debate raging in science fiction art circles: computer art versus traditional methods of brushes and paint. Advances in technology in the computer seem as though it makes anyone an artist. This is not true. It can give someone the **illusion** that they are able to be an artist, but to really be a good illustrator—painter or draftsman—it takes many years of practice and observation. A computer and the various programs can be excellent **tools** if that is what you wish to create with. But, one has to have the basic skills and, I believe, the talent to breathe life into one's chosen subject. If the talent is there and the skills are honed, the style, expression and communication will show through any media. My personal feeling is that I like a painting—a physical piece of art to show for what I have done. Many publishers have entirely gone to using digital computer art. The idea of doing an original painting seems to be viewed as quaint. In fact people are genuinely struck that I "still work the old way." Interestingly, I get calls to do illustrations because I **can** do them "the old way." We are approaching a time when there will be fewer and fewer original, physical paintings and drawings. Conversely, digital storage is not as permanent as one would like to think it is. Computers, programs and storage media go out of date faster than yesterday's newspapers.

I do believe that using digital can be a good thing, if used in tandem with creating an original painting. This works especially well in doing concept art for motion pictures. Working for motion pictures is quite an experience, because unlike doing a single illustration for a story or a book cover, the artist is asked to do **many** pieces of artwork, usually working the same idea over and over again to find the ultimate vision that speaks with its own "voice." Scripts change, directors and producers change their minds; it is an ongoing process of creation and re-creation. It's less important to do a finished illustration than it is to come up with a lot of ideas. And usually, it has to be done quickly. More ideas are better, and even ones that are discarded give life to still other ideas. But, it is no different than the basic idea of communicating.

In regard to health, it is important for the artist to

get out and exercise. Good health is good for creating. Breathe the air, see the sunset. The more you see "reality" the better your fantastic imagery will be because it is grounded in something people can understand. Quite often when I am stuck on a solution I find just such breaks extremely helpful not only to my state of mind, but in finding the best idea for a given assignment. The danger can be like a Chinese finger trap—keep pulling your fingers and you won't get much but panic and confusion. Relax, and the trap loosens. However, and I make this solid and beneficial suggestion: try to keep "working hours" within a regular schedule, say nine to five, as it were. And, unless it's really necessary, don't work weekends. Try to do something for yourself or with your family then to avoid burnout. Balance is very important: the well-being of the creative spirit as well as the physical body.

Being an artist is like a jester doing the juggling act. While the idea that an artist sits in his or her studio creating illustrations and the world falls at their feet is a romantic one, it is certainly not the reality. The reality is balancing life around that—making sure the bills are paid on time, the laundry is done and the dishes washed; to sleep, eat and breathe. And you **still** have to make those deadlines.

I try to suggest to people something that does work for me—be the best artist **you** can be; don't worry about being the best there is. You'll be a lot happier in the long run. Later on, history will judge your work to be the work of some genius—or not. Then again, it could all be the Camembert cheese.

SCHROEDINGER'S HUMMINGBIRD

Written by
Diana Rowland

Illustrated by
Daniel Harris

About the Author

It's taken six years for author Diana Rowland's winning entry to finally make it. Even when Diana was first e-mailed about her winning entry, it was a major struggle against the forces of nature. Diana couldn't be reached because Hurricane Katrina had struck her New Orleans home only days earlier. Diana evacuated safely with her family and PC notebook (housing her precious writing). When she returned a day after the storm had passed, there was widespread damage: no power, no e-mail, no phone service, and lots of cleanup work to be done. As a law-enforcement computer forensics and crime-scene investigator, Diana was placed on patrol searching through mud and grime looking for bodies and survivors. It was a couple of weeks later that the happy message came through. Diana's life has settled down somewhat (she has all utilities and a new roof). Lately she continues to hone her skills and is now cowriting and shopping a fantasy series with another writer.

About the Illustrator

Illustrator Daniel Harris doesn't consider himself a heavy gamer, but gaming has had an enduring impact on his artistic life. It gave him an artistic moniker after inventing the character "Hyptosis" to rescue one caught at the bottom of a well in a multiuser game in the early 1990s. Everyone seemed to like Hyptosis better (though ten years later he wishes he'd picked a "cooler" handle). Daniel wants to be a viewer's artist who speaks directly to the viewer through his work instead of simply creating art for art's sake. So far, Daniel has had success in smaller, amateur projects working with writers and publishers. He credits fantasy and comic strip artists Joe Mad, Brian Froud and Amano for his appreciation of art. Now he's actively working on a professional portfolio while completing art school in Sarasota, Florida.

It didn't matter who'd left the safety gate at the top of the stairs open. The result was the same, the tragedy still there in twisted limbs and broken bones. But whoever's fault it had been, it had happened, and so she'd tried to fix the mistake— making an even bigger mistake. Guilt on top of guilt. Had she been the one or not? But of course now it was too late to ever really know for sure, since Mark's memories of it were gone. How could he have a memory of something that would never happen?

<back>

The cup crashed to the floor, spraying over-sweet tea and sharp shards of fine china across the pale blue-flowered pattern of the linoleum. It had only been a momentary lack of concentration—but then that's what had caused all of the problems in the first place.

This time her gaze had been intent on the hummingbird whirring green and blue wings at the bright red plastic feeder she'd put out the day before. That long-ago day before. She barely remembered that yesterday anymore, it had been so long since she'd lived it. But her thoughts had been scattered as she'd tried to gather herself for yet another go at getting it all right, and she hadn't been paying attention to where the table was when she set her cup down, and had placed it half off the edge.

The hummingbird was right, she remembered that

much. She wasn't sure if it mattered, but she knew by now that she had to try and do everything exactly the way she had before, and try and reduce random changes.

But breaking the cup had not been part of it. The ruins of the cup that had once been her grandmother's still quivered in the aftermath of the destruction, shards slowly spinning to a stop. She could hear the water running in the bathroom. Mark would be finished with his shower soon, and he'd be coming into the kitchen. If he found her cleaning up a mess of broken porcelain that would throw everything off.

Carol looked down at the Rorschach blot of brown tea on the blue flowers of the linoleum. She'd have to do it again. Just a small one though, not even a minute long, just long enough to make sure she didn't break the cup. Better to do it now than wait and see if breaking the cup messed all of the rest up. There were only so many times that she'd be able to go through this. Only so many times she could stand to go back and start over.

Soon it will work out though, she told herself. Soon I'll get it right. Soon I can end this.

<back>

Nothing ever happens the same way twice. You can't say you changed the future if the future only happened to you.

<back>

The hummingbird flitted around the feeder and she lifted the intact cup to her lips. She took a sip of the too-sweet tea—just the way she liked it, and sweet enough to cause Mark to make a face when he sometimes picked up her cup by mistake. She slowly let her breath out and smiled with relief and a touch of triumph. It had worked that time; she hadn't gone back

Illustrated by Daniel Harris

too far—her constant terror now. She took another sip and then set the cup carefully down—making sure that it was completely on the table.

Carol looked up at the hummingbird just as it sped off in a blur of emerald wings. Her smile flickered. Last time it had stayed and fed awhile. Perhaps the wind was slightly different this time, and had brought a scent of something more appealing than stale sugar water. There was always something that changed, some randomness that she couldn't keep constant no matter how hard she tried.

Enough of that. It was just a hummingbird. She washed the cup and dried it, stroking her fingers slowly across the raised texture of the pattern along the rim, twining roses in cream on white. She'd caught up with her last go-back now—past the point where she'd begun it—and now she just had the other larger one to deal with, to finish.

She heard Mark come into the kitchen behind her as she reached to put the cup away in the cabinet.

"Here," he said, taking the cup from her hand. "Let me get that." He placed it on the high shelf and then dropped his hands to her waist, caressing her through the satin of her robe. His lips nuzzled her ear and she smiled and leaned back against him. This was how it was supposed to happen. He'd come into the kitchen before while she was putting the cup away and he'd nuzzled her and they'd ended up on the kitchen floor.

I was right to do that small go-back, she thought, as his hands explored her front. Otherwise he'd have come in while I was picking up shards and cleaning up sticky tea, and we certainly wouldn't have had sex among the porcelain fragments. It will work this time. I'll get it right.

<back>

One cup of tea was so like another, and one day was so like any other. So how was she to know, to remember, that she'd sat in the chair by the window and sipped tea more than that one time. Gazed out at the hummingbird feeder and pondered bright futures almost three years earlier as well. More than once, more than just that one terrible morning. It had seemed safe enough to go back to that.

The wrong morning. Too far back.

<back>

Mark held her close that night, his hand spread flat on her belly. "Maybe that was it," he said. "Wouldn't it be great if it was? What a story to tell the grandchildren—I got your gramma pregnant on the kitchen floor."

She rolled over to look at him, surprised. "I am," she said before she could censor herself.

He gave a soft laugh and slid his hand around to the small of her back, pulling her close against him. "A bit too soon to be sure, don't you think, Carol?"

No, she thought. I do know. This is the sixth time I've lived through this. Each time we've done it on the kitchen floor I've ended up pregnant.

And each time they hadn't, each time it had been someplace else besides the kitchen, or a time other than the morning, nothing had come of it, and she'd had to start all over again. Go back again and try to make it right, because the only way to go forward is to live it out.

We did it on the kitchen floor, she wanted to say, with the tile cold on my back and you laughing and complaining about how the hard floor was bad for your knees. It was almost the same this time, except you laughed and complained about your elbows instead.

But close enough, she thought as she clung to his warmth. Surely it's close enough.

<back>

Back when she first realized what she could do, she'd tried to do what everyone dreamed of doing. Go back. Make the right investments. The right bets. But there are more random factors in the universe than she'd ever considered. And the longer the time frame, the more the random factors intruded until it was nothing at all like the way she'd remembered it.

She lost six months of her life that way—six months that had never happened except in her memory, back during college when she'd first started going back. One terrible semester that she'd decided to do over. Just go back and start from scratch, but she hadn't counted on all the lost experiences—things that had happened only to her and only existed in her own memory now. She'd even lost her best friend, Maria. She'd met Maria in the six months that never ended up happening, and though she tried to recreate the circumstances that had led to them being such good friends, it had just never clicked the second time around.

<back>

The doctor confirmed it three weeks later, to Mark's surprise.

"How did you know?" he asked after they got home. He had a pleased smile on his face that couldn't come close to matching her delighted grin, but there was still a curious look in his eye. "You've been positive ever since that morning in the kitchen."

But she didn't make the mistake she'd made once before. Once she'd tried to explain to him what she could do, tried to prove it. He hadn't believed her, of course. How could he? And she'd gone back and gone back a half-dozen times, exhausting little ten-minute episodes, trying to prove it to him, getting him to guess a number and then showing that she knew it. But he'd guess a different number each time—the random differences inherent in every go-back affecting even his thought processes. And he couldn't remember that she'd just tried to prove it to him—each memory being wiped away every time she went back, so each time she was starting from scratch. She'd finally had him think of a number that wouldn't change, that she wouldn't also know—a friend's birthday, or a childhood address, or a combination to a lock. And even then he hadn't really believed her. How could he?

"I just wanted it so very much," she said to him this time instead of an explanation. And that was the truth, though she could never tell him just how badly she wanted to be pregnant again, how desperately she wanted it to work this time so she could end this episode and have things back the way they were supposed to be.

But each day was a tiny bit different. Every day more random factors intruded until there was little left that resembled that first time. The real time, before the first terrible mistake, and then her other terrible mistake.

<back>

Was it possible to grieve for something that had never happened except in her own mind? Sometimes she felt that was the hardest part—knowing that she was the only one who remembered, who knew. She had to grieve for her losses by herself. The memories of that precious smile and the delighted laugh. The bright blue eyes and the slobbery kisses. Mark had lost too, but he didn't remember. It had never happened for him. All erased in the go-back.

<back>

"You'd be immortal," Mark had said after she'd tried to convince him she could go back. "If it looked like you were about to die you could just go back and live your whole life over again."

Then he'd paused, his brows drawn down into a thoughtful expression. "Of course you'd still only be immortal for the years of your normal lifespan."

Will I ever see my entire lifespan? she'd thought. Too easy to stop and go back. Too many mistakes to go back and fix.

<back>

Time was never the same each time, she realized, she'd discovered. The atomic events, the natural radioactivity changed probabilities in a thousand different ways. Even people's thoughts were different. And she'd discovered—to her intense disappointment—that even betting sports games was worthless, because the more people in the mix, the more random factors occurred. A quarterback might slip one time, and not the other. The pitcher might throw a perfect curve, or the batter might gauge it perfectly this time and smack it out of the park. Or not. One time Schroedinger's cat would live, and the next it would die.

Small go-backs were safest, she'd found. Those were the most effective. The shorter the duration, the fewer random changes could intrude, and the more chance she had of changing what she wanted, without too much else changing without her wanting it to.

She'd only wanted to go back just a few minutes. To that morning when she'd sipped tea and watched the hummingbird. Just enough time to run upstairs and close the gate.

<back>

She didn't want to go for the ultrasound, but she

had the first time, the original time, so of course she had to now, and Mark wanted to know so badly that she couldn't bear to disappoint him. Besides, how could she explain to him *why* she didn't want to know? It was too terrifying, too depressing. And the guilt piled even higher.

Six times now. This was the sixth time she'd lived through this episode, the sixth time she'd gone back to what she now called the beginning, the morning with the tea and the hummingbird. It was the wrong morning, but it was done, and now she had to live with it and work with it. The first two times she hadn't gotten pregnant, and she'd gone back to the "beginning" the instant she'd known it wasn't going to happen. Starting over to fix the mistake. Mistakes on mistakes.

It happened on the third time around. Everything had gone right, and she and Mark had made sloppy, laughing love on the kitchen floor. This is it, she'd thought. Just keep going now.

She'd known what to expect from the ultrasound. She'd been there before. She'd see his perfect little hands and feet. "There's his little penis," the doctor would say.

Mark couldn't understand why she started crying when they saw the ultrasound. The doctor paused with one hand pointing to the screen, and looked at Carol with a perplexed look on her face. "But she's perfectly healthy and normal," the doctor said to Carol. "There's nothing to worry about."

It's not the right one, Carol wanted to scream, and she didn't even wait until they left the office before going back. Right there on the exam table, half-naked and her belly smeared with goop. A breath later she watched the hummingbird come in to feed.

She lifted the cup of too-sweet tea to her lips with a hand that shook and listened for the sound of the water stopping in the bathroom.

<back>

Was it abortion if she never gave it a chance? A daughter instead of a son. Was it abortion if she simply never allowed it to happen?

But it's not the same. Not right. Go back and keep trying.

<back>

"Here, let me get that," Mark said, taking the cup from her hand for the fourth time. But she was still trembling, and even his arms around her couldn't warm her. It had only been minutes ago for her that she'd been lying on her back on a sterile examination table with Mark's hand in hers. And now Mark was here again, but he didn't know, couldn't remember what had never happened for him.

Should I have just kept going? she couldn't help but wonder as she clutched at Mark's arms. Would that be giving up? I could start all over, just keep going.

How much harder to live with the mistake?

This isn't working. Go back and start over.

<back>

A perfect little boy with perfect hands and perfect feet that were just beginning to walk. A gate at the top of the stairs to prevent accidents.

Too late now to even try to live with the consequences of that mistake. Another span of time that existed only in her memory.

<back>

How many countless random factors are involved in the fertilization of an egg by a particular sperm?

<back>

"There's his little penis," the doctor said.

<back>

"I'm not immortal," she'd said. "I merely have a potentially endless life."

<back>

Mark's hand slowly stroked the swell of her belly as they lay curled on the couch together.

"A boy," he said, his voice barely audible.

A boy, her thoughts echoed. It's going to work this time.

<back>

The fifth time the bleeding had started in the fourth month. If she'd believed in a god she would have thought that it was punishment for not letting the girl have a chance. Going back after that one was easy. Mark's face so full of loss when he had to come into the hospital room and tell her that she'd lost it. She had to go back just to get away from that horrible pain in his eyes. It was the one time she felt relief to be able to erase time.

She watched the hummingbird come to the feeder and wondered what he would have done if he'd known about the accident. Whose fault was it? Either way that pain had never happened for anyone but her. That pain was gone for him.

Too gone.

The wrong morning, she thought. Too far. Before he was a baby. Before she'd been pregnant. Before he'd even been conceived.

She set the cup down, half off the table.

<back>

The hummingbird flickered around the faded red plastic feeder in a blaze of emerald wings and ruby throat as she sipped her tea and pondered the bright futures stretching before her and her wonderful family. Sped away as she heard the high-pitched scream and then the crash. A streak of blue and green away from the window as the cup slipped from her hand and smashed to the floor as she ran to the foot of the stairs. Blue and green and red.

<back>

She'd set the cup down the instant she'd gone back and ran upstairs to get the gate closed. But there was no gate. And when she looked in the nursery there was a desk and boxes and the horror of the memory of what the room had looked like before she'd gotten pregnant.

Three years.

<back>

"Carol?"

She stood in the living room and looked up at the staircase. Mark came up behind her and slipped his arms around her waist, gently stroking his hands over the swell of her belly.

"Carol?" he repeated. "Is everything all right?"

We should move, she thought. We should get into a different house, a safer house.

But now she was thinking of changing things, when she'd been trying so hard all along to keep everything the same. Which was right?

"It's not the same," she murmured.

"What's not the same?" Mark asked her, but just then the baby kicked under his hands and his gasp of pure delight forestalled the words in her throat.

This. Me. You. I can't make it the same. I can't get it back.

<back>

There'd been hardly any blood, but it didn't matter. She knew it was bad anyway. She knew that joints weren't supposed to bend that way or heads to turn that far.

Mark must have heard the noise too, for she heard his running footsteps. And she couldn't remember, didn't know whose fault it was. But did it matter? She could fix it, she knew. She could make it right. He didn't have to be twisted and broken. But she didn't want Mark to see, even in an existence that was soon not going to have happened. So she went back.

To a morning when she sat and gazed at the hummingbird at the feeder. A morning that was safe, still fresh in her memory.

<back>

She covered Mark's hand with hers and looked at the staircase. She could feel the baby move again, feel Mark's breath warm and comforting on her neck as he stood behind her, holding her close and safe.

He'd never kicked this much before—the first time, the real time.

What was real now?

"He's not the same," she breathed.

"Carol?"

She turned to face him and looked long at his eyes, his chin, his nose. That first child had had all of them. So like Mark.

That first child long gone in an existence that had never happened.

"It's never going to be the same," she said. "It's impossible. I'm never going to get him back."

Mark frowned, worry darkening his eyes. "Carol, you're not making sense. Who are you talking about?"

I'm immortal, but I'm not living, she thought.

<back>

So much harder to keep going forward. So much uncertainty, so many mistakes that could be made. The only way to go forward is to live it out.

<back>

"Carol? What's wrong?"

If she told him he would think she was raving, but she knew that she was finally approaching something akin to sanity.

I'm trying to fix something that can't be fixed, she thought.

Was it better to live than to be immortal? How many years had she spent trying to recreate something that could not be made again?

She looked up at him. It could have been worse, she realized. What if she'd gone back so far that she'd lost him?

"Carol? You're just tired," he said, taking her hand and guiding her to the couch.

She went with him. "More tired than you can know." Too many years. She sat against him as he wrapped his arms around her and stroked her belly, and she grieved the son he would never know again.

ON THE MOUNT

Written by
David John Baker

Illustrated by
Tamara Streeter

About the Author

Science fiction and philosophy go hand in hand in the world of winning writer David John Baker. As he sees it, both subjects examine what is essential to humans and what happens when we strip away some of our limitations. Add physics to the mix and the result has led to his winning the prestigious Robert Clifton Memorial Prize for philosophy and publication in the journal Philosophy of Science. *His science leanings gained him a Phobos Award and appearance in the anthology* Hitting the Skids in Pixeltown. *David is a National Science Foundation fellow and has conducted research at the Fermi National Laboratory in Illinois. He is currently a graduate student in the philosophy department at Princeton University, New Jersey. His winning story reflects yet another interest—the philosophy of religion. In it, he includes a quote from Blaise Pascal's* Pensées, *which he believes contains some of the most beautiful prose ever written (by a philosopher, at least). Other interests of note include film and poetry.*

About the Illustrator

Illustrator Tamara Streeter admits to being very reclusive and shy about showing her work to people. Yet something motivated her to enter the Illustrators Contest and we are the luckier for it. This Halifax, Nova Scotia, resident has been drawn to graphic novels and comics from an early age. Her favorites are independent and alternative comics created by artists like Daniel Clowes (Ghost World), Craig Thompson (Blankets), and Chris Ware (Acme Novelty Library). While she has always liked drawing, Tamara pursues it in solitude, often working late into the night alone. As inspiration for her work, Tamara continues to be an avid reader, though she admits to no longer reading as much science fiction and fantasy as she once did. Tamara has been too busy, completing a graphic design degree at Nova Scotia College of Art and Design University. Having finished her degree, Tamara is still exploring different media, including work on herself. As a self-described "henna enthusiast," Tamara likes drawing anywhere she can reach.

The Holyman

The day before he met the holyman, Minur was visited by his brother's spirit for the last time. His brother had been a wise and virtuous man in life, and the spirit was doubly wise. It was his counsel that led Minur to Ev-Sheh and the holyman.

Minur was watering his uhlul when the spirit came to him. He felt a breeze at his back—cold, so unlike the desert air even here at the oasis. The uhlul pushed away the water sack with its nose and kicked its single hind leg, turning its eyes warily toward something behind Minur's back. Minur turned and there stood his brother's form, nude, with holy light tracing the edges of his body.

Minur touched a finger to his forehead and lips. "In the sight of Ehl'e Ehrew the All-Father," he said, "I greet you, the abiding dead."

"Ehl'e is just," said the spirit, his voice coming not from his mouth but from the sky all around them. Minur knew from the chastening tone that this was as much a reproach as it was a greeting.

He understood. "I cannot return to Siphenaya."

"Do you think that by spurning her now you can undo your past wrongs?" said the spirit. "No. She deserves a place in our household."

"It's not that, Brother," said Minur. "After dishonoring you, I cannot bear to be with her."

The spirit sighed, eyes turned far away and yet perceiving Minur as they perceived all the world—perfectly. "You don't know how it is to watch the light of Ehl'e upon the Mount, to see His glory. And if you do not leave the path of vice now, you will never see it."

Minur knew it was true. He felt tears forming at his eyes' edges, tiny clean droplets that cleared away the sweat and dust as they crept down his cheeks. He did not want his life to end. "Ehl'e made my heart, and yet I haven't the strength to obey His commands. I am doomed, Brother."

"If you cannot obey your God, then you truly are doomed. But you do have the power to obey. You loved Siphenaya when she was my wife. Now she is rightfully yours, and you ask me to believe you cannot take her?"

Had he loved Siphenaya? Minur couldn't tell. They'd shared stolen moments, secret glances—was that the stuff of love? It didn't matter. Whatever connection they'd once felt was soured now by their disgrace. "I truly cannot love her," he said.

"It is not your place to judge her, or even yourself," said his brother's spirit. "That is Ehl'e's right and His alone."

"Do you think I can come to love her now, at your command or Ehl'e's, because it is right and proper? I told you, I did not make my own heart."

His brother's spirit did not answer immediately, but turned its eyes along a familiar direction. Minur followed the gaze, and there it was—the great dark cone of the Mount, filling half the horizon. Rippling canals in the rock traced the paths of the Worldtears

shed by Ehl'e when this land was new. And at the top
was the Spark of the Divine, the near-unbearable light
of Ehl'e, which left a green streak across his field of
vision as he turned to regard it.

"You believe you have turned away from God,"
said the spirit, "yet I find you here, at the foot of His
mountain. You are seeking a way back to Him."

Minur could not deny it.

"Go to Ev-Sheh," said the spirit. "There you may
end your search."

Minur had meant to pass the city by. "Father called
it a den of evil," he said.

"So it is," said the spirit. "But evil can be the source
of virtue, or Ehl'e would not permit it to exist."

"What will I find there?"

The spirit's lip quirked up in serene amusement.
"Such questions are not mine to answer, Minur. Would
you like to hear the whole tale of your existence, from
birth until death? I could recite it for you. Ehl'e has
shown me everything." The shining figure began to
rise and fade. "Better that I say no more."

Minur became conscious of the uhlul's reins.
Motionless for a time, they jerked in his hand now that
the spirit was gone. The beast had been as transfixed
as he was by the soul's body of light.

"*Yach yanim*," he said, words he often used to calm
the creature. He offered it more water, more of what
it needed. "Soon you can rest," he said. It would be
only a day's journey to Ev-Sheh.

•••

At dusk Ehl'e's Spark outshone the moons and the
Mount became the desert's bright center. Nothing
else rose very far above the landscape; dunes made

up the only significant geography. Still, the Spark's light was far weaker than the sun, and so Minur did not see the Lylahr demon in his path until it was only a few dozen paces ahead. He should have noticed it sooner, but the Lylahr were colored pure and uniform black, and so could be very difficult to see at night.

Minur tried to subdue the fears that slashed through him when he saw the Lylahr. The demon would do as it pleased—it would kill him or ignore him, and Minur could do nothing to hinder it. Turning to flee now would only mean a frightful chase if the Lylahr wanted his head. So he kept walking, urging on his protesting uhlul.

The Lylahr did not move, only stood with its great long arms at its sides. He could not tell if it was watching him—the Lylahr had no visible eyes. As he came closer he saw no features at all, only the great black body, the same shape as a man but half again his size. In a rich man's home Minur had once seen jewels made from obsidian, black volcanic glass that gleamed despite its darkness. The surface of the Lylahr had just the same sheen. He recalled from the Testament that the Lylahr were forged by Ehl'e in the Mount's first eruption.

As he passed the Lylahr he closed his eyes. The deathblow, if it came, would be imperceptibly swift. He silenced his thoughts, all but one: God on high, permit me to live. Five steps later, when he was sure it was behind him, he opened his eyes and looked back.

The Lylahr had turned its faceless head toward him, but made no further motion. The deadly hands were stayed—they were not meant for him. He nearly fell over with relief.

He had seen Lylahr before, but only in cities. They tended to remain near large groups of people, where

God's will needed doing. To encounter a Lylahr alone could easily mean your doom, for the demons were never without a purpose, and humans drew their attention only when their purpose was to kill.

But now the ordeal was over. Minur was not far from Ev-Sheh. He would reach the city before the third moonrise. Now he returned to the road, prodding his uhlul, and saw that he was no longer alone here. Another man was traveling this same road, headed away from the city.

"Hail, friend," Minur called.

"Hail," said the stranger when he came closer. There was caution in his tone. "You mean to reach Ev-Sheh tonight?"

"I do."

"Have you any weapons?"

Minur answered carefully. "A short sword in one of my packs."

"Wear it when you come into the city," the stranger said. "If the mob sees you are armed they may leave you be."

"What mob, friend?"

"Looters. They were just beginning to gather when I fled. The city's Guardian was murdered an hour ago. I'd have been next if I stayed—I was his apprentice." The stranger shook his head. "Whatever else may be said of Ev-Sheh's people, they are fearless. None of them will run. Not until they've stolen all they can in the chaos."

Minur could not believe what he heard. This was the most violent and terrible sin—and sin was death. "Have these people read nothing that Ehl'e has written?"

The stranger studied Minur. "You are from the East," he said. "The Writs and the Testament are life's blood to your folk, and God blesses you for it. It is different here. These people have never seen the angels, and most will never join God on the Mount. To them death is death, and so they live desperately."

Minur was shamed by the stranger's words, for in truth he was no pious Easterner. He would die the true death himself if he could not regain his virtue. This road to Ev-Sheh was his path back to Ehl'e. "I would turn back now," he said, "but I go on the advice of my brother's enduring spirit." That was reason enough, he told himself.

"Then you are in good hands, friend," said the stranger. He looked past Minur, toward the waiting Lylahr. "You have passed by the demon already?"

Minur nodded sadly. The terror of passing by the Lylahr had nearly taken his heart from him. Now the stranger would face the same trial.

The stranger smiled bracingly for a moment, resigning himself to what must be. The Lylahr could not be escaped or hindered. "There will be more travelers down this road tonight. I shall live or die now, as God pleases." He started down the road once more.

Minur watched in frightened wonder as the stranger approached the black figure. He would be safe, thought Minur. There were many Lylahr in the city, he was sure. If this had been the stranger's dying day, wouldn't one of those demons have taken him already?

But this made him wonder—why would the Lylahr wait alone on the road at all? If it meant to kill tonight, why did it dally here instead of seeking out its prey? He could think of one reason, perhaps. His eyes searched the landscape, following a line perpendicular to the road until they caught a spot of black, almost out of sight. Another demon.

The stranger was passing the Lylahr just now.

"Stop, friend!" Minur cried out.

The stranger turned to look over his shoulder at Minur, but—horribly—did not slow his pace. Behind him the Lylahr moved. Half a step brought it within arm's length of the stranger and its hand reached for him, palm open. Its elbow turned in a sweeping motion and the open hand arced like a slow axe head toward the stranger's neck. Where the fingers met flesh they passed through it as if through air, and the stranger's head rolled off his shoulders and into the sand. Blood burst from the open neck in a tall, dark fountain. The body fell.

The Lylahr's arm returned to its side and the demon was still once more.

"No!" Minur dropped to his knees and pounded the sand with his fists. If he'd realized a moment sooner, the stranger would have lived. If only he'd turned back!

Minur had heard of this before. The Lylahr had surrounded the city, isolating it, keeping the population trapped within. Some plan of Ehl'e's was in motion, and until its completion no one could be allowed to leave. This was why his brother had sent him to Ev-Sheh. Something will be revealed here, thought Minur. Revealed to these people. He is drawing them back into His light. And I will be there. I will be saved along with them.

Minur raised his hand toward the stranger's corpse, blessing him, hoping that the angels of the Ehrewat would gather his soul and raise it to the Mount. "God's will be done," he said, and so it would be.

•••

It was not for men to judge, Minur reminded

himself. Judgment was a right Ehl'e had reserved
for himself. If a man did wrong, his corpse was left
to rot by the angels and his soul died with it, the true
death. Noble souls were lifted by the angels of the
Ehrewat to the Mount where they endured forever,
as Minur's brother did, in the light of God's Spark.
To reward or punish was Ehl'e's privilege, for Ehl'e
knew the hearts of men. No human could presume
to know the same.

It was not his place to call these men of Ev-Sheh
evil. But even with his mere mortal vision, he could
tell that they were vile.

Night in the desert was normally cold, but here the
air was heated with an orgiastic energy. There were
no fires or torches burning. The houses and tents were
shadowed structures, the windows cracked open to
make way for staring eyes. From the alleys there came
whispers, sounds of creeping and dashing. In the dark
places at the edges of his vision, behind half-open
doors, he had impressions of bodies coiled in some
corrupt rapture.

He felt exposed and conspicuous at the center of
this darkness, wishing he could quiet the thumping
steps of his uhlul. He knew they could see him, the
sinners who cavorted at the edges of his sight.

He came upon a woman with hands bound behind
her. There was a rope around her neck, leashing her
to a post meant for pack animals. She feared him; he
could see that in her face. He cut her free with his
sword and she ran, disappearing near the shadowed
end of the street.

It was then that he thought to wonder: where were
the moons? There had been two in the sky not long
ago, and a third should have risen by now. Now that

he thought of it, now that he looked above his head, he could see no stars either.

"You cut her free," said a voice from behind him. Minur turned.

The man behind him had a shaven head and a beard that covered only the tip of his chin. He wore a plain robe and held a staff made of white material that looked like marble. On his finger was an amazing object: a ring that blazed with light like a star's. "I wish I could say you saved her," he continued.

"Where are the city folk?" said Minur.

"Hiding. The shrouded sky is their warning, I think. Something is coming."

"But you stand in the open?"

"I have my own ways of hiding." The man peered at Minur's face, searching with quick motions of his eyes. "And you—why not conceal yourself?"

Minur sighed. What could he say? He hadn't the time or the eloquence to tell his story—the betrayal, his brother's counsel, the pilgrimage that ended here. He thought he understood. The time had come for him to face Ehl'e's vengeance, to witness the fate of these sinners who waited on God's mercy.

The robed man nodded as if agreeing with these unspoken thoughts. "You've come to meet the angels," he said.

A tall shaft of flame crackled up from the ground at the far end of the city. Burning fragments of wood and red-hot stone flew away from the spot. There were lights in the sky now, suddenly alive—angels of the Ehrewat.

Above Ev-Sheh they streaked, stabbing starlight down at the corrupt city. More tall fires rose where the light struck wood and stone. The city's silence, induced by the threat of their coming, was now broken by their descent. The once-silent sinners thronged into the streets. Minur felt a streak of pain along his palm as his uhlul reared, wrenching its reins from his grasp. The animal fled, joining the chaos of the crowd.

The robed man still studied Minur, concerned no more with the mobs of city folk than he was with the ravaging Ehrewat. It was as if he expected something, as if he hoped to resolve some conjecture. The stable behind him was blown apart by an Ehrewat's flame, and for a moment Minur cringed, certain the man would be hit by one of the burning scraps—but his eyes must have deceived him, for the hunk of wood careened over the robed man's shoulder. As it flew past, he didn't so much as flinch.

"Ehl'e is destroying this city," said the robed man at last. "Everything and everyone."

Everyone. It was true; the angels would be thorough. Had his brother's spirit sent him here only to die? If so, it would be a true death. He had not yet regained his virtue. His soul would be consumed along with his body—an end to all of this.

He was struck from behind and nearly fell. Two people pushed past him, a man and a woman, hand in hand. The robed man gave them a glance as they ran, coolly watching their desperation as they strove against death. One of the Ehrewat swooped down, almost level with the ground. Minur could see its half-transparent, shifting surface, the painful brilliance of the lights that spun within.

The fleeing couple went opposite ways, but were only a few steps apart when the angel struck at them with its rays of light. The beams passed through them, piercing their flesh as easily as the Lylahr's hand had cut the stranger on the road. And then the angel, God's hand on Earth, came for Minur.

It shifted forward, still near to the ground, passing the falling bodies of the dead couple. Minur had to shield his eyes from the divine light as it approached. Another moment and the light would become deadly, strong enough to cut through and kill him. Now he knew—these were the last moments of his life. This vision was nearing its end. Very soon there would be nothing left of him.

He felt fingers on his shoulder, a firm grasp.

The angel stopped moving. It turned its lights left and right, pulsed them for a moment, then shot upward, leaving a comet streak of brightness to linger in front of Minur's eyes.

He turned to see the robed man with the staff holding his shoulder. "We are leaving," said the man. "Take hold of my robe, pilgrim." Minur did so. "If you let go, the Ehrewat will kill you."

"There are demons outside the city," said Minur.

"Lylahr," said the man. "They employ the same sensors as the Ehrewat."

"What does that mean?"

"I can hide us from their sight as well."

"You are a holyman," said Minur.

"Is that what you think?" The holyman searched his face once more, pausing in the midst of the flaming city, not eager to flee. Fearless, yet sorrowful. Minur saw solemn tears forming in his eyes, shed for the dead of Ev-Sheh, perhaps because he could not save them all. Such serene sadness in the face of rampant death; such quiet contemplation even while the raging angels of the Ehrewat spiralled above. This was no ordinary man.

But Minur was ordinary. A woman not ten feet in front of him was struck by the angel-flame. Her head and shoulders disappeared in a puff of red vapor; the rest of her sizzled like meat thrown into a fire. If he let go of the holyman's robe, that same end would be his. Just the loosening of his fingers could do it. His hand trembled. "I can't stay here, holyman," said Minur.

The holyman frowned. "If you need a word to call me by, use my name. Sean."

"Please," said Minur. "I can't watch this any longer."

"I understand," said the holyman. He wiped his eyes with the back of his hand, clearing away what remained of his tears.

The killing light of the angels, the only brightness in the shrouded sky, lit their way as they started toward the outskirts of Ev-Sheh. *Brother*, thought Minur as he left the dying city, *you knew what I would find in Ev-Sheh—a great man of God, who will lead me from fire and into grace. I thank you!*

Age of Doubt

Michelle Farweigh called upon the fields. It was time to leave this geodesic path—free fall was too slow a course for her purpose. She opened her eyes and the fields were at her command, connected to her mind through the neutrino channels. There was air around her now, and not just stratosphere. Breathable air. She opened her mouth and nostrils.

The air of Enru's world. Michelle breathed it thoughtfully, as if the old master had hidden some message for her in the wind. Anything was possible with Enru.

She used the fields to shape a new trajectory that carried her down toward Enru's mountain lodge. This was his retreat, where he could find time away from the Allach N'tal's Holy Hunt and those Destineers who still followed him. This was the home of which he had written:

Rock parts you from the earth.
This was never my choice—
I only made you
And then fell, slowly as snow, to you
With each homecoming.

No snow fell beside Michelle today. It was summer on the slope: the air was only a little cold and the pines rustled rather than shuddered when the wind blew through them. In the middle of it all was Enru's lodge, a gently triangular home with windows covering one face, parted from the earth by the sculpted mountainside. A ring of tall, narrow poles surrounded it—Onglatna sunsplitters. All this was of Enru's making.

Coming to stand before the door, she touched her feet to the ground—his ground, the master's. She was an Oracle, a Destineer of the First Circle, and had no right to feel trepidation—but she did feel it all the same. At the moment of her footfall the door opened, swinging in rather than dilating, following an old fashion.

Enru M'hehuy had not come to the door. At first she saw no one, but then noticed a presence near her feet and looked down. There stood a diminutive creature: a lenmir, a small apelike being native to the planet Onglat. Lenmir were dumb animals, but this one watched her with awareness and spoke. "Now here's a pretty girl."

Michelle laughed out loud. To be addressed in this way by an Onglat ape!

"I suppose you've come to see the Holy Huntsman," said the lenmir.

"I have," said Michelle.

"I thought so. No one visits to hear my wisdom, though if you listen you'll find my prophecies come true more often than his. I've foreseen that you will step through this door and follow me." The lenmir turned and went into the lodge. As he predicted, Michelle followed.

They came into a sitting room, furnished with human-style couches and the small, flat beds Onglatna preferred to recline on. "A Destineer Oracle has come to call," the talking lenmir announced. "I see you haven't entirely lost the respect of the august Circle."

A tall figure appeared in the doorway at the other end of the hall. Enru was Onglatna—his skin was pale, his head crowned by a crest which arched from his forehead to the back of his neck. "I hope you've shown her the respect she is due, Shayach. You were made to taunt me, and cannot be blamed for it. To treat others the same way is only excess."

"My creator blames me for the will he gave me," said the lenmir. He squatted and left a mound of foul-smelling feces on the gel floor. "That was your doing," he told Enru, and scampered out.

The lodge's fields disintegrated the excrement at Enru's signal. "Forgive Shayach," he said, stepping into the room. "He has been struggling to understand the importance of Sean Adaro's discovery. As have I."

"What is he?" said Michelle.

"A construct of mine. Sean calls him my familiar." Enru held out the first two fingers of his right hand, offering an Onglatna handshake. Michelle saw on his middle finger the twinkling starstone ring, symbol of the Allach N'tal. "He speaks of you often, Michelle. Sean does. It is a delight to finally meet you." Still her eyes followed the bright ring—the same as the one Sean Adaro now wore.

Michelle knew there'd been a time, two millennia ago, when no Destineer could have risen to the First Circle without first meeting Enru M'hehuy. He had been the first Hari-Hinyenar, the first to foretell the Age of Joining that united humans, Onglatna and the other races of the Milky Way. His Destineers, once a secret society formed to end the wars between humans and Onglatna, grew into a great order of scholars and peacekeepers.

But Enru also saw the coming millennia later of the Alyuch Luchann—the Age of Doubt that now gripped the galaxies—and sought his answers outside the Destineer Order. Now the God Hunters of his Allach N'tal searched the galaxies for evidence of the creator they hoped could deliver them from ignorance.

Sean Adaro had left the Order as well, buckling beneath the weight of his own doubt. Enru's Allach N'tal, his hunt for divinity, had lured Sean away from the Destineers. For a time Michelle had tried to blame their estrangement on his dissent. She'd since come to understand that Sean's apostasy hadn't caused their marriage's end. Both arose from the same chaotic force that overtook him as he recoiled from all he'd once trusted.

Now Enru, the mythmaker of Onglat, was Sean's teacher and his only confidant.

"I can't tell you what an honor this is," she told Enru.

He smiled for a moment, showing just the tips of his long Onglatna fangs, but she knew sorrow when she saw it. He wanted no more honor from the Destineers. Pointing to the center of the room, he summoned a field construct, a glowing machine built from swellings

of force and gravity. "Let me show you what Sean
has found," he said.

•••

Outside it was darkening. The sun was low, just
barely cresting the pines at the upper edge of the
mountain's treeline. One of the sunsplitter poles
stood between Michelle and the sun, its narrow
black silhouette dividing the light in half—fulfilling
its function, the foundation of ancient Onglatna
meditation rituals.

Watching the light, she recalled the Spark of the
Divine blazing atop the Mount. Sean's memories still
seethed in her mind. She turned away from the window.

Enru watched the sensorium, remaining raptly
joined to Sean's recorded memories. Sensing that he
had her attention, he lifted his eyes and dismissed the
field construct.

Her memories of Ev-Sheh were fresh, as if she'd
been there herself only a minute ago. Just now she had
seen the angels' fire consume weak, natural flesh. The
planet's inhabitants were native humans. Recalling
the slaughter at Ev-Sheh, she understood at last what
this meant. Old age, disease, mortality. "How many
are dying?"

At last Enru woke fully from the sensorium trance.
He frowned. "Sean estimates more than one thousand
each day."

She would have guessed that many herself, but
it still shocked her to hear it. In a typical year in the
twelve inhabited galaxies of the local group, fewer
than five hundred sentient lives were lost to accident
and misadventure.

"It's not quite so brutal as it sounds," said Enru.

FREE

Send in this card and with any order you will receive a FREE POSTER while supplies last. No order required for this special offer! Mail in your card today!
❑ Please send me a FREE poster!
❑ Please send me information about other books by L. Ron Hubbard.

ORDERS SHIPPED WITHIN 24 HRS OF RECEIPT

___ *L. Ron Hubbard Presents Writers of the Future*® volumes: (paperbacks)

❑ vol I $7.99	❑ vol II $7.99	❑ vol III $7.99
❑ vol IV $7.99	❑ vol V $7.99	❑ vol VI $7.99
❑ vol VII $7.99	❑ vol VIII $7.99	❑ vol IX $7.99
❑ vol X $7.99	❑ vol XI $7.99	❑ vol XII $7.99
❑ vol XIII $7.99	❑ vol XIV $7.99	❑ vol XV $7.99
❑ vol XVI $7.99	❑ vol XVII $7.99	❑ vol XVIII $7.99
❑ vol XIX $7.99	❑ vol XX $7.99	❑ vol XXI $7.99

___ *Master Storyteller: An Illustrated Tour of the Fiction of L. Ron Hubbard* hardcover coffee-table book $49.95

OTHER BOOKS BY L. RON HUBBARD
___ *The Kingslayer* audio CD $25.00
___ *The Ultimate Adventure* hardcover $22.95 ___ audio CD $25.00
___ *To the Stars* hardcover $24.95 ___ audio CD $25.00

Mission Earth® series (10 volumes paperback) $7.99 each
___ vol 1 *The Invaders Plan*   ___ vol 6 *Death Quest*
___ vol 2 *Black Genesis*   ___ vol 7 *Voyage of Vengeance*
___ vol 3 *The Enemy Within*   ___ vol 8 *Disaster*
___ vol 4 *An Alien Affair*   ___ vol 9 *Villainy Victorious*
___ vol 5 *Fortune of Fear*   ___ vol 10 *The Doomed Planet*

___ All ten volumes paperback $79.90
___ *Mission Earth* hardcover $22.95 each
___ *Mission Earth* audio cass $18.00 each
specify volumes:_____

___ *Battlefield Earth*® paperback $7.99 ___ audio cass $29.95
___ *Fear* paperback $7.99 ___ audio CD $19.95
___ *Final Blackout* paperback $6.99 ___ audio CD $19.95

SHIPPING RATES US: $2.00 for one book. Add an additional **TAX*:** _____
$.50 per book when ordering more than one.

SHIPPING RATES CANADA: $3.50 for one book. Add an **SHIPPING:** _____
additional $1.00 per book when ordering more than one. **TOTAL:** _____

CHECK AS APPLICABLE:
❑ Check/Money Order enclosed. (Please use an envelope.)
❑ American Express ❑ Visa ❑ MasterCard ❑ Discover
★ California residents add 8.25% sales tax.
Card#:_____

Exp. Date:_____Signature:_____

Credit Card Billing Address Zip Code:_____

NAME:_____

SHIP TO ADDRESS:_____

CITY:_____ STATE:_____ ZIP:_____

PHONE#:_____ EMAIL:_____

Call toll free: 1-877-8GALAXY or visit www.galaxypress.com

BUSINESS REPLY MAIL

FIRST-CLASS MAIL   PERMIT NO. 75738   LOS ANGELES, CA

POSTAGE WILL BE PAID BY ADDRESSEE

GALAXY PRESS
7051 HOLLYWOOD BLVD
HOLLYWOOD CA 90028-9771

"Only about a third of these are true deaths. This self-styled Ehl'e Ehrew rewards those who please him with eternal afterlife in a mindform database."

"But the others are gone forever?"

"An old Earth notion: 'The wages of sin is death.'"

She looked at the image of Ehl'e's planet above Enru's table. Ehl'e, whoever he was, had taken the name of the ancient deity of Onglatna myth, and now was father-god of a world. The inhabited area was small—a ring of desert that surrounded the mountain home of the self-made god. A thousand deaths there, every day. "How could he destroy so many lives?"

"He must be very confident in the rightness of his undertaking," said Enru. "And I am very curious."

Curious, he'd said. Not outraged, not incensed. "Why?"

Enru crossed the room to stand by her. "Sean and I, the rest of the Allach N'tal—we are searching for the beings who created our universe. This Ehl'e has done something similar. We must know his motives, his methods, the relationship he has formed with his creations. All of these are clues to what we may find at the end of the Holy Hunt."

"I see." It made a sort of sense—but the price of these clues, measured in human lives, mounted each day. And yet the price of intervention could be even greater. Who could say what Ehl'e would do if a Destineer fleet came to liberate his people? He might destroy them all. Perhaps by learning the mind of this god, as Enru sought to do, they could avert such disaster.

"Sean showed great trust in you by telling you of his discovery," said Enru. "I ask you to extend us that same trust. But it is your choice. Tell me, will you bring this before the First Circle?"

Enru is asking for my help. This thought moved her;

she couldn't deny it. She had always envied Sean his chance to work beside the old master.

"No," she said. "The Hari-Hinyenar is often rash. If she knew of this, she would call upon the forces of Stonespire at once. For my part, I don't know if a war can be avoided, but I'm willing to try."

"Thank you," said Enru. The subtones of his voice revealed his relief to Michelle's trained senses.

She had more to say. "In Sean's memory," she said, "he was holding a foamic field scepter."

"He built it himself," said Enru with a look of persistent innocence. "There is no edict against his having one."

"No, of course not," she said. Possessions were only objects; in the age of the foamic field, one had the right to whatever material one desired. "But it's rare for even an ordained Destineer to carry such a powerful artifact. What if Ehl'e were to capture it?"

"Its power would be nothing new to him. He maintains fields over his world already."

"A planetary generator of modest strength, no threat to Destineer ships. But a scepter..." Its field, powered by a miniature foamic vacuum reactor, could reach a density of eighty GeV per Planck cube, a match for most large intergalactic vessels.

"Its ethical intelligence will prevent it from being used against us."

"EIs can be circumvented, given time." Michelle shook her head, even as her heart ached. They were talking about Sean's only defense from Ehl'e's whim. Without the scepter, the self-proclaimed god could kill him at will. Although the thought of it was more than she could bear, she went on. "As you said, it's his choice to carry it. But I'm a Destineer—my duty is to defend these galaxies. I'll help you, but my condition is this: Sean must promise to destroy the scepter if he can't protect it from Ehl'e."

•••

Minur and the holyman were still on the move when the sun began to rise. They had passed quietly by the Lylahr demons that night and now roamed deep in the desert. "You can rest now, if you wish," said the holyman.

"Here, on the open sand?" Minur was caught by a sudden fear. His uhlul was lost in Ev-Sheh, along with all his provisions. The holyman carried no food or water that he could see. They had gone into the desert like fools, without the barest means of survival.

But the holyman lifted his long staff into the air. A cloud of thick vapor formed overhead, blocking the direct rays of the rising sun and cooling the air around them.

"Sean," said Minur, for the holyman still insisted on being called by the name of Sean Adaro, "I have never met a man so favored by Ehl'e."

"Ehl'e doesn't know who I am, Minur."

"You're wrong," said Minur. "Our meeting was predestined."

"I believe that too," said Sean, "but that doesn't mean Ehl'e had anything to do with it."

"But it was foretold by my brother's departed spirit."

"Your brother's spirit?"

"He dwells on the Mount with Ehl'e," said Minur. "He visited me yesterday, told me that I would find redemption in Ev-Sheh."

"A vengeful soul," said Sean with sadness and wonder. He watched Minur as the spirit had just a day ago, his perception somehow flawless and deep. "Your brother can't have foreseen my coming. He meant for you to die in Ev-Sheh."

"That can't be." The spirit had wanted the best for Minur, had wanted him to marry Siphenaya.

"What did you do to your brother, Minur?" It was as if Minur's thought of Siphenaya had been audible to the holyman.

"He is a spirit," Minur protested. "He lives in the light of the Divine Spark. He is virtue itself!"

"He can't have known that I would be in Ev-Sheh. I'm invisible to the angels—Ehl'e's earthly eyes. You saw that. God Himself can't have known."

"No…" Minur was the sinner, the fallen one. His brother had lived by the Writs all his life. What was the holyman saying? That after a life of virtue, after ascending the Mount into the glory of God's light, he would then turn to pettiness and vengeance?

"Minur, why would he want you dead?"

"His wife, Siphenaya, and I…" He found it impossible to go on.

"You were lovers?" said Sean.

"Until the day he died. He never knew, while he lived. Even after he died she was unrepentant, but I could no longer stand the sight of her."

Sean understood. "She reminded you of the betrayal."

"Yes. But all the same it was my duty to marry her, and her right as his widow to keep her place in our household. So Ehl'e taught us in His Eighth Writ." He hung his head. "I couldn't do it."

"Come here, Minur." The holyman beckoned to him. Minur approached to within arm's length of him, and Sean reached out. "Stay still for a moment," he said.

He opened his hand and pressed his fingers against Minur's shoulder. Instead of meeting resistance they passed through the fabric and into his flesh—or so it seemed to his eyes. He felt nothing at all against his skin.

"God on high," exclaimed Minur, flinching away from the ethereal touch.

"Please be still," said Sean. He dipped his phantom fingers into Minur's shoulder once again, inches deep. After a moment he withdrew his hand, and Minur saw a tiny object between his thumb and forefinger. It was round and made of dull metal.

Sean pressed on the little metal ball with his fingers, crushing it flat, and dropped it in the sand at his feet. "You won't be hearing from your brother again," he said.

"Not ever?" said Minur.

Sean smiled at him warmly. "You're eager to forgive and be forgiven." He put a hand on Minur's shoulder, and this time his touch was solid and comforting. "It's possible that you'll meet again. Much will have to change before that can happen. While you're with me I won't let you die, the true death or otherwise."

Could it be true? And even if Sean could protect him forever, was that a sin in itself? "What's wrong?" said the holyman.

"It was Ehl'e's will that I die last night, or the Ehrewat would not have turned on me."

"It couldn't have been acting on its own volition?"

"The angels have no will of their own, separate from God's. They haven't the freedom to disobey Him as men do."

"Do you envy them?" Sean wore a knowing smirk now.

Minur shrugged. "They can do no wrong."

"Even when they kill?"

"Their deeds are Ehl'e's doing, and He gave us the Writs. How could He do wrong?"

"He made those people of Ev-Sheh, knowing full well what they would do with the lives He gave them. Were they somehow freer than the angels? Are you?"

"Right and wrong are His to create, like all else."

"But He forbids the inevitable. The angels are innocent, as you said. Ehl'e is the author of their actions. But what about yours? Think of when you met your brother's wife. Could you have done anything but love her?"

"I could have," said Minur, "if I'd had the strength."

"And who gave you your strength?" Sean scanned the sky overhead, breathed in the air. "Everything here is His doing. Every detail of this world bears His mark."

• • •

"I've found ninety-four likely suspects," said Michelle. "All are missing and assumed to have left the Local Group, perhaps for the Virgo Cluster where Ehl'e's world is located. All are known for their eccentric fascination with Onglatna theology." A list of her suspects' names and faces spiralled above Enru's display. Additional information was transmitted on neutrino bands to her and Enru through their ocular receptors.

It had been her task to search the Destineer archives for former members of the Order, expatriates who might have become the being now calling himself Ehl'e. The archives were public, of course, but a detailed search by Enru or the other God Hunters might have drawn attention from the First Circle.

"Now narrow it further," said Enru. "You're an eldermind. Use your intuition."

"I already have," she said. Long life had made her accustomed to the universe, to the behavior of sentient beings especially. She could anticipate their actions. Informed guesswork was all it was, but even so, eldermentality rarely failed. She gestured and the display changed.

The image above Enru's display depicted a human face, a man with a long, thin beard and sharp eyebrows. "This is our 'Ehl'e,' if my subconscious is to be trusted," said Michelle. "Isaiah Camrin, formerly of the Destineers. Aged 7,344. A student of Onglatna theology during the Age of Joining, when the two cultures first came together. He expressed great disappointment at the end of Onglatna theocracy. Firm critic of Destineerism very early in the Age of Doubt, then left the Order and the settled galaxies quite suddenly at the end of the last millennium."

"I've met him briefly," said Enru.

"So have I," she said. "At a gathering Sean and I held when we were first married."

"Show me."

She obliged, dumping the memory into the room's public sensorium and re-living it with him. She wore a crystal dress in the re-life, a long garment made of soft fluid diamond. It had been a gaudy century. Sean was beside her. He touched her cheek. It embarrassed her to realize that Enru was seeing this and feeling it—she sped up the memory until Isaiah Camrin appeared.

He was speaking with Sean about the Allach N'tal. The God Hunters were young then, newly created by Enru's proclamation. There was no starstone on Sean's finger yet. He'd only just begun his drift toward Enru's new teachings.

"I don't see why you call this an Age of Doubt," said Camrin. "I have no doubts about knowledge or meaning. Only certainty that we have neither."

"But what about divinity?" said Sean. His eyes were alight with the zeal of new belief. "Descartes was only sure that the world around him was real because he believed God would never allow us to be deceived. What if Enru does make contact with whatever force created this Universe? Could he achieve the same certainty that Descartes claimed to have?"

"It isn't possible. If God had given us a world of truth and meaning, would He have hidden it all from our sight? I don't see how we could ever create truth for ourselves, even with the help of our own creator."

"It wouldn't be creation. The real God could show us the truth He made."

"I know now that there is nothing certain in my life, nothing that I can't question. Any truth for me would have to be made whole, from nothing." With these words from Camrin, the encounter was all but over. Michelle and Sean moved on to other guests, other conversations.

As she let go of the memory, Michelle realized that not once during the entire evening had Sean left her side. How he'd loved her then!

It was over, and she regarded Enru across the display table.

"Truth built from nothing," he said. "A worthy thought."

Miracles

When Minur woke it was midday, and the holyman was eating sand. His left palm was full of it, and he scooped the grains into his mouth with the fingers of his right. The brightness of his ring lit up his mouth from the inside as he ate.

"What are you doing?" said Minur.

Sean looked up and finished the remainder of the sand in one swallow. "My body can take its nutrition from all sorts of matter," he said. "Sand is as good as anything. But I imagine you'd like some real food."

He handed Minur a loaf of bread. "I made this while you were sleeping."

Minur took a bite. "You make objects out of nothing—the vapor, the food."

"So could you, with a staff like mine and the right sort of eyes."

"Several times you've known what I was thinking without my telling you."

"Faces become easier to read as you get older." Sean scooped another pinch of sand into his mouth. "What's your point?"

"You are a prophet of God!"

"If I had anything at all to do with Ehl'e, would I hide myself from the Lylahr and the Ehrewat?"

Minur had nothing to say to that.

Sean stood up. "Follow me if you like. It will be the safest thing for you. But I can't bring you back into the grace of your God." He picked up his staff. "I'd like to move on when you're done eating. I hadn't realized how slow it is, traveling on foot."

"Where are we going?"

"To the Mount, eventually. Our next stop will be Osh Ilu."

"If you are not a prophet of Ehl'e, what business do you have on His mountain?"

"Finish your food, Minur." Sean stepped out from under the cloud of vapor he'd summoned, and the sunlight covered him. Minur finished the bread slowly, watching him. He looked back and forth across the horizon, up at the blue expanse of cloudless sky. A distant wind drove up some sand, which caught his attention for a moment. Then he turned his face toward the full brightness of the sun, which would've blinded a normal man. He didn't blink. His every action was miraculous.

Minur finished his bread and stood up. The cloud above him wafted away into nothing, exposing him to the sun. "Come on," said Sean.

They turned toward the Mount. The holyman—Minur still thought of him that way—kept his eyes trained on the glowing Spark, still dimly visible even in daylight. They walked quietly for hours.

"There's no point in my keeping secrets from you," Sean said suddenly. "To answer your question, I'm here to learn about Ehl'e. I want to know what he's done here, what sort of world he's made and why."

"The Testament tells the story of His creation."

Sean shook his head. "Lies and allegory. He didn't build this world out of the Mount's eruption. He used tools, like the scepter I carry."

Minur nearly stumbled when he heard Sean's words. Not even the foulest sinners dared to speak blasphemy against Ehl'e. To call Ehl'e a liar…he had never heard such words! The Testament told tales of men who'd offended God far less and still burned for their crimes.

But Sean had the power to hide from the angels. How could Ehl'e's justice ever be brought down upon him? It seemed impossible. Within himself, Minur was glad for this. He didn't want to see justice done upon Sean, any more than he wanted to die the true death himself. Sean had saved Minur from the fires of Ev-Sheh when Ehl'e's servants would have killed him. Pious though he strove to be, he could not wish Sean harm.

It distressed Minur that his own failings, his own strayings from the path of virtue, arose from inescapable loyalty to others—Siphenaya, Sean, his brother. It was his duty to love other men; more than a duty, it seemed to give purpose to his being. And yet he must love Ehl'e above all. He could not help admiring other people more than he should. Each day he saw them, touched them, heard their words. Ehl'e was distant by comparison, a dim light atop an insurmountable peak.

But Ehl'e was wise. When Minur spurned the truth of His Writs, he brought sorrow upon himself and those he loved. He thought of his brother, who had wanted him dead for what he'd done. Would they ever meet again?

"I know it isn't easy for you to question him now," said Sean, "but someday soon, Ehl'e's dominion over you will end."

This time Minur stopped in his tracks, Sean's words the focus of all his thoughts. Who could this man be? There was no longer any question. His words of rebellion had made undeniable what Minur should have known all along. To think he'd been standing by Sean for most of a day, watching his acts of glory, and only now grasped the truth!

What Sean had said was true, just this far: the world was changing, and would soon be turned on its head. Here on the sand was one who would change the balance between God and man. Sean's words were prideful now, but before his fate had run its course he would earn the goodwill of Ehl'e for everyone living.

"You are the Heyouran," Minur said raptly, "the one who was promised to us." It would never be right that he fall to his knees before another man, but how he wanted to! He was the first to be delivered.

Sean's staff fell from his limp grasp into the sand. A flaring of his nostrils showed how Minur had shocked him. He didn't know! Now the truth struck him like a mighty blow. He ran a hand through his hair, all the while staring at Minur as if he might laugh and admit he was joking. But this was no joke. A laugh did escape Minur now, but it was sheer reverent joy that produced it. The Savior of Man was here, alive, his journey to grace already begun.

Sean's expression stifled Minur's rapture just then. He had seen the holyman's face run the gamut of familiar emotions: sorrow at the slaughter of Ev-Sheh, cold condemnation at the thought of his brother's betrayal, kind appreciation of Minur's thanks. But he had not seen fear there, not until now.

It was Sean who went down on his knees now, head shaking, as if imploring God to pass this destiny on to someone else. "Damn it, Minur." That was all that he said for quite some time.

•••

Minur and I have stopped for the day in a settlement called Osh Ilu. We are now four days' journey from the foot of the Mount. I've enclosed all mnemonics recorded since you last heard from me. No telling at this stage what will be significant.

My companion proclaims to everyone we meet that I am the Heyouran who will earn their people the forgiveness of Ehl'e. Examining the relevant passages of their Testament, I find it impossible to repudiate him. The text speaks in vague terms of a powerful man who will challenge Ehl'e's dominion over His people, but will later approach Him in supplication on behalf of all men. The Heyouran will help Ehl'e to win a war in heaven (referring, perhaps, to the space battle which may occur when Destineer forces come to liberate this world) and earn forgiveness for the sins of the people.

Although the records gathered by Michelle make no claim either way, I think we must conclude that Ehl'e (i.e., Isaiah Camrin) is capable of dreaming precognition, and so has foreseen some part of my mission here. We may also suppose that he either has foreseen, or (more likely) plans to bring about, my defection to his cause. Examining our memories of past encounters with Camrin, it seems to me that he must consider his creation here to be something powerfully real and significant, rather than some sort of experiment or simulation—"truth from nothing," in his terms. He is fully dedicated to preserving the order he has created. He has already proven willing to kill for its sake, since any reasonable ethic would hold him responsible for every death that occurs here.

With regard to the scepter, I will gladly destroy it before I let it fall into the hands of Ehl'e.

Sean Adaro finished his message for Enru, etching it into the fabric of the fields that surrounded him and linking it to the batch of recorded memories he'd just prepared. He called upon the powers of his scepter to cast a Keating wave through hyperspace, toward Enru's world. When he was done he kept his hand on the instrument, his attention captured by the thrumming waveform of local spacetime.

The scepter was a channel to the entire foamic spectrum, linking Sean's will and senses to the subquantum waves that underpinned space, time and matter. Its connection to this substrate was forceful and controlling: it generated a field of foamic ripples, suspended in space all around him, a great machine of interacting energy that could mold and change any object it touched.

Through the scepter he perceived the leading edges of other fields that ringed this planet, doubtless controlled by Ehl'e. He couldn't deny the slightest bit of sympathy for a being who, wielding such mighty energies, felt no remorse at proclaiming himself a god. But even on Ehl'e's terms, there were many more powerful gods in the settled universe—hundreds of trillions of them, filling the uncounted worlds and Dyson spheres under the protection of the Destineers and the sovereignty of the Pax Sapiens. This god's power was nothing special. Only his act of creation was unique.

Creation. Sean swept his eyes over the dusty path that passed for a street in Osh Ilu. They surrounded him now, the folk of this world, walking and talking, buying and selling. Their voices were loud: their ears were too weak to pick up speech at the volume Sean was accustomed to.

These people were made for a purpose. They knew it. How, Sean wondered, could that possibly feel?

Minur was sleeping at their encampment. He would be awake soon if he wasn't already, and would probably want water. Best to get it the old-fashioned way, Sean thought. Small miracles were too great a risk in the cities where Lylahr roamed.

Sean started down the street toward the well. From time to time a passerby stared at him just a moment too long—someone Minur had evangelized, perhaps, wondering if the stories about Sean were true. He sighed inwardly. Minur would keep quiet if asked, but what would be the point? Thanks to Sean's concealing fields, Ehl'e could not know his precise location, and Ehl'e's dream vision had already revealed the inevitability of Sean's coming. Minur's tales did him no harm.

The street opened into a dusty stone walk which surrounded the well. Rivulets of water ran between the stones, darkening the dust, centered around the deep hole. A leather bucket hung from a rope and pulley above the well's opening.

The crowd moved on and Sean was alone, except for one person. A tall young woman sat at the edge of the well, a full bucket of water resting beside her. She dipped one finger into the bucket, watching the ripples in the water's surface, not yet noticing Sean. Her hair was black and curly, something he hadn't seen since landing on this world. It reminded him terribly of Michelle Farweigh.

The girl was perhaps nineteen terranormal years old; Sean Adaro was 3,619. She was a different sort of creature from the women he knew, young and weak in both body and mind.

"Hello," he said to her.

"Hail, friend," was her response, and with it came a smile that released feelings he'd hidden from himself. How could she be so like Michelle? This was not a trick of his memory. There was a real and remarkable resemblance between this woman and the one he'd loved for half of his long life.

Hinla was her name, she told him. She lived with her mother here in Osh Ilu. She came to the well daily for water, often lingering there for a while. Her father had helped to dig the well, and it reminded her of him now that he was gone.

Sean's enchantment with the girl only heightened. Strange ideas came to him. He wondered if Ehl'e had arranged their meeting. Was his control over his creations so precise? And to what purpose…?

He felt it through the fields before he saw it with his eyes: one of the Lylahr was very close to him now, approaching. It couldn't sense him—his scepter cloaked him from its sensors—but here it came nonetheless. He stood and spun the scepter into a ready position.

"What is it, Sean?" said Hinla.

It came around the corner then, Ehl'e's construct, black as the spaces between stars. Its posture was straight, long arms swinging with its steps. Through the lens of the fields, Sean could see gravitational eddies surrounding the Lylahr. It was surprisingly massive, bending the spacetime close around it—something like a walking black hole.

Hinla's face fell to pale ash, her fear so palpable, so like the emotion he'd seen in Michelle. The Lylahr paid Sean no heed—perhaps it couldn't see him after all. Instead it advanced on the girl.

"Run home," said Sean.

Hinla trembled but shook her head. "No one escapes them." Just like that, she was ready to die. Fearful, but ready. This was her god's will.

Ehl'e's intentions meant nothing to Sean. He interposed himself between the girl and the demon, scepter at ready. A negative energy gulf should do it, he thought. A little drop in potential and the Lylahr's mass would radiate away. He tipped the scepter up, erecting an EM barrier to protect Hinla from the gamma-ray bursts.

The black creature reached out with a heavy arm. Sean spun his scepter, stepped forward and left, and swung upward. His weapon came up underneath the Lylahr's elbow, slicing the arm there and freeing energy in a great surge of light. The severed forearm fell through the planet's crust and was gone.

The Lylahr pulled back the rest of its arm and stood

still, its program obviously confused. It saw Sean now, saw the raging fields around him, but perhaps could not fathom how he'd managed to harm it. Did it even know how to defend itself? Perhaps it was programmed to take its imperviousness for granted.

"I can protect you," said Sean. "Run home! I'll follow when I can." Hinla obeyed at last, jumping to her feet and dashing off. She stumbled against her bucket as she ran, spilling the water out over the stones.

The Lylahr crouched and raised its left arm, perhaps receiving orders from Ehl'e himself. Sean retreated two steps and held his staff to the side, baiting the creature forward. He knew he could win. The scepter's power was irresistible.

The demon came at him.

•••

When Hinla came home without her bucket, face white as a corpse, her mother Kehi knew something was terribly wrong. "Dear," she said as the young woman ran past her into their hut, "dear, what's happened?"

"Lylahr, Mati," said Hinla. She told her story— how she met the stranger Sean, how the demon came for her, how the strange man held it at bay. This last part was beyond belief. No human force could resist the Lylahr, and only a man would even think to. God's servants did not battle one another.

Kehi became angry. "Tell the truth, girl!" No man could take the arm of a Lylahr. No man could so much as touch a Lylahr without harming himself. She couldn't believe Hinla would lie about such things, but this had to be falsehood.

"It's true, Mati." Another sob came from Hinla and

286 DAVID JOHN BAKER

she hid her face in her hands. "I'm worried for him," she said. "The Lylahr might still take his head."

"I'm sure it will," said Kehi. She put a hand on her daughter's shoulder, kneading the skin there, trying to calm her. She had to know one thing. "Tell me, dear, if this much is true. Did you run from the Lylahr?"

"It's all true!" Hinla almost screamed.

"Just tell me truly, did you run?"

"Yes."

"Oh, my dear. Oh, my girl." Kehi lifted her hand to her daughter's hair. "I've told you, haven't I? Their will is God's will. We cannot run. We cannot resist."

"I know," said Hinla. Her crying had stopped and her voice was even, as if she understood what was to come. Kehi hoped she didn't. Understanding would bring only meaningless fear, fear that could never save her.

"It's all right, Hinla." Kehi put an arm around the girl, lifting her to her feet. "Come. Your hair is all in a tangle. We'll comb it now while we wait for your friend."

"Yes, Mati." They sat together, mother behind daughter, and Kehi took out her grooming kit. She ran the fine wooden comb through Hinla's hair, always such a chore with these thick curls. She sang an old hymn, one of Hinla's favorites, while hiding her tears from her daughter.

Around the bend I'll find my fate.
Until it's time it kindly waits.
Ehl'e, take me if I'm pure
Upon the Mount, to glimpse Your fire.

Kehi laid down the comb. Beside it was the long razor she used for cutting hair. This she took in her hand while she lifted Hinla's hair away from her neck. The tears flooded her eyes, seeming as if they'd never stop. She'd always loved her daughter so.

"God's will be done," she said.

• • •

The great crowd was centered on the village well. Their noise and shuffling filled the air. They were astonished, each and every one.

Minur pushed his way through toward the center, toward the well. He knew he would find Sean there. The voices spoke of a man matched against a demon. Sean was the only man Minur had ever seen with power over the Lylahr.

As he neared the well, the crowd opened up and Minur saw Sean. His white staff was at his side. There was no sign of the Lylahr. He noticed Minur at once, met his eyes with a look that Minur could not disobey. "Come," he said, and began walking away from the village. The crowd parted to let him through, leaving a wide berth for the demon-slayer.

"Where is the Lylahr?" said Minur, following at Sean's heels.

"Dead," said Sean. "Its body sank to the earth's center."

"I thought you were invisible to them!"

"I was protecting the life of another." Sean kept his eyes fixed on the path ahead of him. Minur thought he looked anguished, as if he'd made a terrible mistake and was only now coming to realize it.

Minur saw that the mass of people was following, perhaps twenty feet behind them. Now they will believe me, he thought. Only the Heyouran could fight a demon and win! For his own part, Sean seemed to take no notice of the people. Minur saw a hut on the sand ahead, directly in Sean's path. Their destination.

An old woman sat on the ground outside the hut, hands covering her face. Her shoulders shook massively with each breath. As they came closer, Minur saw that her clothing was drenched in blood. She was badly hurt! Was this the one Sean had fought to protect?

Sean stood over the woman, not moving to help her. When his shadow came over her she looked up. Minur saw no pain in her face, only sorrow. Perhaps the blood on her dress was not her own.

"Where is Hinla?" said Sean. "What have you done to her?"

The old woman let out a terrible wail which lasted until she had no breath left.

"What have you done?" demanded Sean.

"I had to," said the old woman, the words quivering with sobs. "Another demon would've come!"

"I'd have killed it," said Sean, grasping her shoulders in a dire grip.

"It was Ehl'e's will," she cried, head bowed.

Sean pounded the wall of the hut with his fist. A single blow was enough to crack the clay. He spoke a curse Minur had never heard before, in a voice that made his bones shudder. Then he went into the hut.

Minur looked around at the wary crowd, then gathered his strength. If he could help Sean, he would. He followed him in.

The entire floor was covered in blood, more blood than he'd ever seen, even at Ev-Sheh. Lying in front of a wooden chair was the body of a young woman. Her dress and hair were wet and red and slick. Her throat was cut open.

Minur shrank away from the furious figure of Sean, afraid for a moment that he would let out another great bellow. Instead he spoke quietly, through gritted teeth. "He is trying to force my hand."

"Who is?" said Minur.

"Ehl'e. He's trying to bring me into the open, to make me use my powers."

"Then why don't you?"

"He is evil!" Sean's voice was thunderously loud once more. He pointed at the dead girl. "This is his doing! This and every death you've ever seen. Every tear ever shed on this world was his fault. And you would have me do his will, cower in misery at the foot of the Mount with your people? Never!"

The blasphemous words were so moving that Minur could not help but believe, if only for a moment.

"He knows me," said Sean in a small voice. "He made her to tempt me. Don't you see, Minur?" He looked up, pleading Minur to understand the feeling behind his rushing tears. "I can't let this be."

He touched a hand to the dead girl. Light flooded the room, as if the sun were there, shining in Sean's fist. Minur blinked but couldn't turn away. The torn flesh around the girl's neck curled up and joined together, binding itself like heated metal in a forge. It was over in moments. She sat up quickly.

Despite the miracle, Sean's tears had not stopped. He knelt beside the girl and took her hands in his. "Nothing will ever harm you again," he said.

Minur beheld the glory and could not speak.

He turned and left the hut, dazed by what he'd seen. When he was through the door, the girl's mother rushed inside. Her cries of delight stirred the crowd and they came forward. Behind him, Minur heard their chanting.

"He is come," they said as one. "The Heyouran is come!"

God Hunters

"Wake up, pretty girl."

For a moment Michelle thought it was Sean's voice she'd heard. *Pretty girl*—she wasn't sure if he'd ever called her that.

It wasn't Sean's voice, anyway. It was the ape, Shayach. Now that her eyes were open, she saw him hanging by his hands just above her face. "What do you want?" she said.

"Enru is sulking," said the lenmir. "I thought you might try to snap him out of it."

"What does he have to sulk about?"

"Oh, he's never without his *doubts*. They consume him night and day, or so he tells me. He should get a life. But this time there's something more. A message came from Sean Adaro."

She turned her eyes to the sensorium and lived the memories Sean had sent. "Oh, no," she said when she was finished.

"It seems Ehl'e's written Sean's script for him," said Shayach.

"The script was written by the real god," said Michelle, "whoever that may be. But it seems Ehl'e's had a peek at it." She stood up from the Onglatna flatbed where she'd been dozing. "Where is Enru now?"

"Out there." The ape gestured toward the door. Michelle heard rain beating steadily against the window.

"All right," she said. On her way out she raised a small field barrier to protect her from the rain.

It was dark and cold on the slope, details she noticed

but did not truly feel. Sean was in terrible danger. If Ehl'e had foreseen his defeat, there was nothing that could be done for him. If he'd only glimpsed some of Sean's future actions, there was hope, but perhaps not much. Ehl'e would know just how to react to Sean's every move. He'd had centuries to plan his strategy.

Something within urged her to contact the First Circle now. Sean could already be Ehl'e's prisoner. If he died, it would be in part because of her, because she'd hidden the truth about Ehl'e's world from the Destineers.

But Ehl'e's Testament had claimed that Sean would join his cause in the heavenly war. She couldn't believe he would ever betray the Pax Sapiens. But if he did turn, if Ehl'e's story turned out to be true, calling down the wrath of the Destineers could bring his doom.

If Sean died now, while they were still estranged, because of some mistake of hers…she truly didn't know what that would do to her.

It was not difficult finding Enru. On a night like this he would be on foot, and there was only one path down the mountainside. She came upon him on a mossy ledge that overlooked a stand of evergreens. Further below was mist and darkness. He held his hands clasped behind him and seemed deep in meditation. Behind the clouds lay the moon's dim brightness. She thought his eyes must be focused there.

He had no umbrella of fields over him, she realized. His skin and clothes were soaking.

"Do you think Sean is caught in Ehl'e's vision?" she asked him.

"If he is, there is no help for it. What will be, will be." Enru was right, of course. The dreams came to them from the future itself, which was already real and waiting to be discovered.

"We have to try to help him," she said, questioning the words as soon as she spoke them.

"While he bears the scepter, Ehl'e cannot harm him."

"But he can still be drawn into a trap. Ehl'e could find some leverage against him, force him to lower his guard."

"I am willing to leave the choice up to him," said Enru.

"And you're asking me to do the same?"

"It will be difficult. You love him. If you can't let him endanger himself, I will understand."

Enru's words frustrated her. "I don't see what you hope to learn from Ehl'e. He's a mad rebel on a frontier world. What could he ever teach you about the real God who made this universe?"

"What could bring a being to create others, inferiors? What does he owe his creations? What can he offer them?" Enru turned to watch her for a moment, then back toward the night. Still, he had more to say to her. He recited: "'For, in fact, what is man in nature? A Nothing in comparison with the Infinite, an All in comparison with the Nothing, a mean between nothing and everything. Since he is infinitely removed from comprehending the extremes, the end of things and their beginning are hopelessly hidden from him in an impenetrable secret; he is equally incapable of seeing the Nothing from which he was made, and the Infinite in which he is swallowed up.

"'What will he do then, but perceive only the middle of things, in an eternal despair of knowing either their beginning or their end? All things proceed from the Nothing, and are borne toward the Infinite. Who will follow these marvellous processes? The Author of these wonders understands them. None other can.'"

Blaise Pascal had written this in his *Pensées*, she knew.

"Fascinating," Enru added, "that a child of thirty years, living nine millennia ago, should have foreseen so well the trouble of our times. The story of science, the history of our discoveries, comes near to its end. Soon the last experiments will be finished, the last data recorded. And we will be as ignorant as ever of our purpose, left to stare endlessly at our measurements and wonder: is this all there is?"

"I understand," she said. "But to risk Sean's life—"

Enru interrupted her. "What is Sean's life worth? What is the value of life? Without God's help, we have no answer—only feelings, hunches, all of which arose out of cold evolution."

"We are ignorant, I admit. But we must go on living all the same. What else can we do but hold onto the way of life we've already built?"

"This is why you remain with the Destineers." Enru spread his hands. "I am sorry. I respect your beliefs, but I can't help hoping that my teachings were as transient as anyone's. What I helped to build will not endure. I pray for that."

"Do you really wish the Destineers had never been?"

"No," he said. "They served a great purpose once. Earth and Onglat were at war. But that generation—and the entire age that followed—became tainted with such certainty. I thought I had put into words the great truths of existence." His laugh was a rasping hiss typical of his species.

"Even within the Order, I've met no one free from doubt."

"Then why carry on as if nothing is wrong?"

Michelle hadn't thought it would be like this. Enru

had been known for his serenity once. But she should not have been surprised. His tone only echoed his recent writings—his rage against the world that hid its truths from his sight, the creative powers that eluded him.

She suddenly wanted to feel what he was feeling. She let go of the field umbrella above her head, and the rain poured upon her. In moments her hair was stuck against the back of her neck, her eyelashes heavy with droplets. She hadn't felt rain on her skin in years.

She stepped forward to stand by Enru and put her arm around him. He seemed to relish the contact and the forgiveness it implied.

"Do you blame my teachings for the end of your marriage?" he said.

"No."

"Perhaps you should. I know how it happened. It was the same with my Ahwena. Eventually there was only doubt in my heart, and no room left for her."

She shut her eyes and cried a little. Sean had said the cruelest things to her. *I'm starting to question the worth of these biological drives,* he'd said. Like anything else, love was evolved behavior. He'd expected her to argue with him, as if she could present some proof or derivation to show that their feelings meant something.

She couldn't argue and she couldn't agree.

"Sean is changing," said Enru. "I can feel it in the memories he sends us. There is hope for the two of you." He turned to embrace her. "I won't let him die."

The rain still fell over them in cascades, flushing through the trees and striking the stone hillside. The water's own forceful fall brought it splashing up again like clear flame from the rock. Through the fields she could imbibe all of this at once, if she tried. She let them wash in, all the tiny events, and found herself anticipating each raindrop a moment before it struck her skin.

All of this, the whole beautiful planet, was of Enru's making—but only within limits. In this universe, nothing was lost or gained. Energy, matter, space and time—all flowed from one form to another, and this could be controlled. But from nothing, nothing ever arose. This was the lot of humankind, as Pascal had written: frozen midway between all and nothing, controlling the powers of change but never creation or destruction. What Ehl'e called *his creation* was nothing of the sort. His fields had built a world out of the matter he'd found, floating free.

Seeing through Sean's eyes the work of this so-called God, his crimes and follies, Michelle understood at last why the Allach N'tal sought after real divinity. After all Ehl'e had done, so vast a gulf still stood between him and any real creator, any being who could begin with nullity and from it fashion reality. She lifted her palm in front of her face and watched the rain fall and burst against it. A single one of these drops, summoned newborn from a void, would be a greater miracle than Ehl'e's entire world.

For the first time in her life, Michelle stood in awe of her maker, unsure all the while whether any such being existed.

• • •

In the city of Anumar there dwelt a man named Ohr, who the people called Lord Protector. He held no official title or office; such things were not permitted among mortal people. Ohr was simply a man of great wealth and influence who also possessed a kind public spirit. His riches were spent to the benefit of those around him, and so he was loved and respected by all.

It was to the Lord Protector's court that Sean insisted they go. Minur asked to gather the other followers, but Sean told him no. Only the two of them would visit Ohr's court.

To a simple man of the East, Ohr's estate was splendid. On their way to his hall, Sean and Minur passed gardens of sculpted bushes and strutting nylu birds. The hall was built from the finest stone. Carved upon the walls were murals depicting Ohr's ancestors—the Lord Protector came from a great line of adventurers.

Sean had been so quiet, so somber ever since healing the girl Hinla. It was time, he'd resignedly told Minur, for his presence to be felt in this world. From village to village they moved at the head of a mass of disciples that Sean neither rallied nor dismissed. Everywhere they went he healed all the sick and injured, eased the pain of the old, created feasts from empty air and water from the sand. Those who asked him to preach were told that he would end the evil suffering brought upon them by their false God. To those who did not ask, he said nothing.

When they saw who had come to their door, Ohr's servants offered Sean an immediate audience.

The Lord Protector sat upon a raised chair that was built from plain wood. Doubtless a symbol of his humility—there could be no thrones for men. "The Heyouran is welcome in my home," he said.

Sean stood before the raised chair, the focus of all eyes, with Minur at his side. No one looked away from him for more than a moment. "I would prefer you use my name," he said. "Call me what you like."

"You roam deserts and cities, healing and working miracles. Are you not a messiah?" A skeptical lifting of Ohr's eyebrow showed that he was willing to listen.

"No," said Sean.

"What are you, then?"

"An ambassador from a faraway nation."

"A land of miracle workers?"

Sean shrugged. "My countrymen have the same powers as I. Ehl'e was one of us once, before he created your world."

Ohr glanced away uncomfortably. "A blasphemer. You are surely the one God told us to expect."

"I am a worldly man, Lord Protector. Just as you are."

"What do you presume to know about me?"

"Only what your deeds suggest," said Sean. "You care about the good of your people here on Earth, while they live. Their livelihood. This has earned you their respect and allegiance."

"You make me sound like a ruler, something I am not and have never tried to be. There must be no kings among men. God the Father is this land's only sovereign."

"In my nation there are no kings. Public respect is all that makes a leader." Sean stopped abruptly and cocked his head sideways. His white staff lifted just a little. Minur touched his shoulder. "What is it?"

"A Lylahr is coming." Sean turned again to Ohr. "Ehl'e has become jealous of your influence, Lord Protector. A demon approaches."

The Lord Protector came down from his chair and Minur took hold of his upper arm. "Wait here, my lord. He can protect us."

Sean motioned with his hand for Ohr and Minur to back away from the wall. The courtiers and servants cleared away in a panic. Sean paid them no heed. He kept his eyes on the wall, resting his staff in the crook of his arm.

A black spot appeared on the stone. Minur saw that it was the hand of a Lylahr. The rest of the creature followed close behind, passing through the wall as if it were nothing, leaving a cavity shaped grotesquely like its giant body as it entered the room. Another spot of black appeared to its left, and then another to its right. Two more Lylahr followed close behind. As they came through, part of the ceiling above them collapsed as the wall weakened further. The stones that fell upon the demons disappeared into their bodies.

The first Lylahr stood back in a fighting crouch, hands spread out in front of it, while its two companions began to circle around Sean. The holyman did not let this happen. He sprung at the leftmost demon, a jump made impossibly high and fast by his power, and came down upon the dark creature's head with his staff. The Lylahr raised an arm to block. When the staff met the arm the entire room seemed to shudder, light burst too bright for Minur to watch, and when it cooled away the demon's arm was gone. Its other hand came around to strike, but Sean tapped it aside with a swirl of his staff.

The lead demon came from behind him and Sean jabbed backward without needing to look, striking it in the chest with the bottom tip of his staff. Its hands clenched and its limbs bent as if its body were wracked with terrible pain—it almost seemed as though the silent creature was trying to scream. It fell over onto its back and kept falling through solid earth, leaving behind a pit with no visible bottom.

Sean stood at ready, threatening the remaining two Lylahr with his staff—and to Minur's amazement, first the wounded one and then the other simply turned and left through the holes they had made in the wall. They were no match for Sean, and it seemed that they knew it.

A collective breath was released and then drawn in by Minur, Ohr and the watching servants and courtiers. A force they'd once thought invincible had been bested by their savior. Minur had never before seen anything so much as slow a Lylahr's step. Now one had died before his eyes.

Sean let his voice grow, speaking not just to the Lord Protector but to the entire cavernous room. "Tonight I send word to my people of Ehl'e's crimes. A fleet of their ships will fill the sky."

"The war in heaven," said the Lord Protector.

"Ehl'e will not win." Sean came closer to the Lord Protector, and Minur barely heard his next words. "He will not win, but the battle could ravage this world. If he sees his own people turn against him, he may surrender to us. You must rebel."

"You would have me lead an army against God?"

"Not an army. A pilgrimage. On the day of the fleet's arrival, I will bring my followers up the slope of the Mount to supplicate Ehl'e, to demand that he give himself up."

"The Mount is too steep to be climbed!"

"After what you've seen, do you think I can't cut a path in the side of a mountain? The Lylahr will resist us, and so will the angels of the Ehrewat. Let them try! Nothing in this world can check the power of my scepter." Again he leaned, whispering to Ohr: "Ehl'e's creatures would have killed you this day. What do you owe him now?"

Ohr chuckled. "All that I have." He climbed up to the raised dais where the splinters of his wooden chair remained, smashed apart by falling stone. "Can I believe that you hail from a land of miracles? Maybe not. But if you are the Heyouran, surely it is Ehl'e's wish that I follow you. And to see His Spark atop the Mount with my living eyes...Yes, I will come."

Hearing this, Minur wondered at his own thoughts and motives. Sean was righteous and confident, more so than any man he'd ever met. How could he ever be made to serve Ehl'e, who was not a god to him, but an equal? And why should Minur himself serve God when it was Sean who had saved his life, healed the sick and fed the starving—Sean who had the will and, it seemed, the power to bring an end to death and pain throughout the world?

But life and comfort were not the same as virtue. They were not good in themselves; so he'd been taught all his life long. Could it really be so? If all good lay in virtue and piety, why did men seek other things?

Sean smiled broadly as he shook the Lord Protector's hand, but Minur could not be free of this turmoil. Ehl'e, he thought, how am I to know if you've lied to me?

On the Mount

The view from the very foot of the Mount was imposing.

Straight above Sean's head the slope looked almost sheer to him. Although the Spark of the Divine was not itself in sight, its light washed out over the edge of the slope like the ring of sunlight around an eclipse. With a sweep of his scepter he cut stairs into the mountainside, a wide spiral of them that led to the burning seat of Ehl'e's power.

He turned to his assembled followers—twelve

thousand, a quick estimate told him. "Come, friends. You will be free!" He started up the stairs.

Minur was beside Sean, just where he'd always been. Soon, thought Sean, you will have everything you've ever wanted. Joy, my friend—joy among the galaxies! Here on this wretched world, he wondered at his own sorrows of old, his doubts. They all seemed like madness now.

And all the mad words he'd said. Young Hinla had only now reminded him. He remembered the day he divorced Michelle Farweigh. He'd loved her, then and always, but oh, the words he'd said: *So far as I know, love means nothing. You think what we have is something special, something to make a life out of? It's animal behavior, left over from a dead era.* She had shed two tears then, one from each eye. They'd fallen down to linger at the edge of her lip like teeth.

Those tears were his doing. Now he climbed to his death, perhaps—a fate he now knew he deserved. She'd offered him boundless love and pleasure, and instead he'd enslaved himself to his doubts. The bright starstone ring he wore left etchings of light across his vision as he moved. Now he knew—he'd been a fool when he first put it on.

He had the time, now, to transmit one last message to Enru. It took only a moment to compose, and when it was finished he knew he could bear whatever destiny awaited him. *Michelle must know,* he signaled: *I love her.*

The rest of the climb seemed to pass in just moments. Twinkling angels filled the night sky, but kept their distance. Beyond them he saw distant flashes, the leading edge of the Destineer armada. Justice would soon be done.

Around the bend ahead the light was at its brightest. He rounded the corner and there was the Spark of the

Illustrated by Tamara Streeter

Divine, a point bright as a naked star. He saw Minur and the others shield their eyes. Using his scepter he raised a dimming field in front of him, allowing them all to look directly at the avatar of their god.

Sean spoke, letting the scepter carry his voice to all his thousands of followers. "Ehl'e! Isaiah! You who call yourself a god! I have come on behalf of the Destineer Order and the Pax Sapiens to end your dominion here."

A voice came to him through the neutrino receptors in his eyes. Thoughtspeech. {You are here on your own behalf, Sean Adaro, and no one else's.}

"Speak aloud so these people can hear you," said Sean.

{This is My world, Sean. Here My fields are a match for yours. You do not dictate the terms of our meeting.}

Sean tested the local fields with his scepter. Sure enough, the energy density surrounding the Mount was strong enough to resist his own fields. A powerful short-ranged generator. They were at an impasse.

{A Destineer fleet will be here by sunrise,} he thoughtsaid.

{I have detected them,} thoughtsaid Ehl'e.

{Then you must know there is no point in resisting.}

{Not without your help.} The voice came slyly into his mind.

Sean was stalwart. {Your prophecy is false. I would never aid you against the Destineers.}

{You *will* aid Me, Sean. You are Allach N'tal, a God Hunter, a seeker of the divine. I am what you have hunted for these long centuries. I have written my truth in stone!}

{I can't see how you've made anything but pain, Ehl'e. Pain and death.}

The voice of Ehl'e's mind was disdainful. {Pain?

Death? Show me the evil in these—you know you cannot. Compare them with the agony of nihility, which is all you and I have ever known. We came from nothing, Sean! There is no truth for us. Would you inflict the same doom on my people?}

{You think you give your life meaning by lording over them?}

{My life can never have meaning. I am uncreated, alone. But my people, they have the truth I made for them, the laws I revealed at their world's birth. The purpose is theirs, not mine.}

"You are mad!" Sean said out loud.

{If you turn your back on me, you doom Minur, Hinla and the rest of them.}

Sean returned to thoughtspeech. {What do you mean?}

{Do you truly think that these nations will survive the passing of their Living God?}

{The Destineers will treat you harshly if you harm them.}

{The Destineers will never kill anyone, no matter how heinous his crime,} Ehl'e thoughtsaid. {But I will kill these people.}

{I won't let you.}

{You will weaken your fields if you try to protect them. Even your mighty scepter grows weaker at a distance. Perhaps you can defend these pilgrims you've brought to the Mount. No matter. My Ehrewat have surrounded every city and village on this planet. If you try to save them all, you will become too weak to defend yourself—and I will take the scepter.}

Sean saw too late that it was true. His fields would attenuate if he spread them over the planet. Ehl'e's own power would be more than enough to overwhelm his defenses and wrest the scepter away from him.

And with the scepter, Ehl'e could stand against the Destineer fleet…not forever, perhaps, but maybe long enough to escape.

If he protected himself, Minur and the others would die. But if he protected them, he could not stand against Ehl'e.

{I have a solution,} thoughtsaid Ehl'e. {I thought of it long ago, when I first envisioned our meeting. Turn to my people and tell them the truth: you are my chosen one. You have healed them, you have led them to the slope of my mountain, and now you will win them my forgiveness by giving your scepter to me.}

The Mount erupted then, a wave of light spiraling upwards out of the Divine Spark. Spirits. The souls of all the virtuous dead surrounded the pilgrims in holographic form, exhorting them to turn back to their All-Father now. One soul hovered near where Sean stood—Minur's brother, he was certain.

The spirit spoke to Minur. "He's accused me of trying to murder you, hasn't he, Brother? Nonsense! God was not ignorant of Sean Adaro's coming. I knew you would join him, pilgrim. There is still a role for you to play. He trusts you. Tell him what you know to be true: he is Ehl'e's servant, the same as us all."

Minur turned to Sean, his face ablaze with feeling. Every nuance of it was clear to Sean's trained eye: this was the truest moment of Minur's life. "Before I met you," he said, "my every thought and act was the work of Ehl'e. Do not turn back. Free us!"

Freedom, Sean thought. Can I even offer you that, Minur? Ehl'e's hand has steered your life since that first moment, the birth you can't even recall. Will I strike that hand away now, only to replace it with my own? No one is free from the influence of others, nor from the slow but sure influence of the world around him. Your false god ruled you once, but now you follow me.

Your life was planned by your maker, the mind behind this Spark. My own was determined just as surely by inevitable nature, a thousand tiny impulses. I am no freer than you, Minur. Neither of us will ever be free. Not from each other, not from the whims of this world.

Except perhaps when we are gone from it. Sean realized he'd been terrified until now, cold within and unready to die. Understanding the fear, he found it ebbing away at last. Though it may mean nothing, he thought, I will end Ehl'e's rule. Then I will live or die as fate pleases, just as it's always been.

Taking the scepter in both hands, he held it level in front of him and brought it down upon his knee. Summoning its energies for one last time, he snapped it in half. Those around him saw nothing at first, but for Sean the release was phenomenal. His senses, linked to the scepter, were stifled. His powers left him. The light of the Divine Spark blazed in his face and his eyes streamed with tears. He put up his forearm to shield himself.

The voice of Ehl'e spoke calmly in his head. {I never saw how it would end, Sean. My vision never showed me your death.}

Powerless now before the Spark, Sean spoke what he supposed would be his last words. "If you think the suffering and death you've given these people is some sort of gift, then bestow it on me as well." It was neither jest nor bluster: if this was his fate, he wanted it.

But the raging light of the Spark dimmed. Sean opened his eyes as an audible voice came from all around him. "No. There is no point in vengeance. No point to anything, anymore."

The angels above flew up into far darkness, gone to meet the Destineers in doomed battle.

• • •

Enru was waiting for him on board the Destineer flagship *Night in Motion*. As the ship's fields lifted him into orbit, Sean saw flights of robot warcraft go past, ready to secure all inhabited areas of the planet. The people were being gathered into space as quickly as possible while medical personnel stood by. There would be no more deaths here—not one.

Enru was there when he came through the hatch. They embraced.

"The Hari-Hinyenar is not happy with me," said Sean.

"Nor with me. I was Hinyenar myself once. You'd think I would have more sense than this," Enru said. "She told me what the scout ships have found. Other worlds like this one, dozens or hundreds, perhaps. They were scattered throughout this galactic cluster. It seemed Isaiah Camrin was not the only former Destineer who'd experimented in divinity. He was only the first of a multitude, a secret society of living gods."

"I've signed on with the fleet," Sean said. "I suppose I'll be a god hunter in the literal sense from now on."

"I suppose so." Enru smiled sadly at Sean. Things had changed for the two of them. Sean was a Destineer now, Allach N'tal no longer. He wasn't sure if his doubts would ever be answered, but he could no longer allow them to control his life.

He could no longer imagine a meaningful bond between man and God—any such thing now seemed cruel, imbalanced and stifling. How could he ever relate to a being who'd shaped his life and his world, or put his trust in a creator after what he'd seen? No one could create truth. Ehl'e had tried, and his poor people had suffered for it.

The real God, whoever created this mysterious, wild universe, had done a thing Sean could barely comprehend. He had made dark vacuous gaps that cried out to be filled and sorrowful hearts that slowed and stopped with time's passage. Heat and light were scarce, life and love scarcer yet, and all would one day disperse with entropy into a single meaningless cloud. He could just as well have made joy, thought Sean, real and lovely exultation—but He left that to us.

I don't want to meet God, Sean realized. Not any longer. If He is truly greater than we are, He's done the same wrong as Ehl'e by creating His inferiors. And if He's no greater, we have nothing to learn from Him that we can't discover for ourselves.

"I'm sorry, Master," he said.

"Sorry?" Enru put an arm around Sean once more. "I only wish I could follow where you're going. I regret that I can't." He sighed heavily. "My doubts remain. Joy will have to wait a while longer."

Just past the hatch was a padded bench where Michelle Farweigh awaited him. He sat down next to her and took hold of her hand where it lay beside her.

"I got your message," she said.

"I'm glad."

She squeezed his hand as if holding on for life itself. "Does this mean you've come back to me, Sean Adaro?"

"My wandering is over," he said. He gazed down at his finger, reminding himself with satisfaction that the starstone ring was gone. But there was something he didn't expect leaking between his fingers—the gleam of starstone. He lifted the hand he held, Michelle's hand, and saw a ring.

"We've had opposite epiphanies," she said. "I was standing on Enru's world, thinking of you and your troubles, and of Ehl'e. All at once it became crucial to me. I have to know who God really is."

She had waited this long for his homecoming, only to become a God Hunter herself. He feared her answer to his next question: "Have we passed each other by?"

He couldn't fault her, he supposed, for taking up the cause he'd followed himself. But for her to leave the worldly life he'd only just rediscovered, to fall into that same haze of doubt and questing that had kept them apart—she didn't deserve the pain of it, although perhaps he did.

But she shook her head quickly. "We can't just abandon everything we're unsure of. That was your mistake, Sean. I won't repeat it. I won't stop breathing just because I have doubts, and I won't leave you alone."

He wouldn't be without her any longer. It was all Sean needed to go on with this life. Here it was, life itself: the sky outside the window was black and piercing white, stars all around him for as far as space went on. Not even an hour ago he'd been powerless before Ehl'e, prepared to die. It seemed like an age had already passed since then. He owed that hour's expanse, and all the time that followed, to the mercy of the false and fallen god.

Michelle was here. She loved him. Perhaps there was something worthwhile in the Holy Hunt after all, if she saw fit to join it.

EIGHT THINGS NEW WRITERS NEED TO KNOW

by
Robert J. Sawyer

For Doug and Helen —

Robert J. Sawyer is the author of the Hugo Award–winning Hominids, *the Nebula Award–winning* The Terminal Experiment, *the Seiun Award–winning* End of an Era, *the Aurora Award–winning* Starplex, *and thirteen other science fiction novels, including, most recently,* Mindscan, *for which he won the John W. Campbell Memorial Award. His books are top-ten national mainstream bestsellers in Canada, and they've hit number one on the bestsellers list published by Locus. His short fiction has appeared in* Analog, Amazing Stories, *and* Year's Best SF 5. *Rob first entered the Writers of the Future Contest in 1984, and he became a judge for the Contest twenty years later. He lives in Toronto.*

Best wishes!

1. Not Everyone Is Going to Like Your Work

And that's okay. Your job as a writer isn't to be blandly acceptable to everyone; rather, it's to be the favorite author of a narrow segment of the population. If you try to please everybody, you'll end up pleasing no one. Good book reviewers know this: their job isn't to tell you whether they like a given work (which is a datum only of interest to them personally); rather, it's to say if *you* like this particular sort of work, then this book will be to your taste—or not, if the book has failed at what it set out to do. Which brings us to…

2. Your Fiction Should Be About Something

Theme is the story element beginning writers spend the least time on, and yet it's the single most important aspect. Nothing drives this home more clearly than the success of Dan Brown's *The Da Vinci Code*. The book is poorly written in almost every way—and yet, on its own, it has been read by more people than read all the books published last year by all science fiction and fantasy publishers *combined*. Why? Because it's *about something*. In particular, it's about the suppression of the feminine in Catholicism, and a reinterpretation of the Christ story that is new to most readers. The quality of the plot (formulaic chases), the characters (made of the same stuff as the paperback's cover), and the prose (pedestrian at best) are all forgiven, because Dan Brown had something to say—and you should too. Which means...

3. Your Job Is to Tell *Your* Stories

Too many talented young writers waste time writing fan fiction (such as stories set in the universes of *Stargate Atlantis* or *Star Trek: Voyager*). This is a waste of time; worse, it's a *seductive* waste of time, because they get all sorts of feedback praising their "skillful handling" of the characters, which makes them think they're much better writers than they really are (since creating your own memorable characters, not aping someone else's, is a key part of a writer's job).

Once you start publishing, you may be offered the chance to write a media tie-in; don't do that, either. Your job is to establish *your* name; you are branding yourself in a competitive marketplace, and you do that by telling unique, original stories about characters and events you've devised while exploring issues that you are passionate about. Many experienced writers of media tie-ins do so under pseudonyms—precisely because they don't want the association with hack work to taint their own original writing. And, for Pete's sake, don't even think about *starting* your career with a media tie-in; they are *not* entry-level work in this field; rather, they are dead ends. No, to launch your career, write your own wholly original first novel. But be aware that...

4. First Novels Are Hard to Sell

So don't make it any harder. The number one reason first novels are rejected is that they're poorly written; you, of course, don't have that problem!

The number two reason first novels are rejected—that is, the reason the vast majority of well-crafted, polished, tightly written novels are not bought by publishers—is that they aren't easily categorizable. Almost no one who is involved in the selling of your novel will ever actually read it. All they will know is what the editor says about it at the publisher's sales conference in perhaps sixty seconds, plus maybe 150 words of copy in the publisher's catalog.

What the sales force wants to hear about a first novel from the editor is, "This is a Heinlein-esque military-SF novel that will appeal to fans of David Weber and David Feintuch" or "This is contemporary urban fantasy, in the mold of Charles de Lint." Save your cross-genre impossible-to-categorize novel for later in your career, for the time when all the sales force needs to hear is, "This is the new novel by *you*."

In my own case, my first novel, *Golden Fleece*—which grew from a shorter work submitted to Writers of the Future in 1986—was a hard-SF novel about a murdering computer aboard a starship. It clearly echoed Arthur C. Clarke's *2001: A Space Odyssey*—and that's how the editor presented it. Of course, as with almost all first novels, I had to write the whole thing before I could sell it.

But for my twelfth novel, *Calculating God*, which I sold with just a conversation on the phone, I said I wanted to write a novel in which two people sit in a room and debate evolution vs. creationism without ever getting really angry in the process. I never could have sold that book as my first novel—but it was easy later in my career (and it hit number one on the *Locus* bestsellers list, and was a Hugo finalist), because by that point all that mattered was that it was a new book by an established name. That said...

5. With Your First Book, Knock Their Socks Off

Many people read a bad book then say, "Heck, I can write that well!" and then set out to try to do so—and they succeed, producing a bad book of their own. Set your sights high. For my own first novel, I wanted to do something that I'd never seen done well before: a book from the point of view of an intelligent computer (and I guess I pulled it off, because in his review of my book for *The Magazine of Fantasy & Science Fiction*, Orson Scott Card said I'd created "the deepest computer character in all of science fiction"). It's important to have ambition: you should be aspiring to greatness, not mediocrity, and your best inspiration is the top works in the field. Because the truth is...

6. If You Want to Write It, You've Got to Read It

When I meet someone at a convention who tells me they're trying to break into science-fiction writing, I ask a seemingly unrelated question: "Have you read anything by me?" It seems self-absorbed, perhaps, but it's actually a useful little test. See, I've been lucky enough to win the field's two top awards—the Hugo and the Nebula, both for best novel of the year. If you want to sell in this market, you need to know what the market considers to be the best work. When people say no, they haven't read any Sawyer, I smile politely and walk away—because they can't really be serious about breaking in. After all, if they were, they'd be reading not just the Hugo and Nebula winners, but also the nominees each year; doing so is a key part of knowing the marketplace. Which brings us to…

7. Your Best Market Guide is a Bookstore

Sure, there are lots of web sites with writing advice (including my own at sfwriter.com), but to sell in this field, you have to know the market inside and out—and the best place to learn about that is in a bookstore.

Trivia question: what do the writers Cory Doctorow (Tor), Nalo Hopkinson (Warner), Tanya Huff (DAW), Robert J. Sawyer (Tor), and Michelle West (DAW) all have in common? Answer: we all used to work at Toronto's Bakka-Phoenix, the world's oldest SF specialty bookstore, and Michelle *still* works there, even though she hardly needs the booksellers' wages—because being in a bookstore keeps her finger on the pulse of what's happening in the SF&F marketplace.

Forget about online market listings. Rather, you should spend hours looking at actual books, studying what sort of work each publisher puts out. A wannabe author should be able to name not just their five favorite contemporary SF&F authors (and if the best list you can come up with is Asimov, Clarke and Tolkien, you're not reading enough new stuff), but also instantly be able to name who each of their publishers are—and understand *why* they were published by that house and not another.

There is a world of difference between a Baen military-SF novel by John Ringo, a Del Rey contemporary-SF thriller by Greg Bear, and a Tor literate fantasy by Gene Wolfe. If you send your manuscript to the wrong editor, you're wasting not just the editor's time, but your own—and with editors taking a year or more to respond to an unsolicited submission, it behooves you to do your homework. Because...

8. Ultimately, It's All Up to You

Editors do care, and agents can help. But, in the end, it's only you who really has a large, vested interest in whether or not you succeed. Some established authors think it's their job to discourage newcomers, because the faint-of-heart might not do well in a rough, competitive marketplace.

Ultimately, I think that's short-sighted. Yes, the marketplace *is* harsh and uncaring, but what a loss it would be to our culture if the only books published were by hardened, thick-skinned, tough-as-nails types. There's a place on bookstore shelves for the shy and the delicate, too.

So, take what advice encourages you, smile politely and ignore advice that discourages you, and, most of all, don't give up. More than talent, more than luck, more than anything else, this is a game of perseverance—and the only sure way to lose is not to play.

LIFE ON THE VOODOO DRIVING RANGE

Written by
Brandon Sigrist

Illustrated by
Katherine Hallberg

About the Author

Winning writer Brandon Sigrist grew up in Minnesota reading the likes of Burroughs, Tolkien, Heinlein and Niven, among many. When he enrolled in a creative writing class in college during the early 1980s, he decided to try crafting such stories himself. It wasn't long before Brandon thought that his science fiction work deserved publication. Publishers, however, didn't agree, but fortunately the writing bug stuck.

Professionally, Brandon sought another type of craft, earning a masters degree in architecture, which he has practiced for two decades. Other adventures have seen him hitchhike from coast to coast, climb Devil's Tower in Wyoming and hike the Inca Trail to Peru's Machu Picchu. He's even been kicked off a freight train in world-renowned Havre, Montana. These days he travels with his wife whenever he can get away from the perpetual job of restoring their 100-year-old house. For the past three years, Brandon also has been writing and submitting for publication, still loving the genres of the fantastic.

About the Illustrator

Winning illustrator Katherine Hallberg takes great pride in being a self-taught artist. She is currently attending university studying fine arts, anthropology and German language and culture. As a student, Katherine now explores folklore, mythology and human behavior in general.

It was Katherine's love of storytelling and narrative that first got her interested in illustration. Katherine credits ancient Norse and Native American stories as well as more modern tales by authors like Lackey and Bradbury for spurring her imagination. While her peers influence her artwork most directly, she has also studied art from all time periods. Early Christian, Renaissance and Early Modern are particular favorites. She says she spends a "ridiculously" great deal of time drawing when she's not doing loads of homework or working at the local library. Then again, she is just now making headway into the world of dolls, portraying her own original fantasy creations in the 3-D physical world.

My name is Andy Griswold. I live down by the Mississippi in my van. It's a big Chevy from the turn of the century, boxy and sun-faded blue. There are plenty of extra tires strapped on the body. I don't drive much, what with the oil crisis and all, unless the city has tow trucks out prospecting for steel.

It rained again last night, so hard the van about washed down the bank and floated me home to Louisiana. The sky was clear in the morning, the riverbank a mess of fallen branches and melting hailstones. I went out scrounging at first light. Old Ben Trippen was up and at it too, poking around the grass on the far side of the Broadway Bridge.

"Morning, Ben," I said, after I'd crossed over. His grocery cart was half-full of crushed cans and torn up metal siding. The cart was bouncing around pretty hard between all the gravel on the street and the spastic way Ben has about him.

"Screw you, retard."

"Nice enough day for it," I said cheerfully. "Got some cans myself." I took out the plastic bag of cans I'd been holding behind my back and gave it a shake.

"Lousy thief!" he said, his voice rising. "Them's my cans. Mine!"

That's old Ben for you. He walks around like he's fighting off a hive of bees, and doesn't have a single

nice word to say. My friend Latisha thinks it's some
kinda brain damage that makes him talk so foul, but
I can't find much sympathy for him anymore. Ben
called Latisha a reefer whore to my face once, so I
don't feel too bad about picking cans.

I walked away, spinning the little bag in my hand.
Ben followed after, cursing and twitching. He'd catch
me if he left his cart behind, but that wasn't too likely.
He sleeps with one arm around the wheels of the
thing. A guy like that better hang on to every bit of
civilization he can. Otherwise he'll be carrying cans
around in his mouth, like an animal.

Across the river valley, the downtown skyline and
the warehouse buildings were lit up orange from the
fat morning sun. I squinted, and saw a black sedan
pull up real slow behind my van. A big guy, dark as
molasses, got out and put on a tall hat. He started
walking around my van, and that got me upset. I had
to stop and count tires in my mind. Let's see…I got
five on the roof—no, six with that Uniroyal from Basset
Creek—three on the driver side, four on the passenger
side.…

It happens sometimes. People like me collect things,
and get stuck on counting them or putting them in
straight lines. One guy I heard about had to save
garbage, no matter how bad it smelled. With me, it's
tires. I could be worse off.

When I was finally able to stop, Ben had caught
up and was still cursing me out.

"Stinking turd with legs!"

That's one thing you got to give Ben. As long as
I've known him, he hasn't used the same insult twice.

He was standing a couple of paces away, tying my
bag of cans onto the side of his cart.

"Go count your moron fingers somewhere else!"
Ben said, shaking a fist at me.

I thought about taking his cart away from him
then, but it's wrong to steal from people who are nuts.

• • •

The tall man was still messing around my van. I
ran back over the bridge as fast as I could, my lungs
pounding. A man without spares is wide open to life's
cruel arrows—just one flat away from going nowhere.

I had to stop and lean on my knees for a minute
when I got back on my side of the river, and just
then the big sedan rolled by, quiet as a ghost. I had a
glimpse of his big hands on the wheel and something
that seemed to crawl out of his sleeve and onto the
dash. Maybe it was just a sunbeam, but it sure looked
like a little mouse, bright green and glowing like a
firefly.

I hurried back to the van, and looked it over. Didn't
find anything wrong, except a funny sweet smell, like
cheap candles.

• • •

When it gets close to lunchtime I meet up with
Latisha at the Voodoo Driving Range. She's my partner,
leastways most of the time, when she ain't off getting
high with that guy of hers.

Latisha and I figured out the driving range this
spring. It was mostly her doing, but I helped. I was
cooling my hands in the mud at the river's edge after
work, watching this old guy practice his woods. I felt
something smooth and round and pulled a golf ball

out of the muck. I found a few more, and went to see if the old guy wanted them. They were pretty sliced up, but he still gave me a dollar.

A few days later, I brought up some balls for a lady who was sitting on the bench watching her husband drive hooks into the water. This young tramp walked up and asked the lady if she wanted a painting of her husband on one of the balls for a souvenir. That was the day Latisha and I met. She wasn't much to look at, kinda skinny and unwashed, but she had charm, and anybody who took the time could see it.

Latisha drew a funny head on the ball, with big ears and little nose, comb-over and razor stubble, just like the husband looked, only more so. The lady smiled and gave her two dollars for it. Then the lady got up and took the club away from her husband, teed up, and hit the little round head in a nice straight arc to the far side of the river.

"That felt good," she said, and sat back down on the bench.

Word got around, and people started to come down with photos of their boss, or ex-boyfriend, the president or whoever, and Latisha would draw a sketch for them, and do some incantations. Latisha calls herself Maman Ti when she's working. She charges two dollars a ball if they bring their own, three dollars if they don't. The people belt little voodoo balls of their fears and cravings, and I wade around and bring the balls back, washed clean by the mighty Mississip.

•••

I walked over to the Quik Pump store, hoping they would have something on the shelves, and got a triangle sandwich and a jar of olives. A Shadow Tramp family I knew was waiting in the gas line when I came out. They park their black Suburban about half a block up from me. Living in a Motel 8, we call it, because of the number of cylinders. The father waved me over.

"Hey, Griz, you seen a guy with a top hat and a big black Lexus around?"

"May have."

"Well, you want to keep away from him. The jerk sprayed us with some kind of crappy perfume last night. Didn't say a damn thing. Now the kids got a rash."

"Nothing bad, I hope?"

"I don't know." He shrugged, managing to look worried and pissed at the same time. "Hope not. You see that creep you let me know. I'm about ready to knock his head off."

"Sure," I said, "I'll keep a lookout."

I felt sorry for the guy. That car of his can't get more than a hundred miles on a good day's pay, so most of their money goes into the tank. He spends his free time looking around for a second job, but he ain't found none yet. I hear the kids crying at night 'cause they're hungry. His wife has started putting her hand out beside the freeway. You can tell every dime she gets puts another hole in his pride. I'll be surprised if they make it to winter.

•••

I went back to the river and found Latisha sitting in the tall grass on the bluff. It was a fine day, with them high faint clouds my foster mother used to call angel's breath, and a warm breeze from the coal plant blowing out of the south. There was a gull hunting for scraps of bread in the trash floating along the bank.

"The marks are going to be out today," Ti said, standing up and stretching out her back. I had a hard time keeping my eyes away from the way her bosom pushed out. She caught me looking and gave a little wink.

"You best stay focused today, Griz. No counting tires."

"I'll be okay. I just get concerned, you know, and…"

"You got plenty of tires, Griz. You hear me? You got no worries on that account."

Latisha is still a young woman, the sun and wind haven't beat the looks out of her yet, although her piece-of-dirt boyfriend is doing his share. That morning her eye was starting to purple up, but her skin was so dark from the sun and the road dirt that it was hard to see the bruise.

"Ray's been at you again, ain't he?"

"It's nothing, Griz."

"Just say the word, Ti," I said to her, "I'll let him know what it feels like."

"Ain't his fault," she said, "I was pushin' him again, like the fool I am."

The two of them are from around here, kids that never made it from the start. She sleeps with him under the railroad bridge most nights.

We spent the afternoon at the driving range and made some pretty good pay. I spent my money on a good dinner and a nice steel-belted Michelin.

•••

Larry Parsons explained to me once how gas got

scarce a few years back because of the Oil Peak. That's when people want gas faster than them oil guys can find it. Now we got to burn coal to make up the difference, even though we ain't gonna run out of gas for years. Larry says coal don't burn clean, which is why the weather is so bad.

Larry used to bed down around here until he got the bug to ride the freights to Idaho. Said he wanted to get out there while the diesel was still flowing. Larry was a history professor before he sorta unraveled, but he still knew a lot. There's a rumor going around that he ended up dead in a boxcar in Minot. Somebody stuck a shiv in him for his tennis shoes. I hope it's not true. He did have some nice shoes though.

● ● ●

Over the next couple of weeks we kept hearing stories about the tall man in the black car. Everybody calls him Shiny Lex now. He looks high class, like somebody that runs their own business, or maybe even owns a house. He's got a different suit for every day of the week and a gold watch. You would think he was a Shadow Tramp, like Alicia, who works in a high-rise downtown, dresses neat as a pin, and puts all the money she makes into her kid's college fund. She's smart about it; rolls in quiet after dark in her gray Mazda, never parks in the same place twice. A pretty woman with a young daughter can't be too careful.

But Lex doesn't work, as far as anyone can tell. He spends all his time washing his car, and spraying any of us tramps who come near him. He never leaves the area, or says a word of sense to anybody.

I didn't think he was going to last at first. A flashy

car, and getting on everybody's nerves with them
spray bottles of his. He tried to get me one day, but
I ducked fast and I think he missed. Plenty of folks
around here know how to boost a car and turn some
nice change. I was eyeing his tires myself. But, Lex
has an edge going for him, what with the silent act,
and the mice that live in his car. At night, they flicker
around the inside of the Lexus, each one glowing like
a light bulb. Things like that will set a person back
and make 'em think.

•••

One night in early August, I woke up to the sound
of Latisha crying. She was outside the van, a trickle of
blood drying at the corner of her mouth. It was misting
out, but there were rumbles of more weather in the
distance. I got Ti inside, and saw that Ray had knocked
out one of her teeth. It is some kind of sacrilege to
put a hole in that beautiful smile. I found her a couple
aspirin and got her set up to sleep in the van. My tarp
and bedroll made a decent shelter under a fallen locust
tree down by the water.

After I figured she was asleep I went looking for
Ray. The wind picked up and it had started to rain
by the time I found the bastard under the Plymouth
Avenue Bridge, sitting around a small fire with a
couple of his dope-head pals. I walked into the light
and told him to hit the road come morning, get down
south, and leave Latisha here.

He started dancing around me about ten feet out,
waving this dinky knife and talking a bunch of crap. I
was on top of him before he got done lookin' surprised,
and introduced my foot to his ass a few times. Most
guys who decide they gotta mix it up with me figure

I'm slow, because of the way I talk, and because I'm about as wide as I am tall. Truth is, there ain't nobody within thirty yards I can't put my hands on, and make 'em regret it. They don't call me Griz for nothing.

I didn't mess him up too bad. I been in that kind of trouble before, and who needs it. Besides, I wanted him to be able make tracks.

•••

It was coming down buckets by the time I got back. The storm lasted two days straight. My tarp sprung a leak long about noon the first day. At least it didn't hail much.

Latisha stayed a couple of days. I tried to get her to move in permanent, so maybe I could clean her up some. If I stayed down under the locust trees for a week or two, then maybe she would let me move in all proper. I figured, what's Ray got that I ain't? He doesn't even have no wheels like me. But she took off anyway.

I guess she saw him later on, and the sight of his swoled-up mug was pitiful enough to let her forgive him. Lord, does that woman have an excess of sympathy. That and the meth or whatever it is he uses to keep her on his hooks.

I still see the scum around, though you can bet he keeps his distance. I haven't killed him yet. I guess that would make Latisha unhappy. He don't hit her no more, that I know of, and I keep that knife of his in my hip pocket. I use it to clean under my fingernails when they get dirty. It works good enough for that.

•••

By the end of August, the heat and the Oil Peak really started to kick in. Lots of new faces around the hobo hearth at night, lots of familiar faces gone and hardly two words about where they went. I guess we ain't the kind of folks people miss.

A tramp name of Torelli showed up, a real drinker, not too smart, drunk or sober. He had a mean streak about him and started hassling Shiny Lex right off, just for the fun of it. Nothing major at first, just some pranks like throwing mud on his windshield. Then he tried to start Lex's tires on fire. Lex put it out with a big can of river water, calm as could be. Then he opened his coat and the inside was all pockets, like a Rolex salesman. He picked out this little bottle, real careful, and Torelli just stood there while Lex sprayed him up one side and down the other.

Torelli turned up green a couple of nights later, just like the mice. He didn't last long after that. It's hard to hide from the cops when you glow in the dark. They picked him up for vagrancy and nobody has seen him since, though some claim that he's locked up in a lab down at the Mayo clinic, getting poked and studied up good. Everybody keeps well clear of Shiny Lex now.

•••

A week to the day after Latisha went back to Ray, I got back from the driving range and found the van broken into, the driver's window smashed. The inside was a mess.

I cleaned it up as best I could. There was a sheet of plastic stuck in a tree down the bank, and I still had enough duct tape to cover the broken window. Nothing they stole was worth much, to anybody else, that is. They just took personal stuff like my toothbrush and my one towel. Now I had to air dry. I figured Ray for the break-in, and made up my mind to send him off for good, Latisha or no.

I worried about her all the same. I even made up a couple of voodoo balls for her, but I don't know if they worked. I drew a monkey with a crack through him on one, and a monkey jumping up and down on a heart on the other. They were supposed to be her crack monkey and her Ray monkey. I hit them into the water with a board at midnight. I wish I could get Ti to do it herself, because she's the one who really knows how to say the words and all. I probably just gave a real monkey somewhere a heart attack.

•••

The next morning I went down to the river and washed up as best I could. A man that don't keep himself clean is on a downward slide, and that's a fact. The sun was out again, and the day was shaping up to be a real keeper, clear and cool. It was so nice, it was hard to stay bent up about the van and all. There was even a sparrow singing somewhere off to the south.

Dripping and whistling I headed off to get an early start scrounging balls. It was a half-mile walk, and I ambled along, enjoying the deep slanted sunlight. As I came up to the last bend before the driving range, I heard splashing and a familiar voice. I slowed down and crept up behind the rushes. Sure enough, there was Ray and his cronies, fishing around in the water and dropping our golf balls into plastic bags. I had to stop a low growl in the back of my throat. There was a stand of sumac right down to the water between us, and I used it to get as close as I could without being seen.

The edge of the sumac was a good sixty yards away from them. I worked my way uphill a bit, getting up to the last skinny trunk, slow and quiet, and then charged from above, using the down slope for extra speed. I almost got my hands on one of them, but my foot slipped in the mud right at the river's edge, and all I got was the skin of his heel under my fingernails. That and one of them spilled half their bag of balls. I grabbed an orange Arnie Palmer and pelted him in the back as he crested the hill.

I fished around the river and came up with a few more balls, then hid out in the sumac grove. To pass the time until the marks came out at lunch, I pictured each of the balls getting stuffed down Ray's throat until he had a belly like ten pounds of potatoes in a five-pound sack.

When Latisha came around, she was carrying two heavy bags. Even a dummy like me could figure where she got them. I went up to her, feeling stupid with my dirty teeth and little bag of balls. She had on big hoop earrings and some colorful cloth wrapped around her head.

"Hi, Ti," I said.

"Hi there, Griz." She wouldn't quite look me in the eye. "I...got all the swamp balls I need today."

I couldn't even say a thing. I just stood there thinking about how I was only one flat away from going nowhere, then I started counting tires. There were five, six, seven on the roof, what with the Michelin and the Uniroyal. Four on the back door. No, the right front had picked up a nail in the shoulder a few days back, and there was no fixing it. I had used one of them from the back to replace it. So, that's just three on the back...

By the time I came out of it, the lunch crowd had

started to show up with their troubles, and Latisha had moved away from her usual spot, to get away from me. I could tell by the way nobody looked that I was making them nervous. I stood there anyway, just 'cause this was my place. I had been here first, and to hell with them. But, what was the point? Without her scarves and spells and smoky eyes, it was just me fishing balls out of the water. No voodoo magic without Maman Ti.

• • •

I ran into the guy in the Suburban Motel 8 as I was dragging my sorry ass back to the van. He looked different than I remembered, kept cocking his head at me funny. Maybe it was because I was having trouble with my eyes watering. I didn't remember that oversized nose either. It looked sharp as a tack, same as his wife and kids.

When I got back to the river, the city was towing my van.

• • •

The law says you can't park for longer than a week on city streets. They didn't use to enforce it so much. As long as you had enough gas to move when they painted your tires, you were okay. That was before the steel got scarce.

The van was halfway up the tow truck ramp. The operator had one hand on the butt of a shotgun the whole time, while the driver stayed in the cab with the radio on. They never come down here by themselves. I tried telling the operator a funny story, to soften him up, but of course they took it away. They never let them back down once they're on the ramp. I got a tire off the side as they were pulling away, a snow tire with some good tread left in the middle.

A beat-up little station wagon pulled into my spot, and the cars parked around were unfamiliar. It was like being lost, like the world had shifted under my feet. Everything was different except the river. I wasn't going nowhere anymore; I was right there. Five, six, seven, the Michelin, the Uniroyal, all gone. The three on the back, gone. The four on the passenger side, nowhere. Oh, Lord, could that be right? Let's see…six, seven, eight…

It was dark by the time I was able to stop, my legs were tired from standing so long, and the shiny black Lexus was idling in the street next to me. The window rolled down with a smooth hum.

"Hey, Mr. Griz," Lex said in a rich baritone, "why don't you get in and sit a spell?" He had big smile full of gold fillings.

"I didn't know you could talk."

"Of course I can talk, Mr. Griz, when I'm of a mind to. Now get yourself in."

"Say," I said, stalling for time, "we've never been introduced proper. My name's Andy." I did not want to get in that car.

"Call me Papa Obeah."

I felt a chill blow up the back of my neck. "I know that name. Ti says it in her chants."

"Yes."

One of them mice came out of the back and walked up his arm to the top of the steering wheel, bright as a Christmas tree bulb. I had a strong urge to turn tail and get out of there, but I was afraid to turn my back.

"That's kinda unusual, I mean the mice and all."

"Jellyfish glow, spliced into their genes."

Illustrated by Katherine Hallberg

"What did you do that for?"

"I did not. I took them in. They, like you, will be returned to the Great Mother in their time."

"What's that supposed to mean?"

"It means that Technology Man has had his day, rising high on liquid black magic. Nothing left now but dirty coal magic, storm magic." He lifted up the lapel of his long coat with one big hand and slid the other inside.

"Soon, there will be room for the quiet folk again, the wild ones who came before. That's where you come in, Mr. Andy Griz. Now get over here a bit closer. One more whiff should do the trick."

He lifted up a spray bottle then, brushed metal with a black cap. I tried to run, but the mist settled around me and things got confused. I heard Papa Obeah saying something as I stumbled around.

"A lot of weather coming, Griz. Time to start counting fishes now, you can forget about tires."

Then I passed out.

● ● ●

I woke up at dawn, down under the locust trees, and the whole world smelled. It wasn't bad exactly, just stronger, more distinct, like my nose had gotten ten times bigger. My eyes were a mess though. Everything was a blur. I could see close up, but I must have had some kind of double double vision, cause there was four times too much hair on my arm.

I was thirsty, and went down to the water. My knees weren't working right, so I had to go on all fours. I scooped a small carp out of the water with one hand. It was easy to do, cause my fingernails had grown long and sharp as claws. I started looking around for something to start a fire, but the smell got to me first. I ate the whole thing raw. It tasted better than you would think.

I caught scent of Ray and Latisha a few mornings later, sheltered under one of the…I can't remember…one of the dry sky rocks above the river. Ray woke up at first light. He couldn't seem to find air, and flopped around on the bluff until he slipped from his bag on a trail of sweet-smelling slime. It seemed like his arms were stuck to his sides, and he couldn't get his legs apart. Latisha screamed at the sight of him, but I thought he looked pretty good. Made my belly growl anyway. Ray flipped and twisted his way down the bank and into the big water. He looked a lot more comfortable there, and swam off with a quick swirl of his palms. See you sometime, Ray.

Latisha still lives under the dry sky rock with some other people. They spend a lot of time making smoke out of sticks. I think she is going to be all right. I went to see her once, but they all cowered away at the sight of me, and I stepped on their smoking ground and hurt my paws. I stay away from people now. There is a scent of lady in the north, musky and strong. When the scent tells me, I'll go and say hello.

•••

My name is Griz. I live in a den by the fast water. There is sumac and buckthorn all around. One cold day, old Ben came along. I couldn't see him, but I recognized the smell, and the sound of his cart full of cans. He was mumbling to himself, and having a bee-chasing fit. A minute later, I heard the smooth hum of a machine pulling to a stop. All of a sudden I could smell Papa Obeah.

"Mr. Trippen," he said.

"Go suck a duck." The old man sounded angry, but scared too.

"Time to give up the shopping cart, Old Mister Ben," said Papa Obeah. There was the rattle of a metal ball in a can full of liquid.

"Keep your hoodoo crap. I'd rather be dead."

"So be it," said Papa Obeah.

The car door shut, and the Lexus drove off. Old Ben just kept saying, "Go suck a duck," over and over, until he started coughing. Pretty soon he was gasping and choking something pitiful. A clatter of cans came down the hill, followed by something heavy.

I poked my nose out of the sumac. The Ben smell was down by the water now. I followed the scent and found him face down. I got my head under his side and turned him over, but his eyes were staring and filled with mud.

It rained hard the next day, and the spot where he ended up had some logs and trash washed up, so nobody found him, until the Suburban guy brought his family down. They were all looking quite feathery now, and very sharp-beaked. The kids let out a few rasping caws and pecked out Ben's eyes. I guess they'll make it after all.

AT THE GATE
OF GOD

Written by
Joseph Jordan

Illustrated by
Eldar Zakirov

About the Author

If at first you don't succeed, try, try again are
bywords that Joseph Jordan follows. He began
writing science fiction stories at fifteen and sent them off to
the big speculative fiction magazines of the day, racking
up a mountain of rejection slips, including a stack of
handwritten critique rejections from the editor of the
early Asimov magazine. By twenty-two, Jordan had
moved from Lititz, Pennsylvania, to Baltimore, Maryland.
He joined the U.S. Navy, married a woman from Naples,
Italy, and had two children (now twenty-two and
nineteen). It was in 1990 that Joseph first heard of the
Contest. He dutifully submitted a short story but later
received yet another handwritten rejection from then
Contest editor Algis Budrys. It would be Joseph's last
short story for fourteen years. The family moved to Italy
two years later. When Joseph went to work in Bosnia-
Herzegovina for a U.S. defense contractor maintaining
U.S. Army helicopters, his family remained in Italy. Joseph
decided to occupy his down time by writing again. His
persistence has paid off with this winning entry.

About the Illustrator

Winning illustrator Eldar Zakirov has been on a flight of fantasy since he first discovered science fiction art as a teen in Uzbekistan. At sixteen, Eldar felt electrified after seeing a collection of American and British science fiction and fantasy drawings. Suddenly, drawing, painting and art history each combined into a new passion for speculative fiction illustration. Eldar credits the rich history of art as his teachers—from Renaissance, eighteenth and nineteenth century surrealists to contemporary fantasy illustrations of today. As a result, he uses many techniques and materials in his painting—oils, acrylic, watercolor, pen and ink, and computer graphics. Most recently, Eldar added airbrush to his arsenal.

An avid reader of science fiction books, Eldar began studying the history of science fiction illustration at the Institute of Architecture and Construction in Tashkent and focused on its influence in twentieth-century book design. Now when he creates an illustration or views work by other speculative fiction artists, Eldar says he's like a traveler moving through past, present and future. Such works are not simply illustrations to him, but windows to other realities altogether.

> *And the Lord said, Behold, the people is one, and they have all one language; and this they begin to do: and now nothing will be restrained from them, which they have imagined to do.*
>
> *Genesis 11:6*

Beneath his clericals, Father Jose Sanchez wore a gold chain adorned with a gold pendant in the shape of $10^\wedge-43$. Few people knew what this number represented. Father Sanchez's mother had been one of them. She had given her son the chain and pendant as a gift when he completed his candidate year at the Moreau Seminary, years before his ordination as a Roman Catholic priest.

"I'm so proud of you," Jose's mother had said to him after the ceremony. With the Sacred Heart Basilica and Notre Dame's Main Building filling most of the Indiana sky in the background, she leaned up and gave Jose a big kiss. She didn't even try to hide her tears. "I just wish your father were still alive to see this."

But Jose's father had passed away over twenty years earlier, when Jose was only three years old. He could never forget his father's friendly face—not with the dozen or so photographs cluttering Jose's childhood home in South Bend—but he could not recall any of the moments he had spent with the man.

Soon after her husband's death, Jose's mother used the life insurance money to pack up her household and move to Indiana, abandoning the gangs and the crime and the discrimination of Chicago's Humboldt Park community. Stripped of his paternal influence and the Hispanic culture of his birthplace, Jose clung to his mother as he grew and matured, making her the center of his world.

Because his mother was a devout Catholic, so was Jose. As a child, he accompanied her to Mass every Sunday and on most Holy Days of Obligation. Later, he became an altar boy. But not until he took elementary cosmology in his second year of college did his faith strengthen, when he realized the significance of 10^{-43} seconds. Only then did he hear God's calling.

And now, at forty-eight years of age, his mother a year in the grave, Father Jose Sanchez no longer heard God calling him. Science no longer instilled in him the sense of faith it once had, even as he embarked on a pilgrimage to the newest shrine of physics, the most powerful ion accelerator/collider ever built.

Father Sanchez did not feel any of the excitement that he knew swelled within the hundreds of other physicists who would attend the three-month residency at the Brookhaven Energy Laboratory's new accelerator, even now powered up in preparation for its inaugural run a week from now. Father Sanchez had not wanted to go, but he was a celebrity in the scientific community, an astrophysicist credited with the famous theory of quantum gravity—even though he had played only a minor role—and his invitation to the residency had come personally from the BEL chairman himself.

"We'll be achieving energy levels up to 10^{24} electron volts!" the chairman had crowed, his holographic image looming high over Father Sanchez in the Notre Dame teleconference room. This man was the one most responsible for the success of commercial nuclear fusion, a man so powerful and influential that he had created his own national laboratory, the BEL, from the Energy Science and Technology Department of the Brookhaven National Laboratory.

"We should be able to observe the grand unified theory symmetry at the BEL Accelerator."

"Impressive." Father Sanchez already knew about Dr. Nimrod's claims for his new facility. The priest had been following the BA's progress for years with considerable concern. "Let me discuss the matter with my superiors. I had been planning to take a sabbatical from the university to do missionary work."

Dr. Nimrod frowned. "This turn of events is unfortunate. The pope assured me that you would be available."

The pope! Father Sanchez had forgotten that the chairman was Catholic.

After the teleconference, Father Sanchez went to Father Oliver Johnson and requested a transfer. Father Sanchez had last sought counsel with his immediate superior in the weeks following his mother's death, when he began losing his faith.

Just as he had during their first session together, Father Johnson listened, and he understood, but he was firm. In the rectory of the Basilica of the Sacred Heart, Father Johnson placed his hands on Father Sanchez's shoulders and denied the request. "I believe it is God's will that you attend the BA residency."

And so, Father Sanchez made the journey to New York, caressing the gold pendant beneath his clergy shirt the whole time. As his flight from Chicago descended to JFK International Airport, he could see the sprawling metropolis of New York City, while his ultimate destination, Long Island, lay hidden to the east by the early morning haze. When his plane finally landed, Father Sanchez found the airport thick with travelers. It took him a long time to recover his luggage, a surprising amount for a priest on a three-month trip. A porter helped him with the load and accompanied Father Sanchez to the airport's basement where the Long Island MagLev Train System awaited to carry the priest to Babylon Township.

The train station platform was also packed. Father Sanchez scanned the crowd, wondering how many of these people would be attending the BEL residency as well. Then he noticed a group of three men who appeared to be of Middle Eastern origin. Two of the men wore business suits, while the third man sported a black tunic under a dark gray jacket, a red and white checkered ghutra covering his head. One of the men watched intently as Father Sanchez descended the escalator. The man tugged at the sleeves of his companions and gestured for them to look up. All three of them stared at Father Sanchez. The first man continued pointing. Although too far away to be heard, he seemed to be talking excitedly as he pointed. The man beneath the ghutra nodded calmly.

Father Sanchez had no time to ponder the incident, for at that moment the MagLev train arrived, its massive body hovering above the rail beams until its wheels descended to the pathways and the train came to a halt. The awaiting passengers rushed forward, blocking his view of the three men. The porter politely but firmly urged Father Sanchez to board his assigned train car. In the confusion, the priest did not even notice if the Middle Eastern group had boarded the MagLev train or not.

•••

On the day she left Chicago behind, Jose's mother stopped speaking Spanish in her son's presence. What little he had picked up as a young child soon faded along with the memory of his father. English became his natural language, and later, in the Catholic schools he attended while his mother slaved away at multiple jobs to keep up with tuition payments, Latin became his second language.

More to make his mother proud than any other motive, Jose did well in school. He kept out of trouble and he kept his grades up, even as he tackled difficult subjects in high school such as calculus and physics. Between his grade-point average and test scores, Jose was assured a scholarship and a post at any university in the state of Indiana. Of course, there had never been any doubt that he would attend the University of Notre Dame.

After graduating with a degree in physics, Jose made the big decision to attend the Moreau Seminary. When he told his mother, he feared she would be upset at the prospect of never having grandchildren.

"Don't you worry about that none," she had admonished. "I have plenty of nieces and nephews back in Chicago, and they're starting to have children themselves."

She gave Jose that smile that always filled him with joy. "You go and carry out God's will."

For Jose, God's will resulted in an unusual career for a priest. After his ordination into the Congregation of Holy Cross, Father Sanchez was surprised to find how willing the Congregation was to let him return to his alma mater to teach and to pursue a doctorate in astrophysics. Afterward, he was offered an assistant professorship. Five years later, he became a fully tenured professor within the Center for Astrophysics.

And now, Professor Sanchez would represent the University of Notre Dame at Dr. Nimrod's residency to research the results from the BEL's very expensive and very powerful toy, the BA.

$10^24 \, eV!$

It had been decades since anyone claimed the ability to attain significantly higher energy levels from a particle accelerator/collider. During Jose's early days of college, the large colliders had fallen out of favor, replaced by the less expensive compact linear colliders. These lab-sized systems could attain the same energy levels and better luminosities than their multibillion-dollar, multikilometer-sized counterparts. The compact collider experiments proved so accurate that physicists were able to make badly needed revisions to the standard model, the bible for fundamental particles and their interactions.

Funding dried up quickly for the larger facilities. Most of them ceased operation years before originally planned. And now a new accelerator had been built that would supposedly surpass the most powerful of those old dinosaurs by a magnitude of twelve! Father Sanchez feared what scientists might find with such power at their disposal.

•••

Over the past decade, Long Island had become Dr. Nimrod's domain. Back when he was merely the head of the Nuclear Energy and Infrastructure Systems Division at the Brookhaven National Laboratory, his group had taken advantage of advances in nanotechnology that enabled the assembly of new materials with properties not previously possible. They developed a plasma chamber with a novel shape and wrapped it with a blanket capable of absorbing the energetic neutron radiation created by the deuterium-deuterium fuel cycle. Soon afterward they performed the first successful test of sustainable nuclear fusion with a Q factor greater than twenty. Dr. Nimrod's group proved that nuclear fusion could be an economically viable energy source.

After that, things progressed rapidly on Long Island. Dr. Nimrod rose through the ranks of the BNL until the Brookhaven Energy Laboratory was created. To accommodate the throngs of international travelers who descended on the BEL to participate in the nuclear fusion experiments, and to appease the vocal anger of residents who complained about the saturation of their highways and airways, the state government built the MagLev Train System, a massive infrastructure project with underground vacuum tubes extending from JFK to the opposite tip of Long Island.

One of those trains carried Father Sanchez at close to six hundred kilometers per hour to the MagLev station in East Babylon. Once there, BEL representatives herded him and other delegates onto buses. Father Sanchez once more saw the three Middle Eastern men, but they boarded a different vehicle. The small fleet of buses plodded through the overdeveloped township of Babylon, taking almost an hour to reach the new BEL facility in Farmingdale.

Although the BEL Accelerator was located in Brookhaven, Dr. Nimrod had not been able to find enough land at the BNL site to build a place suitable for the hundreds of visiting scientists he envisioned. Thanks to the MagLev Train System, Long Island was dotted with disused regional airports. Dr. Nimrod snatched up the abandoned Republic Airport and spent hundreds of millions of dollars to build the Babylon Center, one large building that was part control center for the BA, part research laboratory, and part dormitory for resident scientists.

Father Sanchez saw the building from his window long before the bus arrived at the Babylon Center's restricted perimeter.

The ziggurat-shaped structure was tall, towering over all other buildings in the region. Dr. Nimrod had publicly defended his choice for the tall design by pointing out the paucity of real estate in the area, but everyone knew the chairman had eccentric taste and a propensity toward things larger than life.

Later in the day, after the resident scientists claimed their dormitory rooms and took the time to unpack their belongings, they were invited to attend a reception in the lounge on the ground floor of the Babylon Center. It was there that Father Sanchez finally met Dr. Nimrod in person.

• • •

Professor Webster had been one of Jose's more jubilant instructors in college, a man who loved cosmology and who managed to instill enthusiasm into his students despite the mind-boggling math that accompanied the subject.

"Cosmology is a marriage between the macroscopic science of astrophysics and the microscopic world of particle physics, with a healthy dose of theology mixed in to make the whole thing work."

All through the semester they analyzed the big

Illustrated by Eldar Zakirov

bang timeline, working backwards like detectives looking for clues from a crime already committed.

"The matter-dominant universe that surrounds us today did not come about until three hundred thousand years after the big bang." Professor Webster paced the stage as he spoke through a microphone projecting his voice to the hundred or so students in the auditorium. At the front of the large room a video screen almost two stories high displayed the spectacular computer graphics designed to accompany his lectures.

On the screen, solar systems evaporated. Galaxies rushed toward each other, reverting back to their primitive, quasar states. Massive black holes unwound themselves and matter coalesced as the universe reversed itself like an old film threaded backwards through a projector.

"Before then, the primordial universe was made up of plasma. The transition from the plasma era to the matter era caused the release of photons that today we view as the cosmic background radiation."

Once the universe became one big ball of light, Professor Webster's graphics depicted highlights at the microscopic level.

"Even the lightest of elements, hydrogen and helium, did not come into existence until the nucleosynthesis epoch began, about ten seconds after the big bang.

"Hadrons themselves, the very protons and electrons that make up the atoms, did not appear until energy density levels cooled to a reasonable one giga-electron volt, about 10^{-6} seconds after the big bang. Before that, there was only plasma made of quarks and gluons."

The professor smiled widely, his pale face seemingly pink from the reflections of the red-colored quarks in his graphics. "And then things really become interesting. At about 10^{-10} seconds, the electromagnetic and weak nuclear forces went their separate ways."

Lightning flashed, representing the symmetry breakdown. Thunder rolled from the audio system, causing many in the auditorium to jump and others to giggle.

"At approximately 10^{-37} seconds, we believe that the strong force decoupled from the combined electro-weak forces. Even more bizarre, this symmetry breakdown most likely caused the inflation era, a brief instant when the universe expanded from a singularity to a macroscopic-sized dimension that would eventually grow into our current universe."

A student pressed the call button to ask a question. Professor Webster gazed at the callboard to see who it was.

"Yes, Linda?"

"Professor." The young woman had to move closer to her microphone to be heard. "Professor, doesn't the inflation theory imply that the universe expanded faster than the speed of light? Isn't that impossible?"

"Excellent question, Linda." Professor Webster stopped pacing the stage and stood perfectly still, a gesture the class had learned meant he was about to say something very important. "You see, the known laws of physics are bound to matter and energy *inside* our universe. What we are talking about here is the universe *itself*—the entire space-time continuum—expanding. That is why it appears to astronomers that many faraway galaxies are rushing from us at speeds greater than C. Those galaxies are not actually moving that fast: it is the space-time continuum carrying them away as the universe expands."

It was difficult to tell if his response satisfactorily answered Linda's question, or whether indeed anyone in the class understood the professor's explanation. But he pushed on.

"Finally, we arrive at 10^{-43} seconds after the big bang, when gravity itself decouples from the other natural forces in the first symmetry breakdown, a moment we call Planck Time."

When it became clear that the professor would not elaborate beyond this point, Jose pressed his call button.

"Yes, Jose?"

"Professor, what happened before 10^{-43} seconds?"

"That, young man, is where theology comes into the picture." The professor shrugged. "Because only God knows."

• • •

The Babylon Center lounge was filled with enthusiasm and the smell of fresh paint. Father Sanchez sat alone in a corner, avoiding the crowd, sipping from the flute of champagne that someone had thrust into his hand, until a booming voice accosted him.

"You cannot imagine how delighted I am to see you here, Padre!"

Father Sanchez looked up to see Dr. Bartholomew Nimrod approaching. Amazingly, the man appeared even larger and more intimidating in the flesh than he had in the teleconferencing room. As he waded through the sea of people in the lounge, the chairman shouted hellos and shook every hand that sprung toward him as though out of nowhere. When it was finally his turn, Father Sanchez offered his hand and the two men shook.

"As you can see," Dr. Nimrod said, "I am much in demand around here."

"Yes, I see that."

The chairman parked himself next to the priest. The group of smartly dressed assistants who had been following behind suddenly found themselves standing by with nothing to do.

"Now," Dr. Nimrod resumed, "isn't this a lot better than traipsing around the Third World?"

"I wouldn't know," Father Sanchez answered.

"Oh, come now, Padre. You're not still upset with me, are you? It's clear the Holy See wanted you here. I didn't insist. Besides, I'm sure you won't regret it. We expect to find gravitons! It would further vindicate your discoveries in quantum gravity...."

"They were not my discoveries!" Father Sanchez spouted the words too harshly. He apologized immediately. "I do not mean to sound ungrateful. It's just that I've been so embarrassed—I mean, I was merely a participant in the research. It is unfortunate that Dr. Mahajan's accomplishments have been eclipsed by my own notoriety."

The chairman waived his hand impatiently. "Always so modest. Doesn't matter, though. Your presence here is"—he paused to find the right word—"inspiring!"

An anonymous voice called out from somewhere in the lounge. The chairman scanned the crowd, found the source of the call and nodded. Turning back to the priest, he said, "My apologies, but I must go. Why don't you contact my secretary and make an appointment for sometime this week so we can talk in peace?"

"Very well." Father Sanchez attempted to shake the chairman's hand in parting, but the large man was already several meters away, his entourage trying desperately to keep up with him.

"Professor Jose Sanchez?"

Father Sanchez almost didn't hear the soft, heavily accented voice over the din of the lounge. When he turned, he found a man much shorter than himself, dressed in a tunic and ghutra. It was one of the Middle Eastern men Father Sanchez had seen staring at him on the MagLev Train System platform earlier in the day. The man offered a hand in greeting. His grip was as soft as his voice.

"Forgive the intrusion. I am Dr. Awwad Moussa Zihlif, from the University of Jordan." His face held an expression that Father Sanchez could not interpret. "I approach you because I believe we have much in common. In my land I am an imam, a religious leader like you, and an astrophysicist."

"Pleased to meet you," Father Sanchez said. "I did not realize astrophysics was an important discipline in the Muslim world."

"Oh my, yes. Astrophysics, particle physics, cosmology. The pursuit of knowledge is an obligation, and what could be more important than learning the divine origin of Creation itself? We look for *ayat* Allah, signs of God. As it is written in the Koran: '*And He hath subjected to you the night and the day; the sun and the moon and the stars too are subjected to you by His behest; verily, in this are signs for those who understand.*'

"For example, we see your theory of quantum gravity as an important sign."

Father Sanchez sighed internally, although he managed to retain his smile outwardly. "You realize that Dr. Somatra Mahajan was the principal investigator on that project. They were *her* hypotheses we investigated and proved."

Awwad looked around the room. "Yes, but the good doctor is not here this evening." He smiled at Father Sanchez. "Besides, I do not believe she is a religious leader."

Father Sanchez raised his eyebrows in surprise, but before he could say anything further, the imam continued.

"I saw you talking with Dr. Nimrod a few moments ago. Do you know him personally?"

"We've talked in the past, though this is the first time I've met him. He personally invited me to this residency. In fact, he asked me to make an appointment to see him."

"The chairman is Catholic, is he not?"

"Yes."

Awwad smiled. "Good."

Before Father Sanchez could ask why the chairman's religious preference was *good*, Awwad changed the subject.

"How did you come to be involved with Dr. Mahajan's quantum gravity project?"

Father Sanchez downed the rest of his champagne and prepared himself for a long talk. He was asked this question all too infrequently.

•••

Even as Jose Sanchez was beginning to dabble in cosmology and redefining his faith, veteran cosmologists were still wrestling with the problem of dark energy. What was causing the universe to expand at such an incredible rate? NASA and the European Space Agency sent numerous satellites into space to chase down this problem, including the Laser Interferometer Space Antenna and the Inflation Probe.

These two sensors alone sent back to Earth enough data to keep astrophysicists busy for years. Notre Dame was one of many universities with access to these data through the Goddard Space Flight Center. But the resulting research brought only suspect theories and more unanswered questions. About this time, Father Sanchez became an associate professor at the Center for Astrophysics and Notre Dame acquired one of the first-generation ultracomputers from IBM.

And then came Dr. Somatra Mahajan.

She was the consummate absentminded professor. Intelligent, of course: she did complex algebra and calculus in her head. She had brilliant ideas, too, but they spewed forth in such a scatterbrained fashion that her colleagues could not follow them. She was such a disorganized researcher that no one at Notre Dame could figure out how she had managed to put together a winning proposal for a fellowship from the National Science Foundation. But she did. And she decided she needed an ultracomputer for her work. The University of Notre Dame was willing enough to accept the fellowship money and to sponsor her research.

Father Sanchez and a few of his graduate students had been "put at Dr. Mahajan's disposal," but the department chair confided that Father Sanchez's main job was to "ensure she stays out of trouble and doesn't break anything around here."

It took much patience to deal with the woman, to follow her disjointed instructions and to fulfill her confusing requests for ultracomputer time. But after a few months it became clear that, not only was there method to her madness, there was sheer genius to her method. In less than a year she tied together most of the disparate theories about gravity that had sprouted over the past decade into one theory that finally connected the force of gravity with quantum mechanics.

Furthermore, her theory of quantum gravity showed that the force of gravity interacted differently with the vacuum energy of the space-time continuum than it did with matter. In other words, just as Newtonian Mechanics was only valid within the local environment of Earth's gravitational influence, Einstein's theory of general relativity was only valid within the gravitational influence of the local superstructure of galactic clusters. In the vast stretches of vacuum energy between galactic clusters, gravity behaved differently, acting as a repellant, explaining why the expansion of the universe had renewed acceleration six billion years ago. Astrophysicists and astronomers finally ended their search for dark energy.

Having corrected discrepancies in Einstein's work should have made Dr. Mahajan the most famous scientist in history. But the attention bestowed upon her by the scientific community frightened her and caused her to disappear, reportedly back to her home in India, leaving Father Sanchez to publish the theory on her behalf and to explain it to the world. He became the de facto point of contact for the theory of quantum gravity and, because he was a Roman Catholic priest involved in scientific research, Father Sanchez became an international media celebrity as well.

"So you see," Father Sanchez concluded, "my role was not only minor, it was mostly administrative."

Awwad did not seem disappointed. "Still, you followed and understood the results from her research?"

Father Sanchez nodded, remembering when he first realized what those results indicated. Despite his modesty, he had been the first to point out how Dr. Mahajan's theory of quantum gravity related to the vacuum energy.

Awwad acknowledged Father Sanchez's nod by saying, "Very good."

Clearly, Awwad had not approached Father Sanchez out of mere admiration. Father Sanchez said as much.

Instead of answering, Awwad changed the subject again. "Professor, have you ever heard of the Schoef theory of cosmological symmetry?"

Father Sanchez rifled through his memory. "I have heard of it, but I don't know much about it. There are so many theories out there. If I remember correctly, Schoef's theory is not widely accepted."

Awwad nodded. "As you can imagine, the University of Jordan does not have a lot of money to spend on expensive scientific equipment. In our astrophysics department, we take advantage of grid computing. The high schools have been particularly helpful, providing us their unused CPU power while participating in larger academic projects. We use this virtual computer for theoretical research. We take lesser known, sometimes fringe, theories and rigorously investigate them, to see if they have merit. While eighty percent of the theories we dismiss as useless, some of them are actually ahead of their time, awaiting an improved technology or discoveries in some other discipline before they can be properly explored.

"Schoef's theory did not show much promise until after you—pardon me, I mean Dr. Mahajan—came out with the theory of quantum gravity. We substituted her equations for those used by Schoef based on the knowledge of gravity in his day, and suddenly his cosmological symmetry came to life." Awwad's eyes widened. "With results that would most likely astound even Johan Schoef if he were still alive."

"This is all really interesting." Father Sanchez glanced at his watch. "But is that the only thing you wanted to tell me, that a theory I worked on helped you to understand another theory?"

"Not at all." Awwad looked around the room conspiratorially. He lowered his voice to the point where the priest could barely understand him. "Schoef's theory has some very disturbing facets that I need to discuss with you." He pulled up the sleeve of his tunic to look at his own watch. "Not now. I must meet with my colleagues. Would you be willing to come to my room tomorrow after the scheduled events? What I must tell you is so incredible that you'll want to see the proof."

Father Sanchez reluctantly agreed.

•••

Father Oliver Johnson was a legend, famous not only within the Catholic Church but also throughout the world. The media often referred to him as a modern day Mother Teresa. Before being assigned as provincial superior to the Indiana Province of Holy Cross, the priest had spent most of his thirty-year career serving the neediest of God's children in the impoverished reaches of Central and South America. He first came to international fame after leading a successful revolt against the notorious coffee cartel.

Father Sanchez had not known what to expect when he first met his new superior. Wild rumors had always accompanied the extraordinary priest, including the latest one that he had been pulled from his post in Central America because of death threats from local organized crime elements. When the two men finally met, however, Father Sanchez saw immediately that the myths behind the man did not come from Father Johnson's physical size or from an overbearing demeanor. Although tall, Father Johnson's body was slender, almost frail-looking. He turned out to be an easy-going man with a soft-spoken voice.

It didn't take long for Father Sanchez to realize that Father Johnson's strength came from within. Here was a man who truly believed in God. His faith had not come to him on the coattails of another person, nor did it need some gimmick to prove itself. For many months after his new superior came to Indiana, Father Sanchez could not stop talking about him.

"I know he's a good man, Jose," Father Sanchez's mother said one evening as she prepared dinner. "But I don't understand why you go on so much about what he's done. You're a good man, too."

"He's not a good man, Mother, he's a *great* man." Jose sat at the dining-room table, wringing his hands together. He knew better than to ask if his mother needed help in the kitchen. The woman lived for the two or three evenings a week that she was able to cook her son dinner at his childhood home, one of the advantages of Father Sanchez being assigned to the University of Notre Dame. "He brought down a rogue business consortium."

His mother carried a casserole dish to the table. "Well, what about you? It's not every day that someone proves Einstein wrong."

"But Mother, it wasn't—"

"And don't bother talking to me about that Indian professor," she interrupted as she took her seat. "What a strange one *she* was. If you hadn't been there to organize things for her, she wouldn't have found the laboratory, much less that vacuum gravity stuff she was looking for."

She dished out a small portion of the casserole then pushed the dish toward her son. Father Sanchez remained silent as he filled his plate.

"And anyway, what can you do about it now?" His mother kept chewing as she talked, a habit she had developed in her senior years. "You're pretty much settled at Notre Dame. You're tenured and everything."

Father Sanchez played with the food on his plate for a few minutes before speaking again. "I've been thinking about requesting a missionary assignment." He looked up to see his mother's reaction.

She stopped chewing. Her eyes widened for a second, but just as quickly they returned to their normal size. The panic was brief but discernible, and Father Sanchez felt terrible for having induced it.

"Probably not." He finally spooned some food into his mouth. "Just something I'd been thinking about."

His mother resumed eating. "Well, I don't think you need to prove yourself in any way. But I'm sure whatever you decide to do will be God's will."

She seemed all right after that. A little pale, perhaps, but it was difficult to tell in the dim light of the dining room. Father Sanchez thought no more about the occasion until two days later when he was summoned from a lecture he'd been giving at the Nieuwland Science Hall. He was surprised to find Father Johnson waiting for him in the administrative office.

"Jose, it's your mother. She's in the hospital."

•••

The second day at the BA residency was a blur of activity. Throughout the Babylon Center there were various lectures, work groups, and demonstrations that the visiting scientists could attend. First item on the agenda, however, was an indoctrination session in the main auditorium, the only room large enough to hold all five hundred of the researchers. And everyone was expected to attend because Dr. Nimrod himself would be leading the indoctrination.

The chairs in the auditorium were overly comfortable, each with its own retractable computer terminal. Father Sanchez settled in and waited for the show to begin. He knew that everyone present understood the basics of the BA and were already familiar with its capabilities, so the session would be more than anything a chance for Dr. Nimrod to boast in front of a large audience.

Suddenly the lights dimmed and the chairman came bounding out on the stage, moving more lithely than one would imagine considering the man's girth. Before anyone could react to his abrupt appearance, Dr. Nimrod announced, "Welcome to history in the making!"

Sound feeds lining the stage picked up his voice and amplified it across the auditorium. A holographic image of the Babylon Center appeared, hovering over the stage. Clearly no expense had been spared in creating the auditorium's audiovisual capabilities.

An enthusiastic round of applause erupted from the crowd. Dr. Nimrod stood smiling, basking in the ovation for a few moments before continuing.

"The Brookhaven Energy Laboratory welcomes

you, and we thank you for sharing with us the first run of the Advanced Relativistic Heavy Ion Collider—which everyone seems to prefer calling simply the BEL Accelerator. Well, however you choose to say it, the BA is not only the most powerful particle accelerator/collider ever built, it is also the most significant international project ever undertaken."

Father Sanchez quickly realized they would be entertained with a highly edited version of the BA's history. The chairman failed to mention that it had been CERN who first announced that the time had finally come for a new generation of large accelerator/colliders. Exploiting advances in nanotechnology and ultracomputing, they had proposed building a new facility in the twenty-seven-kilometer trough of their old Large Hadron Collider, one that would achieve energy levels rivaling those of the most energetic cosmic rays, approximately 10^{20} eV. CERN revived the International Committee for Future Accelerators and began seeking worldwide participation.

The following year, emboldened by his success with nuclear fusion, Dr. Nimrod made the audacious claim that he could build an accelerator/collider reaching energy levels of 10^{24} eV. What's more, he said that he could build the facility in the four-kilometer tunnel of the BNL's original Relativistic Heavy Ion Collider, that he could do it in six years, and that he could do it for just a little more than CERN's proposed budget. CERN lambasted Dr. Nimrod's proposal, pointing out that the schedule depended on technological breakthroughs that had not yet materialized. But the U.S. Department of Energy backed Dr. Nimrod, making available to him the resources of all the national laboratories. Soon the major universities of North America pledged their support for the BA as well.

The European Union could not hope to match the money the U.S. was prepared to put into Dr. Nimrod's hands. Reluctantly, the International Committee for Future Accelerators endorsed the BA, and CERN was reduced to becoming a participant in Dr. Nimrod's scheme.

The chairman chose to ignore these complex and controversial facts in favor of a more streamlined explanation of events. "We made it on schedule and within budget." He feigned a pained expression. "Well, mostly within budget."

The expected laughter emanated from the audience.

"And now, after a year of testing, the BA is ready for production. The magnets and RF systems have been powered up for almost a month in anticipation of next week's run, so unfortunately we can only provide you a virtual tour of the facility."

As though on cue, the stage hologram changed to an aerial view of the ring at the Brookhaven National Laboratory, site of the old RHIC and now the new BA. The display zoomed in and then descended into the depths of the BA's tunnel where two shiny tubes stretched to the limits of the curved corridor's line of sight. A diagram of the entire BA superimposed itself on the view of the tunnel. Dr. Nimrod drew everyone's attention to a line on the diagram that intersected the ring at about seven o'clock.

"Here's where it begins. The Electron-beam Nuclei Kinetic Injector, or ENKI, a linear accelerator with its roots in the most advanced of the compact linear colliders. Intense electric fields from laser-produced plasma will inject bunches of uranium ions into both of the BA rings at a velocity so close to the speed of light that, if we could view them, the ions would appear as flattened discs.

"And then there are the rings themselves, built from a specially designed material that conducts electricity and magnetism better than any alloy.

"The magnets themselves are nothing short of magic."

An understatement, Father Sanchez knew. The magnets had been at the core of CERN's objections, and had almost derailed the entire project, until, at the last minute, the Argonne National Laboratory came up with the technological breakthrough needed and saved the BA. Dr. Nimrod, of course, made no mention of Argonne during his lecture.

"These superconducting magnets operate at room temperature, yet they produce a magnetic field hundreds of thousands of times more powerful than the earth's own. These magnets will keep the ion beams focused and accelerated to the speed required to produce collisions with 10^{24} eV worth of kinetic energy."

The stage hologram transformed itself again. It now showed a monstrosity of metal, several stories high judging by the size of the technicians who scrambled around it on scaffolds. Father Sanchez recognized the image as being MERODACH, the single detector on the BA rings. The name was an odd collection of acronyms describing the various experiments built into the detector. There were the Microvertex detectors, the Electromagnetic calorimeter, the Ring imaging Chernkov detector, the Octagon multiplicity detector, a traditional Drift chamber, an Advanced spectrometer, the Chamber array (a series of large volume gas-drift chambers), and finally the Hadron-blind detector. Together these sensors made up the four-thousand-ton piece of equipment that further testified to Dr. Nimrod's love of grandiose designs and his philosophy of putting all the eggs into one very important basket. He spent nearly half an hour describing the function of each experiment.

Finally, toward the end of his presentation, Dr. Nimrod revealed why he had invited them all to this residency. "No less amazing than the physics behind the BA is the computer system that will control all the functions." He walked back and forth across the stage, gazing over his audience, pausing for dramatic effect. "We have expert systems monitoring all aspects of MERODACH. Not only will these systems record the petabytes of data from each collision event—yes, you heard me right: petabytes! Not only will the expert systems record and archive data for future research, they'll feed the data into BAAL, the most advanced artificial intelligence ever developed."

Father Sanchez knew that the AI's name had been given in honor of the engineers who designed its principal algorithms, Benoit Auclair and Andre Legault. Another accolade that Dr. Nimrod failed to provide.

"BAAL will analyze each collision and provide preliminary results immediately." The chairman then waited the appropriate amount of time to build suspense. "Therefore, you are all welcome to attend the ten-hour beam run right here in this auditorium, using the terminals built into your seats to monitor the status of the run and to investigate the collisions in *real time!*"

With that remark, the audience began clapping again.

"This is just the beginning, my friends." Dr. Nimrod did not wait for the applause to subside. "Together we will uncover God's best-kept secrets. Nothing can stop us but our own imaginations!"

Father Sanchez clapped as well, but just to be polite, with little enthusiasm.

•••

On the day he first sought counsel with his superior, almost a month after his mother's death, Father Sanchez was in spiritual shambles. After her collapse, Jose's mother had hung on to life for several more weeks, but she never recovered, never even managed another coherent sentence before succumbing to heart failure. When consulting with the doctors, Jose learned that his mother had been receiving treatment for heart disease for several years. Father Sanchez would never understand how or why she had kept the illness a secret. Nor did the news alleviate any of the guilt he felt for having caused his mother's collapse in the first place.

In contrast to the turmoil troubling Father Sanchez's mind, the weather on the Notre Dame campus was calm. The sun shone warmly on both priests as they strolled toward the Basilica of the Sacred Heart. At one point, as he gazed up at the stained-glass windows, Father Sanchez realized he was standing almost at the exact location where decades earlier his mother had presented him with the gold chain and 10^{-43} pendant.

"Jose," Father Johnson said after listening to Father Sanchez ramble, "I understand your sorrow. The only comfort I can offer in this moment is reassurance that it is quite normal for you to feel this way. The loss is too great for you to realize that your mother is now in a far better place. That realization will come eventually, gradually."

Father Sanchez exhaled loudly. "It's not just that. It almost feels like—I don't know. It seems like when she left, she took my faith with her."

A long silence descended over the priests, interrupted only by the songs of birds and the mumbled greetings of passing students. Father Johnson stopped walking before he spoke again. "Faith is not a jug that you can fill up or empty. You either have it or you don't. And if you have it, the faith is always there. During trying times such as these, it may seem more difficult to access."

"But I feel so useless. I can't say Mass. I can't…" Father Sanchez raised his arms then dropped them again, as though he couldn't remember why he had raised them in the first place.

Father Johnson laid his hands on Father Sanchez's shoulders. "Listen, I can pray with you. I can hear your confession. I can do many things for you, but in the end you must reach inside, find your faith, and cure yourself."

• • •

By the end of the second day at the BEL residency, Father Sanchez's head was so full of facts and figures that his head hurt. All he wanted to do was settle in the lounge with a cold beer. But Dr. Awwad Moussa Zihlif tracked him down before he had a chance to order the beer.

"Please, Professor Sanchez, I would not insist if this was not urgent."

Awwad's expression contained so much fear and desperation that Father Sanchez could not refuse. He accompanied the imam scientist to his quarters on the third floor of the dormitory. Once inside, Father

Sanchez noticed that Awwad had not even unpacked. Apparently the man had been living the past day and a half out of his suitcase. An assortment of toiletries and clothes covered much of the furniture.

"I apologize for the mess," Awwad said without looking at his guest. He cleared away the clutter from two chairs, offering one to the priest. "I have spent all the time working with my colleagues to prepare this material, to make it suitable for your viewing."

Awwad sat down in the second chair. He held a computer tablet in his hands, an older model with only a two-dimensional viewing screen. "I see you have your tablet with you, Professor. If you turn it on, I can make the appropriate files available to you."

Father Sanchez maintained a neutral expression as he unzipped the leather pouch holding his tablet. After he activated the device, it automatically communicated with Awwad's tablet.

Awwad spoke as he made the necessary private network connection. "Professor, up until now, what has been the highest energy density ever achieved by a collider?"

"That would have been the CERN Large Hadron Collider during lead-ion beam runs. About a thousand tera-electron volts, if I remember correctly."

"Yes," Awwad concurred. "They recreated the universe as it was approximately 10^{-20} seconds after the big bang. And now, presumably, this new accelerator will reach 10^{24} eV, equivalent to 10^{-37} seconds after the big bang."

He looked hard at the priest. "What occurred between 10^{-37} and 10^{-20} seconds?"

"Well, for those who believe in it, the inflation era."

"Does anyone actually doubt the theory of inflation anymore?"

Father Sanchez shrugged noncommittally.

"There," Awwad finally announced. "Now you are logged onto our mainframe back in Jordan. You can follow along with me.

"To make a long story short, Johan Schoef played with a concept that became popular at the beginning of the century, that the space-time continuum is closed—but not that it contracts. Rather, it moves from a state of highest order to a state of lowest possible order, or absolute zero."

"The old alpha to omega idea," Father Sanchez offered.

"Yes." Awwad smiled, clearly pleased that the priest was following him. "Schoef believed then what we know now: the galactic black holes will eventually consume all normal matter and emit the mass back into the vacuum energy of the space-time continuum as virtual particles."

Father Sanchez sighed. "Awwad, these events will occur so far in the future that I fail to see…"

Awwad waived his hand. "Please, I will get to the point. Schoef tried to prove this idea mathematically, but because he had incorrect information about gravity, his models always failed. Before reaching absolute zero, they stalled. Schoef died an unhappy man.

"However, once the theory of quantum gravity came out, his theory began to make sense. As the amount of vacuum energy grows in the universe, gravity's repelling force increases until it reaches infinity—in other words, the model finally reaches absolute zero."

Father Sanchez blinked several times in confusion.

Awwad tapped away at his tablet's touchscreen. "Here, it is now easier for me to show you. There, on your computer display, I will show you a model of the universe as it expands in accordance with Schoef's formulas, using Dr. Mahajan's equations for quantum gravity."

The model started from the singularity of the big bang and progressed rapidly, expanding as Awwad provided commentary.

"See how the black holes consume all matter as the universe ages? And then the matter is regurgitated back as virtual particles. And always the amount of vacuum energy increases until the entire universe is nothing but vacuum energy. The universe achieves absolute zero. It closes."

Awwad paused long enough for Father Sanchez to study the model's display and the accompanying equations.

"Do you see? The space-time continuum ceases to exist. Space has no more meaning: there is no more here or there. Time does not stop—it simply disappears! There is no more then or now."

Father Sanchez nodded in comprehension.

"Now, we will let the model continue, and look!"

The entire model seemed to reset itself. The big bang started anew.

Father Sanchez blinked several times. "What just happened?"

"Professor, I assure you that nothing artificial was added to the model. It occurs spontaneously. Once the universe reaches absolute zero—I know this is an oversimplification of quantum mechanics, but gravity seems to *borrow* all the vacuum energy and spits it back out through a new singularity. The big bang repeats!"

Father Sanchez realized he had been holding his breath. He exhaled. "It keeps going?"

"Yes." Awwad studied the priest's expression. "I

invite you to review the equations on your own, to convince yourself. But you realize what this means, don't you?"

Father Sanchez looked away from his display, at Awwad. There were so many implications that he didn't know where to begin.

Awwad continued. "The big bang was not really the beginning. At least, not the beginning of Creation: just the beginning of the universe we currently inhabit." He smiled. "Science must never contradict religious doctrine, and now Allah has given us this clear sign that reconciles the theory of the big bang with the fact that He has always existed and always will."

Father Sanchez felt his heart beat faster. "Yes, this is amazing. I'll need to study the equations thoroughly. We have a computer back at Notre Dame suited for this type of modeling."

But Awwad did not appear pleased by this prospect. "Dear Professor, you may never have that opportunity."

Father Sanchez frowned. "I don't understand."

"Let me show you a revised model."

An expanding sphere representing the universe once again appeared on the display of Father Sanchez's tablet. Then, suddenly, a new white dot appeared inside the sphere, a singularity that expanded into a second sphere that overrode the first one.

"What was that?" Father Sanchez exclaimed.

"I arbitrarily introduced a new inflation era. It spontaneously sucked in all the vacuum energy from the first universe, creating a new one."

"But how…"

"Professor Sanchez, that is not the proper question." His eyes widened so far that Father Sanchez could see white all around Awwad's irises. "The question is, what happens when the BEL Accelerator creates a new inflationary period?"

Father Sanchez laughed out loud. "Are you trying to tell me that, when the uranium ions collide and create an energy density of 10^{24} eV, the BA is going to *borrow* all the vacuum energy from our universe and create a new one in its place?"

"I did not believe this at first either, when my colleagues brought this news to me. They were terrified. They wanted me to show them their error, console them that Allah would not permit such a thing."

Awwad still had his eyes open wide. His mouth seemed to tremble. "But I saw nothing but the horrible truth."

Father Sanchez sat back in his chair, not knowing what to say or think.

"Pursuit of knowledge is our duty," Awwad added. "But the BEL Accelerator is an abomination. It is the sorcery of Satan. The Koran says: 'Call upon your Lord with lowliness and in secret, for He loveth not transgressors. And commit not disorders on earth after it hath been well ordered.'"

"I-I never realized before that these words should be taken literally!"

Awwad's voice changed then, becoming calmer, almost as though he were talking about something totally unrelated. "We tried publishing the theory. We showed the results to other universities. Everyone was interested in the idea of recycling universes, but no one took us seriously enough to believe in spontaneous creation.

"Dr. Nimrod will not see us. His secretary claims all appointments are booked. So, Professor Sanchez, you are our last hope."

"M-Me?" Father Sanchez felt numb. He could not

share Awwad's angst. How could anything so absurd
be allowed? "What can I do?"

"You must talk to Dr. Nimrod. You must convince
him to halt this experiment. He is Catholic: he will
listen to you."

Father Sanchez almost laughed again. He realized
that being a religious leader in the land of Islam must
still carry some weight. Poor Awwad sincerely believed
that a man like Dr. Nimrod would be influenced
by one of his own religious leaders to shut down a
multibillion-dollar project. Father Sanchez wondered
what the chairman would say if the pope himself tried
to order the BA experiments stopped.

Awwad grasped the sleeve of Father Sanchez's
clergy shirt. "Professor, you must not fail. The Koran
makes many references to a fiery and violent end for
disbelievers.

"'Are We wearied out with the first creation?'" he
then said, once again quoting the Holy Book. "'Yet
are they in doubt with regard to a new creation!'"

The skepticism must have shown on Father
Sanchez's face, for Awwad continued. "I see that you
must first convince yourself. Please, go to your quarters.
All the information at our university is available to
you. Study the equations and play with the models.
You will see that everything I tell you is true."

Father Sanchez looked up from his tablet. "And
then what?"

"Then pray, like you've never prayed before, in
the name of Allah, the Compassionate, the Merciful."

•••

The second time Father Sanchez sought counsel
with his superior was after the invitation to the BEL

residency. Father Sanchez did not want to go. For the longest time he had been questioning his role in the church, his usefulness to humanity, his very morality. It was time for a change, he decided. Surprisingly, his superior balked at Father Sanchez's request to be assigned missionary work.

In the rectory of the Basilica of the Sacred Heart, Father Johnson made his argument. "Jose, you do wonderful work here at the university. You fill young people with an appreciation of God's Creation."

The remark stunned Father Sanchez, who had assumed that spreading the gospel to the impoverished masses was the ideal religious work. "Father, I have been at Notre Dame my entire adulthood. I took a vow of poverty, just as you did, but I have been surrounded by opulence my entire life." Father Sanchez waived his hand to indicate the grandeur of the basilica and of the surrounding campus. "I have never experienced hardship. Considering your own accomplishments, I feel ashamed."

"I see the problem now." Father Johnson had just poured coffee for Father Sanchez and himself. He stirred his own coffee slowly. "Jose, you may feel you have been overly blessed, but there is no need to feel shame. You have had little say in your assignments. From the very beginning your career has been guided by the U.S. Conference of Catholic Bishops."

Father Sanchez had been preparing to raise his coffee cup to his mouth but stopped. He could not hide his surprise, causing the other priest to smile.

"The Catholic Church is very keen on keeping up to date with science and technology, and we officially endorse cosmology. A big bang is exactly the way we would have expected God Almighty to create the heavens and Earth. So, we rejoice when one of our own has the ability to understand something so profound.

"The pope is very interested in this new accelerator, and I know he would want a representative there. You are the logical choice. The Vatican itself has been following your career since your quantum gravity discoveries...."

"Father, I didn't..."

Father Johnson raised his hand to stop Jose's interruption. "Yes, I know, and I appreciate your modesty, but we take whatever advantage we can. After all, do you really think I brought down the coffee cartel?"

Father Sanchez's eyes widened.

"Jose, the cartel was a group of coffee importing cooperatives gone bad, backed by financial institutes with ties to organized crime. What in the world could I have done against such odds? Law enforcement agencies from over a dozen countries had been working on that case for almost a decade. When they finally closed in on the key players, I knew that residual cartel members would seek revenge on the most vulnerable of the victims, the coffee growers themselves. All I did was gather together the farmers for spiritual pep talks, to help them prepare for the worst. The news media caught my speeches on camera about the same time the cartel ringleaders were arrested, and the rest is distorted history."

Father Sanchez finally took a sip of his coffee as he absorbed his superior's words.

Father Johnson continued. "We let these little misconceptions slide because we need the attention. Religion is no longer at the center of people's lives, so we must shout to be heard, to keep people focused on their spirituality. And every time one of our members is internationally recognized for a positive achievement, our recruitment of new clergy increases worldwide."

After finishing his coffee, Father Johnson rose to his feet. "Tell you what: when it's over, if you still feel the same way, let me know. I can recommend a few pitiful slums in Central America where you could be useful." He placed his hands on Father Sanchez's shoulders. "But for now, I believe it is God's will that you attend the BA residency."

•••

Father Sanchez sat in the reception area outside Dr. Nimrod's office, desperately wondering what God's will was in this moment. His hands trembled slightly as they clutched the computer tablet's leather case. He stared intently at a digital clock along the far wall that counted the seconds and minutes away in blood red numbers.

The secretary, who had made the 10:00 a.m. appointment for Father Sanchez, saw him watching the clock as it approached 10:15. "I apologize, Father. I'm afraid the staff meeting is running a little late."

"No problem." Father Sanchez did not remove his gaze from the clock. He was not concerned about being delayed. He watched the clock not out of impatience, but out of fear. The seconds ticking away seemed like a reverse countdown to Armageddon. The first beam run was scheduled to start at the BEL Accelerator at 10:00 a.m. tomorrow.

Father Sanchez had no idea what he was going to tell the chairman beyond explaining Schoef's theory and showing him what would happen to the universe if an impromptu inflation era sprang forth from an ion beam collision. He had spent the past days studying Awwad's data, and of course praying.

Would Dr. Nimrod see the same end? Father Sanchez had to convince the chairman. But how? He considered the fate of others in the Bible who had faced such challenges from God: Noah and his ark, Moses leading the Israelites out of Egypt, and so on. Not only did he *not* feel up to the task, Father Sanchez felt ridiculous trying to draw analogies between himself and those personages.

At that moment, the large wooden doors to Dr. Nimrod's office opened. A group of people dressed in expensive suits and dresses poured from the room.

"You may go in now," the secretary announced.

Father Sanchez stood, using his free hand to smooth the fabric of his black cassock. He had chosen to wear the tunic that was normally worn under vestments during Mass, rather than his clerical garb, as a way to emphasize his position with the Catholic Church. His appearance had the desired effect as the important people departing the office acknowledged his presence with greetings and stepped aside to allow him access.

Inside, the office was spacious, as Father Sanchez had expected. Dr. Nimrod's desk was a mammoth of solid wood. The chairman greeted the priest and they both seated themselves on their respective sides of the desk. Dr. Nimrod began. "Well, what do you think of the BA so far?"

"Impressive," Father Sanchez replied curtly. "But I'm afraid this is not merely a courtesy call, Mr. Chairman."

"Oh?" Dr. Nimrod seemed surprised that the priest had taken command of the conversation.

"Have you ever heard of Johan Schoef's theory of cosmological symmetry?"

The chairman nodded. "Yes, I have. I believe there's a group of Arab scientists here to see if our experiments will help prove Schoef's work."

"Well, it's not exactly like that." Father Sanchez pulled his computer tablet from its pouch. The device immediately synchronized with the pervasive network of the Babylon Center. Father Sanchez quickly found the connection to the display device built into Dr. Nimrod's desk. "I have something I must show you."

A holographic image appeared above the desk, surprising Father Sanchez in its size and clarity. The lights in the office dimmed automatically to further improve the image.

Dr. Nimrod watched intently as Father Sanchez went through the expanding universe model. The simulation appeared even more dramatic and horrifying on the chairman's holographic display. At the point where the space-time continuum ended and the big bang recreated itself spontaneously, Dr. Nimrod smiled. "Amazing! And you've confirmed their work? Well, we'll certainly have some interesting things to prove during the first beam run, won't we?"

"That's where the problem lies."

Father Sanchez then proceeded to show the chairman the other model, the one that implicated the BA as an instrument of doom. It took a while for the chairman to realize what the priest was insinuating.

"Padre, this can't be right." Dr. Nimrod continued looking over the equations that appeared beside the model.

"Believe me, I wish it wasn't. I've been all over those equations and the models. It all fits."

"You can't be serious." Dr. Nimrod was still smiling. He studied the priest's face, looking for some sign of humor. When he saw none, his own smile faded. "You are serious. And what do you propose we do about this?"

"It is clear, Mr. Chairman. The data is in front of you. The beam runs must not proceed."

Dr. Nimrod seemed flabbergasted, and he was obviously not accustomed to feeling this way. "Padre, let's be realistic. Look, accelerators have always brought fears that violent particle collisions could somehow disturb the vacuum state. These fears have always been put to rest, first theoretically and then by running the accelerators."

"You and I both know that all previous facilities were deemed safe because their energy densities did not even reach the level of natural cosmic rays. The BA not only goes beyond cosmic rays, it goes beyond the inflation era."

"Yes, but the mass of the particles involved is so small that the absolute power of their collisions is meaningless. The snapping of fingers disturbs the universe more than those collisions will." The chairman snapped his fingers to demonstrate. "The duration of any effects from the collisions is so short…"

"But mass has nothing to do with this. We're not talking about an explosion. We're talking about the universe spontaneously recreating itself. And duration has nothing to do with it, either. According to the equations, once an inflationary period begins, nothing can stop it!"

"Now calm down, Padre." Dr. Nimrod tried to collect his thoughts. "I find all this rather outrageous, but I have tremendous respect for your accomplishments, and out of deference to the church I would like to reason this out with you. Now, let us assume this theory—and I emphasize that it is only a *theory*—leads where you say it will. Don't you think that God would prevent such a thing?"

"Mr. Chairman, God gave us free will. And the Bible is full of examples where disasters occurred because man chose the wrong path: the great flood, the destruction of Sodom and Gomorrah, the plagues in Egypt. 'Let no man say when he is tempted, I am tempted of God: for God cannot be tempted with evil, neither tempteth he any man.'"

Dr. Nimrod was clearly not impressed by the reference to James I. His face turned red. "I can't believe this! We are on the threshold of the greatest scientific experiment ever, and you spout Sunday school stories to me?

"Do you realize what it took to build this facility? I had to unite scientists, universities and governments from all over the world, get everyone speaking the same language so we could dedicate the needed resources to get this thing done."

Dr. Nimrod jumped from his chair. The holographic image above the desk disappeared automatically as his face penetrated one of the display planes. "And now you want me to close down the whole place because of a—a fairy tale?

"Goddamn it, Padre, what is wrong with you?!"

Silence followed his outburst. After a few moments, Dr. Nimrod's scowl faded. He suddenly looked surprised that he was standing. He eased himself slowly back into his chair. "Dear me. I've never talked that way to a priest before."

Father Sanchez remained quiet himself, not sure what to do next.

Dr. Nimrod drummed his heavy fingers on the

desktop. "You understand that what you ask is impossible."

Father Sanchez nodded.

After a long, awkward pause, the chairman sighed. "Before you go, Father, would you hear my confession?"

"Of course." Under the circumstances, it seemed the most important thing Father Sanchez could do.

• • •

The next day, while most of the guest scientists went to the main auditorium for the BA beam run, Father Sanchez remained in his quarters. He knelt at the bed, rosary in hand. He imagined that Awwad and his colleagues were in their own quarters as well, bowing in the general direction of Mecca and asking Allah to be merciful one more time.

When 10:00 a.m. arrived, Father Sanchez knew that billions of uranium ions were entering the alternating rings of the BEL Accelerator. The two separate beams would then rush toward each other at an intersection on the far end of the rings. While most of the ions would avoid a collision during the ten-hour run, millions would not survive. Most of the hits would be peripheral collisions, crashes where two ions only graze each other. Even so, the results would be devastating, creating temperatures so high that protons and neutrons would vaporize into quarks, antiquarks, and gluons. The quark-gluon plasma would not last long, condensing quickly into new particles, exotic baryons and mesons that would then fly into the awaiting net of multiple experiments built into MERODACH.

But some of the hits would be central collisions,

head-on crashes creating energy densities far beyond anything occurring in nature since the big bang itself. And according to a theory that Father Sanchez had helped to develop, such a collision would destroy the reality where he existed.

Was that God's will?

Father Sanchez had always seen Planck Time as an insurmountable barrier where none of the physical laws known to man made any sense, where scientists could not even intelligently speculate, much less investigate. The 10^{-43} second barrier had seemed like a wall between the knowable and unknowable, the worldly and divine, man and God.

Now science was on the verge of crossing that barrier. The BA was like a bridge stretching toward the divide, a tower reaching up to Heaven itself. And as punishment for its arrogance, humanity would suffer the ultimate wrath. Before they could uncover the secret of Creation, God would simply replace it!

And here knelt Father Jose Sanchez, begging God to reconsider.

Jose laughed.

He was surely one of the most pathetic priests to ever wear the collar. He had always attended Mass, accepted the Eucharist, and gone to confession, but Jose had gone through these rituals more out of love for his mother than out of true faith. Only after he learned of Planck Time was he filled with an intense belief in God, like Saint Thomas placing his fist into the pierced side of the resurrected Jesus.

God had surrounded Jose with devout believers all his life: his mother, Father Johnson, and countless others. But Jose had needed *proof* before giving himself to God, making him more arrogant than even Dr. Nimrod.

No, Jose was a blasphemer, and as such had no right to ask God for anything.

And yet, even as he sank into despair, he remembered the prayer of another devout believer whom God had sent to him, and there he found salvation.

In the name of Allah, the Compassionate, the Merciful.

Yes! God was severe, but not vengeful. He was compassionate. Merciful.

Forgiving.

Father Sanchez reached beneath his collar and yanked the gold chain from his neck. He tossed the necklace with its pendant to the floor. Even though it had been a gift from his mother, the device was no longer needed. He now saw the inner faith that Father Johnson had said would be there. Father Sanchez asked God to forgive his transgressions, especially his lapses in faith. Then he prayed.

And prayed.

He lost track of the time. He did not eat, drink, sleep, or even go to the bathroom for the entire duration of the BA beam run. As colliding uranium ions challenged the very fabric of existence, he remained on his knees, pleading with God to bring the BEL Accelerator experiment to a different conclusion.

•••

Sweat poured down Father Sanchez's face. It dripped from every pore, soaked his clothes, and made his hair perpetually wet. The moisture drenched the pages of the Bible as he carried on his lessons. The Costa Rican sun did nothing to help him keep the attention of his teenage charges.

Half-naked in the unbearable heat, the children sat in a circle around the priest, who also wore the minimal amount of clothing needed to maintain decorum. While Father Sanchez tried to use an ancient parable to instill morality into his class, the boys seemed more interested in pointing out the budding maturity of the girls. The girls, for their part, seemed more interested in the attention the boys gave them.

Despite the futility of his lesson, Father Sanchez smiled. He was just glad to be alive, happy that the children surrounding him and indeed the entire universe around him still existed. He could not feel anger. He merely soldiered on, carrying out God's will in his own way, the best he could.

"Father Sanchez!" One of the local brothers called out to him. "There is a call for you."

Father Sanchez closed the Bible and looked at his class. "Very well," he said in the Spanish that he'd had to relearn over the past months. "You children get a break, for now. But be back here in twenty minutes."

With no functioning clock in the village, Father Sanchez knew he would have to track down each student individually to get the class back together. They were already halfway across the village before the priest could even get to his feet. He walked through the mud to the tent where all the mission's communications equipment was located, running off a generator they could only operate a few hours a day due to fuel rationing.

Inside was an old computerized workstation connected to a satellite broadband transceiver. Awwad Moussa Zihlif's face smiled out from the computer's display. Father Sanchez sat down on a rickety chair, positioning himself so the tiny camera built into the monitor would capture his face.

"Hello, Professor Sanchez. You are a difficult man to find."

Father Sanchez sighed. "Yes, I'm a long way from the likes of New York. There is poverty and misery here that I never knew existed."

The imam scientist laughed. "And you, Priest, have never been happier, right?"

Father Sanchez smiled instead of answering.

"But I am not spending fifty dollars a minute here just to chit chat. I thought you would be interested in hearing the latest about the BEL Accelerator."

Father Sanchez had not kept up with news since leaving the United States three months earlier. He had almost forgotten the whole ordeal, except for the inner faith he had found there, the same faith that pushed him to rise from his wet cot every morning and to go through the same rituals every day to save the indigenous villagers in spite of themselves and in spite of the Costa Rican government's indifference to their plight.

After Father Sanchez's prayer marathon at the Babylon Center, the universe, miraculously, still existed. It wasn't until the next day that he and Awwad discovered why. Everything had gone as scheduled. The BA had operated properly. Uranium ions collided with each other in record numbers. But the expected energy densities never occurred. Father Sanchez had studied the luminosity graphs. As the peripheral angle of the collisions decreased, the energy levels rose, but never high enough. It seemed as though an invisible hand had restrained the energy densities from surpassing the critical threshold.

When it became clear no new science would be learned from the first beam run, Father Sanchez had convinced Father Johnson to recall him from the residency. As promised, his superior assigned Father Sanchez the first missionary post that came open. Before he departed for Central America, Father Sanchez learned that the entire BA residency had been disbanded.

"There was a federal investigation by—I believe you call it the General Accounting Office," Awwad explained. "There was never any indication of a malfunction. All hardware performed to design specifications. Software logs showed no errors. The investigators concluded that the basic theories behind the accelerator must be flawed. They now believe that generating the advertised energy levels is impossible, prohibited by some law of nature we do not yet understand. You know, like the theory of special relativity prohibiting travel faster than light."

Awwad suddenly laughed. "The Europeans and Asians are furious! They are demanding a refund for their investments. Anyway, all foreign participants have withdrawn support, as have all the universities. The Brookhaven National Laboratory will gain control of the accelerator, while the Brookhaven Energy Laboratory will focus exclusively on nuclear fusion. Dr. Nimrod has gone into early retirement."

Father Sanchez absorbed all the information, relieved that the ordeal was truly over. Now that Dr. Nimrod's plans had been thoroughly confounded, his resources scattered, there was no more worry that humanity would overreach its bounds—at least not within the realm of particle physics.

"Of course," Awwad added, "the news media accounts never mention what you and I know."

"What? You believe it was divine intervention? You don't agree that it's simply a physical impossibility?"

Awwad shrugged. "Possible or impossible: what is

the difference? Nothing in the universe occurs without Allah's intercession. 'Not the weight of an atom on earth or in heaven escapeth thy Lord.'"

Father Sanchez recognized the famous verse from the Koran. But he no longer needed proof to bolster his own faith.

"Well, my time is up." Awwad smiled one last time. "May God bless you, always. Goodbye."

"Goodbye, friend," Father Sanchez replied, but the display had already gone blank.

ARE WE AT THE END OF SCIENCE FICTION?

by
Orson Scott Card

Orson Scott Card is the author of the novels Ender's Game, Ender's Shadow, *and* Speaker for the Dead, *which are widely read by adults and younger readers, and are increasingly used in schools.*

Besides these and other science fiction novels, Card writes contemporary fantasy, biblical novels, the American frontier fantasy series, the Tales of Alvin Maker, poetry, and many plays and scripts.

Card was born in Washington and grew up in California, Arizona and Utah. He recently began a long-term position as a professor of writing and literature at Southern Virginia University.

Orson Scott Card has been a judge of the Writers of the Future Contest since 1994 having earlier served as a guest instructor at the Writers Workshops, both at Sag Harbor, Long Island, and at Pepperdine University in Los Angeles. He was also the featured essayist in volume four with his essay "The Write Kind of Writing Workshop."

In the following article, Card speculates on the current state of science fiction and the role of the Writers of the Future Contest in the genre.

These aren't the best of times for science fiction.

The magazines, from the venerable *Fantasy and Science Fiction* to the once-dominant *Isaac Asimov's Science Fiction Magazine* are at astonishingly low circulation levels, and even that bastion of idea-oriented ("hard") science fiction, *Analog*, is hurting.

But those are the short stories, and they have long been an anomaly inside the genre. Long after short stories became a dead issue in popular reading, and the old fiction magazines either died or found new kinds of content, science fiction stories persisted. It's possible that the decline of the magazines only means that science fiction is catching up with—or falling down with—the rest of the literary world.

When you look at the science fiction section of the major bookstores, it can seem that science fiction is doing just fine. In Borders and Barnes & Noble there's a healthy section labeled science fiction, with lots of titles and…

Oh, wait. It's labeled science fiction *and fantasy*, and when you look at the covers of those books, what do you see?

Trees. Horses. Mythical beasts. The only sheet metal seems to be on medieval armor.

What happened to the science fiction? Oh, wait—there's a Benford. And ah, yes. We have a spaceship here on this Niven, and that Barnes, and…and the very fact that we can count the covers with a science fiction look tells us something.

It's a conspiracy! Fantasy is crowding science fiction off the shelves!

Relax. There are no conspiracies, except insofar as capitalism might be considered one. Bookstores and publishers are in the business of making money by selling books. If the reading public were snapping up science fiction books in numbers anything like the sales of big thick fantasy trilogies (or infinite series like Jordan's *Wheel of Time*), then science fiction's space on the shelves would not be declining relative to fantasy.

The only part of the science fiction market that seems impervious to this decline in sales is that portion devoted to *Star Wars, Star Trek*, and other media-based fiction. And in some ways those are the opposite of science fiction.

For science fiction has long functioned, not as a predictor of the future (we usually get it wrong), but rather as a rehearsal for it.

That is, when readers plunge into a science fiction novel, they set aside at least some of their assumptions about the present reality and try to absorb a new set of rules. Whether it's the physics, the biology, the psychology, or the history of the world that is transformed, the very thing that makes it science fiction is that the story takes readers out of this world and into another.

The very process of picking up the cues and learning how the world differs requires that readers be observant and analytical—they have to notice changes and induce new rule sets and deduce new conclusions (or, reasoning backward, premises) in order to navigate in this invented environment.

In effect, then, the process of reading a science fiction novel prepares you to adapt to the changes that are coming at a rapid pace in our world. That's one reason why adolescents are much more likely to read science fiction than adults are—because that adolescent's world is already in flux, as is their role within it, and exploring alternate realities is in some ways closer to the practical issues of an adolescent life than strictly realistic fiction.

But science fiction is not, contrary to some assertions, a branch of children's literature. There have always been adults who continue to thrive on the fiction of reinvention and transformation long after their adolescence is behind them. The best science fiction is almost always written for those adults, and adolescents only adopt it as their own after the fact. (There are exceptions, of course, like the great William Sleator; nor can we forget Heinlein's and Andre Norton's "juveniles" from fifty years ago.)

So…what has happened in the past decade or so?

The world hasn't stopped changing. The need for transformative literature can't have disappeared.

I've heard (or thought of) several speculations:

1. Science Has Moved On. The cutting edge of science has moved to theoretical or submicroscopic or beyond-cosmic levels that don't lend themselves to storytelling—because they don't lead to new machines or cool new creatures. We don't even understand the science when you do try to use it in a story. So we turn to fantasy or alternate history to give us interesting stories contrary to the present reality. Therefore science fiction isn't so much dying as changing clothes, because we ran out of science that was accessible to readers.

2. We Used Up the Ideas. All the really cool stories that were possible within science fiction have been written. With the exception of Carter Scholz's unforgettable "The Nine Billion Names of God by Arthur C. Clarke," you really can't rewrite the classic idea stories. "Nightfall" and "I Have No Mouth and I Must Scream" and "To Serve Man" have already been written. Now we're just getting retreads of the same old stories: Another time-travel paradox story, another persecuted mutant story, another meet-the-aliens-and-find-out-they-really-are/aren't-trying-to-kill-us story.

3. The Good Writers All Got Old (or Died) and the Younger Ones Suck. Depending on whether you class me as old (I'm over fifty) or young (compared to Bradbury or Clarke), I can't help but take this one rather personally. Still, the idea is that without the real masters to lead us, we've lost our way, and now the best new writers simply refuse to keep company on the bookshelves with a genre that has become so much worse than it used to be.

4. Science Fiction Was Always Lousy. I really hate this one, but I hear it a lot, so I have to include it. Science fiction was never good, but it felt new, so it attracted a lot of attention. Now it doesn't feel new anymore, so it's more obvious than ever how very bad it has always been.

5. Print Sci-Fi Can't Compete with Computer Graphics. Readers are now impatient with science fiction that can only hint at fantastic new worlds; they're used to *seeing* those fantastic places and devices and creatures on the screen. So the audience that used to read in order to see wonders in their minds' eye now buy DVDs or video games to get that thrill.

6. Women Prefer Fantasy. This might sound sexist, but it's a publishing reality that most books are bought by women. For decades, however, science fiction remained a bastion of primarily male reading. Women began reading sci-fi in greater and greater numbers from the sixties on, and they brought their tastes with them, so tech-centered stories began to give way to character-centered stories. But character-centered stories can be written as easily in a fantasy world as a science fictional world, and so the women readers have caused fantasy to rise as a portion of the speculative fiction genre.

7. Writers Are Lazy and Fantasy Is Easier to Write. After all, you don't have to know any science, you just make stuff up. In fantasy, *anything* can happen.

8. The Audience Has Moved On. The new generation of readers is either too lazy to do the work required to process science fiction, or has such elevated tastes that sci-fi is now beneath them. I hear both theories, and sometimes from the same people.

Which, if any, of these explanations is true?

1. Yes, a lot of exciting science is in areas where it's hard to explain them to readers and harder still to find a compelling story to tell. It's not as if you can put your characters back at the big bang. (I refuse to count the story where a spaceship slips into a black hole, goes back in time, and *causes* the big bang.) But the fact is that there are still plenty of great stories left to tell in all of the subgenres of the field. We haven't thought of every alien race or transformed human society; we haven't dealt with every scientific point of interest or every biological oddity that might be thought of. We have not run out of science.

2. Nor have all the good ideas been told. It's true that the pure idea story, in which characterization does not matter—"Nightfall," "The Star"—is harder to come up with nowadays, in part because the more obvious ones have been taken. But there are still inventive writers who spew out ideas like a leaky firehose. To claim that the good ideas are used up is to be like that legendary patent official who resigned in 1800 because everything had been invented.

3. It's simply not true that the younger generation of writers cannot compare with the older ones. Good new writers come along every year, and great ones show up, too.

4. It *is* true that when you go back to some of the early sci-fi that first created an enthusiastic audience for the genre, much of their work does not hold up well. E.E. "Doc" Smith's work does not hold up well compared to later writers. But it's worth pointing out that he was helping invent a new genre, pioneering new ground. As was once said of the classics: "If we see farther, it is because we stand on the shoulders of giants." When they were busy inventing science fiction, our literary forebears did not think of everything at once. But it is an arrogant epochist who sneers at older writers for not being modern. I personally find *Slan* unreadable—but Van Vogt changed science fiction and like it or not, I am one of his heirs. There was an audience for my work because he created it. Besides, what does that have to do with today? Anybody who knows the average quality of high school and college graduate today has to laugh at the idea that the new generation is so sophisticated that they've finally caught on that sci-fi has always been lousy.

5. This one has some truth to it. When a new art form emerges, it sometimes forces the older art forms to adapt or die. The advent of movies began to kill vaudeville, and talkies threatened to kill theater. Why see local actors perform when you could see world-famous movie stars every time? And once

color film came long, neither plays nor fiction could compete for sheer spectacle. Once you might read a book in order to imagine faraway or magical places. Now you just went to the movies. In response, plays stopped trying to be realistic and concentrated on dialogue, while books retreated to the one place where movies can't go: inside the characters' minds. The same thing happened to movies when television came along—the intimate comedies and dramas became far more rare, since television could take you closer to the actors and put them in the living room or bedroom; movies became dominated by the movies that showed things you couldn't put on TV. So now, with computer graphics allowing movies and games to show things that have never existed and could never exist, print science fiction has less to offer. It has to find something that films or games just can't do in order to continue to exist.

6. Blaming the decline of sci-fi on women is just silly, I think. It might explain why fantasy sells *more* than sci-fi, but since I don't know of any women who've gone around killing male sci-fi readers, their entry into the audience can hardly explain the *decrease* in sci-fi readership.

7. Maybe there was once a kind of fantasy that was "easier to write," but it sure isn't the mammoth eternal epic that is selling in such vast numbers today. Today, in fact, what's making the best fantasy literature so good is the fact that fantasy is finally being written to science-fiction standards. That is, instead of stealing the tropes of Robert E. Howard or J.R.R. Tolkien, changing the names, and pumping out words, fantasy writers today are required by their readers to account for the economy, to carefully think through the rules of magic, to create plausible multilayered societies—in short, to fully invent their worlds, just as good sci-fi writers have to do. It's every bit as hard to do what Robin Hobb or George R.R. Martin do in fantasy as to do what Larry Niven or Jerry Pournelle do in science fiction. (And it's worth pointing out that even less talented writers usually sweat just as much blood to create mediocre fantasy novels as mediocre sci-fi novels.)

8. Today's college and high school grads are, in fact, less well educated and seem, at least, to be lazier than their predecessors. I have written diatribes elsewhere on the reasons why our schools are training a lot of kids to hate literature; this isn't the place for that. But this still wouldn't explain the *relative* decline of the science fiction audience. While those graduates who do strive to be part of the literary elite have always despised science fiction or appreciated only those sci-fi stories that are least like sci-fi and most like li-fi, and as li-fi writers and editors will tell you, *that* audience has not increased in numbers at all in recent decades.

There are some vaguer theories, too—so vague as to be impossible to prove or disprove. Like the idea that sci-fi is declining because instead of being excited about the future and eager to move on into it, the general public is now more likely to be discouraged and pessimistic, especially with science-centered futures, since science in so many ways seems to have failed to live up to the high expectations that people were led—in part by older sci-fi—to expect.

I suspect that it might also be a generational thing. It is still possible to write great science fiction, but many young writers may *feel* that the field has been saturated, that they cannot compete with the great ones who went before. So it's possible that a higher proportion of our talented young writers are simply moving into other genres where they feel it's more possible to do important, original work.

Or it might be a different generational shift. Maybe it's just that fantasy seems to offer clearcut moral decisions to a world that has lost hold of any sense of universal verities. While some kinds of religion make a lot of news, the fact is that in the Western world, belief in traditional religion and scripture has radically declined in the past decades, leaving people hungry for religion but unable to believe in the old ones. Good science fiction doesn't fill the void, but good fantasy can. So fantasy isn't a replacement for sci-fi, it's a replacement for the Bible.

Or it might be that sci-fi has simply run its course and it's time for another revolutionary wave to transform American literature. Just as science fiction was the revolution after modernism ("post-modernism" is just modernism with a new tie), perhaps the new wave of realistic character-centered mysteries are the revolution after sci-fi; or perhaps the new realistic fantasies are; or both. And perhaps the next literary revolution already has its seeds planted somewhere else, and we simply haven't noticed it yet. These things move in cycles that are beyond our control and are rarely identified until well after the fact. Maybe sci-fi simply got old and is now on life support simply because the life cycle of literary revolutions is only forty to sixty years and we've already had longer than we could have hoped.

Pick-your-speculation is a game we could play all day without coming up with a useful answer.

But let me suggest another set of possibilities:

1. Maybe most or all of these ideas contain some speck of truth, but the *real* fact is that all we need is some brilliant writer to bring science fiction back into preeminence, the way that J.K. Rowling put children's literature at the top of the *New York Times* Bestseller List for so many months that the big whining babies in the New York literary scene were able to pressure the *Times* to create a special children's list in order to get Harry Potter out of the way. (To which my response is, why not give Stephen King, Mary Higgins Clark, Tom Clancy and John Grisham emeritus status and open up even *more* slots on the list to those pathetic, needy writers who think somebody is *cheating* them out of their rightful measure of fame?) All it would take is one great writer to make all the hand-wringing about the death of sci-fi seem…premature.

2. Maybe the writer who will do that has just had his or her first story published in the annual *Writers of the Future* anthology, which continues to thrive, continues to discover eager and talented new writers, and continues to please thousands of readers who become the audience for yet another generation of sci-fi writers.

Science fiction has always happened first in the short stories. Novels bring each new movement to fruition, but the new ideas, the new trends, the new techniques have always surfaced first in the short form.

And if newsstand science fiction dies, maybe that's because the newsstand itself is dying; maybe the internet will eventually become the new home for sci-fi short stories.

The internet—and Writers of the Future. I tell my writing students that they owe it to themselves to submit their stories to this Contest and, therefore, this anthology *first*. Because Writers of the Future actually delivers on the promise. When you win, it can build you an audience; it can lead you to a career.

So. Maybe science fiction *is* dying. If it is, you'll find the best last gasps of the field here in these pages.

And if it *isn't* dying, it's in large part because of this book, this *series* of books devoted to the science fiction short story and the newly hatched writer, revivifying the field year in and year out. Perhaps not quite like the Nile flood or the monsoon, but at least like the April showers that bring May flowers.

For Doug and Helen

Richard Korblae

Have a good time!

BALANCER

Written by
Richard Kerslake

Illustrated by
James T. Schmidt

About the Author

Down-under author Richard Kerslake wrote his first science fiction tale, The Time Traveler, *at age eight and still has it. As a youngster, he delved into SF films and books such as* Land of the Giants *and* Time Machine *to Arthur C. Clarke's novels and C.S. Lewis's Narnia series. Much older now, our Sydney, Australia, resident has been writing in earnest for the last four years since reading Stephen King's* On Writing. *Richard relies on his physics degree and varied interests in technology, music and ancient history to create a rich blend in his own writing. His stories have been featured in e-zines such as* Dark Moon Rising *(darkmoonrising.com),* Antipodean SF *(antisf.com), and* Borderlands, *one of many Aussie fiction print publications. A prior semifinalist of Writers of the Future, Richard claims that the experience has been a fantastic boost for his writing. Richard is now completing a novel in addition to his other commitments, which include more speculative fiction writing, his family of girls and his executive day job with an international service company.*

About the Illustrator

When illustrator James T. Schmidt was little, he was always drawing. He continued drawing—in between doing homework and exploring the outdoors. The only inspiration he remembers at the time was his envy of a friend of his brother's who could draw 3-D letters. So James kept on drawing straight through high school and the local community college. There, he took advertising classes and learned the valuable lesson that advertising wasn't for him. Now he's working full time at a veterinary clinic which he loves ("Animals are awesome," he says). He also looks forward to enrolling in those art classes he missed as a boy. He still sketches and is looking to become a full-time artist/illustrator. His current inspirations are Tim Burton, Leonardo Da Vinci, Raphael and those individuals who enjoy his work. When he's not busy sketching or taking care of animals, James enjoys dancing, being outside, and traveling whenever possible.

"Time," said Balance-Master Sedra, "is an infinitely branching network of arteries, hanging down from a heart."

Beside me in the forest-class listened another boy and three girls.

"Imagine the heart pumping the blood down those branching arteries, toward the bottom. But the blood chooses only one path, leaving all other capillaries empty."

Master Sedra reached out and illustrated this on the blackboard, driving away a brilliant gold hummingbird that flitted around his chalk. A dozen white lines branched like an inverted tree; then a thin red line led from a heart-shape at the top, down an aortic trunk and along many branches to the end of a single capillary. "This red blood is the flow of our causality; the tree, all possible paths that the universe, the earth, could take."

"So our world is most probable?" asked a girl, Vanra.

"No. It will be a long while before you're ready for the Most Probable." The schoolmaster chuckled. He drew a horizontal line, and circled its intersection with the red artery. "This—here and now—is True Time: the ideal, Balanced, AD 1765 world."

"Then," I said, "who—?"

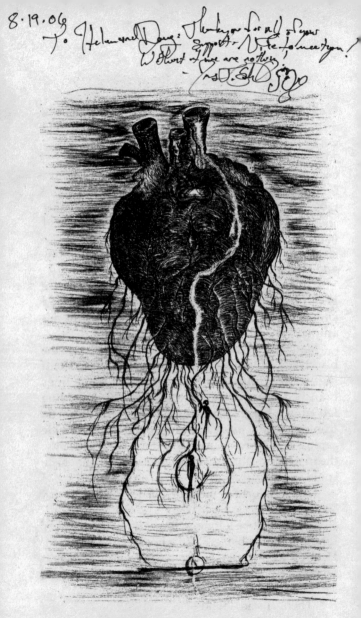

Illustrated by James T. Schmidt

"You, Hendri." Master Sedra smiled. "You will continue to ensure that the blood flows to our perfect 1765—here…So we need people to help." He drew a tiny human figure at a higher fork of red and white capillaries. "That could be you, back in AD 20, Canterbury, just twenty years After Democracy, ensuring that Ambassador Julius Caesar signs the Romano-Druidic Truce…or in AD 150, influencing Livinna to try sulfur in her saltpeter mix." He sketched another figure, higher up, closer to the heart. "Or you, Vanra, a thousand years earlier, preventing the birth of a would-be historical figure: harrowing work, denying life to innocents.

"Welcome to the life of the Balancer. Without us guarding the time probability junctions, entropic wormholes would redirect our causal blood. We'd jump, our very memories changing, away from perfection—toward that terrible, Most Probable artery.…"

•••

That was my twelfth birthday, my first Temporal School lesson.

We later learned that not all arteries other than our True Time were white. A few were salmon, even rose pink. On those anemic capillaries waited other children, other Hendris, Ghosts, who wanted nothing more than to steal our hard-won causal blood and replace our red-blooded present with theirs.

•••

As Spartacus emerged from the new People's Assembly, the Romans cheered. Modest as usual—although a free man for a decade—he bowed his head toward the spectators before making his way across the Forum, flanked by three bodyguard soldiers, ex-gladiators like him.

I thought: even after all these years, Spartacus abhors the publicity, hates being a figurehead. It took all of Gunra's Balancing efforts to entice him back from Thrace after his victorious slave revolution. Yet he's a signatory to the Declaration of Freedom, and can read well enough now to help draft Rome's new constitution. After this morning's swearing-in, he's the Roman Empire's newest consular candidate. Spartacus is well loved, with many to help him.

Freedmen comprised most of the crowd. Despite the painful process of replacing slavery with suffrage in the Roman Republic, few Roman patricians would accept the new order or publicly acknowledge Spartacus as a candidate to rule their empire. Yet the patricians' influential days were numbered, the Senate already reduced to a rubber-stamp upper house with filibustering, but little veto, power. I had helped see to that, whispering in suitable ears, dropping covert, future-forged gold into sweaty palms, aiding in the assassination of dangerous men like Crassus—inducing subtle chain reactions to ensure that this nascent Spartacus time-capillary would survive, flowing its causal blood toward our True Time eighteenth century.

It was tough Balancing work, my first assignment since graduating from Temporal School six years ago, and greatly rewarding.

Here in old Rome I was Barus the barber, Vanra my good wife Fulvia: minor figures whose mysterious entrance to, and exeunt from, Rome's stage was set in self-consistent historical stone; like those two prophets whose return to our future had been recorded as heavenly ascent in Judaean scripture.

"How did you go, Hendri?"

I turned to see Vanra, her pale face serious as usual. She wore the plain brown dress of a freedwoman: no rich togas or *stolae* for us, merely my tunic and her simple dress.

"It went well," I replied. "I kept the three senators talking. Did you divert the assassins?"

"I hinted to their contact that Spartacus would follow the Via Labicana, and they believed him. Those cutthroats should be arrested there by the guards—ninety percent probability. I'm monitoring."

"So another un-True artery stays white." I nodded. "Come with me for a wine."

She took my hand. Twelve Balancers, hailing from various eras, were stationed near this arterial intersection of time—most of them here in the Roman Empire, preventing the deadly slide toward the Most Probable World that would have followed the quashing of Spartacus's rebellion, his death at Crassus's hand. But rarely did I see another Balancer than Vanra-Fulvia.

I kissed her as we walked, home to the Via Fallorca and our marriage bed.

In the past six years, like true Roman and wife, we had fallen in love.

•••

Spartacus's candidacy was only ten days old when a Ghost, a dark Balancer from Other Time, crossed my path.

Crassus had been assassinated that spring: a busy time for Vanra and me. Now with Crassus tracked down and gone, the Freedom Party had removed its greatest obstacle, new democracy, but we still faced enormous challenges before Spartacus could prevail. The Forum seethed with dissent, patricians raised private legions in the provinces, and opportunistic Gaul rebels had besieged Massalia.

Paralus I knew to be a Balancer, but I hadn't discovered his true name. Through our quiet network we had found each other, and received our joint orders through leg-screens and mind-alerts: to detain a senator in the Helena Baths for two extra minutes. Thus the senator would avoid meeting in the street a treacherous, silver-tongued Senate colleague who would sour his judgment: a tiny, unwanted, renewed bloodflow toward the despotism Marcus Licinius Crassus had craved.

"We should each delay him separately," said Paralus, as we sat alone at the rear of his master's kitchen. "I'll speak to Senator Metellus in the baths, offer him wine. Then you come along and offer him a free haircut."

Paralus was a kitchen servant, and although Rome now had no slaves, the status of his ilk had risen little. He smelt—taking authenticity a little far—and his dark, Cappadocian eyes darted to and fro beneath thick brows.

"All right," I agreed. "You first, with the wine. But be subtle. If the senator asks why you are offering, what will you say?"

For the rest of the day we planned our mission, Paralus irritating and forthright; and I observed a change in him. He became quieter, sly, and his eyes stopped darting.

When I saw him glaring at me in outright hostility, thinking my attention distracted, I asked, "Is everything all right? You seem annoyed."

"Oh no, good Barus. Just concentrating on the mission to hand."

Yet my suspicions were aroused.

As we walked to the Baths, Paralus was still changing. He grew taller and younger, as though his new self hailed from one of those Other-Time arteries where people pursue longevity goals. I knew him for what he was—a Ghost of the true Paralus, invading from a different timeline, trying to rescue his particular future.

I watched from a steamy *caldarium* alcove as Paralus approached Senator Metellus and offered him wine from an amphora. The fat senator nodded, thanked him and drained the glass—obviously one of the new, rare patrician order willing to converse with plebs. Then Paralus leaned forward to whisper in Metellus's ear.

"You must leave here at once—" I overheard. Shaking his head, the senator stood. I stepped forward, eyes fixed on Paralus, and placed a hand on Metellus's rubbery, puce shoulder.

"Senator, can we talk?"

Metellus scowled. "Sorry. Must be about my business."

"Yes, you must," urged Paralus, face tense. "You must meet—"

"Do you know who this man is?" I smiled at the senator. "He's my tricksy brother, and he just put a sleeping potion in your wine."

"What?" The senator stared at the empty glass on the bench. "Surely not—"

"Oh yes," I said. "But it can be cured if you go back to the warm room for ten more minutes."

Metellus's lips tightened. "Who are you two?"

For another minute I held the senator's attention

with sheer forced eloquence, while Paralus was reduced to tugging at his sweaty arm.

"Please…" cried the Paralus-Ghost in unforgivable British. "Barus, I must save my time. Your timeline does not understand how man must become machine, fill the…"

"Senator, relax and sweat here a few more minutes."

"Young man—"

"Solar system with humanity…"

"I'm a barber—let me offer you a complimentary shave."

"No!" Metellus tore away, grabbing his towel, and stalked to the *frigidarium*.

His street appointment had come and gone. Whatever anti-Spartacan scoundrel would have accosted Senator Metellus in the street could no longer do so.

Paralus slumped against the tiled bath wall, eyes again darting, restored to his True self. "Ah—fireball," he moaned, in British. Then, remembering authenticity, he whispered to me in Latin: "A Ghost took me. Yes?"

So our mission was successful, and we closed the door on Ghost-Paralus's anemic time-capillary.

Yet Other-Time Ghosts were the bane of Balancers. In my Rome career I'd encountered several, and if they succeeded in overthrowing True Time, they could destroy our society, render me an unknowing serf in some bleak alternate eighteenth century. We must always be on the alert. Even Vanra—hadn't she lately been a little different, subdued…?

"What are you frowning about?" asked Vanra (Fulvia), gazing at me over intricate needlework that evening.

I broke from my reverie. "Nothing."

"It wasn't nothing. You were worrying."

"Planning, love."

"No, *worrying*, Barus. About what?"

Her tone was acquiring its investigative edge. Smiling at her, disconcerted, I went to the front of our shop and began to sweep away my day's hair-cuttings.

"If it's to do with that Ghost today," she called, "I'm not turning into one."

● ● ●

One summer day when I was thirteen, I witnessed the birth of Balancing.

I sat with my four classmates in the Cave of Alternate Vision, venue for all the most important temporal lectures during a student's seven hard years. So real, so three-dimensional were the Cave's wormhole-accessed images that I'd come to feel we could simply step through to those other times and live our lives there—as after graduation we would.

"Here we are, 1325 After Democracy," said Master Sedra. "The Birth of True Time. The castle of Edward of England, President."

Under a gray sky a tall man paces dour battlements, his square, stern features vivid across four and a half centuries.

A blood-streaked, gaunt young man appears. One minute President Edward paces alone, the next the wild-eyed Dawn Balancer stands in his path.

"Here—" he gasps, pushing toward Edward a small black box. "I have no time here, but take—"

President Edward recoils as if from a snake. Perhaps he's also fearful that the dirty young man might soil his resplendent blue robe. "What are you doing here? I'm calling the guards. Sergeant!"

He shouts into an old-fashioned radio-necklace, and running feet can be heard. The president draws a gun and levels it at the visitor's chest.

"No time," repeated the Dawn Balancer. "Yours is the most promising time channel. Woodlands, democracy..." he stares around, eyes wide. "Beautiful..."

"Time channel?" says Edward. He takes the box. "What does this do?"

"The data's all there...You must preserve your time artery. I'm from 2134, different capillary, hellish...Yet I helped invent this technology, discovered your world. Astounding...you're up to late industrial age already...."

"I see," says President Edward. He glances around; a sergeant, aiming a rifle, has appeared on the battlement. "So...this has to do with time travel?"

"Yes, and—"

"Come down with me. Tell me more."

"No time. My presence here is unstable. Entropy, wormholes, are eating me, pulling me away. Mine's the most probable—"

He vanishes, leaving Edward gripping the black box.

The air-screen went blank. I breathed again.

"The Dawn Balancer was from Most Probable World," said Master Sedra. "That breathless, anonymous man on the castle top found our time-capillary, already by chance nearly perfect. He gave us the means to secure and Balance our fragile time-lines. That black box, after a century of computer and N-spatial advancement, yielded the Temporal Methods, then our profession. By 1426, we had sent our first Balancers back to the key capillary junctions to ensure that the correct past happened—as, of course, it must have done for Edward's advanced society to exist at all."

•••

The summer of the year 1 BD drifted past, three eventful months for Rome but—after the Paralus-Ghost—quiet ones for Vanra and me. With Spartacus's campaign gaining momentum, and his consular election nearing, we could watch the flow of history take its True course, stepping in only occasionally to muster the precious causal blood back into the proper capillary.

Spartacus was hated and adored, a quiet and uneducated man. I often watched him from a distance; his public speeches were brief, unpolished and forceful as he spoke with abhorrence of slavery and oppression, vowing that Roman provinces would soon elect their own governors and promising more taxes on patricians. His trusted bodyguards accompanied him everywhere.

I, of course, never spoke to him, my authorized Balancing influence being several rungs down the pecking order from the great ex-gladiator, and several more still from Gaius Julius Caesar, his main electoral adversary. Spartacus did at least speak to ex-slaves and humble barbers like me, asking about their families and wants. Caesar never did: his votes would come from the patrician nobility, the burgeoning trading class, even perverse ex-slaves who wished Rome back to its old slave-taking glory where they had had no responsibilities.

In this period were three assassination attempts, two on Spartacus and one on Caesar. Both failed, but the second on Spartacus would have succeeded but for Vanra and me.

Buried in the skin of each Balancer's left upper thigh was a patch of cells that acted as a duplex screen, enabling communication with the Grand Balancer in our future. The Grand One, or any Balancer, could observe the past through this aperture and I, in turn—although it was awkward to be hitching up my tunic too frequently—could download information from our time-web. Vanra and I had spent a thousand Temporal School lessons understanding how those intricate time-flows connected, influenced one another, and could be subtly diverted.

The assassin, posing as a distraught petitioning mother with baby, would try to accost Spartacus one evening on Via Flavia. Beneath the assassin's brown maternal cloak would lurk a dagger that would, on current Most Probable time-capillary, find its way to Spartacus's heart and usher Rome into two centuries of orgiastic despotism. This I studied on my leg-screen, sitting in the shadowed rear of my shop.

Aware of our duty, Vanra and I set out to truncate this Probable future.

Vanra, gossiping in the market with friend Calpurnia, let slip a tale of riotous youths near an inn on the Via Flavia.

"Dreadful, they are," Vanra said, while Calpurnia nodded in sympathy. "A gang of about five, drinking ale and fighting. I heard they stole cakes from Lorano's bakery...."

Calpurnia's husband was a baker. She told him Vanra's contrived Lorano story and warned him to be on his guard against marauding, cake-stealing youths. Her concerned husband mentioned it over supper to his brother, a constable of Rome's fledging law brigade, and asked if he could patrol a little longer each night in the Via Flavia. Thus, when Spartacus was passing with his retinue and the assassin mother emerged weeping from the shadows to accost him, the nearby constable was alert enough to see an odd manliness in the mother's tread and to block "her" way.

Earlier, I had sneaked to a nearby stable and dropped into the manger six extra handfuls of hay. This hay, as modeled through our Balancer database, would enlarge the equine resident's next meal, causing her to pass stools exactly a minute earlier, and of slimier texture, than was More Probable. The horse thus evacuated midway along the Via Flavia, and when the assassin took a step backward from the approaching constable...

As a bystander helped the manure-stained "mother" from the ground, the baby bundle unwrapped to reveal a shiny blade. The miscreant tore away and ran, knocking pedestrians flying; the constable and one of Spartacus's guards gave chase and caught him near the Forum. Questions followed. The would-be assassin spent the last five nights of his condemned life in a cell.

And so...our subtle seedling acts, Vanra's gossip to Calpurnia and my slippery tactics, allowed Spartacus to live another day, just as the myriad time tendrils on my leg-screen had foretold.

•••

Even far ahead in our perfect eighteenth century, some laymen question why Balancers like Vanra and me work on time with such zeal. Our sense of duty, of course, but more than that. What drives us is the horror of the Most Probable World that ours could become if we fail.

Vanra and I witnessed this at nineteen.

So that it strikes home, Temporal School leaves the Most Probable lesson until last. When we don our yellow Balancer graduate robes and stride into the past to direct causality toward True Time perfection, we do so with its images engraved on our very souls.

We students, on our final day, filed into the Cave of Alternate Vision. On stage between the stalagmites, recognizable at once from his busts and 3-vids, stood the Grand Balancer himself. At his gesture, we sat.

The Grand One readied the air-screen. "At last," he said, "you will see AD 1765 as it should be."

In the air, dimmed by the number of temporal junctions from True Time, appeared scenes.

Forests falling to men's axes: animals fleeing.

Horses, of the ordinary dumb kind, being flogged by red-coated hunters in pursuit of a terrified fox.

A city full of beggars and pockmarked faces, its citizens dropping filth into the street from hovel windows.

"London," remarked the Grand One. "Near this very spot. Capital of a monarchy, trees gone, crowded with a million people who possess religious opiate but no awareness."

Starving ragged children, thieving and running through septic alleyways.

A raped woman screaming.

A man, strangling with a noose about his neck amid a jeering crowd.

The cheeks of two girls gleaming with tears.

"Most Probable 1765 had no airboats, medicine trees, or intelligent super-horses. Its history was not democratic progress like ours, but a millennium of religious discord and war."

Hopeless gaunt people, toiling in slums at handlooms and forges.

Cannon, cavalry, impaled youths shrieking from battlefield mudholes.

People abducted, chained, groaning in the bellies of ships, perishing amid their own filth.

The air-screen darkened.

We blinked.

"Remember. That is what we will become if we lose vigilance, if entropy prevails: if time-wormholes from present to past are permitted to erode that past. And the AD 1765 that you saw is only part of the downward slope, for in AD 2134, the Most Probable World ends."

● ● ●

Election day came with trepidation. I awoke on our straw bed convinced that I had had a bad dream, a true augury in Roman superstition; but try as I might I could not remember it.

I left Vanra still sleeping, and walked out stretching and yawning into the dawn-lit Via Fallorca. Around me donkeys pulled carts of wares to early market, and my neighbor shopkeepers were raising their blinds for the day's bustle.

An elderly man, tapping the ground with a stick, shuffled past me—and disappeared.

I gasped and stared around. None of the other pedestrians, even those adjacent to that vanished old fellow, had stopped to stare or seemed surprised.

Their time-paths were unchanged.

Time was changing around me. I and my whole Balanced future had flicked to a less True capillary branch of 1 BD. Almost certainly a Balancer, a Ghost, was near, filling a less-than-perfect capillary with causal blood, adulterating my future toward his.

Or hers…I glanced back into my shop. I walked to the rear room, relieved to see Vanra still sleeping peacefully. Yet surely, it couldn't be her. I could imagine no future reality wherein my beloved Vanra, even an alternate Vanra, would fight to preserve any other future than our own True one, with verdant Earth and disciplined philosophy.

But if it was a *close* Ghost-world to ours…?

I shook my head. This suspicion would get me nowhere, and Vanra and I had a full day's work, ensuring Rome's first election commenced without More Probable terrors occurring, blocking the alternate debacles our leg-screens had displayed. A Ghost would be a challenge, but one that we were trained for, and almost to be expected on such a historic day. We would find and eliminate him, as we had others.

I awoke Vanra. We breakfasted quickly on rolls and fruit, and I told her of the suspected Ghost.

"Very well," she said, "I will look for any reality shift pattern that may reveal our Ghost-friend's location. You concentrate on our main mission." She studied her leg-screen, running fingers over the skin to run scenarios, noting the positions of the nine other Balancers who today worked in Rome.

This morning at the election, as I confirmed on my own screen, renegade unemployed legionaries would Most Probably attack the polling house where Spartacus was to register his own vote. If True Time failed they would ransack the building, capture Spartacus and lynch him. Within a week those soldiers would be proclaiming Julius Caesar dictator of Rome; within a month the People's Assembly would be a burned and blackened memory.

So this election day was critical. All efforts of our highly trained Roman Balancers were bent toward its success, chaperoning in the first whiff of democracy that would within a century become a model for Persia and India.

We walked across the Forum toward the first polling house, where swelled a raucous crowd. Abruptly the house's gray tiles changed to reddish brown.

"Aha!" said Vanra. She glanced down, limping as she surreptitiously inspected her thigh. "That house was built with tiles from the…Arimus Quarries. The Balancer who influenced a particular shipment out of those quarries…was me. Five years ago: I had to change the masonry of—"

"I remember." I felt tense. I could see Spartacus on the polling house steps and rough-looking soldier types at the edge of the crowd that thronged around him; my mission would be to block the way of a certain tall ex-Praetorian with murder on his mind. I might be wounded, but I was determined—

"So, mine is the area that the Ghost is disrupting," said Vanra. "The usual attack mode against True Time, trying to eliminate us Balancers before invading the time-capillary in earnest. It's affecting *my* impingement on the past…five years ago. So something the Ghost is doing—maybe jeopardizing my ancestors—has potential to change me in the future…stop me becoming a Balancer, even destroy me…" Her voice stayed matter-of-fact. "What's the matter?"

I stared at her. An odd, rising sense of horror assailed me. Vanra dropped her skirt as one or two people in the crowd began to stare. Then I *felt* my legs move me toward a corner of the polling house.

Yes, felt my legs move me. Something had seized my will, and as I began to run, sensing Vanra following me, I knew that I had to kill a particular Spartacus bodyguard, and felt a sick certainty that the unfortunate man must be Vanra's ancestor.

After him, I would kill Spartacus himself.

I was the Ghost. I knew…and I faded out.

•••

I am Hendri 4-G, just now created, sent here by time-wormhole. My memories tell me my future: I must divert time's causal flow into my pretty wives Jayn and Sara, into me, and into our tremendous civilization, Earth of 1,800 years hence: an urban utopia, capital of a stellar empire, conqueror of a hundred worlds.

I stab a Roman bystander, one I know is ancestral to one of the Meta-Balancers, originating from a limp green version of the second millennium, who plague this reality. The ragged young man dies under my dagger-prosthesis, and the polling house architecture flickers and changes. Time alterations made by the stabbed man's descendant, Meta-Balancer Paralus, vanish, and although Spartacus still stands there a free man, the crowd is different, angrier. My data-organ tells me that even one of Spartacus's own gladiator followers will now prove treacherous; and two thousand miles away, the Persian Empire strengthens in cruelty, budding nemesis to Rome's fledgling democracy.

But Persian intervention will be needless, for Rome's soldiers will in eight months reintroduce slavery and appoint a militaristic general. That Roman general's grandson will rule the world from Atlantica to Cathay, and his grandson will inaugurate a scientific and industrial expansion that will put soldiers on our moon within a millennium.

As the bystander's thin, blood-slicked body drops to the pavement, people scream and dodge away from me.

Now for Spartacus's bodyguard, the fair-haired gladiator

Briton Theodosus, a sixtieth generation grandfather of Meta-Balancer Vanra.

In two strides, I am beside the bodyguard, holding my dagger ready.

I can no longer hear Vanra behind me. The impending certainty of her ancestor's death must already have erased her, rendered her a Ghost.

Fair-haired bodyguard Theodosus turns to me.

I raise my dagger…and unexpectedly meet the grim eyes of another, bearded man. Standing before Spartacus, oddly armoured in silvery plate, he blocks my way to Theodosus and the consular candidate. Spartacus peers past his bodyguards, frowning as a group of spectators lift my ragged victim's bleeding body.

The bearded man keeps his stern, gray gaze on me. He takes from his armor a shiny pistol, rather like those used by our Centaurian Guards, and points it at my face. A green beam emerges, I smell burning and—

Darkness…

● ● ●

I open my eyes and sit up in bed.

"There, lie still," says Vanra. "You're still not yourself. We kept you asleep for ten hours, until you looked safe."

I gaze at her, then around our familiar bedroom. Except the décor is somehow different.

"Not quite yourself," repeats Vanra—or Fulvia—I remember. "We Balancers are still repairing the damage your Ghost-self caused."

"But…I thought I was doing right."

"You"—she inspects her leg-screen—"started out as a laser-burned corpse, face down before Spartacus, with ugly metal cyborg parts in your body. The Grand One was first on the scene: he went back along that capillary, arrested your Ghost-self's progress across the square, prevented the murder of my ancestor, dragged the world back toward True Time, reinstated me. Of course, from my current point of view we simply completed our successful mission at the first polling house—you tripped up some ex-Praetorian who wanted Spartacus dead, and the constables arrested him. Then Spartacus gave his speech, and you became comatose. My memories are reverting to True Time too."

I lean up and kiss her. "Very good, sexy."

"But with all our efforts, our future is still different—and hence you are. At this moment the Ghost's residual impact is making you a deprived child, and our future AD 1765 has less prosperity than it should. Paralus and the others are working on it...but you are a coarser, lewder, bitterer individual than in True Time. Give it a few minutes."

I spit a foul taste from my mouth. A core of inner bitterness and temper does indeed eat at me. "So? Do I just wait to be restored?"

"Hello!"

I twist my head toward the voice, and see standing in a shadowed corner the Grand Balancer.

"Grand One."

He emerges into the light: a short hawk-nosed man in a gray tunic, like any Roman servitor, in clothes if not demeanor.

"And yes, you just wait. In five subjective minutes this capillary will be True again."

I bow my head, difficult to do when sitting in bed. This is the first time, since my revelatory Probable

World lesson six years ago, that I have met the Grand One, except on screen.

He sits on the bed. "Let me tell you what your Ghost did."

He relates to me the final seconds of my Ghost-Hendri, the reality he—*I*—so nearly unleashed.

"You realize, of course, that the bodyguard with the anachronistic light-gun was a Time Spy. He waited in that untried capillary, and several million others simultaneously, in case a Ghost like yours should divert some causal blood from True Time to one of the miserable realities he guarded. Now he will be reassigned. Albu is his name, born AD 1787…and his life-timeline consists of brief flashes of action, when a capillary he is stationed in happens to activate. You'll recall that one Spy is assigned from each class?"

I nod, remembering my relief when another classmate, not Vanra or me, had been nominated for the lonely path of Spy. "He—Albu—did well, Grand One."

"Yes. He stopped your other Hendri admirably. I'll reward him with an interesting set of Other Times, maybe that little-known arterial branch of expansionist, enslaving Mayas; they invade England in about AD 1200 and make it a Mayan province. How are you feeling?"

"Good."

The bitterness, my memories of Other-Time childhood abuse, are fading.

Vanra leans down and kisses me.

When I look up the Grand Balancer, too, has gone.

I clamber out of bed. "Well, what do we do today? What's our mission?"

A distant cheer arises from the direction of the Forum.

"No mission today," Vanra replies. "That was the election announcement—Spartacus is consul of the empire. No special adversity in the time-capillaries, at least today. For the moment, our True future is assured."

"Rome has its democracy? We get the day off?"

She nods.

I take her in my arms and pull her toward the bed.

THE BONE FISHER'S APPRENTICE

Written by
Sarah Totton

Illustrated by
Kim Feigenbaum

About the Author

Originally trained as a wildlife biologist, author Sarah Totton has worked many odd jobs: counting wild birds, chasing raccoons, and tending to the needs of pythons and monkeys at a zoo near Canterbury, England. Seeking steadier work, Sarah entered veterinary school and is now a licensed veterinarian. She works for the Marwar Animal Protection Trust which seeks to eliminate rabies from India's stray dog population. Meanwhile, Sarah has occasionally entered the Writers of the Future Contest over the past eleven years. After graduating from Odyssey writers' workshop in 2003, she "buckled down," began taking her writing much more seriously, and started entering the Contest every quarter. This is her seventeenth submission. Over the past two years, she's also sold works to Realms of Fantasy *magazine and several other anthology publications. She currently divides her time between the city of Jodhpur at the edge of India's Thar Desert and her Canadian home of Guelph, Ontario. Sarah may have caught her literary white whale but continues to practice wordcraft on unsuspecting story ideas.*

About the Illustrator

Illustrator Kim Feigenbaum simply opens her front door to get inspired for drawing. Residing within the beautifully forested Appalachian Mountains, Kim enjoys viewing wildlife and exploring the many diverse habitats of this awe-inspiring region. Her forested views feed Kim's admittedly unorthodox imaginings of organic forms commonly found in her work (though she also claims to just like drawing big monsters). Kim has been drawing for as long as she can remember while growing up in the suburbs just outside Atlanta, Georgia. She recently graduated from Appalachian State University in North Carolina with a major in studio art. Though her formal concentration there was painting, Kim's skill at drafting and her growing interest in fantasy literature has prompted her to pursue a career in illustration. Before studying studio art, Kim had also wanted to be a writer. She feels that illustration provides a career that combines the best of both interests.

The Bone Fisher could slip his hand into water without throwing a ripple. It was an art his apprentice was still mastering.

Sitting down to dinner, sharing the dead seagull they had found on the beach, the apprentice watched him spoon the meat from the gull's body. He did it neatly, without cutting and without touching its feathers. He didn't wait for it to cool before he ate it. Dealing with being burned was another art the apprentice was learning.

"Tell me about people," said the apprentice.

"There are three kinds of people," he told her. "The first kind—the oldest kind—want to be rescued." Another spoonful of steaming gull muscle disappeared into his froglike mouth. "The second kind want to do the rescuing." He went on chewing.

"And the third kind?" she prompted him.

"The third kind want to be left the hell alone. And God help you if you bother one of them."

"Which kind am I?" she asked. She knew very well which kind she was, but whenever she asked, he would tell her the story of how he found her....

• • •

It was the custom in that day and age to bring unwanted babies—those born out of wedlock, the unwanted, the misshapen—to the beach and leave them there for the tide to take. The Bone Fisher took no notice of them. As living, innocent beings with no memories, they were of no use to him. One particular gray morning, however, when he went out with his bucket looking for lures, he stumbled across a bassinet lodged in a rock outcropping on the edge of a tidal pool. It was apparent why the child had been left there; it had a misshapen head, and the hand that grasped the edge of the bassinet had only three fingers. The child was still alive, though not crying, only blinking its clear eyes. It had been tied securely into the bassinet with two gray ribbons crossed and knotted below its chin. The bassinet itself had been unstably set on the edge of the tidal pool which the Fisher himself knew to be waist deep. The pool never emptied completely even at the neap tide in the hottest and driest of years.

As the Fisher watched, the child moved and the bassinet tipped, spilling the child into the depths. It sank immediately. The child's mother had obviously taken care to weight the bassinet, leaving nothing to chance.

The Fisher watched slow bubbles breach the surface, tendrils of slipgrass stirring in the child's wake until they went still. He watched for a time before turning away and going back across the sands to the harbor. A few steps he took, then he stopped. Then a few more. Then stopped. One step. He watched the bucket swinging from his hand. He dropped it, and the swag spilled out across the sand. And then he turned and walked back to the tidal pool, stepped into the water, warm as soup, and reached into its depths until he felt the carapace of the bassinet with a great softness of baby inside it. He pulled it up. Then he took the child home.

The Fisher knew nothing of children or of how to look after them, so he fed her body on beach carrion and her mind on the dreams of the elderly to give her wisdom, cynicism, the strength to resist hope. Hope was valueless and potentially dangerous, innocence more so.

He also tried to instill in her, as much as her nature would allow, a toughness of character. He did this by acquainting her with the world's sharpest edges early on. He discovered that though her body was misshapen, and she quite lame, her eyes were keen and sharp, and very tender to the beautiful things hidden among the sand and stones on the beaches. Before she was very old, he began sending her out to gather lures for his nightly fishing. She learned quite young that the best time to go out was at dawn when the beaches were empty, because sometimes when people saw her, they threw stones at her. She was a reminder of the worst that could happen. She learned to take the Fisher's cloak while he slept and cover herself with it whenever she went out. It was so big on her that when she wrapped it tight around herself, no one could see her at all; oh, they knew who she was, but they behaved more respectfully when they couldn't see her deformities. No one would ever attack her directly, of course; they were all too afraid of her master.

So the years passed, and the apprentice grew into young adulthood via a life of ritual: nights of dreams seeded with stolen thoughts, mornings searching and collecting, evenings of questions over a scavenged or stolen dinner. And always the question, "Tell me about people." But never did the Bone Fisher answer her question: *What kind am I?*

• • •

On an early morning in summer when the apprentice was seventeen, she was crossing the pebbled beach with her bucket as the sun rose. The lure bucket was small and ceramic, black enamelled on the outside, white on the inside. She would feel the pull of it in her shoulder joint as she carried it, even empty. The tide was ebbing—the best time for searching, as the stones at the water's edge were still wet. There she would find bits of glass, translucent and smooth or frosted. The Bone Fisher thought the green ones best for his purposes—the ones that most appealed to those drifting in dreams. For many people, green was the color of paradise.

The Fisher sent her out for glass, but she also collected colored pebbles, odd ones, blue ones, green ones, ones with fossils embedded in them, peculiar shells. These were for her. She would put them in the pockets of the Fisher's cloak till there was no more room, and it was time to go home.

On this particular day, she had massed a few handfuls of glass in her bucket and one or two notable pebbles, when she found a golden heart in the sand between the stones. When she picked it up, she saw that the heart was a golden locket attached to a fine chain, like the kind lovers give each other. She dipped it into the sea to wash the sand away. The chain was broken, probably how it had come to be here. She tried to pry it open, but couldn't manage it. Pebbles and glass were the enemies of fingernails, and hers had lost the war long ago. The Bone Fisher occasionally used gold for its powerful mesmerizing properites. She should have put it in the bucket for him. Instead, she slipped it into her pocket with the pebbles.

That night, she lay awake trying to imagine the faces of the lovers in the locket. Who were they? Were they people she had seen before, at a distance on the beach? Were they still in love? Were they dead? A week later when she found herself alone in the old watchtower where she lived with the Fisher, she pried the locket open with a knife from the kitchen. There was nothing inside it but a few grains of sand. She was disappointed. It was like some of the pebbles she found on the beach which looked so beautiful and colorful when wet, only to become dull, gray things when the sea had dried on them.

Not long after she found the locket, she made a discovery of another kind. She had just finished her morning's lure hunting, and the bucket was nearly full of bright nuggets of glass. They were clean because she'd taken a great deal of care to rinse them in the sea, standing there in her shorts while the water flooded the tops of her rubber boots. She always washed the glass just before coming home. It was the best part of her day, to count the fruits of her labor, but it was also the most stressful. By the time she reached this stage, it was well after dawn, the most likely time she would be discovered.

She had just finished washing the glass and was wobbling on the stones, one-footed, emptying the water out of her rubber boot when she saw a man down by the bitches. The bitches were what the townsfolk called the jagged rock islands off the end of the point that lay just under the water at high tide and would rip the bottom out of a boat if you weren't careful. At low tide, they stood right at the water's edge, bared to the gums. The man was sitting on one of these rocks with his bare feet braced on the opposite one. She couldn't tell at first what he was doing. Wisdom dictated that she leave before she was seen, but he seemed so innocuous sitting there, and she found herself suddenly curious to see what he was doing. She moved closer.

He was playing with something long and dark on the sand. Coming closer, she saw it writhing there, glistening, silver and black. It moved like an eel, but didn't look quite like one. The man pinned it to the sand with his toe, and it curled around his foot and slithered up to encircle his ankle. The man pushed off the rocks and turned to go back up the slope. The eel—or whatever it was—looked like a ribbon now, still around his ankle. He caught sight of the apprentice and stopped. The apprentice pulled the cloak tight around herself. The man came toward her. He managed the pebbled slope very well for someone without shoes. The apprentice backed away from him. As she did, the wind caught her hood and blew it back from her face.

She had never seen another person at such close quarters before. He looked perhaps old enough to have small children.

The apprentice pulled her hood up quickly.

"I've seen worse," said the man. He said it like a challenge. "What's your name?"

She knew about the concept of naming; she swam in enough dreams and nightmares to know it. "I don't have a name. I'm the Bone Fisher's apprentice."

"What's in there?" said the man, pointing to her bucket.

"Lures, for the Fisher," she said. "I collect them." She wasn't sure whether this was strictly a secret. No one had ever asked her before.

"Oh," said the man, as though he had solved a puzzle. "You're like a bowerbird."

"I gather them for a different purpose than a bowerbird does."

"How do you know what a bowerbird is?" said the man. "They don't live in this part of the world."

"I've seen them. I've seen the world through a thousand eyes," she said.

"I've seen a bit of the world too," he said. "Through my own."

"What's that thing around your ankle?" she asked.

"A thought-sliver," said the man. "It'll be gone in a minute or so."

The Bone Fisher had mentioned thought-slivers to his apprentice, mostly to complain about how they clogged the dream-weave. They were ephemeral, unimportant, so he said, but potentially dangerous for the untrained mind. The Bone Fisher had never let her handle one, or even see one up close.

The apprentice was about to speak, to ask this man what he was doing with it, but he spoke before she did. "I'm Bellan, by the way. Hello. And goodbye." The thought-sliver disappeared like smoke and then he turned and, in a peculiar gingerish run, he hurled himself up the slope of rolling pebbles and left her there on the beach.

•••

The next time she saw Bellan, he was floating in the cove at dawn in a little coracle, like the ones she had seen the fishermen use, though none of the fishermen dared use this cove—it belonged to the Bone Fisher. And they never hunted for what the Bone Fisher caught.

Bellan stood in his coracle. "Hello, little bowerbird," he said. He did not look up at her. He was too intent with what he was doing. He leaned over the edge of the boat with his hand outstretched over the water. He knew enough to find a calm patch of water, but he was clumsy and unskilled. When he thrust his hand into the water, he drew a splash, and he pulled up a thick ribbon of green that immediately turned bright pink and dissolved between his fingers. He swore and shook his hand. "That burned!"

"It would," said the apprentice, "unless you fix it quickly."

Bellan put his hand in the water to cool it. "You know about these things?"

"Of course," she said. "I've been years learning them."

"Will you teach me?"

"Why?" she said.

"I want to learn. Will you teach me?"

"It would be dangerous."

Bellan paddled his coracle to the slipway where she stood and jumped out next to her. "I know a little," he said. "I've read about it, studied it. Most of the skills are practical though, and I need someone to show me."

The apprentice suspected what the Bone Fisher would do if he found anyone trespassing in his little cove, let alone angling for his knowledge. "The Bone Fisher would kill you," she said. "Eventually. But first he'd strip out your soul. You really shouldn't be here now. He could find out."

"He doesn't have to know."

•••

He was a long time convincing her, and eventually, she agreed. She spent hours showing him how the lure was tossed so that it would twirl as it sank. She instructed him how to wait, leaning over the water until your back screamed at you, and longer, until pain didn't matter. She taught him to cone his fingers before darting his hand into the water so as to break the surface silently. When he had learned all of these things well enough, she went out with him in his coracle and had him try. The first time he succeeded, he caught hold of a nightmare. He screamed and kept screaming long after she'd shaken it free of him and brought the boat aground. Afterward, he cried like a small child, but he was still sane. He must be of very strong character to have stood it and survived, she thought.

"That was awful," he said, wiping away tears.

"I know," she said. "I caught my mother's nightmare once."

"She must regret…the guilt she must feel."

"Not guilt," she said. "She dreams me as a monster seeking revenge. She thinks I have fins and fangs. The most hideous thing she's ever seen. She—"

"Stop it," said Bellan. "I can't stand it."

•••

For a long time after that, the apprentice hardly saw Bellan, and when she did, he seemed reserved and cautious. Every time the apprentice went out onto the beach in search of lures, she looked for him. While on one of her trips, hoping for a sight of him, she found a little green crab in a tidal pool. Because there was room in the bucket, she filled it a little with water and put the crab inside and took it home. It became a fixture in her room. She put it into an old bucket and changed the water every day, and she took it out onto the beach with her and let it play on the sand. She had nothing else on which to lavish her affections. Lately on some days, the excess of feeling nearly drove her mad.

•••

After a week of not seeing him at all, she set off across the sands when it was dark enough that no one would recognize her. She went into the little cove halfway along the pebbled beach and squeezed into the crevice in the rocks there. She wormed her way inside until she came to a little chamber. Here, she kept all of her possessions—hidden so the Bone Fisher wouldn't take them from her. She gathered the coins she had collected, found on the beach and hoarded over the years. She took all of them, half a hundred of them—she did not know how many she would need—and put them into her pocket. The other thing she took was the cloth mask she had found several years before. It was a rich piece of work, though the tiny jewels studding it were not on tightly and likely to be lost. It was a mask meant to cover the entire head, though hers being larger than most, it was tight to squeeze into. The mask was opulent, likely imported from another place. It was fashioned in the shape of an elephant with a long, baggy trunk that nearly trailed the ground. It had been cast onto the beach, as many masks were discarded on the Festival Night when the real celebrations began.

She donned this mask along with her usual clothes, and a pair of gloves, also found on the beach. She had stuffed the finger and thumb with rags so that no one would know she was lacking them.

For the first time in her life, she braved the company of other people. For the first time in her life, she had reason enough to brave the company of other people. Dressed as she was, she fit in amongst the contrived grotesquerie of the others. No one paid her any mind.

She was at first overwhelmed with the feeling of people, so many people around her. She was surprised at the warmth of their bodies, pressed against her in the crowds. She found it strange at first, then unpleasant, and she pushed and poked her way through to a less crowded place. She had thought that it would be easy to find him, that no matter how he was costumed, she would recognize him. But she had not imagined so many people, so many colors, so much clutter, so much *noise*. One little child, dressed like a monkey, took hold of her trunk and tried to swing from it. The apprentice had to snatch it away. She stopped to catch her breath, looking for a way of escape back to the beach, but she was blocked by columns of people, five and six deep. There was no escape, except behind her, where she found a scarlet tent with an opening large enough for her. She slipped inside. Here, it was quiet, and there were no crowds. Only one woman, sitting, waiting expectantly, not pressing herself on her like the others.

"Tell your fortune, miss?" The woman indicated a large red cushion opposite.

The apprentice sat, and produced her bag of coins. She set them in front of the fortuneteller. The fortuneteller's eyes widened when she looked inside. She set the bag aside and said, "May I see your palm?"

The apprentice hesitated, and extended her hand. The fortuneteller sighed and before the apprentice could protest, she had pulled off her glove, revealing her three-fingered hand. The fortuneteller sat in silence, looking at her hand, but she neither shrank from it, nor did she seem repulsed. And then the apprentice

Illustrated by Kim Feigenbaum

noticed that the other woman's throat was mottled with deep green skin beneath her twists of scarf. She was a monster too, though one who could pass for normal.

"Will you not read my fortune?" said the apprentice.

"I can see it quite plainly."

"What must I do to win him?"

The fortuneteller shook her head.

"Tell me," said the apprentice. "I can wait a lifetime, if I must—"

"No," said the fortuneteller. "He will never love you that way. And if you continue to demand of him what he cannot give you, he will come to hate you."

"What can I do, then?"

"You can do nothing to change his mind," said the fortuneteller. "At least, not to turn it toward you. You have two options. The first is to go on as you are. You will live, possibly love another man. But you will not win that one either."

"How do you know?" said the apprentice.

"I have experience in these matters," said the fortuneteller.

"What's the second option?"

"To stop going on as you are."

"You mean…die?"

"Not necessarily," said the fortuneteller. "But you must change yourself somehow."

The apprentice went home with her thoughts. Crossing the beach, she stripped off the elephant mask and dropped it onto the sand. It had been one of her most prized possessions, but it had served its purpose.

•••

The Bone Fisher had noticed that for some time

now his apprentice had been eating less and less, toying listlessly with her food. Moreover, she had been, of late, morose and sullen. More of a concern, she had been bringing in fewer and fewer pieces of glass, which seemed odd as she seemed to be spending more and more time on the beach. She kept her secrets well, but he knew she must have some. He had always respected her sleep, all her life. He had protected her dreams, warded away the nightmares which would surely have preyed on her young mind, fed as it was with the worst memories he could find for her. Her dreams had, until now, been sacrosanct to him. But as he watched her from day to day wasting away in front of him, saying less and less, he decided that he must find out what the trouble was. So that night when he saw her coming back across the sands when she ought to have been sleeping, he waited until she did sleep and then he delved into her dreams. Straightaway, he found Bellan in her memories. In fact, there was little else among her dreams but images of him. When she went out on the beach these days, she wasn't searching for glass, she was searching for her heart, watching for a lone figure on the lip of the tide. The Bone Fisher was surprised and somewhat revolted by his discovery, and he abandoned her to her pointless dreaming.

Who was Bellan? The name was a ghost in his memory, but then, he knew so many names. He knew everyone's names.

He went out in his seashell boat with the choicest pieces of glass, the palest green ones, in the quiet of pre-dawn, though the waters and dreams were more turbulent than he would have liked. They always were after the Night of Masks.

The Bone Fisher found Bellan after a bit of searching. For some reason, the young man's dreams were muted,

quiet things. Not weak, but still and focused. Who
was Bellan? Bellan had dreamed a thousand dreams
in which he was the hero, in which he rescued children
and the helpless from danger. This was not unusual,
but about Bellan, there was plenty which was. In
none of his dreams did the apprentice figure, nor any
maiden, young, beautiful or otherwise. Nor could the
Fisher find, as happened in some such cases, a desire
for young men. There was simply no desire of that
type for men or women in this man at all. And yet
Bellan was neither innocent, nor damaged. He was
whole, complete. He didn't love the apprentice at all,
had no capacity to do so. The Fisher was disinclined to
instill such desire in him, even had he known how it
could be done. No, the Fisher's anger had dissipated
at this revelation. He did not understand Bellan, but
he was intrigued enough to let him sleep, at least
another night, perhaps longer, so that he could study
him.

•••

The morning after the Night of Masks, while
walking the beach and searching for Bellan, the
apprentice contemplated her situation. How many
days would she spend like this, yearning, suffering
to no purpose? How much futile dreaming? Life had
been pain enough before this, but it had been a quiet
pain. Now, it roared so loudly she could hardly sleep,
hardly think. Yet it was the noise of nothing, a complete
fantasy. If the fortuneteller had counseled her correctly,
she should stop going on the way she was. How,
though? By ending her life? She suffered, but she did
not want to die. She felt more alive now than she ever
had before. What other way was there to change? The

Bone Fisher might be able to do something. The Bone Fisher was a powerful man…Would he deny her this one request?

As they sipped soup from the skulls of a married couple that evening, she said to the Bone Fisher, "I want my desire for love to die."

"Die?" said the Bone Fisher. He was a wise creature, experienced in worldly things, witness to the world's happiness and tragedies, in the ways of love (he had known it once himself, and it had left him bitter). But he had never encountered such a wish as this one, nor had he expected this request from her.

"I want my desire to go," she said. "I want you to take it away. I was happier without it. I want to stop wanting."

He had raised her to be strong, tough. He had not expected to be confronted with this cold practicality. A part of him felt suddenly very sad. "To take away your memory of him, you mean?" he said.

"No," she said. "I want to keep my memories. But I want them uncolored by this…this curse of wanting."

"To take away your hunger would kill you," he said. "To take away your appetite, you would have no will to eat."

"What I hunger for, I can live without," she insisted. "If I must live without it, I would rather not hunger for it too."

That she was damaged, inside as well as out, was clear. He could not heal her. He was no healer. But she was not asking him to heal her. She was asking him to break her even more until the inside no longer hurt. If that could be done.

The Bone Fisher nodded. He would try to grant her request, though he was not sure how he would do it.

He thought about it many days, and then one

morning, he asked her to join him in his seashell boat. She had not ridden in this boat since the early days of her apprenticeship when he had first initiated her into the sickness of the world, guiding her through dreams and reality. She sat quietly in the stern, head bowed as though in thought, hands between her knees. She did not move or stir, though the water was rough in the bay, and it jostled the boat. She was very calm, now that she anticipated an end to her suffering.

The Fisher brought the boat into the cove. She stirred herself then and dropped the anchor, holding the mother-of-pearl gunwale to steady herself.

"Get into the water," he said to her.

She took off her shoes and did so. It was late in the fall, and the water was cold and black, but she knew how to swim, and he held her with his skeletal hand by the nape of her neck.

"I will have to hold you under for some time," he said. "You will struggle, but I will not let you go."

She was shivering too much to reply. The water was cold and silent, with a great emptiness below her. She glimpsed green ribbons some way beneath her and remembered Bellan pulling one free. Then the colors faded, and there was a great rumbling, as though the sea bed had opened, and she felt some of the warmth and the light, a pale-colored light, drawn out of her. The cold suddenly slipped into her. Instantly, she stopped shivering and lay limp while the Bone Fisher held her. She did not struggle when he pulled her from the water and put her back in the bottom of the seashell boat. She lay in the boat, quiet now, not even shivering.

The Bone Fisher took off his cloak and lay it over her.

"I don't feel any different," she said, almost angrily. "Am I supposed to feel any different?"

Nor did she feel any different that night when she went to bed. Her dreams were empty, formless things, but then they always were on nights when the Bone Fisher didn't feed her, when she didn't tap the dreams.

On waking the next morning, she at first forgot that the night before had happened. Then she sat up, looked around her little room with its boots, rinsed in seawater and set in the corner upside down, her blue seashirt that she only wore on the windiest days. So ordinary, so normal, she wondered if she'd dreamed the day before, if today was the day of her surrender.

She went out onto the beach. It was later in the morning than she usually went. Perhaps that was why she saw Bellan, for he lately seemed to have been avoiding her. At first, she didn't recognize him, seeing a figure in a gray smock, paddling the coracle out by the point. It was him, and yet…the colors of the day were faded, the sea strange and flat, even the pebbles were like paper. She looked at him and looked at him. "I used to love him," she thought. She peered hard at him, trying to understand what that meant, but her keen eyes could not spot a whisper of charm, and she quickly grew bored. She had glass to collect. And indeed, the Bone Fisher noted as the days passed, that his apprentice brought in buckets heaping with glass, more than she ever had before, even though her trips to the beach became shorter.

One morning, she tipped out her bucket with her little green crab and left him on the beach for the tide to take away. She reached into her pocket and pulled out the golden locket with its grains of sand inside.

There are three kinds of people in the world.
Which one am I?
She threw the locket into the sea.

TONGUES

Written by
Brian Rappatta

Illustrated by
Ozzie Rodriguez

About the Author

Tri-linguist Brian Rappatta's life revolves around language—whether teaching Spanish and German in a small Colorado plains high school or English to adult learners enrolled in a family literacy program. In college, he triple-majored in all three languages and studied abroad in Ecuador and Germany. After receiving an MA in education, he's now getting his second MA in teaching English as a second language.

His love of languages naturally extends to writing and editing speculative fiction. When he was younger, Brian read genre classics like The Lord of the Rings, The Chronicles of Narnia, and a whole lot of other genres as well. In high school he began writing his own stories. By 2004, Brian attended the Odyssey writers' workshop in New Hampshire, studying with World Fantasy Award–winner Jeanne Cavelos and writer-in-residence George R.R. Martin. In late 2005, he was hired as an associate editor for Surreal Magazine. His work has appeared in various small press publications; however, this entry marks his first writing award.

About the Illustrator

Osbaldo "Ozzie" Rodriguez has been fascinated by pictures all his life. As a four-year-old he would watch cartoons and spend hours sitting with crayons and pencils trying to draw his favorite characters. In school, he eagerly took every art class. After school, he read comics, played video games and watched more cartoons. About the same time, Ozzie began to read stories of fantasy and adventure, trying to picture and draw these characters as well. His formal commercial arts training started after his acceptance to an all-arts high school. Ozzie went on to study art at New Jersey City University and then to William Paterson University where painting, printmaking and graphic design became new creative outlets for him. Two years ago, he received a statewide scholarship from the Art Directors Club of New Jersey. This led to receiving his first full-time job as an assistant art director.

That last night on Penitentiary, as the drugs the guards had put in his last meal began to take hold, Seamus knew he'd be waking up a long time later on a new planet and with a new religion.

The emergence from the transit death was always the same: one huge inrush of breath, the lungs jump-starting again after long disuse, the body clawing its way back from death. Disorientation, caused by the blindness of deep stasis. And then the gagging and the puking as the body tried to purge the aftereffects of the slow-trans drugs.

He was not alone this time, though. There were hands, warm on his chest as he shivered. And then a voice, calling to him. "Dr. Martinez! Dr. Martinez, can you hear me?"

He tried to focus on the voice even though his sight would not return for several hours. "Wh——" *Where am I?* was his first question, but his stomach heaved and he vomited. He couldn't tell for certain, but he thought he must have gotten some all over the man who had called his name.

Finally, Seamus managed, "Who are you? Where am I?"

"I'm Reverend Thomas Huntsberger," said the voice. "You're on Onomayu."

Seamus didn't know where Onomayu was, and he didn't much care. "Reverend? What de—de—denom——?"

"I represent the Protestant Union."

Protestant, Seamus thought. *So I'm Christian again.* It should have been comforting. After fifty-two years, he'd finally returned to the church of his youth.

"You can save your time, Reverend," Seamus said. "You might as well send me back to Penitentiary. I'm not converting."

"Oh, we didn't bring you here to convert you, Dr. Martinez. We need your help."

Even worse. Seamus was almost relieved when a wave of nausea rolled over him.

•••

If this was a penal facility, Seamus couldn't prove it by his cell. It was a spacious room, with a real bed, not a poor excuse for a cot like on Penitentiary. It had its own alcove bathroom stocked with towels and shampoo, and when Seamus experimented, the hot water even worked. The entirety of the wall opposite the bed was a screen connected to the terminal set in a small table. He spent many hours catching up on the soccer scores from Saturn's lunar leagues for the past decade.

The second morning, a boy, maybe sixteen years old, appeared at his door. "Good morning," he said to Seamus.

"To you, too." There were no guards with the boy. Odd. "Pardon me for saying this, but you don't look much like a prison guard."

"Oh, I'm not a guard, sir. I'm just—the reverend's assistant. I'm Alan. I'm here to take you to him."

"I see."

"I'm surprised you haven't left your room yet. There's lots to see."

"You mean the door wasn't locked?"

Alan looked aghast. "Of course not. We would never do that."

"Then you won't last long in the corrections business, I'm guessing. Lead on, then. Let's go meet the fine reverend."

Alan led him back down the corridor, past the room where he had awoken. Then the boy stopped at a lift. He pushed the call button, and the door opened immediately. "After you, sir," Alan said.

Sir? This place was already much better than Penitentiary. Seamus stepped into the lift.

After a few seconds the lift doors opened onto an enormous room. The ceiling was high overhead, so high as to be almost mistaken for open sky. At the far end of the chamber was a long metal table and a glass window overlooking a vast panorama of mountains. Seamus's breath caught in his throat; even Penitentiary's rec gymnasium had not boasted this much open space.

"Go on," Alan said. "You can get out of the elevator, you know."

Seamus hesitated for a moment. With the ceiling high overhead and the wide window looking out onto the sky, he had the distinct impression of stepping out into open air. But as he stepped out of the elevator, the floor beneath his feet did not give way.

"I'll let the reverend know you're waiting for him," Alan said. "He should be here shortly." The lift doors closed, and Seamus was alone—truly alone—for the first time in years.

He wasted no time. Practically sprinting across

the carpeted floor beneath him, he rushed across the chamber to the massive display window at the far end.

The window looked down upon a valley formed by mountains of some type of rock resembling limestone. In all his travels, he had never seen mountains such as these.

In the crook of the valley lay a village. He could see the rooftops of a great variety of dwellings. It was hard to get a good read on the architecture from this vantage point, but Seamus thought it looked obviously pre-industrial.

"Impressive, isn't it?"

Seamus started. Such had been his absorption in the view that he'd forgotten where he was, just for a moment. He turned.

Reverend Huntsberger was short and round, with close-cropped graying hair. He wore spectacles, an affectation that made him look somewhat pedantic.

"Dr. Martinez, I'm Thomas Huntsberger." The reverend extended a hand for Seamus to shake. "It's nice to meet you, properly, I mean."

"You're my new contractor?" Seamus asked.

"I am. How do you like our facility? A bit more comfortable than a penal asteroid, I hope?"

"It's…impressive," Seamus admitted. "But I'm a little confused. It must have cost a fortune. Why spend so much money on a penal facility?" Huntsberger chuckled. "This isn't a penal facility, Dr. Martinez. This is a retreat center."

Seamus grunted. "Retreat center? There's a new one." Penitentiary had officially been called a "Rehabilitation Campus."

The reverend smiled and shook his head. "No, I'm afraid you misunderstand, Dr. Martinez. You see, we didn't build this place with the purpose of rehabilitating wrongdoers." At Seamus's frown, he hastily added, "Though we are fully licensed to take on confinement contracts, have no fear. Your sentence is safe with us." He chuckled at his own joke.

"What about those people down there?" Seamus nodded to the little village nestled in the valley.

"The Onomayu. A remarkable people."

"I see. Pre-industrial, I'm guessing, judging by the architecture?"

"Very."

"Did anybody ask them if they wanted a religious resort on their front lawn?"

"You needn't worry about them. We've expressly forbidden our guests any direct contact with the natives. Observation only."

"I see. So it's okay to hang out inside the mountain and spy on them, but not to talk to them."

Huntsberger frowned. "The arrangement is not ideal, but until their civilization develops it's the only way we can learn about their culture. They're quite fascinating, Dr. Martinez."

Seamus took his gaze away from the village in the valley. "Is that why you brought me here?" he asked.

"Of course. Despite your unfortunate imprisonment in the last decade, you're still a fine xenolinguist."

Seamus understood the subtext well enough. "You needn't waste breath on flattery, Reverend," he said. "I take it their language is giving you problems?"

"Yes. They have an incredibly intricate ceremonial language that has completely baffled the computer translation matrices we've set up. Their day-to-day language is fairly straightforward, but…"

"There's not much that's fairly straightforward about ceremonial languages in any culture."

"I see your point. Why don't you take a look for yourself?"

Huntsberger gave a command to the room computer, and the transparent wall began playing video of the Onomayu village. The video opened in a large gathering hall, what appeared to be some form of community hut. Approximately sixty of the natives were gathered around, sitting in clumps on the ground. Then, the entire assembly began chanting one word—*Retauros*—and one man, an elder, by the looks of him, got up and moved to the forefront of the group. The group's chanting rose to a fevered pitch, and then fell silent. All those assembled in the room watched the man, whom Seamus assumed to be Retauros, expectantly.

The man spoke, at first in a lilting, cadenced speech that reminded Seamus of a Scottish brogue. The man Retauros was quite a performer, injecting his performance with theatrical rises to thunderous crescendos and alternating with throaty whispers.

The language seemed to change during the performance as well. Parts of the man's speech were filled with undulating, vowel-heavy utterances while other parts contained the jarring of several harsh consonants together. Seamus could detect no coherence to the language other than an obvious lilting rhythm; through it all, the audience sat transfixed, and at certain points either laughed or wept in a religious fervor depending upon the tone of the performer.

The video ended. Seamus was surprised to find that even though he had understood not a single word of the performance, it had given him goose bumps.

"Well?" Huntsberger pressed. "What do you think?"

"Fascinating," Seamus said. "A very stirring

performance. The Onomayu appear to take their worship very seriously."

Huntsberger nodded. "There is something about the way pre-scientific societies worship, you have to admit. They're so—ardent. They don't have any concept of science to temper their zeal." Seamus was surprised to find that the reverend didn't sound pompous or overblown at all as he said this; rather, he sounded wistful. "There are people who still want that. Sometimes, this is as close as they can get."

"So…" Seamus took a deep breath. "You want me to crack this ceremonial language for you."

Huntsberger nodded eagerly. "Exactly. If anyone can do it, it's surely you, Dr. Martinez."

Seamus sighed. He closed his eyes. This was it. He would have to refuse, and of course they would send him back to Penitentiary. No more private room, private bath—no more private scenery with a real sky just on the other side of the glass…

Before Seamus could open his mouth to speak, Huntsberger spoke again. "Before you say anything, I have some good news for you, Dr. Martinez. I spoke with an advocate on Earth about your case. He's positive he can use your service for the church as evidence of good faith toward your rehabilitation. He thinks he can get your sentence commuted to the time you've already served plus five years' parole."

Seamus's refusal suddenly died on his lips. "What?"

"He thinks he can get your sentence commuted to—"

"I—I heard you." Seamus held up his hand for him to stop. "But—I don't understand. How?" Huntsberger grinned. "We have certain influence with the arbiters on Earth." He flashed Seamus a broad schoolboy grin. "You could be a free man in a very short period of time, Dr. Martinez."

"I—I'm not sure…The last time I worked on a project like this…" *People died.*

"Think of it, Dr. Martinez. If you can submit a full syntactic analysis and a basic lexicon of the Onomayu ceremonial language, the church is willing to submit a post-facto plea bargain for a lessening of your sentence. What do you say?" Seamus felt distinctly like a rat in a maze chasing cheese. That Huntsberger had played him perfectly, with just the right amounts of flattery and temptation, did not escape him. He looked out the window, once again transparent, at the Onomayu village in the valley. What could it hurt?

He considered his words carefully. He did not look at the reverend. "I'm not sure I have the moral fiber to refuse."

Huntsberger beamed. "Excellent. The Protestant Council is expecting the analysis in a month. I'm sure you'll be wanting—"

"A month?" Seamus said. "I can't do a full syntactic analysis and a lexicon in a month. It would take twice that just to make preliminary observations—"

"Normally, yes. But there have been some improvements in ethnographic investigation since your imprisonment, Dr. Martinez. We have a tool that will help you along." He pressed his finger to his ear to activate an implant. "Now, Alan."

The lift doors opened, and a figure emerged. It was a male humanoid, of some race Seamus had never seen. The man's skin coloration was a light olive, and the face contained two bright brown eyes with retinas much darker than a human's; the nose was flattened, with two tiny nostrils that seemed to appear out of nowhere just above a small mouth ringed by darkish green lips. The man's similarity, in structure if not in coloration, to a human from Earth definitively placed his planet of origin as somewhere along the Kzrjemian arm of the Milky Way.

Seamus watched as the man crossed the room to stand before the table. "Well, what do you think?" the man said—in Alan's voice.

"What the—?" Seamus muttered.

"Survey android," Huntsberger said. "State of the art. And damned pricey to have tailor-made. With this you can have full interaction with the Onomayu people, and their culture will never be compromised."

"You're serious?"

"Of course. Cuts down on the observation work considerably. All the anthro surveys into pre-scientific cultures are using them these days."

"Are you seriously considering letting a convicted murderer *interact* with the Onomayu?"

"Come now, Dr. Martinez. You're hardly a convicted murderer. You were convicted as an accessory to murder. It's not the same thing."

●●●

Over the next ten days Seamus, with Alan as his assistant, immersed himself in the anthro team's reports and findings of the Onomayu. He read every word of the logs of each of the team's ten participants, making notes and jotting down further questions, then rereading the survey team's results one more time.

In all, he was astounded at the poor quality of the research team's findings. They'd been on the planet for three weeks and four days, and then had abruptly packed up and left, leaving all their research files and studies open. When Seamus had queried Huntsberger about it, the reverend had merely shrugged. "They were due somewhere else. Onomayu was a low priority."

Although they had a functioning computer translation matrix for the Onomayu's day-to-day language, Seamus spent far too long studying its grammar and syntax.

After two weeks, Seamus had to confront the possibility that he was stalling. He'd learned almost all he could about the ceremonial language, or the *kamin-na*, from covert video surveillance of the Onomayu's ceremonies. The computer was still baffled, and so was he. As far as he could tell, the *kamin-na* had no set structures that he could latch onto as a point of departure. He was tempted to declare it just a load of gibberish and have done with the whole affair, except for the nagging question: how could such an elaborate system of gibberish come to hold such a vital role in the Onomayu society?

On the fifteenth day, Reverend Huntsberger entered the room Seamus had occupied as a lab. Huntsberger took a rather disinterested look around the room at the clutter of computers and monitors. He'd been mostly absent for the past two weeks, leaving Seamus and Alan to their research in peace.

"How's it going?" the reverend asked.

Seamus grunted. He leaned back in his chair and ran his fingers through his hair. "Not well. I've hit about ten brick walls. As far as I can tell, the Onomayu's ceremonial language has no grammar whatsoever."

"But that's impossible, isn't it?"

"Normally, I'd say yes. But I can't even pinpoint a common vocabulary. I have yet to find a single word in common between two people's speech. It's like they've each developed their very own individual vocabulary."

Huntsberger frowned. "Odd."

"Well, religions don't usually make much sense, so why should a language of worship?"

Huntsberger stiffened. "Well, I'll leave you to your work." He turned to leave.

Seamus sighed. "I'm sorry. I didn't mean that." Huntsberger turned back around. "It's just...I'm frustrated. I need more time."

"I wish I could give it to you. But we have retreats scheduled in exactly two and a half weeks. Scores of people will be coming here, and they paid the price of admission to see the Onomayu. I'm sorry. I have no control over that."

"I know," Seamus said. "But have you considered that maybe I'm not the best person for the job?"

"What do you mean?"

"I mean, maybe somebody with more religious background would be more intuitively suited to this project. They might be able to—"

"I have the utmost confidence in your abilities, Dr. Martinez. But if I might ask...why have you not used the survey android? Surely if you were actually to go to the Onomayu village you would have more resources at your disposal. You could interact with the people, ask about their customs."

"We don't know enough," Seamus said. "The survey team did a horrible job of studying the Onomayu. There's no way, based on the data I've got, that I could take that android in there and make it behave in culturally appropriate ways. I need more time."

"I'm afraid I'm not sure what to tell you," Huntsberger said. "This may sound like a platitude to you, but if you trust in God, he'll show you a way."

Seamus glared at the reverend. "That's all you've

got to offer? 'God will show you the way'? With all due respect, Reverend, where was God on Menaus? I ought to know better than anyone: when you traipse in without a full concept of the culture you're entering, people tend to *die*. And there's not much God can do about that."

"This isn't the same situation, Dr. Martinez. If you take the survey android in, the Onomayu will never know they're in contact with an extraterrestrial. Nobody's going to die."

Seamus threw up his arms in frustration. "Fine, then. I'll take the bloody android in tomorrow. But if anything goes wrong, let it be on your conscience. I've got enough on mine already."

•••

Seamus timed his arrival in the Onomayu village just right. He meandered up the main thoroughfare leading through the center of town just after sunup, only shortly before the morning *kamin-na* ceremony was to begin.

A group of children playing in the street greeted him first. They came up to him, laughing and brimming with exuberance, and they took turns taking his elbow—the android's elbow, really, but he felt it just as if it were his own arm—in the ritual Onomayu greeting.

The oldest of the children, a boy analogous to a human adolescent, was accorded the honor of saying the words of greeting. "Be welcomed to Onomayu-eska," he said.

"Many thanks for the welcome," Seamus said, and accorded the boy a polite nod of his head.

Seamus was not too practiced at reading Onomayu facial expressions yet, but he thought the boy looked…ashamed. "I apologize for my rudeness," the boy said.

"Um—" Seamus considered. He hadn't anticipated this. "Rudeness? I do not understand. I have perceived no rudeness."

The boy looked relieved, but slightly puzzled. "I have no *kamin-néa* to offer you. Is it not custom in your village to greet strangers from far away with the *kamin-néa*?"

The android's translation matrix offered no translation for the word *kamin-néa*, but Seamus assumed it meant some sort of words of welcome in the *kamin-na*. "Yes, it is customary," Seamus said, "but I have had a long journey, and I am tired, so I hope you will forgive me, too, if I have no *kamin-néa* for you?"

The boy actually smiled, and Seamus relaxed. So far his instincts had been right. And he couldn't have asked for better luck in making his arrival in the village. Children were an incredible source of information on native customs, and usually were not reluctant in the slightest to answer questions.

"Would you prefer lodging?" the boy asked. "There is room in my hut. You have much gear."

The android was carrying a large pack on its back to cement the illusion of a traveler from far away, but thankfully Seamus had been able to disconnect the load from the android's tactile interface; his own back just wasn't up to it. "Thank you," he said. "I would appreciate that."

The still nameless boy led him toward one of the huts. A few of the children followed behind at a respectful distance. The arrival of a stranger in town was a rare occurrence, but the children apparently observed a protocol of some sort whereby the boy was accorded the sole status of guide.

Two adults, both men, were loitering in front of the hut where the boy led Seamus. As they caught sight of Seamus, they came over to greet him. They took his elbow just as the children had.

"Be welcomed," the taller one said. "You are from far away?"

"Yes. I have come from Onomayu-idru, over the mountains."

Seamus waited. He'd deliberately chosen a village far away, almost a month's travel time on foot. Hopefully, the men would have heard of it, but would not have visited it themselves. It was a gamble. His file on his village of origin was quite thin if they started asking questions.

The two men exchanged a look. "Far indeed," the taller one said. "You have our respect."

"Thank you," Seamus said. Inwardly, he breathed a sigh of relief.

"I am Ceratuë," the taller man said. "This is Aranai."

"It is a privilege to meet the both of you."

"You will be staying here? May I take your pack?" Ceratuë asked.

"Thank you." Seamus surrendered the pack. Ceratuë took it and disappeared into the hut.

"So," Aranai said. "Who is your patron here in our village?"

Seamus blinked. "Patron?"

"Yes. The one who will guide you."

"Oh." *A guide.* Seamus made a mental note to make an adjustment to the translation matrix when he got a chance. "I have only just arrived here. I have no patron."

The man's eyes grew wide. "You have only just arrived? Then…Enkiru," he indicated the boy who had greeted Seamus, "gave you welcome?"

"Um, yes, that's correct."

"Please, forgive us. It was not our intent to offend. The boy has no *kamin-na*." Aranai glared at the boy.

"I have taken no offense. The boy…Enkiru?…has been very welcoming to me." He tried to flash the boy a reassuring grin. He hoped the boy interpreted the expression correctly.

The boy, Enkiru, stepped forward. "I will serve as patron," he said to Aranai.

The older man hissed. "But you…"

"I am old enough," the boy said. He stood tall and proud, as if challenging the man. "It is my right. I saw him first."

The android's receptors rendered *I saw him first* as a rather petulant statement, but Seamus could tell something else was at work here. This was a matter of mores.

Aranai sighed. "Very well." He turned to Seamus. "It is no insult to refuse this boy's offer. He has no *kamin-néa*, nor *kamin-na*."

Seamus looked from the boy to the man. Already, in less than ten minutes in this village, he was out of his depth. What would a real Onomayu do in this situation? What was the culturally appropriate thing to do?

He had no idea, so he decided to trust his instincts. He bowed his head in a gesture of respect to the boy. "I am honored by your offer. Will you please be my patron?"

The boy returned the nod of respect. "It is my honor."

At that moment a bell of sorts rang out nearby. The boy's eyes flickered off in the direction of the sound for just a second. "Will you come to morning *kamin-na*?" the boy asked.

"I would consider it a privilege," Seamus said. He

had to try hard to keep an edge of excitement out of his voice. The android's speech emitters would pick up whatever inflection he gave. But as Enkiru led him through the village, he could not contain a nervous flutter of excitement. This was what he had come for.

•••

Easily a good half of the settlement's four hundred residents had already packed into the meeting hall when Seamus arrived with the boy.

The meeting hall was at the center of the settlement, and it consisted of little more than a thatched roof on a dozen evenly spaced support beams. Low seats fashioned out of some native greenish wood arced around a central dais. By some unspoken custom of the Onomayu, those present had clustered in the back seats, leaving the front ones for those to come after.

At first Seamus thought the gathering hall was curiously devoid of decoration of any kind—strange for a place of worship in any culture—but as the boy led him by the hand into the hut, he saw that his initial observation was wrong. Each of the support beams held intricately carved designs of stunning detail and artistry, most of them depicting what Seamus surmised to be various deities in the Onomayu pantheon.

Enkiru led him by the hand to one of the support beams at the back of the hut. The boy stopped in front of the beam and broke hands with Seamus. Then, he knelt and pressed his forehead to a blank spot toward the bottom of the beam. He remained like this for several seconds, his eyes closed as in worship, then he straightened up. He looked at Seamus expectantly.

Conscious of the gazes of the assembled villagers

nearby, Seamus knelt down and pressed his forehead to the same blank spot as the boy had.

And as he did so, all the background conversations of the villagers stopped. Even though the android's receptors didn't come complete with a sixth sense, Seamus could still feel the stares of all the Onomayu.

After a few seconds, he stood up and turned expectantly to the boy. Enkiru was looking at him in what he assumed was a smile. Interpreting facial expressions on alien species, however humanoid, was always a difficult proposition. Seamus had done his homework, but he was still a little out of his league.

The boy then led him to the forefront of the seats, which were empty. He gestured for Seamus to sit on the front row of benches, which Seamus persisted in thinking of as pews. Somewhat self-consciously, Seamus sat.

Almost immediately, the conversations resumed behind them. The android's audio receptors delivered the hubbub of conversations to his ears, though the translator could not filter out any individual conversations.

Enkiru was watching him expectantly. To fill the need to say something, Seamus said, "If I didn't know better, I'd think they were talking about me."

The humor didn't translate. "They are."

"Oh? What are they saying?"

"They are wondering why you would choose someone with no *kamin-na* to be your guide. They are wondering if you have no *kamin-na* yourself."

Seamus didn't know how to respond to that. Fortunately, he didn't have to. At that moment a crowd of villagers entered the worship hut, and the seats all around him began filling up.

Seamus noted that these new arrivals were mostly older members of the community, some of them with the graying hair of middle age. Seamus cross-referenced the android's visuals with the databases on the aliens, and identified eleven men and women who had spoken the *kamin-na* in the daily gatherings over the past few weeks. He made a mental note of this; if the social hierarchy of the village dictated that the best *kamin-na* speakers sat at the front of the worship, he would have possible means to determine relative quality of each of the speakers.

Those members of the community that took seats around Seamus greeted him warmly, taking him by the elbow one by one. Seamus greeted them all in kind, and was glad that the android was able to keep a memory bank of all their names.

At length, a woman whom Seamus surmised to be one of the village elders got up before the assembly, and all the conversations quieted immediately. Then, she spoke some words that Seamus's translator could not interpret.

Seamus leaned forward as if to hear better, even though the android's receptors would function regardless. This was to be his first close-up witnessing of the *kamin-na*.

But instead of beginning an impassioned fit of babble, the woman turned to him. She said something that the translator couldn't make out. She held out a hand as if in invitation.

Seamus froze. What was she saying? Even though he was not really present in the worship hut, his heart thudded to a frenzied rhythm in his chest.

The woman said something again, something different this time, and beckoned again. Nervously,

Seamus looked to his left and right. All the villagers were regarding him expectantly.

Enkiru took his elbow and leaned in closer to whisper. "She is inviting you to speak the *kamin-na* as our guest."

"Seamus swallowed. "I—but—I don't—"

"Please," the boy said, and Seamus thought he saw such longing there that his protests died in the android's speech processor. "I've never sat here before."

Seamus turned back to the woman. She beckoned again, and said something else in the *kamin-na*.

Seamus stood up hesitantly and took a few strides to where the woman stood. She said something that he assumed was thanks, then took a seat in the audience.

Seamus considered the assembled villagers. They all looked at him expectantly. He pursed his lips, as if he were an actor who had forgotten his lines.

He considered his options. He had data on all the *kamin-na* speeches of the last few weeks. He could pull up any one of those, and have the android's equipment repeat one of those performances verbatim. But as soon as that idea came he discarded it. Every one of the *kamin-na* speeches he had witnessed on the monitors in the comfort and anonymity of the observation room had been different, and infinitely creative in the types of utterances. Given the phenomenal memories of the Onomayu, plagiarism of such a sort might immediately overturn his welcome.

So then what? He knew the computer at his disposal could cobble together a random sampling of all the various types of utterances from the various *kamin-na* speakers and combine them in a completely new and unique way. But that would yield dubious results as well; without syntax, it would be like throwing out random words here and there, and the result was likely to be completely unintelligible.

So Seamus improvised. The *kamin-na* always had a strong rhythm. He rationalized that since the *kamin-na* so far defied all attempts to determine its syntax, it was as good as babble to him. And he could easily babble back to the Onomayu. If pressed, he could always claim that he was from a village where the *kamin-na* was spoken very differently. He doubted any of the villagers had the experience to contradict him.

So he disengaged the android's translator function and spoke the first words that came to his mind:

'Twas brillig and the slithy toves
Did gyre and gimble in the wabe:
All mimsy were the borogoves,
And the mome raths outgrabe.

He'd learned the poem long ago, and the words had stuck with him since. He dredged them from his memory now, giving them the appropriate histrionic flavor with his voice and his gestures, until he was acting out the poem, in English, to a group of aliens who had never heard English spoken in their lives.

One, two! One, two! And through and through
The vorpal blade went snicker-snack!
He left it dead, and with its head
He went galumphing back.

He brought his recitation to a crescendo, and concluded with a bow. Then, he regarded the audience for their reaction.

The entire worship hut was silent for a stunned instant. Then, all the Onomayu began hooting at once in their culture's version of applause.

Seamus accorded the audience a polite nod and returned to his seat. As he took it, he noticed that Enkiru's eyes were shining, and wet around the edges—from pride, maybe? He couldn't be certain, but he knew one thing: the boy was not upset.

•••

After the service, Seamus weathered the congratulations and the elbow-tuggings of scores of the Onomayu villagers. They gave him all manner of accolades, most of them a variation on the theme of "a very interesting rendition of the *kamin-na.*" A few even said something like, "We shall have to visit your village to hear more."

Seamus was relieved that he had not inadvertently made a cultural faux pas in his hasty speech, but still he was no closer to unraveling any of the rules governing the *kamin-na.* He realized he had an incredible resource in Enkiru: you could ask children things that you couldn't adults—not without seeming odd—and children would almost always give you honest answers. But it was impossible to get some time alone with the boy; Seamus was continually besieged by villagers who wanted to meet him and comment on his unusual speaking of the *kamin-na.*

Luckily, it was already evening. Only a few hours after the worship ceremony, Enkiru steered him toward the hut where he had stowed his gear. Among the Onomayu, sleeping was a social experience. They slept on the floor of the hut. A pallet had been prepared for him next to Enkiru's.

At the same time, all the Onomayu men and women took off their simple garments and settled into their bedrolls. Seamus followed suit, glad that the android had been made anatomically correct, just for such situations.

Before the last candle was blown out, Enkiru rolled over on his side and addressed Seamus. "I thank you," he said.

Seamus was taken aback. "For what?"

"For accepting me as your patron, even though I am not whole."

There wasn't much Seamus could think to say to that. "You're welcome."

Seamus stayed connected to the android until all the Onomayu began to drift off to sleep. When he deemed it no longer necessary to interact, he hit the disconnect button on the android's control panel in front of him. The visual of the Onomayu hut disappeared, to be replaced by the bare interior of the retreat's control room.

"Well, that went well," Alan said. He'd monitored the entire scenario on a side monitor. Not quite as immediate as being hooked into the android's receptors, but still he could tell what had happened.

"I got lucky," Seamus said. "That could have been a complete fiasco."

"Lucky thing you knew that poem," Alan said. "They seemed to like it."

"No," Seamus corrected. "They didn't know what to make of it. It was complete nonsense to them."

•••

"Will you walk with me?" Seamus asked Enkiru

the next morning, when the village was just beginning to wake up. "Would you show me your valley? It is very beautiful here."

The boy agreed. They dressed and left the hut. Enkiru led them through the village, past the various huts where men and women were just beginning to stir. On the way, they passed the worship hut. Enkiru walked immediately to the same blank spot as he had the previous evening and pressed his forehead to the smooth section of beam. Then, he stood back and waited expectantly for Seamus to perform the ritual.

When Seamus was finished, Enkiru asked, "Do you miss your god?" Seamus frowned. Was this a personal question? "Um—I'm not sure what you mean."

"Do you miss touching the face of your god? In your home?" *Oh.* Slowly Seamus understood. "I guess so," he said at length.

Enkiru accepted his answer, and led on. They began to head north, out of the village and toward the mountains.

"May I ask you a question?" Seamus asked when they were far enough out. "A personal one?"

Enkiru frowned. "You need not ask to ask. I am your patron."

"Oh. Well, tell me—how is it that you have no god?" The boy looked at the ground. "I have no god because I have no *kamin-na.*"

"But how is it that you have no *kamin-na?*" Seamus pressed. "Please, I wish to understand. There are many things in your village that are different."

The boy seemed to accept Seamus's explanation. "I have no *kamin-na* because no god wishes to speak through me."

A definition? Seamus thought. "So is the *kamin-na*

the god speaking through you? Are they the words of the god?"

The boy looked puzzled, as if he were being asked to confirm that the sky was blue. "Of course."

"I see. Forgive me if I pry, but why is it that no god speaks through you?"

Enkiru shrugged, a mannerism that struck Seamus as particularly human. "Because I am not worthy."

"But why not? What makes you unworthy?"

"Because I have no *kamin-na*."

Seamus considered. The circular logic apparently made perfect sense to the boy, and by his expression, he thought it should make perfect sense to Seamus, too. "So how does one get the *kamin-na?*"

Enkiru regarded Seamus shrewdly. "You are *hanní* in your village, aren't you?"

Seamus frowned. "What is a *hanní?*"

"One who asks questions that everyone knows the answers to."

Seamus was becoming more confused than ever. He cursed Huntsberger for throwing him into contact with this species so soon. "Why would anyone do that?"

"To lead the people to wisdom that they don't know they already have. You *are hanní!*" Enkiru suddenly grabbed Seamus's wrist and pressed it to his forehead.

"Perhaps I am a *hanní*," Seamus said, "but I would like that to be our little secret, all right?"

Enkiru frowned. "For what reason?"

"Because I have very little wisdom to give, most of the time. I am…not always a very good *hanní*."

To his relief, the boy laughed. "Very well. I won't tell."

"Can we stop here a moment?" Seamus asked, indicating a convenient patch of rock to sit on. "I am older than you, and I am tired." In truth the android could keep up the hike all day, but Seamus wanted to sit. So they sat.

"So you have not answered my question," Seamus said. "How does one come by the *kamin-na?* How do you get the god to speak through you?" Enkiru answered far more readily now that he thought Seamus was a *hanní.* "When you are of age, your god chooses you."

"And then what happens?"

"You begin to speak the *kamin-na.*"

"Immediately?"

Enkiru nodded. "But the beginners aren't very good. Not right away."

"How do you know they aren't very good?"

"Because they only have a few sounds."

"And what are these sounds?"

"The sounds of the *kamin-na.*"

"Such as?"

Enkiru stood up straight, as if reciting a school lesson. He uttered a basic vowel: æ. Seamus noted it in the android's memory.

"I see. And what is this sound?"

Enkiru shrugged. "I do not know. I have no *kamin-na.*"

Seamus sighed inwardly. This could take all day. "But the sound—does it mean something?"

"Yes."

"What does it mean?"

"I don't know. I have no—"

Seamus decided to try a different tack. "How do you know it means something, if you do not know what it means?"

"Because it is part of the *kamin-na.* It comes from the gods."

"All right." Seamus resisted the impulse to shake the boy. "What do you *think* it could mean?"

"It could be one of the elements," Enkiru said.

Now we're getting somewhere, Seamus thought. "And what are the elements?"

Enkiru made a face. "Do you want me to name all of them?"

"I want you to name the ones you can."

Enkiru could name every one of the elements, it turned out. He rattled them off without so much as a pause, evidencing even further the spectacular memory of the Onomayu. Most of the qualities were abstract concepts such as love, peace, happiness; Seamus knew he was receiving only the translation matrix's crude approximations of these concepts, so he resolved to devote considerable study to fleshing out his understanding of the sixty-two elements. For thirty of the words that Enkiru mentioned the translator had no definition.

The boy finished and watched Seamus for approbation, as if he were a student coming to the end of a recitation for his teacher.

Seamus's mind was working so fast he almost forgot that the boy was there. Sixty concepts. A similar number of phonemes in the Onomayu language.

"So," Seamus said, understanding, "each sound is paired with one of these qualities?"

"Yes, *hanní.*"

"But…how is the pairing done? It is different for each person, yes?"

Enkiru nodded. "You must listen to the voice of your god to help you interpret the words of the *kamin-na.*"

I see, Seamus thought. "And…how long does that take?" "All your life. It is a very private, very sacred process." Enkiru looked away from Seamus. "My god has never spoken to me." He took a deep breath, then looked back to Seamus. "Tell me, please…how you arrived at your *kamin-na*."

Seamus stirred uncomfortably on his rock. "Um, much as everyone else," he hedged. "My process was…not special."

"But it *was* special!" Enkiru said. "It had to be. You possess qualities in your *kamin-na* that no one else possesses. Surely you are blessed by your god."

"I—" Seamus stammered. He replayed Enkiru's words: *you possess qualities in your kamin-na that no one else possesses.* What could that mean?

The answer was plain: *'Twas brillig and the slithy toves…*the Onomayu language contained no *V.* In his haste to speak the *kamin-na,* he'd unwittingly used sounds the Onomayu had never heard before.

Surely you are blessed by your god.

Enkiru leaned in closer. "Teach me, please," he said, and his voice shook with an earnestness that transcended species. "Teach me how you learned to speak the *kamin-na* with such authority. Teach me so that I needn't spend my whole life broken."

Seamus could not avoid Enkiru's eyes. He tried to pull away from the naked need he saw there, but he couldn't.

"Please," Enkiru said.

Seamus's breath lodged in his lungs. He'd heard those words before, years ago, on a distant world, light-years away, from a being with a much different set of vocal chords, but the need had been much the same.

Teach me. Please.

"I—I—"

Seamus severed the connection with the android. In an instant all the vista of the mountainside went blank, to be replaced by the bare walls of the retreat center's control room. Last of all faded Enkiru's face, though the eyes remained long after the image was gone, the eyes that pleaded with Seamus more eloquently than any words could.

"I can't," Seamus muttered.

• • •

Several hours later, Huntsberger came to his room. The reverend pressed the door chime. Seamus heard it, but did not answer. He merely remained sitting on his bed, staring at the blank wall.

Huntsberger did not ring again. Instead, he opened the door and stepped inside. He looked at Seamus. Seamus did not look back. A brief silence ensued.

Seamus finally broke the silence. "I solved your mystery."

"Oh?"

"It's really very simple. Anybody could have figured it out. Just a simple matter of sixty-two abstract concepts, each of them attached to the phonemes of the Onomayu language, assigned by association over a period of adolescence to old age. The rhythm conveys the tone, but each listener constructs the meaning for himself. It's like linguistic mood music."

"I know," Huntsberger said. "I reviewed the data from the android."

Seamus finally took his eyes off the picture to look at the reverend. "That's it. There's never going to be a grammar for the language. The syntax and the semantics both are completely constructed by the recipient. It's a purely internal process." He turned to look back at the picture on the wall. "Anybody could have figured that out, if they'd bothered to take the time. You didn't need me."

"No, I suppose I didn't."

Seamus pried his eyes off the picture again. He regarded the reverend. "But you knew that already, didn't you?"

"I suspected," Huntsberger admitted.

"Then why did you bring me here?"

"Honestly? Because xenolinguistics is a hobby of mine. Almost the entire linguistic community believes you were wronged by the investigation into what happened on Menaus. It's our duty to right injustices where we can."

"I was convicted as an accessory to seventy-eight counts of murder and inciting a rebellion."

"You were just the scapegoat. You know that."

"You don't understand. I deserved my sentence."

"I don't believe that."

"You should. Because it's true. I knew that what I was doing would very likely start a civil war on Menaus. I knew that if I did what I did those people I called my friends would be in danger. But I did it anyway."

"Because you thought it was the right thing to do."

"Yeah," Seamus admitted at length. "I thought so, anyway."

"Maybe it was."

Seamus shook his head. "It wasn't."

"You've surely not kept up on the newsfeeds due to your imprisonment. Perhaps you don't realize that Menaus eliminated their slave castes last month. Not bad for a caste-dominant society. Slavery has been completely abolished. They're struggling, but they're making progress."

Seamus felt as if the reverend had wrung out his intestines. "You—you mean it?" Huntsberger nodded.

"So perhaps some good came of your decisions

after all. Only history will be the final arbiter of your judgment. And God, of course."

"But…I don't really believe in God."

"I don't believe you," Huntsberger said. "After all, what is God for if not to help us decide the right thing to do?" Seamus had no answer to that.

"I'll leave you to your thoughts," Huntsberger said. "I just thought you should know…the Onomayu have been tending to our android since you disconnected. They think he had a stroke of some sort. The villagers are praying over him even as we speak." He paused. "They are a remarkably spiritual people, you have to admit."

The reverend withdrew, leaving Seamus staring up at the picture on the wall.

• • •

The android's eyes blinked open. Seamus reestablished the optical connections, and he saw what the android saw.

He was lying on a pallet in the Onomayu hut where he had bedded down the night before. The hut was gloomy; it was heading toward evening on Onomayu.

The hut was empty save for one other. Enkiru bent over the android, his hand clasped in the android's. When he realized that Seamus was stirring, his face lit in a beatific smile that Seamus didn't need to be an Onomayu to interpret.

"*Hanní!* You're—are you—are you all right?"

"I'm fine." Seamus could have sat up right then, but given that the boy had apparently kept this vigil over his sickbed, he thought it best not to overdo it. "I'm fine, really. Just—an old man's health. Nothing to worry about."

Enkiru studied his face. "Your god looks out for you," he said. "You are lucky to return from such a fit."

"Yes," Seamus admitted. "I guess he does."

Enkiru leaned in close to whisper, even though no one else was nearby. "I know now why you left your own village."

"Oh?" The boy nodded. "You left to die, didn't you? You left to kiss the face of your god?"

Seamus considered. "I guess you could say that."

The boy stood up quickly. "I must go tell the others you're awake. They're entreating their gods for your health in the worship hut." He sprinted to the entrance of the hut, but turned around at the threshold. "You will be all right, won't you?" Seamus nodded.

"I just need a good night's rest, that's all. Tomorrow I will teach you how to begin to speak the *kamin-na*."

The boy beamed, and left the hut. Seamus lay back on the pallet and stared at the ceiling. He almost wished he had a personal god he could entreat for help. He had absolutely no idea how he was going to teach this boy to speak a language that had no rules.

•••

The next day, at morning worship, several of the Onomayu who were invited to speak the *kamin-na* performed their version of giving thanks to their deities for Seamus's quick recovery. The health of visitors was of paramount importance to them, and Seamus's recovery was occasion for great joy among the villagers. It was proof that their deities had heard their prayers and had seen fit to grant their requests.

Seamus listened to the speakers of the *kamin-na* with renewed appreciation. He heard now the tell-tale repetitions of various sounds as the speakers poured out their souls in messages that played like a dance of random ideas, united by sound and rhythm into melodious sermons that only the speakers understood. The audience members were equally enraptured; never mind that the messages they received were by design far removed from the intent of the speakers—that was the nature of the *kamin-na*. For in the *kamin-na* the wisdom was as much in the receiving as it was in the speaking. It was a belief based on randomness as the true conveyor of cosmic import.

But as the *kamin-na* speakers tended toward long-windedness, Seamus fidgeted inwardly. Soon enough the morning service would end, and a young boy would look to him for religious instruction. If there was ever a more ironic case of the blind leading the blind…

•••

The worship service did end, and Seamus and Enkiru ascended into the mountains again. The boy stayed at Seamus's elbow the entire trek, a worried look in his face.

"Don't worry," Seamus reassured him. "I can guarantee I will not be suffering any more attacks today."

Enkiru did not ask him how he knew this. The boy proceeded eagerly, his pace brisk, eager to begin his instruction. Although the android could have easily outpaced the boy, Seamus kept his gait to a leisurely stroll.

They reached the rock where they had sat the previous day. Seamus sat next to Enkiru. The boy regarded him expectantly.

At length Enkiru spoke. *"Hanní? Hanní,* would you instruct me?" Seamus sighed. The words were similar to those he'd heard those many years ago, on Menaus. The words that had begun a rebellion. For the first time in a long time, Seamus prayed to whatever god was listening that he would not take a misstep.

He turned to the boy. "Tell me again," he said, "why it is that you have no *kamin-na.*"

Enkiru frowned. "I told you already."

"I know, but I am *hanní,* remember? I ask questions that everybody knows the answers to."

Enkiru looked away, shame-faced. "Because my god does not speak to me."

"And why does your god not speak to you?"

Enkiru shrugged. "I'm not sure. Probably because I have not proven myself worthy."

"I see. And what must you do to prove yourself worthy?"

"I don't know. If I knew, I would do it."

"But everyone else in your village has heard the voice of their god?"

"Everyone. Even ones much younger."

"And what did they do to be worthy to hear their gods' voices?"

Enkiru's shame deepened. "I—I'm not sure. Perhaps they have more faith."

"Perhaps," Seamus said. "Or perhaps they have less."

Enkiru's eyes went wide. "What do you mean?"

"When a god speaks to one of your people, how do they speak?"

"I'm not certain. The gods always speak privately."

Exactly as Seamus had suspected. "So the only

way you know that a god has spoken to one of your people is when they tell you so?"

"Of course," Enkiru said. "What other way would there be?"

"Probably none." In all Seamus's experience with various galactic religions, there never was any objective proof that a deity would speak with a believer. "But then perhaps you are listening in the wrong way."

"I don't understand."

"How do you imagine your god speaking to you?"

"I'm not certain. I know there are many ways the gods speak. Portents, signs…"

"And you have never seen any portents or signs?"

Enkiru considered. "I suppose I may have seen many. I can't say."

"But you never suspected your god was attempting to talk to you?"

"I—I wasn't certain. How could I be certain a god was speaking to me?"

Indeed, Seamus thought. He regarded Enkiru, who was still looking at him with an expression of wide-eyed hope, as if he could solve all his problems. But how? The boy was ahead of his time, a true skeptic in a society that wasn't ready for them.

"Hanni?" Enkiru said. "May I ask you a question?"

"Of course," Seamus said.

"I know it's improper to ask…but I would like to know…how does your god speak to you?"

Your god. How could he answer that? Buddha, Allah, God, Tkltk…over the last decade he'd been an unwilling participant in a half-dozen faiths, depending upon the institution that had held his confinement contract. But none of them had been *his* god. None of them had ever spoken to him.

"I—"

"*Hanní?*" Could he tell him the truth? He'd told the truth on Menaus, a world that had never conceived of a society without rigid caste distinctions. They'd asked out of politeness for him to teach them English, and when he had, the utter absence of caste pronouns had led to some very uncomfortable questions…and ultimately, to a bloody rebellion.

Ready or not, though, ten years later the caste systems on Menaus were weakening.

It had to happen sometime. It took a cataclysmic jolt to a society's ethos to move them forward. And that jolt usually came from an outsider trying to do the right thing for one individual.

Enkiru was only one individual, but sometimes it only took one. Seamus took a deep breath. "I have no god," he said. "No god speaks to me."

Enkiru's eyes went wide. He got up and took a few steps back from Seamus. "You—you…but how? How can you have no god and still be *hanní*? How can you have no god and still speak the *kamin-na?*"

Seamus couldn't look the boy in the eye. "I didn't, really. They were just words."

A series of emotions played on Enkiru's face. Seamus had never realized before that betrayal looked much the same on every species' face.

Without another word, Enkiru turned and ran away. Seamus watched him go.

•••

He couldn't just fade away, never to be seen again, much as he would have liked to. It was not a culturally appropriate thing to do.

He thanked the villagers for their hospitality, and informed them that he would be leaving first thing in the morning. Enkiru was nowhere to be found.

• • •

Hands shook him awake. Seamus opened his eyes. At first he thought it was Enkiru entreating him to wake, but when he blinked he saw that it was Alan, and he remembered. He'd disconnected from the android hours ago.

"Dr. Martinez! Dr. Martinez! Come quick!"

Seamus sat up, blinking sleep out of his eyes. "What is it?" he asked. His words came out slurred from sleep.

"You have to connect to the android, *now!* The Onomayu village is on fire."

"What?" Seamus bolted out of bed then. Not bothering to dress, he followed Alan out of his room. Together, the two of them sprinted down the corridors of the retreat center.

"What happened?" Seamus demanded on the way.

"I don't know."

They burst into the control center. Seamus wasted no time in buckling himself into the android's harness. He activated the relays—and suddenly he was in the Onomayu village, experiencing an odd case of déjà vu. Someone was shaking the android awake, roughly, just as Alan had woken him only moments before. It took several seconds for Seamus's perception to acclimate to the android's. At length, Seamus realized that it was not Enkiru who was attempting to wake him. It was one of the other Onomayu men.

"At last," the man who was shaking him said. "I was frightened you—"

"What's going on?" Seamus cut him off.

"The worship hut is on fire," the man said. "Come quick."

It was a very short trip from the dormitory hut to the center of the village where the worship hut lay. As Seamus emerged into the open air, he instinctively shielded his eyes from the glare of the blaze.

The worship hut was completely engulfed in flames. The thatched roof sent tendrils of flames into the night sky of Onomayu. All six of the support beams with the carved faces of the Onomayu gods were wrapped in an orange glow that obscured the carvings.

The entire village had come out to see the inferno. Men and women stood, naked, gazing into the flames. Some gazed in silent horror, some moaned, some sobbed silently.

Seamus scanned the crowd. At first he could detect no sign of Enkiru. But then he spotted the boy, standing at the forefront of the onlookers. He gazed raptly into the flames.

Seamus started toward him. He drew up beside the boy. Enkiru's eyes flickered for a brief second as he noted Seamus's presence, but he did not take his eyes off the blaze.

"What happened?" Seamus demanded.

"You helped me to hear. At first I was angry, but then I understood. Your No-god spoke to me. He's been speaking to me all my life, and I never realized."

Seamus felt the words like a physical blow. He moaned softly; the sound of it was swallowed by the crackling of the flames. "Please, Enkiru, tell me you didn't do this."

"It was the only way for them to hear, too."

Seamus shook his head. "No." He fought down

Illustrated by Ozzie Rodriguez

the urge to vomit. "No—" It was the only word that would come, so he latched onto it and repeated it, over and over again.

Enkiru pulled his gaze from the inferno and turned to Seamus. Just as he did so, one of the support beams buckled, and a section of roof of the worship hut caved in. "I want to come with you."

Seamus stared at him in horror. "What?"

"I want to come with you," he repeated. "Be with you on your travels. There's nothing for me here now."

"But—" Seamus shook his head. "You don't understand. You can't go where I'm going."

"Why not?"

"Because—you just can't. I can't explain it to you. Please, listen to me. This—" he indicated the blazing wreck of the worship hut. "This is not what I meant. You must understand…this is not the way to listen to the No-god."

Enkiru frowned. "You don't understand."

"Understand what?"

"Look at them." He pointed to the sobbing villagers, to other Onomayu children crying in their parents' arms. "They understand now. They finally hear me. This is my *kamin-na*."

Seamus could only watch as the fire continued to burn.

•••

Huntsberger found him on the observation deck, standing at the massive one-way window and gazing down into the valley. Seamus heard the reverend come in, but did not turn around to greet him.

Huntsberger crossed the carpet and came to share Seamus's vantage point. "Is the android back?"

Seamus nodded.

"And the boy—is he gone from the village?"

Again Seamus nodded. "They banished him for life. He can never return to his home."

"Unfortunate. Still, I can't say I blame them."

"I can't, either," Seamus said, and sighed.

"I've brought you some good news." Huntsberger raised a data pad he carried in his right hand. He handed it to Seamus. "A judge on Earth rescinded your sentence to eight years under an approved confinement contract, which you've already served. Congratulations. You're a free man."

Seamus took the pad and stared at the document. His eyes read the words, but his mind failed to comprehend them.

"Any ideas where you might go first?" Seamus gave up trying to read his release document. He lowered the pad. "Actually," he said, "if you don't mind, I thought I might stay here for a while."

"Oh?"

"You'll have hundreds of religious tourists arriving here any day looking for an authentic religious experience. Somebody's got to teach them to listen to the *kamin-na*. They've got to know how to listen to it right."

"You're welcome to stay here as long as you like. But may I ask what prompted this decision?"

Seamus shrugged. "People still need a *hanní*."

The reverend nodded, and left. Seamus returned to looking out the window.

THE YEAR IN THE CONTESTS

by
Algis Budrys

Algis Budrys, editor of the anthology, was born in Königsberg, East Prussia, on January 9, 1931. His family came to America in 1936.

Budrys became interested in science fiction at the age of six, when a landlady slipped him a copy of the New York Journal-American *Sunday funnies.*

At the age of twenty-one, living in Great Neck, Long Island, he began selling steadily to the top magazine markets. He sold his first novel in 1953, and eventually produced eight more novels, including Who?, Rogue Moon, Michaelmas *and* Hard Landing, *and three short-story collections. He has always done a number of things besides writing. He has been, over the years, the editor in chief of Regency Books, Playboy Press, all the titles at Woodall's Trailer Travel publications, and L. Ron Hubbard Presents Writers of the Future anthologies.*

he judges for this year are named on the cover of this book. And, as has been true since the beginning of the Contest, these professionals comprise many of today's top names in the fields of science fiction and fantasy literature and art.

This year, we are proud to welcome our *Writers of the Future* volume nine winner, now South Australia Great Award for Literature winner and *New York Times* bestselling author, Sean Williams, on board as a judge. Since winning the Contest, Sean has since gone on to publish twenty novels and over sixty short stories.

The enterprise goes ever forward, and the authors and illustrators in this volume will, in due course, take their firm place in the history of creative arts. For the 2005 year, L. Ron Hubbard's Writers of the Future Contest winners are:

First Quarter
1. Michail Velichansky
Games on the Children's Ward
2. Lee Beavington
Evolution's End
3. Richard Kerslake
Balancer

Second Quarter
1. Blake Hutchins
The Sword From the Sea
2. David Sakmyster
The Red Envelope
3. David John Baker
On the Mount

Third Quarter
1. Diana Rowland
Schroedinger's Hummingbird
2. Judith Tabron
Broken Stones
3. Joseph Jordan
At the Gate of God

Fourth Quarter
1. Brandon Sigrist
Life on the Voodoo Driving Range
2. Sarah Totton
The Bone Fisher's Apprentice
3. Brian Rappatta
Tongues

L. Ron Hubbard's Illustrators of the Future Contest
2005 winners:

Kim Feigenbaum
Katherine Hallberg
Daniel Harris
Laura Jennings
Ozzie Rodriguez
Miguel Rojas
James T. Schmidt
Tamara Streeter

Nathan Taylor
Alex Y. Torres
Melanie Tregonning
Eldar Zakirov

Our heartiest congratulations to them all! May we see much more of their work in the future.

CONTEST RULES

1. No entry fee is required, and all rights in the story remain the property of the author. All types of science fiction, fantasy and dark fantasy are welcome.

2. All entries must be original works, in English. Plagiarism, which includes the use of third-party poetry, song lyrics, characters or another person's universe, without written permission, will result in disqualification. Excessive violence or sex, determined by the judges, will result in disqualification. Entries may not have been previously published in professional media.

3. To be eligible, entries must be works of prose, up to 17,000 words in length. We regret we cannot consider poetry, or works intended for children.

4. The Contest is open only to those who have not had professionally published a novel or short novel, or more than one novelette, or more than three short stories, in any medium. Professional publication is deemed to be payment, and at least 5,000 copies, or 5,000 hits.

5. Entries must be typewritten or a computer printout in black ink on white paper, double spaced, with numbered pages. All other formats will be disqualified. Each entry must have a cover page with the title of the work, the author's name, address, telephone number, e-mail address and an approximate word count. Every subsequent page must carry the title and a page number, but the author's name must be deleted to facilitate fair judging.

6. Manuscripts will be returned after judging only if the author has provided return postage on a self-addressed envelope. If the author does not wish return of the manuscript, a business-size self-addressed, stamped envelope (or valid e-mail address) must be included with the entry in order to receive judging results.

7. We accept only entries for which no delivery signature is required by us to receive them.

8. There shall be three cash prizes in each quarter: a First Prize of $1,000, a Second Prize of $750, and a Third Prize of $500, in U.S. dollars or the recipient's locally equivalent amount. In addition, at the end of the year the four First Place winners will have their entries rejudged, and a Grand Prize winner shall be determined and receive an additional $5,000. All winners will also receive trophies or certificates.

9. The Contest has four quarters, beginning on October 1, January 1, April 1 and July 1. The year will end on September 30. To be eligible for judging in its quarter, an entry must be postmarked no later than midnight on the last day of the quarter.

10. Each entrant may submit only one manuscript per quarter. Winners are ineligible to make further entries in the Contest.

11. All entries for each quarter are final. No revisions are accepted.

12. Entries will be judged by professional authors. The decisions of the judges are entirely their own, and are final.

13. Winners in each quarter will be individually notified of the results by mail.

14. This Contest is void where prohibited by law.

CONTEST RULES

1. The Contest is open to entrants from all nations. (However, entrants should provide themselves with some means for written communication in English.) All themes of science fiction and fantasy illustrations are welcome: every entry is judged on its own merits only. No entry fee is required and all rights in the entry remain the property of the artist.

2. By submitting to the Contest, the entrant agrees to abide by all Contest rules.

3. The Contest is open to new and amateur artists who have not been professionally published and paid for more than three black-and-white story illustrations, or more than one process-color painting, in media distributed broadly to the general public. The ultimate eligibility criteria, however, is defined with the word "amateur"—in other words, the artist has not been paid for his artwork. If you are not sure of your eligibility, please write a letter to the Contest Administration with details regarding your publication history. Include a self-addressed and stamped envelope for the reply. You may also send your questions to the Contest Administration via e-mail.

4. Each entrant may submit only one set of illustrations in each Contest quarter. The entry must be original to the entrant and previously unpublished. Plagiarism, infringement of the rights of others, or other violations of the Contest rules will result in disqualification. Winners in previous quarters are not eligible to make further entries.

5. The entry shall consist of three illustrations done by the entrant in a color or black-and-white medium created from the artist's imagination. Use of gray scale in illustrations and mixed media, computer generated art, the use of photography in the illustrations, are accepted. Each illustration must represent a subject different from the other two.

6. ENTRIES SHOULD NOT BE THE ORIGINAL DRAWINGS, but should be color or black-and-white reproductions of the originals of a quality satisfactory to the entrant. Entries must be submitted unfolded and flat, in an envelope no larger than 9 inches by 12 inches.

All entries must be accompanied by a self-addressed return envelope of the appropriate size, with the correct U.S. postage affixed. (Non-U.S. entrants should enclose international postage reply coupons.) If the entrant does not want the reproductions returned, the entry should be clearly marked DISPOSABLE COPIES: DO NOT RETURN. A business-size self-addressed envelope with correct postage (or valid e-mail address) should be included so that the judging results may be returned to the entrant.

We only accept an entry for which no delivery signature is required by us to receive the entry.

7. To facilitate anonymous judging, each of the three photocopies must be accompanied by a removable cover sheet bearing the artist's name, address, telephone number, e-mail address, and an identifying title for that work. The reproduction of the work should carry the same identifying title on the front of the illustration and the artist's signature should be deleted. The Contest Administration will remove and file the cover sheets, and forward only the anonymous entry to the judges.

8. To be eligible for a quarterly judging, an entry must be postmarked no later than the last day of the quarter. Late entries will be included in the following quarter and the Contest Administration will so notify the entrant.

9. There will be three co-winners in each quarter. Each winner will receive an outright cash grant of U.S. $500 and a trophy. Winners will also receive eligibility to compete for the annual Grand Prize of an additional cash grant of $5,000 together with the annual Grand Prize trophy.

10. For the annual Grand Prize Contest, the quarterly winners will be furnished with a specification sheet and a winning story from the Writers of the Future Contest to illustrate. In order to retain eligibility for the Grand Prize, each winner shall send to the Contest address his/her illustration of the assigned story within thirty (30) days of receipt of the story assignment.

The yearly Grand Prize winner shall be determined by the judges on the following basis only:

Each Grand Prize judge's personal opinion on the extent to which it makes the judge want to read the story it illustrates.

The Grand Prize winner shall be announced at the L. Ron Hubbard Awards Event held in the following year.

11. The Contest shall contain four quarters each year, running October 1–December 31, January 1–March 31, April 1–June 30, and July 1–September 30. To be eligible for a quarter, the entry must be postmarked on—or before—the last day of the quarter. The Contest year ends at midnight on September 30.

12. The winning entrants' participation in the Contest shall continue until the winner of the Grand Prize judging has been announced.

13. Entries will be judged by professional artists only. Each quarterly judging and the Grand Prize judging may have different panels of judges. The decisions of the judges are entirely their own and are final.

14. This Contest is void where prohibited by law.

Journey to Other Worlds and Imaginative Dimensions

WRITERSOFTHEFUTURE.COM

◆

Visit the Writers and Illustrators of the Future
web site and discover the latest news,
updates and successes of Contest winners.
The web site also features:

- **CONTEST HISTORY**
- **DOCUMENTARY**
- **AWARDS EVENTS**
- **CONTEST RULES**
- **JUDGES PANEL**
- **ART GALLERY**

Become part of the Writers and Illustrators
of the Future community today. Sign up for
newsletter updates, buy each of the books in the
series, and get expert tips and advice to find out
how you can become the next winner!

◆

Mission Earth

BY

L. RON HUBBARD

The ten-volume action-packed intergalactic spy adventure

> "A superbly imaginative, intricately plotted invasion of Earth."
> —*Chicago Tribune*

A gripping narrative told from the eyes of alien invaders, *Mission Earth* is packed with hard-driving suspense and intrigue.

Heller, a Royal Combat Engineer, has been sent on a desperate mission to halt the self-destruction of Earth—wholly unaware that a secret branch of his own government (the Coordinated Information Apparatus) has dispatched its own agent, whose sole purpose is to sabotage him at all costs, as part of its clandestine operation.

With a cast of dynamic characters, biting satire and plenty of twists, action and emotion, Heller is pitted against incredible odds in this intergalactic game where the future of Earth hangs in the balance.